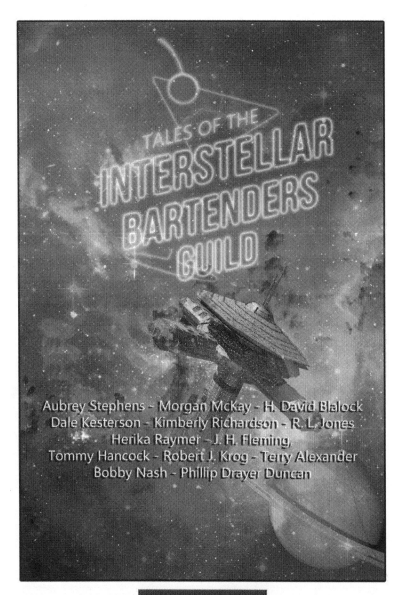

TALES OF THE INTERSTELLAR BARTENDERS GUILD

Aubrey Stephens - Morgan McKay - H. David Blalock
Dale Kesterson - Kimberly Richardson - R. L. Jones
Herika Raymer - J. H. Fleming
Tommy Hancock - Robert J. Krog - Terry Alexander
Bobby Nash - Phillip Drayer Duncan

PRO SE ✺ PRESS

PRO SE PRESS

TALES OF THE INTERSTELLAR BARTENDERS GUILD
A Pro Se Productions Publication

Sam 1701 by Aubrey Stephens
Just a Drop by Morgan McKay
The Game by H. David Blalock
Waltz at the Dancing Pegasus by Dale Kesterson
The Last Stand by Kimberly Richardson
Thanum o'n Dhoul by R. L. Jones
Critters by Herika Raymer
All Hallows' Eve at Midnight Absinthe by J. H. Fleming
Gardner's Hole by Tommy Hancock
Roxy Socksy by Robert J. Krog
The Saga of Snagnar Jim by Terry Alexander
"Ol' Jake" by Bobby Nash
What Do You Have for a Rebellion? by Phillip Drayer Duncan

Editing by Aubrey Stephens, Ernest Russell, Gordon Dymowski

Cover by Antonino Lo Iacono
Book Design by Antonino Lo Iacono
New Pulp Logo Design by Sean E. Ali
New Pulp Seal Design by Cari Reese

www.prose-press.com

TALES OF THE INTERSTELLAR BARTENDERS GUILD

Contents

Introduction

Long ago in a state far away there was a small convention called Pulp Ark 2. I was lucky enough to be attending as a new writer also in attendance was a gentleman that I knew from many conventions in the Memphis area. His name was Stuart Bergman better known to his friends and con attendees as Shorty. At well over 6 feet tall and he could very often be found lumbering around cons wearing a monster mask but behind the mask was a gentle soul. The inventor of the walking taco and the severely alcoholic drink called with a shudder "the blue stuff."

Shorty wanted to be a writer. He talked to editors, publisher, and writers about it. He attended panels about writing. And of course, he asked the standard question, "Where do you get the ideas for stories?" I'm sure he got the same or similar answers many times. At Pulp Ark 2 I was sitting on a panel on writing and there in the audience sat Shorty once again. We had just about finished the panel and had scarcely covered a question along that line when I caught sight of Shorty. For some reason a story idea for him to write popped into my head. I grabbed him as I was going out the door and passed the concept on to him.

Shorty listened to the idea and disappeared into the distance as I headed to another panel. By the time I had finished the next panel and headed back to the dealer's room Shorty had already talked to Tommy Hancock and Alan Gilbreath about the story idea and between them they thought it should actually become an anthology. As the old saying goes "no good deed goes unpunished" somehow I was elected to edit the anthology. In a moment of insanity, I agreed.

The book you hold in your hand is the result of all the above. Most of the authors included in the book knew Shorty or knew him from hearing about him from the rest of us. Some are old hands, and some are new writers.

I regret that there isn't a story by Shorty in the book. Shorty not long after the concept was finalized had the world interfere with his life. A long story involving moving to a new city and family problems, not too long after that his health began to decline and less than a year later Shorty passed away. His friends in the local con circuit remember him fondly, and his creations are still served at Memphis area cons.

These stories are for you, Shorty.

Aubrey Stephens

March 2017

Sam 1701

By
Aubrey Stephens

Sam 1701 felt dwarfed as he walked through the towering building of 'Ein Lein. He had seen the grand embassy buildings that represented the Empire's thousand worlds. All of them made lesser by the Emperor's palace and the silver and gold gilded Guild building. He still had no idea why he was summoned to the Guild Master's Hall. But here he stood just feet away from the massive bronze doors of the Grand Master's receiving room surrounded by busts of past Grand Masters. As he stood looking more than a little awestruck the doors slowly began to open. He advanced uncertainly through the door.

There before him was the largest chair that he had ever seen. Its back had to be at least eight feet tall, and most of it was covered with gold. Draped across was one of the biggest men he had ever seen. Standing the man would easily reach seven feet in height and must weigh at least four hundred pounds.

A deep echoing voice rang out "Pay no attention to the man behind the curtain!"

Sam 1701 whirled around looking for a curtain. He saw tapestries, paintings, and stone walls but no curtains.

The voice called out again, "Just my little joke. So you're Sam 1701."

"Yes, Grand Guild Master," He replied.

"They tell me you're the best record keeper on this planet. Well, are you?" The Grand Guild Master's eyes examined intently.

Sam 1701 stood straighter. "I like to believe so." He started to say more but stopped when the Grand Master leaned toward him. The chubby face stared into his eye, and the words froze.

There was a booming laugh that echoed through the large room.

"Good I hate false modesty. I'm told that you spend time digging through old records."

"I like knowing what has gone on before Grand Master."

The Grand Master lifted a goblet the size of a small punch bowl to his mouth and took a deep drink. "You can call me Sam 1. I used to have another name, but I forgot it about a century ago. Have a drink," he said as he gestured for an unnoticed scantily clad young woman standing just behind his chair to serve Sam 1701. She quickly brought him a goblet to rival the Grand Master's. It wasn't as big but could hold a quart or more.

Rising and giving the woman a nod of dismissal Sam 1 approached Sam 1701. He threw an arm around him saying, "Come with me."

He led Sam 1701 around the large chair to the Grand Master private entrance. They passed into a hallway treading deeper into the bowels of the building. They walked at a steady pace that took them around a corner and downstairs until they arrived at a hall where the floor was cover with a layer of fine dust.

The Grand Master stopped Sam 1701 before a door. He grabbed the bronze handle turning it, so the door opened with a screech from the hinges. As it opened a long unused light flicker on revealing a room.

Sam 1701 gawked at the immense space fully 300 feet long and a 100 wide with shelves running the length of each wall and massive tables filling the space between. He saw that the tables and shelves were filling with boxes and stacks of disks.

The Grand Master grinned. "Welcome to your new job. I want you to be our record researcher. I want you to discover the truth of how the guild was started and where." He gestured to a massive desk sitting in the corner by the doorway. "Get busy. I'll like a report within the next year. Damn my goblet's empty. I'll leave you to it. I need a drink."

Sam 1701 walked through the room randomly picking up files from one place after the other. He placed them on the desk. He got comfortable in the chair and began to read.

Just a Drop

by
Morgan McKay

The shot ricocheted through the faceted glass, sending gold sparks wheeling in every direction. Patrons of the Gemini had hit the deck, while Cimi Daschul shoved herself under the counter, covering her head. Shards of exploding liquor bottles rained onto the bar top as the commotion turned to an uproar.

Even though she couldn't see them, she knew that her bar had suddenly become a battleground. And, with that knowledge, she began to scramble on her hands and knees to the far corner where she kept the good stuff, hoping to salvage the bottle before it joined the others.

Ios—and more importantly Siks—were known for the planetary rivalry, and even more for their confrontations in public spaces. Like her bar tonight, for instance. When she had seen the first of her tables flipped over by the Ios, she should have known what would follow. Now, both she and her patrons were dodging pistol pot shots, fired from each races' respective bunker. The Ios, hulking creatures that resembled dinosaurs of old Earth's past were now shelling the Siks across the way, lobbing her drink glasses and anything else that would pack a wallop. Their feathery opponents, avian creatures from the same planet, shot back. And Cimi used the distraction to collect her bottle of Amenberger's whiskey.

She shoved the false panel aside that sat just under the till and reached in, hoping to God there wasn't anything but a bottle waiting in there. Her fingers wrapped around a familiar neck and she yanked the good stuff into the light for the first time in a long while. It was a bit dusty, and the label was peeling, but it was still the stoutest stuff she knew about. It had been old Jerome's last bottle of whiskey, his insurance policy. One she was about to cash in on. Spinning about, glass crunched under her boots as she waddled her way undercover to the middle of the bar, the place she assumed was between the battling clans. With the bottle in one hand and her other reaching for a small blue shot glass under the bar, Cimi popped up and flipped the bottle with the precision of a master mixer. It rolled over her fingers with a flare, then she gripped it, slamming it down on the bar. Her hand traveled up the great vessel, and she placed her thumb against the cork. It popped off as a pistol shot narrowly missed her shoulder. "Hey! Assholes!"

The Siks and Ios turned in unison to the petite human who manned the bar. Her long black hair draped over her narrow shoulders, dotted with flecks of shattered glass, giving it sparkle like the stars in the sky of Old Earth. It framed her round, pale face and icy blue eyes, eyes that were glaring at the creatures who were tearing up her bar. She tilted the bottle over, loosing the golden liquid into her shot glass and lifting it into the air with a salute. "Cheers."

The sudden screams of horror were music to her ears. Ios and Siks collectively began to scramble together toward the door, covering their eyes, their mouths, and noses. Where once they'd been fighting, they were now working together to escape the stench of earthen whiskey, the most abominable wretched thing they'd ever smelled. It was a nifty trick she'd picked up from Old Jerome back on Europa almost seven years ago. Her old boss had been to the dark part of space, and back. He'd always say, as an Infinity Marine, he'd seen more space than she'd ever dreamed of. Still, the old dodger had a couple of tricks up his sleeve, and this one had become priceless and one hell of an insurance policy.

She took the shot as the last of the battleground fled through the batwing doors. The vicious burn took its time on the way down. Cimi slammed her favorite shot glass on the bar. "You sure knew how to pick whiskey you old bastard."

"And which bastard would you be referring to?" a voice questioned.

Cimi looked up.

Standing in the midst of the destruction and prior battlefield, three men stood, decked from head to toe in brilliant white. The uniforms were easily recognizable, and Cimi had to stifle a groan. Quasin Marshalls. For bartenders, especially on this end of the galaxy, the Marshalls never came for a pleasant visit. Usually, they came for information, but Cimi rarely had any of note. Not many people came to Quilis looking to defraud the Interplanetary Gambling Ring or pirate the commerce ships moving from Earth to Vagabond Row, a long string of planets that stretched from one end of the known universe to the other. So, as Cimi watched the man who'd spoken holster his sidearm, she began to speculate about their visit.

"Old Jerome. The man who owned this bar before me," Cimi calmly stated. "He had a fine taste in Old Earth whiskey."

"Is that so?" the first officer chuckled. "It seems that your prior...patrons didn't particularly like it. Mind if we join you for a few rounds?"

Cimi lifted her hand and offered the men a seat at the bar, at least the ones that were still standing. "What can I get you?"

The speaker of the group, a balding man with salt and pepper hair, flipped open a laser badge. It read Silas Transion, paired with a strong chin and an athletic frame. "You really can't ask that question much longer, Ms. Daschul. You should be offering us what you have left."

"That's true," she said. Then Cimi paused. He knew her name. That didn't bode well. "I've got whiskey for days if you'd rather that than something else."

"That's why we're here, actually," the man told her, pulling a pencil-sized tube from his pocket. He rolled it to her across the black granite countertop. "Do you know this individual?"

Cimi caught the Pentab but didn't peel it open. "What exactly is this about, Marshall?"

The man nodded. "We just need some information. And human bartenders are the best at what they do, and the best at what we need them for. Take a gander at that, would you?"

Cimi tapped the button on top of the device, and it began to project a screen, a medium picture with an animated, rotating figure. She studied it closer, reading the text sprawled out next to it, but she was more interested in who the figure was. From head to toe, it looked like a mouse, with large bristles and grey and white fur. Minsch, they were called, a race of rodent-like humanoids from two planets down. And this one, this one was one of her best friends.

"Her name is Brill Xalo. We arrested her on Talos three days ago for smuggling whiskey onto a dry planet. Do you know her, Ms. Daschul?"

Cimi knew that they were here for more than just an admonition. "I know her. She's one of my night bartenders for the Gemini. I didn't know she was off world."

"She's been off-world for several days," the marshall informed her. "As her employer, you had no idea?"

"Brill comes and goes as she likes. I'm usually here, so I don't count on the young minsch. They're hard to keep in one place anyway. Just how they are."

Cimi placed the pentab down and reached for a rag, calmly wiping the space in front of the men clean. "What do you want from me? I don't make whiskey here, so I don't know where she would be getting it."

"Do you mind if we take a look around then?"

Cimi Daschul stood straight and crossed her arms. "I don't make it here. I don't know where she got it."

"So you're saying you had nothing to do with her extracurricular activities?"

Cimi tossed the rag down. "No. I run a bar. I don't have the time or the money to 'make' whiskey for her to shuttle around. What she does in her own time, that's on her." The two other officers shuffled uncomfortably. "But, if you're insisting, I suppose I'll have to oblige you. Is there a need to search the premises, sir?"

Officer Transion smiled at Cimi. "No, not at all, Ms. Daschul. But I have one more question. Did you know that Brill was working for the Whiskey Runner?"

A spark of surprise lit on Cimi's face. She silently cursed herself as she brought it under control, but it only took that moment to damn her. "What?"

"I'm sure you've heard about the Whiskey Runner. It's been all over Earth. Especially with his recent attacks."

"I had no idea that Brill would be involved with someone like that! Are they still smuggling the bottles in and off world?"

"It's more than that, Ms. Daschul," Transion stated cordially. "They're passing messages. There's going to be an uprising."

"Passing messages? How?"

"Like this," Transion said as he reached for Old Jerome's whiskey bottle. Cimi began to protest, but he held up a finger that told her to back off. No one messed with the Marshalls and didn't sacrifice something. From his pocket, he pulled a blue light, one that hurt her eyes as it flickered on. As he flipped a crystal glass and began to pour, he slid the light underneath, reflecting and projecting the contents of the vial on the ceiling.

There were words... floating around in the liquor. "Seems Old Jerome was a little more than a bartender," Transion chuckled, pulling free the light. He pushed the glass back to Cimi, and she caught it near the edge. "Sucks to be the last one to know, hmm?"

Cimi didn't say anything as they stood up together. The salt and pepper man in the white uniform seemed to smile. "If you know anyone who's aiding this criminal, know that they'll be lumped in with the others at the trial. And trust me," he stated with a tilt of his head, "Vandergarten prison is no place for ladies such as yourself."

The thinly veiled threat made Cimi angry as he turned away, his bright white suit unmarred by the charcoal stains on the stool he sat on. As the batwing doors swung open for the first two, the man paused, and, with a fluid motion, whipped out his sidearm.

Cimi didn't flinch as a single shot rang out, nor did her eyes leave his as Old Jerome's whiskey bottle exploded beside her.

Cimi Daschul had just been threatened.

And Cimi Daschul didn't respond well to threats.

***

After blue skies and oceans, adjusting to the red glow of Quilis had taken some time. But, Cimi was resourceful and had quickly found that blue-hued goggles stifled the effect of the orange sun, which irritated the corneas of her earthen eyes. It was only just rising so she figured it would have been the best time to get out. She was on a mission. Passing the natives, several minsch and a couple of Grelkans, large frog-like beings known more for their copious bellies than their brawn, Cimi drew up in front of the commodities shop in the trade outpost of Terrace Drop.

Owned by the only other human in the general vicinity of planets, Gosling had the monopoly on all things, especially when it came to humans. They were a homesick bunch, and she'd dropped by for more than just supplies in the past. Still, it was a business day, and Cimi stepped through the moving grey doors and into the junk shop.

"Ey Rocko!" she heard a voice bellow, one that belonged to the shopkeeper behind the counter. He stood about two feet taller than her by earthen standards, covered in a photosynthetic slime that gave him his sickly green color. She hated Grelkans more than most, but she had to deal with him today. "Good Morning Crick," Cimi muttered, approaching the counter. "I need to see Rocko."

"This about the Ios you kicked outta the Gemini last night?" he inquired with a laugh. "Pretty pissy group when they came in here to buy the liquor you wouldn't sell'em."

"They started a clan squabble in the middle of the bar, so I'm glad they went somewhere else. I'm still trying to recuperate from that. It'll take me days to get the burn marks off of the walls."

"Rocko's got something for that I'm sure," Crick chuckled, spit flying. He lifted a metal piece, something that looked like an old two-cycle engine from Earth. "He's got a bit of everything nowadays. Whatya need though? I'm sure I can start pullin' it for you. We gotta new shipment of liquors a few days ago."

"Go ahead and fill this then," Cimi told him, tossing him a Pentab. He slid it open, reading the flickering letters.

"They drank all of this?" Crick guffawed, looking up at her. His face was hard to read, but she was sure it was amusement.

"Not drank. Destroyed. Almost half my stock. I hope Rocko's got something he needs from a bartender, else the Gemini won't have anything to sell."

She flipped her long black hair over her shoulder and slid her hands into a leather space jacket that hugged her narrow frame. Skinny pants wrapped around her lower half and knee-high boots laced right below her kneecap. Cimi cocked her hip to the side as the Grelkan read the list, sighing.

"Heard you pissed off a few Siks and Ios last night," a voice chuckled as a familiar face emerged from the back reaches of the store. Rocko Gosling's firm jaw and brilliant green eyes locked that smirk onto a firm countenance marred by acid burns. Still, Cimi found him attractive, and she liked men with a bit of a background. Human men, anyway.

"I was telling Crick as much. It doesn't take long for them to burn the damn place down if you know what I mean."

Rocko nodded and slid his hands into his pockets. His ex-military figure cut an impressive shadow under the periodic lights that adorned the scattered shop. "Well, come on back. I'm sure we can work out something to barter for the booze. Besides, you're the only other human in this quadrant, so I suppose we have to stick together."

He turned, pushing a contraption out of the way, clearing a path for them as they slid into a small office space that was unbelievably neat and organized. It was the quarters of a soldier and one that knew the location of every object he needed to survive. He closed the door behind her and offered her a seat.

She didn't take it.

"You're here about Brill, aren't you?"

The words struck her, but it didn't make them any less true.

"The Marshalls came in here looking for my whiskey stores. Asked to examine them. Then ran both me and Crick through the ringer. You know, they're real fancy bastards in their white suits. I'm gonna invent something to muck 'em up."

"What did they ask you about Brill?"

"They told me she'd been arrested on Talos. She was working for the Whiskey Runner? How could you not know that?"

Cimi swiveled her hips. "Did they tell you anything else?"

"No. Is it true?"

"I don't know Rocko. She was off-world a lot."

"Well," the ex-marine started, "She picked a hell of a cause to join. I don't suppose you keep up with the news? Come on Cim, sit down. You're makin' me all kinds of nervous standing like that."

She obliged him and slid into the leather-like chair across from the desk. He rocked back and slid his hands behind his head. Outside, she could hear Crick grumble, then the clatter of bottles as he tossed them in her bag.

"I was talking to a few of my old buddies back on Earth a couple days ago. Said that the Resistance groups were getting stronger. A lot of the commoners are rejecting the communist agendas and are trying to overthrow several of the regimes. The UK is definitely going to be one of the first republics if the Whiskey Runner manages what he's trying to do."

"Which is?" Cimi queried, unaware of the rumors. "Getting whiskey back where it came from? Or…"

"The messages are hidden in the liquor. I heard Officer Transion shot your bottle from old Jerome."

"Who told you that?"

"Some scrub who was in here earlier said he was in the bar when all the rioting went down."

Cimi rested back this time, crossing her arms against her chest. There hadn't been anyone in the bar when the Marshalls had come calling.

"I doubt Old Jerome had anything to do with it. And if Brill was working for the Whiskey Runner as a smuggler, then she probably tainted my bottle."

The whole time Rocko studied her face. "Or she didn't know about it at all, and someone else planted that bottle."

"What are you getting at?"

"I'm saying," Rocko commented with a grunt, sitting up and clasping his hands on the desk, "is that someone is looking to get you off this rock, just like they are me. Humans out this far are a threat. We could always start a new free colony on some Class E planet and call it the new Earth. Then what would the Marshalls have to do?"

Rocko was right. It could be done, and easily. And it would explain why the Whiskey Runner was usurping non-humans to help. Earthlings were being rounded up like cattle and shipped back home to be watched and commanded.

"They threatened you too, didn't they?" Cim interjected. "Was one of your bottles tainted?"

"All of'em were. So now, the Marshall's think I'm the Whiskey Runner. I have the resources and the commodities docks for this entire quadrant. I'm surprised they didn't arrest the both of us on the grounds of espionage."

All of this made Cimi's stomach twirl in a knot. A tight one.

"I'm not going back to Earth." Her voice was final, deadpanned.

"Yea, me neither. I'm going to get Brill first though."

"Get Brill? Are you insane?"

"Some say that."

"She's in Vandergarten—there's no way you can even get to her."

"No, she's not there yet."

Cimi pulled another Pentab from her jacket pocket, this one disguised as a hairpin. "I've never asked this from you, and you don't have to start. But…"

She tossed it to him, watching as he read the contents and managed a smile. "All of it?"

"All of it…and anything else you might want to toss in as a Hail Mary."

Rocko chuckled. "I want the Gemini. Is that a fair trade?"

Cimi started at that. "My bar?"

"Your list is pretty extensive Cim. And there is a likelihood you won't come back. So, I want the Gemini after twenty-five red cycles. Do we have a deal?"

She pondered for a moment, and never one for indecision, extended her hand. "Alright. Deal."

As he clasped her hand, he stood. "Alright, the warehouse is your playland. Anything you can carry."

Two double doors slid open behind him as she watched him depress a red button on his desk. He motioned to the door. "And I'll get to working on that Marshall's pass for you, Ms. Daschul. Enjoy."

***

Cimi left the commodities depot with lighter pockets and heavier bags. The coarse material chafed against her naked shoulder, having drug open her jacket just enough to expose the freckled skin beneath. She shifted it unconsciously and pulled the black pleather strap higher, walking with a slight dip so that it would rest comfortably on her hip, rather than her shoulder. That left her to look at the rocky ground that made up the main drag of the small outpost known as Terrace Drop. Built into the side of a mountain, the mining outpost had become a haven as of late for all manner of life. Cimi hated what the place had become in the last few years. More and more of the gentle races had fled to greener rocks, and that had left the rough and tumble collection that cowered on Terrace Drop. As she approached The Gemini at the base of the tower lift and wandered her way into the alley toward the back, she groaned as she thought about how long it would take to scrub the laser burns from the walls.

Even if she'd tried to make the bar a gun free space, there was no way she could enforce it. Law enforcement was what you could make of it, and the only time the offenders ever stayed home was when the Marshalls were in town. A night like last night.

A night that had Cimi making plans.

Brill had supposedly been arrested and tortured. She saw it on the Pentab and could see the Marshall's cybernetic eyes narrow as she looked through the holographic image at him. And three? It didn't take three Marshalls to garner that kind of information. They were looking for a fight. But a fight with who?

Cimi could smell the whiskey on her jacket and let her mind wander. She kicked something in the alleyway, and it clattered down through the stink of urine and garbage, landing next to the rusting steel wall of Kigli's butcher shop. The back alley smelled terrible, reminding her of the old days back on Earth when she played in downtown Brooklyn back during the Harpersville Riots. Her parents' store had been burned down soon after, and they'd been put out on the street. Cimi tried to forget that now as she slid the key panel out of the wall next to the back door of The Gemini. Twenty years had come and gone, Earth had been razed and rebuilt, a bright new shining star of equality and poisoned utopia.

And Cimi had been on the first boat out of there.

It had only taken a few years for her to see the truth of what her home planet had become, and she watched from a distance as those that stayed became the impressed new citizens of the Human Republic of Earth. And the Marshalls, the cybernetic watchdogs of the Milky Way. Cimi stayed far away. She had known it would catch up to her eventually.

The barkeep stuck her hand in the contraption, and it turned green, reading her DNA and popping the lock on the back door. A bright white light clicked on, and she pushed the door open, dropping her bag on the floor next to the entrance and flipping on the light. Her room was a horrendous mess. A small cot stretched across the left wall, mussed with tangled blankets and tossed pillows. Her whiskey-drenched clothes from the night before lay hanging on the back of her black vanity chair, and there were more than a few empty food rations lying about. Cimi sighed and pushed the door closed, keeping the steamy atmosphere outside.

Straight across from her, the portal to the actual Gemini waited, but Cimi couldn't bring herself to look over the destruction. Instead, she shed her coat and sat herself down on the corner of the rumpled bed, leaning forward to cradle her face in her hands. She rubbed her weary eyes. "Now what?" Cimi asked aloud. "You've got Marshalls after you, and you basically sold the Gemini for a few rounds of booze. Good job."

She fell backward then, bare arms above her head, her bright green eyes staring at the ceiling. Rust spots decorated the expanse with flowers of bright red and patina, spiraling out from the center and eating the metal in huge swaths. Cimi sighed. Just another thing she'd have to fix.

The roll of a bottle across the floor gave her pause, and the woman shot up suddenly. The pale blue light that hung in the center of her small cell seemed to dim as she stood, reaching for her gunbelt, the one she'd hung over her jacket on the chair. She pulled her pistol from it, edging along the wall toward the door to the Gemini's main floor.

The door had been locked—she was sure of that. No one could have gotten in here without her knowing, and indeed, no one could have broken in. The Gemini and all the surrounding buildings were made from the remains of the ships that had settled the area, so the bulkheads were a foot thick at least. No one could have cut their way in.

But Cimi had a bad feeling, and swiveled herself into The Gemini, her gun leading the way through the barely cracked door.

The main lights were on, and standing in the center of the Gemini was a familiar man.

It wasn't so much that she was surprised by his appearance—she just hadn't expected them so soon. And she surely hadn't expected the pile of whiskey bottles he had lying at their feet.

"Ms. Daschul. Care to explain where these came from?"

She didn't lower her weapon but cast her gaze down. Twenty. Maybe thirty bottles.

She didn't own that much whiskey, let alone know where to get it out here in the far reaches. "I don't know Marshall. You tell me. I just bought my booze down at the Comod. And those bottles don't look anything like what Gosling sells."

"We found them here. Under the bar." There was a click, and Cimi felt the barrel of a laser pistol rest solidly in her black hair, right at the base of her neck. The Marshall sneered, but Cimi didn't relent.

"I would say you planted them here, more like. Every damn bottle."

"But what's your word against ours, Ms. Daschul? It's plain as day for all to see, right here."

He tapped an empty bottle with his foot, and it rolled, gently bumping into hers. "And you've pulled a weapon on me. That. Now that is another criminal offense."

The slender ivory clad man slowly walked toward her, as one of the Marshalls pushed his gun into her skull. "Drop it."

Cimi was suddenly thinking quick, trying to find a way out of this. But there wasn't. She was stuck, blackmailed. And now, headed to Vandergarten.

Slowly, Cimi raised her hand, and the gun was plucked from her fingers. Forcibly grabbing her wrists, the apprehending Marshall turned and shoved her against the bar, locking her hands behind her back in a pair of dark nickel handcuffs.

"Cimi Daschul, by the mandate of the Human Republic of Earth, you are under arrest for conspiring with terrorists and smuggling, as well as threatening a law officer. You may say whatever you wish, but know that it may be used against you in your trial back on Earth."

Cimi's head snapped up suddenly, surprised. "Earth? Not Vandergarten?"

The Marshall smiled, his eyes twitching with electricity as they narrowed. "No, all terrorists will be tried by the masses of Earth as examples. Congratulations Ms. Daschul. You're going home."

A sudden jerk had Cimi on her feet and trudging through the back door into her room. She looked longingly at the small cell one last time, knowing full well it would quickly fall into Gosling's hands once word of her arrest spread.

And as they yanked her into a small transport, Cimi Daschul tried to think of one thing to get her out of this mess. But nothing came. Nothing but hope for a miracle.

***

Marshalls were all the same Cimi mused as she watched them mill about the deck of the transport cruiser. It was a small affair for the trio, a class 2 gate jumper from the Europian shipyards, equipped with only the necessities: a bridge, a brig, and an escape hatch. The only entertainment that she could muster was pulling at the handcuffs binding her wrists and ankles, but that too provided little amusement. She was stuck, like a magnet to a steel plate. The bangles on her wrists had been magnetized to attach to the back of the chair she now sat in, a throne surrounded by superheated laser beams that would easily slice through her skin like butter. Her ankles had gotten the same treatment, and now, she was beginning to ache.

Or, at least she would have if her arms hadn't been numb. She dropped her head with a sigh, staring at her heavy boots and the untied laces. Magnetized or not, the cuffs didn't allow much play, and Cimi tried desperately to stretch her shoulders, fearing that, if she ever did get out of this mess, that they'd be stuck like that permanently.

Footsteps drew her vision upward to an approaching figure, hard to miss in his bright suit against the cold, dismal grey of the ship's hull.

"Come to read me my rights again?" Cimi snorted, flipping the ebony strands from her vision. She winced as she turned her shoulder against the metal and let go.

"No need, you won't really need them," the Marshall retorted, pausing right in front of her. He peered through the sizzling bars and smiled an odd, knowing grin. Cimi gauged the unfamiliar Marshall, giving him a long once-over. Had she been standing, he would be a whole head taller than her. Dishwater blonde, somewhat longer than the others, stood straight up an inch from his skull. He had brilliant blue eyes, so unnerving that Cimi looked at other things.

"Sounds like I won't have much fun back on Earth," the bartender snorted derisively. "Least you could let me have was one last drink."

"Oh don't worry, at your trial, you can have all the whiskey you want, just like the other four we've arrested within the last cycle. Brill being one of them."

"Four? Who are the others?"

The Marshall winked. "Don't worry, you'll find out. We'll be on Earth in half a span. Get comfy. You'll be in that chair for another couple of hours."

Another voice entered the fray then, and Cimi's lips pressed into a hard line. "Back here fraternizing with the enemy?"

"I'm not an enemy," the woman retorted.

"Contrary to popular belief, you are," Marshall Transion replied, stepping up beside the unnamed Marshall. "Septon, head back up and help Excle. We're coming into Republic Space."

The man nodded and turned, but not before he cast the glimmer of a smile at her. At the point she was at now, Cimi believed that she'd suddenly lost her mind and was seeing things.

Transion quickly snapped her out of it. "I've spoken to my superiors. You'll be tried within the week."

"Great. The quicker I can go home."

He chuckled, crossing his arms behind his back in a gesture she was sure was from a movie. And always, the bad guy had done it when he thought he'd won.

"Humans are meant to be on Earth. We aren't like all of these other races. We aren't spread out, we aren't mating with the first compatible creature to walk in front of us. We're pure, we're genetically balanced."

Cimi didn't buy into that mentality. No, not at all. But she entertained him for the meantime, listening to what he had to say. "So you're rounding up all of us, no matter if we're guilty or not?"

"Oh, no, I think you're guilty, just like the rest of them," Transion pointed out. "The Whiskey Runner has many faces, it's just the fact that you didn't even bother to hide your involvement."

Cimi pulled against her bonds. "Because I wasn't involved!"

"The bottles say otherwise."

"The bottles were planted."

"In a bar?"

"In my bar, you bastard."

Transion's grey metallic eyes smiled at her in their own way and condemned her all the same. "Who's going to contest the word of a Marshall, Cimi Daschul?"

She glared at him with her chocolate eyes, staring him down. He leaned forward, his sharp nose barely millimeters from the heat bars. "No one. Not even you."

With that, he turned and casually eased his way back to the bridge, a door that was in full sight of the chair Cimi sat in. The wheels turned in her mind, but they weren't getting a grip. And she was running out of options.

***

Docking, at Bay Nineteen. Memphis. Please wait for clearance before departing.

The woman's voice sounded so familiar, and if possible, so utterly human it made her sick. Cimi heard the air sizzle as the beams were turned off, then the maglocks released. And there was the Marshall, Septon by the badge, helping her to stand on wobbly and numb feet. The smell of Mississippi river water assaulted her first—the muddy, garbage infested swamp odor that had become so prevalent in the time of her youth. But oxygen was oxygen, and there was no better place to breathe it than home.

The back of the small spaceship released with a clank, lowering the ramp down onto the landing pad where it echoed throughout the space. Cimi blinked as the sun came into view, attempting to adjust her eyes to the new yellow light versus the red she was so accustomed to. But everywhere she looked, she saw things that made her cringe. Like the reporters waiting on the outside of the platform, already snapping pictures of a mysterious woman in handcuffs, being led down the ramp and across the pad to a waiting car.

Cimi wanted to look away from all of the stark human faces, their colorful facades, brown, black and white, but it was nostalgic. She'd been away from humankind for too many years to not look.

The public wanted to know, but Septon guided her away from the crowd and back toward the hangar that sat in the center of the pads. With Excle and Transion in the lead and Septon behind, Cimi had determined that it was done. There was no way out of this. Seven hours on the flight from her bar to this place had left her there.

But something happened then that she didn't expect.

The bangles that held her wrists together suddenly popped open as they approached the side of a small personal aircraft.

The familiar handle of a laser pistol slid into her fingers.

And then, Cimi Daschul was running for her life toward the edge of a four-story building, throwing her manacles away and scrambling for cover as hell broke loose in a symphony of laser shots and human screams.

***

The air quickly became a sizzle of bright lights, fired across the landing pad in various directions. She covered her head and hit the tarmac, rolling beneath the body of a helicopter for cover. The smell of asphalt invaded her senses as she lifted her head to peer from beneath the landing gear. From her vantage point, six men hunkered down behind the small aircraft she'd been beside, two in white, the rest in standard military attire. And the crowd they were shooting at were…the reporters?

No, the woman realized. Not reporters. Armed soldiers. Soldiers bearing the Resistance mark under their right eye. The equation.

Coats and various disguises hung on the fighters as they ducked for cover, drawing fire. Cimi saw her chance then as the shots let up and sprung to her feet, running for the side of the tower landing pad. As she did, she witnessed a sizeable white craft float past the edge and level with the tower. Cimi hefted her gun.

Through the glass, she could see a white uniform and clenched the trigger as the firefight behind her erupted in cries and shots once again. She witnessed the side of the cargo bay slid open. The pilot waved her on. And even though he wore the uniform of a Marshall, he also bore the same mark on his cheek. The Equation.

She broke into a sprint.

Her heavy boots pounded the tarmac as she heard Transion's voice order the few soldiers he did command to turn on her. Cimi's long black hair blew into her face as she turned for a split second to look. Transion lifted his gun, and at that moment, Cimi took a leap into a lucky cargo transport with a perfect stranger.

She spun slightly in the air, aiming her gun toward the men. One shot struck Excle in the chest and threw him back against the aircraft. Transion shot back, grazing her cheek with a vicious sizzle. She collided with the steel grate of the deck with a crash and into a pile of boxes. The cargo door slammed shut behind her.

"Get up here! We've got to clear town or else they'll pick us out of the sky!"

Cimi pushed a box off of her, and it fell with a crash. "That's a bit difficult! Keep this boat steady would you!?"

The craft veered hard to the left, rolling Cimi out of the boxes and into the cargo door with a thud. Having dislodged the parcels, they now tumbled on top of her as the cargoheli zipped through the air this way and that. Pretty soon, the bartender turned fugitive covered her head and rolled with the boxes. Hard thuds pounded into the hard metal of the flying machine as the Marshalls caught up with them, reinforcements from the landing pad. There was a loud buzz she'd never heard before, and as the air whined with projectiles, she listened to the pilot curse in several different languages.

"Dammit!" came a cry from the cockpit, and she definitely knew what that meant.

A series of hard clangs and the smell of smoke alerted her before her rising stomach did. Jerking, the craft tried to stay aloft, but the

Marshalls had damaged it past the point of recovery. It began to fall from the sky. Weightlessness overtook Cimi in the weirdest fashion. Even though she'd never been in space without gravity, the sheer feeling made her queasy. Boxes began to float from on top of her and into the compartment, and she pushed off the wall like a floating feather.

A passing body grabbed her though, shedding a stark white uniform coat to reveal a tattered white t-shirt. The man who had once been piloting her getaway car now drug her toward the back of the vehicle by her collar, his hands working the latch feverishly. Cimi made the grievous mistake of looking down, only to see the brown water of the Mississippi River quickly approaching.

"When I get this open, you're going to have to push away from the truck. That, or land on top of it. Do you hear me?"

He grabbed and shook her, drawing her eyes away from the doom below. "Cimi!"

And with that, he released the lock and they were falling, sitting ducks several hundred feet from the mighty river. Somehow Cimi managed to right herself, falling face first the last few feet from the water. The man had gotten them low enough to where the drop wouldn't kill them, but it was about to hurt. She tried her best to plunge into the murky water feet first, though the whipping wind burnt her face and eyes.

And then she was in the water, clawing, scrambling for the surface as every nerve in her body lit up like a spark, sending her near to blackout, reaching for the light through a muddy brown window.

***

The sound of shattering glass startled Cimi into the world of the living.

"Broden! Get your ass in here! You sat the damn bottle on the top shelf, and it raked the others off again!"

It was dark where she laid her head, and the woman didn't move as a figure came tramping into the room. He stood almost two heads taller than her, burly like a Grelkan, but all human. She could see the red in his beard from where she lay, and the style of his dress told her all she needed to know. Cautiously, she rolled over with an unexpected groan.

The fall had taken a little more out of her than she'd expected, and how she'd gotten to the cot in the back of a bar was a mystery. But, if there was one thing that Cimi Daschul was appreciative of, it was that she'd managed to escape. And, that she was alive. That was a plus too.

"Hey, Sevens! Yo girl is rollin' outta the bed in here!"

Cimi didn't try to say anything, just planted her feet on the rotted wooden floor. Her boots were gone, socks too, and the sensation of actual earth wood beneath her bare toes was unique and reminiscent. The place smelled like old hickory wood, doused with a few gallons of booze, and probably a couple fires. But that aroma gripped her like a bearhug. Cimi welcomed it. She grabbed the back of her head to rub the soreness from her neck, noting that her hair was still damp and smelled like river water. All in all, though, she was in one piece.

A figure appeared in the door as the burly man flipped a switch, revealing the whole of the room in more detail. It was a stockroom, that was for sure, littered with old glass bottles of liquors she hadn't seen in years. Some not before the Second Prohibition, and definitely before that. Dust settled on almost everything, but it made her that much more appreciative of the lengths this man had gone to keep it safe.

"Where the hell am I?" she queried, managing her feet unsteadily, holding onto a root that hung from the ceiling.

Wait. The ceiling?

She looked up. As far as she could see, there was a dirt roof. Large veins of roots crisscrossed adjacent to slats of wood, old looking rusted beams and more. "Now that's not what I was expecting."

"You're in Northern Mississippi," the unfamiliar figure said. Her gaze returned to the two men who stood by the door. Even though he seemed vaguely familiar, his accent and face were not. He was clearly Australian. She could have picked that inflection anywhere, having been on Earth or not in the last ten years. He was of average height and build, with sandy blonde hair that was barely peach fuzz. Buzzed in the familiar military crew cut, it did little to detract from the rest of him. Bright, intelligent blue eyes stared at her, hands shoved in the pockets of a black coat with a thousand pockets. Military issue by the looks of it, she noted the double line logo of the resistance under his right eye immediately and eased the tension in her shoulders.

"And how did I get here, pray tell?" Cimi smiled a pained, wry grin, and stretched.

"Well, after we jumped out of a cargoheli and into the Mississippi River, you managed to swim to shore where Herbert and Vander were waiting for us. Then, I guess you passed out. They brought us up here for a round of drinks and a little time to let things die down. Your escape made the news, by the way."

"You mean ours."

"That's semantics. I was sent to retrieve you, and so I have."

"That's great, and I really appreciate it. But...who are you?"

The man chuckled and bent forward a little bit, a look of amusement on his face. "I'm surprised you don't recognize me. I rode the entire way to Earth with you."

"The guy called you Sevens. And there was no Aussie on that transport with me."

"Yea...I go by Sevens when I'm here. They think it's funny, them boys. And I guess it kinda fits. Come on out here. I'll grab ya boots and explain everything."

She waddled her way across the splintered floor and into a common room, one that definitely noticed her. It was a bar. A very illegal one.

A few occupants sat at make-shift wooden tables strewn this way and that, all harsh characters that had their own stories to tell. To her left, a long plank of wood sat from wall to wall, a testament to the old speakeasies of the pre-21 century. Lines of clean crystal bottles sat in the carved out earth on planks, and the rotgut that she could smell in the earth was entrancing. Someone bumped her, and she turned to see the burly red man pull out a chair.

"I wouldn't be walking 'cross this floor without shoes, little lady. Plop down here with that'en, and I'll grab em if they're still up there."

"If they're still...?" The look on Sevens' unfamiliar façade told her all she needed to know. "Ok. Thanks."

She watched him travel toward a silver door set in one of the walls and heard the scrape of a chair as the Aussie plopped down next to her. "Wanta drink?'

"Whiskey. Straight. Old."

"Should be able to handle that. Ey Markie!" Sevens raised a hand and held up two fingers. At least it was a universal sign for the good stuff. The slender white-headed barkeep nodded and began to whip out two glasses he'd been polishing since they'd entered the common room. He turned back and plopped his feet down on the table. "So you've got questions."

"More than a few. You're Septon. Marshall Septon. I don't know how, but, you are."

"Quicker than she said," Sevens snickered.

"Than who said?"

"Your Bartender. Brill Xalo."

"You know Brill? How?"

"I've been working with her for a few months. I'm one of the best smugglers she has."

"Then how have I never met you?"

Sevens seemed to ponder that for a minute. "We have met. Several times. You just don't recognize me."

Cimi shook her head. "No, I remember everyone I meet, especially if they were with Brill."

Two glasses clinked on the table, and Cimi turned. "Thanks, barkeep."

He nodded and turned back toward the bar, wiping his hands on the muddy towel in his back pocket.

"Okay, well do you remember me?"

Cimi lifted her glass and turned, surprised by the tone of voice. And when she did, she almost choked on the shot. It burned all the way down and made her cough, but that was nothing compared to the confusion bouncing around in her head. As she laid eyes on Sevens, the Aussie that sat there before was now a man of the same build and height, but with black hair, a goatee and green eyes. And…he spoke perfect Russian.

"How in the world?…" she marveled. "How did you do that?"

"Ok…what about this one?"

Cimi watched as he shook his head, and everything shifted. Black became blonde, green became blue, pale became tan. His face seemed to melt slightly. Then Rocko Gosling sat in front of her.

"There's no way…"

"Perks of being a Marshall once," Seven replied with Rocko's voice. "I can be whoever I want, so long as they kinda look like me, to begin with. Nanotech from the Grelkan Kindred War. Comes in handy every so often."

And then he was back, that short hair, full face, and twisting smile.

"So you can do that whenever?"

"Pretty much."

"And you were on the flight back from the Gemini?"

"Yea."

"I'm going to need another one of these."

She lifted her fingers, and the barkeep nodded. "So...color me more confused than when I woke up."

Sevens nodded and threw back the whiskey. "Hell of a year, that. Cheers."

The rattle of the door made Cimi turn, and the barback came in, clutching her boots in his hands. "Still here. But it's raining so they might be a little damper than when you took 'em off. Sorry."

Cimi tried her best to look thankful, but as she slid her feet into them with a sickening slurp, she almost yanked them back off. Another round hit the table, and it took a minute for the woman to collect herself. "Alright," she breathed after a period of silence. "Now what?"

"Well, now, I take you to Brill Xalo."

"But Brill's supposed to be in Vandergarten. I just barely escaped prison and a death sentence. Now you want me to walk right back into one? I say there's another way."

Sevens laughed. "No. Brill Xalo is nowhere near Vandergarten. She's holed up in the north, leading the revolts."

"On Earth?" That took Cimi by surprise.

"Who else? She's the only one with the Intel and leadership. The Whiskey Runner is out finding recruits, while we fight the battles for freedom at home."

Cimi downed her second shot, and this one burned the way it should. "And what would Brill want with me? I know you didn't come get me for sentimental value. And I'm sure that she didn't send you after me because I'm a good bartender."

"She knew you were in trouble out there. And getting to you was easy. Getting you here was hard."

She laughed. "Looks like I was coming back in chains or in a body bag anyway."

After a moment's pause, Cimi turned to Sevens, her long hair brushing over her shoulders, damp, but still darker than a Europan night. "Guess it's time to throw in with this little cause since they were the ones who rescued my bacon eh? Find me something to eat, and you can lead the way, medicine man."

***

When Cimi emerged into the light sometime later, it was in the middle of corn. Lots and lots of corn. It stretched as far as the eye could see in every direction, some of it broken or pushed down by the patrons of the Corn Hole. It had been so aptly named that she shook her head, turning to follow Sevens through the field. He wore a new disguise, a man much older than his body let on, but as they jumped in an off-road jeep, she understood why.

Roadblocks.

Though it had been some time since she'd been back on Earth, little had changed about the south. Rows and rows of cotton, corn, and soybeans stretched down long strips of road, and the smell of the summer heat and good dirt brought back memories. Still, as they rolled up to the border between Tennessee and Mississippi, Cimi Daschul took a deep breath and waited for Sevens to do the work.

The officer at the post was a young man, a sheriff from some town they'd passed through twenty or so minutes ago. He lifted his hand as they pulled up and motioned for them to stop.

"Afternoon, officer," Seven said in the most gravelly, smoker voice Cimi had ever heard. "We're headin' up to see my son. He's stationed in the barracks in Memphis. About to deploy, you see."

"Sounds good. Who's he serving with, sir? Might that I know 'em."

"Oh, what was it hon?..." Sevens turned to her with a wink. "201? Ground?"

"That's right Pop. See? You're not getting so old you can't remember things."

Sevens winked at her and turned back to the officer. Cimi smiled, looking back ahead.

"Hey, good to know. Alright, all I need is your handprint, and you can get on up the road."

The officer pulled out a device that mimicked the one she'd had at the bar back in Quilis. And Sevens was about to fail it. They were caught.

"I reckon I can do that," Sevens chuckled. "If you don't mind, hang it on in here. I'm a might stiff from all that drivin'."

Officer Sanders did as Sevens asked, and he played it through to the end. As the transparent plate glowed green, Cimi did what she could to keep from exhaling the breath she had stored. "Alright, ya'll…Safe trip."

He stepped away, and Sevens urged the vehicle forward, passing through the gate with little hindrance, and off onto the blacktop that reached into the southernmost reaches of the Volunteer state.

"Three…"

Cimi turned to him, but his eyes were locked on the road ahead.

"Two…"

"What the hell is going on?"

"One."

Sevens punched the throttle, sucking Cimi back in her seat. She watched his face shift fluidly again, this time a younger man with blonde hair. There was a crisp blueness to his face as the new identity took hold, and he gripped the wheel tighter as they flew down the highway.

"I didn't think about the border patrol. The pad will recognize me, but not as who I looked like. I tipped off the police by doing that. And now, we've got to get out of here as soon as we can before he sends the helis' after us.

"Do these vehicles have trackers? Are they going to be able to pinpoint us?"

"No, we took them out."

"Then why are we going so fast?"

"Because," Sevens said with the most serious face she'd ever seen, "I like to go fast. And I don't want him catching up with us."

And Cimi sat back then and shut her mouth.

***

"So why did the Marshalls come get me?" Cimi asked a little while later after the long drawn fields had become too dull to bear any longer.

"Bait. Hostage. Take your pick," Sevens chuckled. "How best to draw out the Whiskey Runner's right hand but to take her best friend?"

"Why don't they go after the Whiskey Runner? Wouldn't that be their first goal?"

"Not quite," he admitted. "Just from being with them for a few days looking for you, I garnered a little intel. Basically, the Whiskey Runner isn't important. They just want to keep the two from getting together."

"Has the war changed here? Is it the same out in the galaxy?"

"The war here took a turn. It's not even about the trade embargos anymore. At first, we couldn't drink, which is where the Whiskey Runner came in. Smuggling booze became smuggling people, like the old Underground Railroad. People wanted off. Realistically, this war is about being free to do what you want. The Human Republic of Earth has slowly chipped away at those rights."

"Is it influence from other races?" she inquired, genuinely interested.

"Possibly, but we can't see infiltration from this far down. The United Nations has agreed to hear the people only because we've been staging attacks in all the major cities around the world. Only a few have been thwarted, but each time, they see the equation."

"Clever. I wish I'd thought of that."

Sevens laughed, his grin wide. "Supposin' that, we'd all be dead. No offense."

"None taken," she laughed with him. "So where are we going?"

"Chicago."

"Are they still known for their pizza?"

The ex-marine looked at her. "Seriously?"

"I'm as serious as they come. From a social revolution to pizza. What? Can't keep up?"

Silence pervaded the old beat up jeep. "Well. The pizza is okay."

"So where are you originally from?"

"I was waiting on that one. Where'd you think?"

"Boston."

"What?" He turned to her curiously, his face rippling again. It took the form of a middle-aged, road weary marine.

"So I was right."

Seven smacked his hand against the steering wheel, and his face flickered back to the blonde 20-something. "Dammit. No one's pegged that quite as quick as you did."

"What can I say? Bartending on Europa for years...I learned to read people."

Cimi crossed her arms, her black jacket crinkling. "Besides, you really weren't that hard. What do you really sound like?"

"I don't remember," he chimed honestly.

"So you've been doing this for a while, then?"

"Longer than you probably realize."

"Give me a time frame. I'm curious."

The car bumped hard on a bad patch of asphalt, swinging the conversation. "You sure are curious. I thought bartenders were supposed to listen, not ask."

"Oh, well, we are," Cimi said with a ruby smile. "But, that's only on Earth."

"I thought that was a guild thing," Sevens told her. "You know, listen, don't tell? Isn't that right?"

"I suppose. But bartenders are usually the ones you have to look out for. Got a bottle of whiskey in here?"

"Yea, my small bottle is in the back bag."

Cimi climbed over the seat, careful not to let him see what she was doing. "Oh! Dammit! Pull over Sevens. I spilled this freaking everywhere."

"We need to keep going Cimi. If we don't, we won't make it in time."

"Sevens...oh dammit. I got it on all of this equipment."

The jeep yanked over then, and Sevens threw it in park. "We really don't need this now!"

He cracked the door and jumped into the night, coming around the vehicle in blind anger. "You know if Brill didn't ask me to get you..."

He rounded the corner and looked up to find a gun pointed squarely in his face. Cimi Daschul held the pistol, and in her other hand, a small viewfinder. In it, a small red dot blinked like a pulsing heart, bearing a direction and heading.

"You'd what? Take me to Ohio? Toward the Marshalls' headquarters? Don't color me a fool, Marshall Septon."

He snatched his gun quicker than she could fathom and pointed it right in her vision. "I'm taking you where I said I would."

"To who? To Brill? Or to Transion?"

"To Brill. You've lost your mind."

"Oh, but that's not what your orders are, are they, Septon? You already told me the Marshalls were going to use me for bait. What better bait than a Marshall toting it around to keep it safe, and to draw out the one you're looking for?"

Septon's face shimmered in the dark and turned again, this time to the battle-hardened Bostonian she'd briefly seen. "I'm not a traitor."

"Not a traitor to who? It was too easy. You appeared to have a camaraderie with the Marshalls. The story behind your ability to shift into anyone. The sudden turn against your own kind back on the helipad. They all started stacking up against you the instant you walked into my bar. And when I started asking questions..."

She popped the safety on her gun. "My sense of direction doesn't fail me now, and it doesn't fail me, even in the deep of space. I knew we were going in the wrong direction, but I couldn't let you get too far. Drop your gun, and this'll be easier for the both of us, Marshall."

Septon glared at her. "You're the perfect bait, Cimi. And now we've got Brill."

"No, not quite. Even though you told Brill the rendezvous was in fifty miles, I sped things up."

Two huge lights flickered on in the trees next to the road, and the green sights of several high powered weapons pinned his chest. "They were waiting for us to get this far. And now, I've found Brill's mole, and managed to get myself back on the planet at the same time."

"Drop your weapon, Marshall Markus Septon!"

It fell from his fingers. He wasn't an idiot by any means. "How did you know?"

"I told you. You sat at my bar. All your secrets are mine."

Figures emerged from the brush, black-clad Resistance warriors led by a familiar face. Brill.

As they shoved Septon against the truck and bound him, the Minsch woman came to stand next to Cimi Daschul. She stood almost the same height, lithe and coated in a subtle sheen of white, short hair. Her large round pink eyes took in the scene before her. "I knew it was him. But there was no way to be sure."

"You were right in asking for my help. The plan worked out just as we said it would. My passage back onto the planet would have been suspicious. What better way to bypass customs than in the hands of a few Marshalls?"

Septon glared at her, unbelieving. "This was your plan? Plan for what? You're crazy!"

"Eh, they've called me that," Cimi Daschul chuckled. "I have a few other names too."

A set of soldiers approached, saluting the woman as Brill offered her a coat. She slid it on, watching the soldiers pull Septon from the truck after a thorough pat down. "Pull the power cells from the truck and make sure there's nothing left that he can use to call out. Kill his communicator. It's implanted below his right ear. Then I want you to let him go."

"Let him go?" Brill questioned, her long whiskers wiggling slightly. "He's a valuable hostage."

"He might be more trouble than he's worth. But, he's a good messenger." She turned to him, her raven black hair caught in the wind, her face turned into a sardonic smile. "They'll want to hear what he has to say."

As a guard held the EMP against his head, killing his com, Septon crumbled, dizzy. And the woman crouched in front of him, holding his chin. "Tell them thanks for the ride, but the Whiskey Runner is back in town. I won't need any more assistance. Thanks though."

And with that, Cimi Daschul stood, shoved her hands in her long coat, and stalked down the hill to her waiting chariot.

She had a war to finish.

The Game

by

H. David Blalock

"You look like you could use another," the barkeep, a six-tentacled Aldeboran called Keill, said through its translator.

Jeff Halloran nodded and shoved his glass forward. "The same again, please."

Two of the barkeep's six appendages wrapped around the glass and transported it to a dispenser. A golden liquor the Aldeborans called whiskey and humans called beer poured into it to the brim. "What's troubling you?"

He took the beer but let it stand on the bar. He looked along the length of the counter, taking in the variety of lifeforms sitting, reclining, or standing as was their way. An equal variety of refreshments stood before each, some liquid, some solid, some still wiggling and trying to escape their confinement. Hanging over the bar was a portrait of the Emperor. The Aldeboran sometimes claimed to be a personal friend but nobody really believed him, although no one had the courage to call it out on that. The lighting in the bar was just bright enough to prevent drunks from stumbling into the other customers but not so bright as to discourage anonymity. A dizzying array of brightly-colored containers stood on shelves hanging from the wall behind Keill. A low noise of conversation that was a cross between a rumble and a buzz filled the air.

The Interstellar Tavern and Gambling Facility had branches all over this part of the galaxy. Hurl drive ships stopped regularly in front of them to disgorge lifeforms as diverse from humans as humans were from amoebae. Over the past few days, Jeff had come to know the place a little better than he felt he should but there was a lot on his mind and this was the only place he felt he could be safely depressed and not draw undue attention. That, and Keill had seemed to have taken a particular friendly interest in him and his problems.

"I'm supposed to be getting married in three days," Jeff answered. "But I'm not sure I should."

"Ah," Keill's voicebox hummed in sympathy. "Woman trouble."

"We met on a starliner from Rigel to Coriolis V, you see," Jeff said, unable to contain himself and suspecting the Aldeboran whiskey contained something more than just liquor, something chemically akin to pentathol. He tried to stop the words coming but they seemed to have a life of their own. He knew he should be alarmed but somehow he couldn't get up enough energy. "I was being transported at company expense, otherwise I would have had to go by freighter. Anyway, I was taking advantage of the food. Best I'd ever had in my life. She just sat down next to me in the dining hall and started talking. Her name is Christine." The words were coming easier now. Maybe it was the memory of her eyes, the way her mouth curved when she smiled. "We connected almost immediately. We spent the entire trip together, dining and dancing, spending hours in the observation lounge watching the stars. I thought we had something real, something lasting, but when we got to Coriolis I couldn't find her. It was like she'd disappeared into thin air. At first, I was hurt and confused but eventually I thought, hey, a shipboard romance? Maybe I read more into it than she did. You know what I mean?"

Keill tapped the bar. "Your drink's getting warm."

He took a sip of the beer. "Anyway, I had a job on Coriolis as an engineer at the main port. I never really got her out of my mind though I guess I was starting to heal. Then it happened. After a couple of months, I was taking a break at the restaurant there and she came in, looked around, saw me and walked right up and sat down at my table. She started talking as if no time had passed at all. It seemed a bit odd at first and I started to tell her how angry I was she'd ditched me on the starliner, but after talking with her for a while I forgot about it and just enjoyed her company." He sighed. "I couldn't help myself. I had fallen in love with her and no matter what she did, I would always be in love with her." He took another drink, thinking about that conversation, the sound of her voice, the scent of her perfume.

"Go on," Keill said.

He shook himself and put the beer down. "Long story short, I proposed. And she looked at me strangely. I was confused at her reaction but thought maybe I'd moved too fast for her. After all, I didn't really know anything about her. I had poured my heart out to her but it wasn't until then I realized she was practically a stranger." He looked at Keill. "But she said yes. She said yes and I suddenly got scared."

The barkeep had listened silently to his story, idly cleaning the bar and polishing the drinking containers. Jeff's energy ran down as he reached those last few words.

"So, now you don't want to marry her?" Keill asked.

Jeff started. "Of course I want to marry her! It's just..." He stumbled for the words.

"You're not sure you know enough about her?" the barkeep guessed.

"I know enough to know I love her," he said, sadly. "I just don't know if what I have to give her is what she really wants. If only I had a better job, some money. Could give her some security, you know?"

"Does she love you?"

He frowned in thought. "I'm pretty sure she does. I mean, why would she say yes otherwise?"

"Good point," Keill responded. "So, you love her and she loves you. Shouldn't that be enough?"

"I don't know," Jeff gloomed. "Out here on the frontier, things are tough, you know? She just doesn't seem to be the type."

"What type is that?"

He spun his glass in place. "The type to live a rough life. She's very... I don't know. Fine. Delicate."

Keill refilled his glass. "She knows you're working out here?"

"Yeah."

"And she still said yes?"

"Yeah."

Keill made a noise through his voicebox that might have been a chuckle or might have been a raspberry. "Then, what's the problem?"

Jeff sighed and shook his head. "Maybe it's just me. It's like, I don't feel like I'm good enough for her. I'm thinking about going back to the core systems and looking for a better paying job."

"That would be quite a gamble," Keill observed. "Giving up your job out here for a possible position in the core. Competition is very stiff there."

"I know." He passed his hand over his face and took another drink. "It's a tough decision. I don't know what to do."

Someone down the bar called for Keill and the barkeep excused himself. Jeff sat glumly watching the head on his beer slowly disappear. The prospect of being married didn't bother him so much as not knowing if he could be the kind of husband she deserved. Still, what could he do about it?

"I couldn't help overhearing."

Jeff turned to find a black robed, hooded figure sitting a couple of seats away. The man stood, walked over, and sat on the stool beside him.

"I can help. For a price," the man told him.

He stared at the stranger. "A price?"

"One million credits."

He had to laugh. "You're crazy. Where would I get a million credits?"

The figure pointed a gloved hand at the door to the casino. Jeff followed the indicating digit, then turned back and shook his head.

"Look, whoever you are, this isn't a central core casino. Even if I could win that much, which I very much doubt, the house couldn't cover it," he said.

As an answer, the hood turned toward the bar. "Barkeep," he barked.

Keill appeared immediately. Jeff suspected he'd been eavesdropping but what of it? It wasn't like this was going anywhere.

The man handed the barkeep a small blue cylinder that Jeff recognized as a communications ticket normally reserved for very wealthy clients of the Interplanetary Contact Corporation. He'd only ever seen one before, and that was on the starliner when one of the swells at a nearby table called for a communicator to make a business call. Whoever this stranger was, he had some powerful friends. Keill took the ticket and disappeared behind the bar long enough to retrieve an ICC device. Jeff was surprised to see one in such an out of the way place. His expression must have given him away because the barkeep chuckled.

"We have to keep in touch with the latest mixologies, you know," Keill said. "Wouldn't be good to have somebody come in and ask for the latest thing and us not know about it. We might get a reputation as backward." The barkeep pushed the ticket into a slot in the top of the device. He pushed the device toward the hooded man. "There you are, sir."

The stranger's fingers played over the Comm for a few moments. A tone responded and he tapped the control pad another three times. There was another tone and the cylinder ejected. He removed it and motioned to the barkeep he was done.

"What was that about?" Jeff asked.

"This casino has now been connected to the central core for twenty-four standard hours," the stranger announced.

Jeff and the barkeep exchanged startled glances.

"Just like that?"

The hood nodded.

"I don't believe it."

The hooded figure motioned to the barkeep. "Check."

After a moment's hesitation, Keill reached up to his hearing organ and tapped the device fitting there for his intercom. "Look up authorizations to central core, will you?" his voicebox said. There was a moment or two, then his expression told Jeff the stranger was telling the truth.

He looked at the man. "Who are you?"

"Let's just say I'm a gambler who needs a proxy."

A chill went down Jeff's spine. "You're... barred?" What have I fallen into? Jeff thought. Barred gamblers were on the edge of criminality out here on the Rim. They consorted with the darkest elements of society to feed their obsession: people like slavers, murderers, and raiders. Did the stranger think he fit that description? What had he done that the man would think so?

There came no answer but Jeff didn't need one.

"Look, I don't want any trouble," Jeff began.

"Nor would you have any, I assure you," the other said. "As long as I'm with you."

"I don't know if..." he started.

"Son," the stranger put in, "that code cost me a lot. Don't make me think I used it in vain."

The chill was back stronger than ever. A stolen access code to central core? That was worth more money on the black market than he could imagine.

"Alright," he said holding up a hand in surrender. "All right. I get it. But it takes money to make money and all I have is a couple hundred credits."

"More than enough," the gambler said.

Jeff choked back a laugh. "Twenty four hours to turn a couple hundred into a million? It's impossible."

The man leaned in closer and Jeff saw the face under the hood was covered by a one way visor. His own reflection stared back at him.

"Trust me," the man said. "It's more than enough."

Jeff swallowed. His mouth had gone suddenly dry and goose flesh rose on his arms. He leaned back from the man.

" I... uh, all right. If you say so," he managed.

"I do," was the reply. "Now, I suggest you get started. The clock is ticking."

Jeff started to rise then paused. A terrible thought had occurred to him.

"Wait. What if I don't win?" he asked.

The gambler reached into his robe. Jeff nearly jumped but all he produced was a small globe about the size of a pea.

"Swallow this."

Hesitantly, Jeff accepted the item. It looked like nothing more than a tiny plain marble. He glanced from the gambler to Keill. He wished he could read the Aldeboran's expression. It would be nice to know what the barkeep thought.

"Go on. It won't hurt you," the dark man urged.

Keill handed him a full glass of water. With a sinking feeling, Jeff popped the globe into his mouth and downed it.

"Now go."

Jeff wiped his mouth on his sleeve and set the glass on the bar. He looked at the barkeep.

"I just..."

Keill waved him away. "Don't worry about me. We're connected to the core. It's not my money anymore. Good luck."

Feeling slightly ill, Jeff made his way into the casino.

Few players braved the late evening games. He scanned the room, taking in the different possibilities. He hadn't spent much time in gambling halls. He'd never really had enough money to waste. Most of the games were unfamiliar. He suspected they came from places he'd never seen and probably would never visit in his lifetime. There was a good-sized crowd playing at the tables or standing and watching. A light blue haze hung over the room which Jeff suspected was more than just the smoke from recreational drug consumption. Knowing Keill, that haze probably contained something to give the house a little edge, probably a mild mind-altering effect that instilled a false sense of confidence. Not that it would stop the people who frequented the gambling hall. Gamblers usually figure they have a system to beat the house, no matter the odds.

"Hurry up," the gambler's voice came from behind him.

He spun around. There was no one there.

"You swallowed a Comm device. No one can hear me but you."

"Oh," Jeff said.

"Quiet! Don't say anything but what I tell you."

Jeff swallowed again. His mouth was dry once more. He wished he hadn't left his drink on the bar.

"Just do what I tell you. You'll lose some and win a lot as long as you follow instructions."

Jeff took a deep breath. He wasn't sure why, but he did feel better knowing the stranger was backing him up.

"We'll start with the games you know. I can see through your eyes. Don't ask how. Just walk to one and watch for a bit."

He looked around for a moment, then went over to an old roulette wheel. The thing was a true antique, without the digital readouts several of the other tables nearby had. The little white ball ran with dizzying speed around its track. The dealer was busy arranging chips as the wheel spun. Jeff stood behind the two players that sat at the table.

"Just watch. I'll tell you when to bet."

The dealer, a humanoid from one of the Greller systems, looked at him from its central eye. The outer eyes alternately watched the table and the wheel. The rest of him looked normal enough it didn't distract Jeff from watching the game.

"Scratch your left shoulder."

Jeff frowned.

"Do it!" the voice barked.

Almost involuntarily, he complied. The dealer caught the motion, then looked away briefly, scratching his nose.

"Good. Sit down."

Jeff sat. The dealer moved six chips aside and counted out two more as the roulette ball came to rest. The dealer announced the result and pulled all the chips off the table as the players grumbled at their loss.

"Put 50 on 12."

The game was on.

***

Over the next three hours, Jeff won and lost. His chips slowly grew until the gambler told him to move on to the next table. His gaming skills eventually caught the attention of one of the pit bosses. The man, another Greller, followed him from one game to another until Jeff felt a heavy hand on the shoulder.

"Excuse me, sir," the man said politely. "May offer you a drink?"

"Get up," the stranger said in his head. Jeff stood and smiled nervously at the man. "Ask him for a Procyon Century."

"Yes, a Procyon Century, please," Jeff said.

The boss blinked twice. "I'm sorry, sir, but we don't have the right mixture for that."

At the gambler's prompting, Jeff said, "Then how about an Aldeboran Monte?"

"That's a very expensive drink, sir."

"Give him six hundred credits," came the translation. Jeff counted out the chips.

"Will that cover it?" he asked.

The chips magically disappeared in the boss' hands. "I'm sure it will. I'll see to it right away."

"Thanks."

"Move on to the next game," was the instruction.

"What just happened?" Jeff mumbled.

"Never mind. And stop mumbling."

***

He began to draw what amounted to a crowd, some of whom looked at him with what could only be described as criminal intent. Out here on the Rim, the law had a very tenuous hold on society. The patrons were safe in the confines of the bar guaranteed by the bar's bouncers and a variety of security measures with a nasty rep. Once a patron left the premises, however, they were game for whatever predator might think it was strong enough. Jeff became increasingly nervous as the denominations on his chips climbed from three to six figures. The local prostitutes, some not even human, jockeyed for position beside him each time he changed games. The gambler encouraged him to be generous with them, ensuring a flesh wall between Jeff and anyone who might be so rash as to try something stupid.

Seven hours in, Jeff was exhausted physically and emotionally. He was halfway to his goal but the stress was taking its toll. He needed a break or he felt he would collapse, not a pretty prospect considering his sudden fame.

"I'm gonna take a break," he announced. "I need to eat." He turned from the gaming table, hoping to escape from the casino for at least a few minutes.

It wasn't to be. Almost magically, Keill appeared pushing a portable bar along on its anti-gravs. A full menu graced its length. He motioned to Jeff.

"Please, Mr. Halloran," the barkeep said with his interpretation of a smile, "with the compliments of the house."

Only then did it occur to Jeff that in seven hours, Keill had become a rich barkeep. Obscenely rich in local terms. The money had been automatically siphoned off central core to cover his winnings but his losses had reverted to the local bank. He now understood Keill's willingness to go along with the plan. Obviously, the barkeep was sharper than he.

Jeff sat at the bar and ate his fill. He invited his entourage to share his good fortune and nearly smirked when the barkeep balked before giving in. The meal turned into a celebration that would be talked about for years later.

Sated, Jeff wiped his mouth on his sleeve and sighed.

"Tick tock," the gambler's voice came.

He closed his eyes and grunted. The stranger hadn't spoken the whole party. Jeff had almost forgotten about him.

"Okay," he said. The people nearest looked up. He realized he'd spoken loud and smiled at them. Summoning what bravado he could, he rubbed his hands together. "Round two."

A ripple of excitement went through the crowd.

***

For the better part of the next two hours, it seemed his luck had run out. He lost more than he won. People began to lose interest in him and the crowd started to thin. As soon as they did, his winnings started piling up again. As did the attention of those who made him so nervous. The barkeep stayed beside him, deflecting the mildly curious.

Inevitably, his success once more began to attract the attention of the rest of the players. As the hours rolled by, his counters piled up into an impressive array. The gambler advised him to continually upgrade the counters to prevent them from becoming cumbersome when transferred from one table to another. Eventually, even that stopped being a problem as his winnings were transferred through the ITGF's computers. Still, the gambler insisted he use physical counters to keep him engaged in how much he was winning and losing. Without that, Jeff would have certainly lost his place as to where he was toward his goal.

Jeff noticed the bouncers moving among the crowd as his account balance reached one million credits. Even he was surprised when the amount was announced. An immense feeling of relief went through him. He had done it! At last, he could be free of the stranger. All he had to do was cash in and turn over the credits and he could go home.

He was just about to do so when the gambler's voice stopped him.

"Keep going. You have six hours left."

He covered his mouth with a glass and pretended to drink as he whispered, "I have the money. And I'm exhausted."

"Six more hours," came the terse reply. It was obvious he wasn't going to be denied.

Jeff was beginning to resent this whole thing. Even if all he did was make a token resistance to the stranger's plan, he felt he would have won back a bit of his self-respect. He thought quickly and realized there was one thing even the dark man couldn't refuse him.

"I have to hit the head," he said aloud.

He put the glass down and stood up from the table. Instantly, two bouncers appeared at his side. He hesitated and looked at the barkeep.

"Just looking after my customer's safety," Keill said.

Jeff grimaced at him. It was probably a good thing to have an escort but he couldn't help feeling like a prisoner under guard. As he made his way to the service, it dawned on him that for all intents and purposes he was exactly that, at least for the next six hours.

To his relief, they didn't follow him in although they did check the room before letting him inside.

The quiet of the restroom was soothing at first. Then a chill went through him. Without the effect of the haze that hung over the gaming room, he felt the beginnings of anxiety at the situation. He knew that the longer he stayed, he less likely he would be to go back. The pressure of the last few hours seemed to build on him the more time he spent in that quiet place. He almost ran out of the restroom and into the comforting haze hanging just outside the door.

He was surprised and alarmed to find when he got back to the table that the place was emptied of customers.

"What happened?" he asked.

"Your benefactor has rented the casino for the night," the barkeep said.

"Ah," was all Jeff could think to say. At least he didn't have to worry about looking over his shoulder. Even with the bodyguard, the unwelcome attention had been nerve wracking.

"Your table awaits," Keill said, motioning to the gaming table.

Jeff took a deep breath and settled in for the next round.

***

Without the distraction of the crowds, his gaming went uninterrupted. It was soon plain to Jeff that every employee in the casino was in on the scam. Their manipulation of the odds was masterful, never going so far as to trip the automatic protections built into the core computers that would have shut the games down remotely. In the final hours, even he was amazed. Once the accounting was done, he had accrued nearly two and a half million credits. The house had gained significantly more from his losses and the barkeep was in a jovial mood as the casino finally closed. He even bought a round on the house for everybody.

"They'll be in asking for a raise tomorrow," he confided to Jeff as he drafted the script for Jeff's winnings. "For now, free drinks'll keep them happy, though."

Jeff accepted the script, a counter in the form of a plasticene card blazoned with the ITGF logo in bright colors. It was hard to believe such a small thing represented such massive wealth. He stared at it for a moment. If he left now, carrying the script, he might be able to avoid the gambler and run toward the core systems. If he made it there, he was fairly sure the gambler wouldn't follow for fear of the authorities. It would be a simple thing to exchange the script for a hard credit chit. Two and a half million credits could buy a lot of security for himself and Christine.

But then he would be constantly looking over his shoulder. Who knew what kind of reach the gambler might have in the core? Jeff was sure there must be ways that debt would be collected, and in ways he wouldn't survive. Did he really want to live like a refugee for the rest of his life? And what about Christine? If he couldn't reach Jeff, would the gambler hurt her in order to collect on his loss?

Jeff resigned himself to the task and walked back into the bar to find the gambler was seated where he'd left him. The man turned his way as Jeff approached and put out his hand. Jeff handed over the house script without a word. He surprised himself that it didn't bother him as much as he thought it might.

The stranger passed the script to the barkeep. "Break that in half," he said.

Keill took the script and passed it through his accounting, returning two hard credit chits with a flourish. The gambler accepted them, then offered one to Jeff.

"For your trouble."

Jeff gaped at the proffered money. The credit chits were legal tender anywhere in the Empire. He was being offered a fortune far beyond anything he'd ever imagined. All he had to do was reach out and take it. But, was the gambler testing him? Was this some kind of trick? Why would he give it away? It went against everything he'd ever heard about the barred.

"Go on, boy. Take it," the man urged. "That's not bad wages for a day's work."

He took a step backward. Yes, it was a fortune, but it was dirty money. If he took it, he would be the same as the barred. If he took it, he could never look Christine in the eye and not think of what he'd given up to be with her. If he took it, Christine herself would be a reminder of what he had done. If he took it, that beautiful, delicate person he'd fallen in love with would always represent the darkness in his own soul to him.

"I... I can't," he choked out.

"Why not? It's not like the core will miss it," the stranger said. "No alarms went off. It's done, free and clear. You wanted my help. This is it. This will give you and your little lady the security you wanted."

He shook his head. "I didn't want to do this. It wasn't how I wanted..."

The stranger laughed. "What difference does it make how you get the credits?"

Jeff looked at the man holding out the credit chit. Wasn't he different from this man? This man who lived on the Rim because he couldn't live anywhere else? This man who was such a slave to his addiction that he forced others to do things against their will?

A thrill of fear went through him when he considered how the man would react if he refused the money. Had he become a liability in spite of everything? What would the stranger do after he left the safety of the bar? Did he have people waiting outside to teach him a lesson? To make sure he understood what it meant to deny a barred?

Then he thought of Christine. He could never be anything but himself for her. He couldn't touch her fine skin with hands fouled by this. He would be ashamed to take the money and lie to her about how he'd gotten it. How could he ever keep that secret forever, knowing that sometime later this stranger or someone like him would use it against him?

"No... thanks." He took a deep breath. Whatever the consequences, however this went, he wouldn't sacrifice his self-respect. It was all he had. "I can't take it."

The hood tilted a little bit and he had the impression the stranger was thinking about what to do. Jeff swallowed hard as he waited, fighting the urge to dart out the door and run as far as he could away from what was going to happen in the next few seconds.

"Take the chit, boy."

The stranger's tone was terse, biting. Jeff forced himself to stand straight and slowly shake his head.

"Sir, I cannot take that. You forced me to gamble. It was your orders that showed me what to do. I would never have known how to do it."

"I couldn't have done it without you," the dark man said, almost friendly.

"You could have picked anyone in here," Jeff said. "I was convenient. I had no choice."

"Sure you did."

Jeff shivered. "Sir, anyone with half a lick of sense would know not to refuse a barred."

The stranger didn't remark. After a moment, he tucked both chits into his robes and turned back to the bar.

It was then the fatigue hit him. The physical and emotional stress fell on him hard and his knees buckled. The room spun and he found it hard to breathe.

The last thing he remembered was the floor rushing up to meet him before everything went blank.

***

"He lasted longer than I thought he would," the stranger said as the bouncers carried the unconscious Jeff to the office. He turned to Keill. "See to it he's good and rested before he gets on the ship tomorrow."

"Count on us," the barkeep replied. "And thank you."

The hooded man leaned over the bar. "When you came to me with this plan I thought it was insane."

Keill gave the man his interpretation of a smile. "You wanted to know how to test the mettle of the man who was to marry your daughter. It was either this or personal combat and I didn't think you would want him damaged."

The man pulled back his hood and removed the mask. The face he revealed was older and a bit more gray but it was unmistakably the same one that peered from the portrait above the bar.

"I always liked that one," the Emperor said, gazing at the portrait. "It was quite flattering. I gave the artist two systems for that."

The barkeep looked at it as well. "Yes, I like it, too. It brings back good memories."

The Emperor laughed. "Ah, the misspent youth. Remember the time..."

They spent the next few hours reminiscing while Jeff dreamed of a happily ever after.

Waltz at the Dancing Pegasus

by

Dale Kesterson

Alixa sighed as she saw the five beings gathered outside her pub. Most were human, but there was one who looked like a halvsie. And they were coming inside. She had regular customers, but these men were strangers.

She glanced down behind the bar to make sure she was ready for anything. Standing two inches over five feet tall and with a small frame, Alixa needed what she called her tools when trouble threatened. Halvsies, the results of interbreeding between the male human mine workers and the Gencoan females, often meant trouble. They tended to be quick-tempered and not overly bright, which is not great when combined with alcohol.

The strangers were having a conference but entered. The two tallest had a menacing look. She had been hearing rumors that other bars in town had been having some trouble with a group of strangers with a halvsie in tow. She guessed it was her turn now. And she was ready. She just wished that she had some back-up, but it was too early for her regular trade to begin.

"What can I get for you," she asked in her best 'mistress of the pub' voice, staying safely behind the bar. She carefully kept her hands on the counter and continued wiping the surface with her small towel. "It's a bit early for drinks, but I have coffee-sub brewing."

If she had real coffee, Alixa thought, she'd have to beat people away with a baseball bat. The real stuff was too expensive to import to this backwater berg of a planet. Gencoa was only fifty light-years from Earth, but it wasn't exactly New Copenhagen. Hell, it wasn't even New Edinburgh. Even with Jones-Drive, most ships bypassed it as too industrial. So coffee-substitute was all that was generally available. Luckily, tea wasn't hard to procure, which she preferred anyway.

Two of the humans, evidently miners just off-shift judging by the dirt on their hands, approached the bar while the other two humans and the halvsie found seats at one of the round wooden tables placed around the open room. They chose the large table by the window, rather than the large one near the hearth of the fireplace.

"We don't want nothin' right now," the taller and older of the two stated. "We're waitin' on someone. Anyone from the mine been in here in the past ten minutes?"

"You're the first from this shift," she replied. "Just got off work? The washroom's over on the side if you want to clean up a bit." She nodded off to her left at the door plainly marked as the pub's lavatory. Both men could use a thorough dose of soap and water, even if the water was standard tap – and cold.

"Tank ye," the other man replied. Shorter by a few inches than his companion, he was stockier. "We will. My name is Leander, and this here is Max."

Alixa nodded and watched as the two men disappeared into the facilities, then turned her attention to her other three customers. She noted that the humans were not miners; at least they hadn't worked the day's shift as the first two had, and they were relaxed. If she had to judge, they looked like old-fashioned goon muscle. Probably about as bright as the halvsie. Speaking of the halvsie, he looked nervous. And that made her nervous. She mentally blessed the training she had gotten from Nyall Prysen when she took over the pub's day-to-day business.

"There will be times," he had told her, "when spotting trouble before it starts will save you." And he had proceeded to teach her what he knew, including how to turn the tables in spite of her size and sex. He also took care to make sure she learned enough to take care of herself. Human women were rare on Gencoa. However, he had also told her, this may be a backwater, but that didn't mean you had to act like Neanderthals. He took great pride in what was proper and taught her correct speech and manners. When she was older and had observed the people around the city, she had stated that humans may be among the stars now, but that didn't mean they weren't human – with all the negatives following along. She had learned her manners anyway, along with a lot more.

Gencoa was a rough world; there was no doubting that fact. The only industry, if you could call it that, was the company mine, Quinterium Universal. The quinterium, the single asset of the planet, was mined here, quickly processed – but not refined – and shipped off-world where it was used in the construction of energy production plants. The only people getting rich from mining were the corporate officers. Big surprise. Workers came from Earth looking for jobs and more often than not got stuck on the otherwise barren world. There were few human females around, hence the halvsies. Gencoan males tended to die out quite young; the theory was the male line was genetically weak. Alixa was amazed that the male halvsies managed to live out almost-human lifespans. There were female halvsies, but they rarely reached ten years of age, too young to even consider breeding.

The Dancing Pegasus – named after the ancient human mythological flying horse by the oddly-romantic Prysen – was one of a handful of bars in Quint City, which was the only major city on Gencoa. Alixa herself was Earth-born. Her father had brought her with him after he accepted a management position with QU, following the early death of her mother. Fifteen years ago, when her father drank himself to death, Nyall had taken her in and raised her as his grandchild. Despite her petite size, she felt confident to handle whatever came through the door. She had been running the pub for about a year and had managed to create a homier atmosphere than the other watering holes in the district. If she was going to live here, she wanted it that way. She had informed Nyall, when he objected to her changes, that it was his fault for teaching her manners. Besides, the atmosphere had increased their business. Now business was as good as could be expected, maybe just a tad better.

She shook her head suddenly to break her reverie. It would not do to get caught spinning daydreams. Life in Quint City was too cheap for that. She eyed her five customers, the first two having rejoined their fellows. No one was talking, no one was moving. They were waiting. Not comforting at all.

"Hey, Alixa!" came the booming voice of Sev Drummond, as he entered the pub. "Start a batch of Rock Pounders! There are three more behind me!" He had a boyish face, powerfully built but relatively short man who looked far less dangerous than he was. He had made it known to her that any time she wanted help – or love – she was to call him first. They were good friends.

"You got it," she said as she laughed, watching four of her regular customers file in, dirty and damp from the almost constant drizzle outside. "Who's buying? Jerred, Mako, or Reive?"

"Me," replied Sev, digging into his pocket as he came up to the bar. "I even washed up at the mine." He put money on the bar and held up his hands, which were clean.

"You are buying? This is an occasion!" She smiled as she put the money in the till, and started to gather the ingredients for his favorite drink – the Rock Pounder was a simple recipe, combining off-world vodka with two local brews. Vodka was the cheapest off-world liquor, so it was often used in drinks to add punch. Sev liked the drink because he swore that it makes him able to pound rocks with his bare hands. She didn't mention that it was early for hard drinks; she was grateful that he and the other three were there. "What are we celebrating?"

"I got a bonus today!" Sev grinned. "They even did a presentation. What do you think of that?"

Bonus wages from the mines were doable, but generally required a lot of extra work, which was not Sev's style. Alixa opened her mouth to reply, but her response was cut off by the sound of three chairs falling over. Max, Leander, and another human had stood abruptly, the chairs falling in the process. Sev raised an eyebrow at Alixa, who shrugged.

"They told me they were waiting for someone," she whispered, leaning over the counter. "Didn't order any drinks."

The tall stranger, Max, took three long steps to Sev. He topped Sev by over eight inches, and probably 50 pounds. Alixa knew that wouldn't bother Sev.

"That bonus is mine."

Sev drew himself up to his full height of five feet eight and tried to glare at the man in front of him. Alixa noted that the halvsie was now on his feet and that Sev's friends were still seated but exchanging glances.

"Uh-oh," she thought, "here we go." She moved carefully and slowly towards the end of the bar in preparation for joining the fracas she was certain to come, figuring that attention wasn't on her but on the two men facing each other.

"Stranger, I earned that bonus by pulling extra duty and taking extra shifts. There's plenty of work for all, and no need to get upset. Have a Rock Pounder on me." Sev gave the man his most disarming smile, knowing it had worked before to get him out of tight spots.

"Nope. Me and my buddies are movin' in, and what is extra is ours." The tall man leaned forward, almost pressing his chest in Sev's face. "We won't take regular pay, just the extra. Better get used to it. Now hand over the money."

Behind the corner of the bar, unnoticed by everyone but Sev's friend Jerred, Alixa bent over and removed her shoes. She put on her special pair and came around the bar. She was now a bit taller. Jerred caught her eye, nodded slowly, and winked at her.

"Sev, if you want me to, I'll go get the constable." Alixa smiled up at the tall stranger. "I take it that this is the man you were waiting for?"

"Girl, keep your nose out of this," said Leander, moving to stand with his friend. "And stay put. No cops. We don't want no trouble, just his money."

"Hmm," Alixa mused to herself. The men actually spoke like cheap hoods from a vid about old Chicago on Earth. Definitely not good.

"This is my place, and I won't have it wrecked – by anyone," Alixa replied, "friend or stranger. Why don't you two sit down and have a couple of drinks on the house while you discuss this? I'll make a pitcher of Sun Wukongs – it's the specialty of the house, created by the man who built this place." She stood to the side of the two men. Sev noted that she was only four inches shorter than he was instead of the usual six. And he knew what that meant.

"Sun Wukongs? I've heard that somewhere. It's a fancy drink, right?" Leander's face reflected the effort he was making to think. No one paid him any attention, even Max.

Sev's friends were slowly moving to position themselves in striking distance of the rest of the strangers. Alixa saw that Jerred was getting ready to tackle the halvsie. Jerred was smaller than Sev, and not as strong. She would rather Reive do it but noted that he was targeting a larger human. If that's the way, they wanted to play it, okay. Forcing down a shudder, she stepped even with Sev, to his right.

"How about it?" encouraged Sev. He slipped his right arm around Alixa, his hand on her hip. "Her Sun Wukongs are even better than Nyall's were. And she uses real orange juice for special occasions." His back was to the bar, and his left arm was lying casually on the counter. Sev was left-handed. He also had a partially artificial hand, the result of a mining accident.

"Nyall? Nyall Pyrsen built this place?" Max took a look around. Sev's friends froze in place. The lighting in the pub was dark enough to shield them, and they knew where the shadows were. "He done pretty well for himself."

"You know Pyrsen?"

"His old man and my old man was once friends. Now I can make up for him, what happened." He frowned. "Yeah, that's fair. I think I'll take this place over."

"Wait just a damned minute, friend," Alixa warned, "this is MY place now, and not up for grabs by anyone. Especially not some stranger. I took it over from Nyall fair and square. If you have a quarrel with him, take it to him. Leave me and my place out of it, Max."

"Nah, Nyall is history. The name is Maxfield. Calder Maxfield. Most people call me Max. I always take what I want." He smiled, or thought he did, with his lips closed. "You're a feisty little thing, ain't you. I'll take you along with the bar." Max rested one hand on her shoulder. "Bet you can keep me warm at night." He ignored her reaction to his hand.

"We got in from Earth last week." Max continued, lightly rubbing her shoulder. "I tried working in the mine, but I don't like it. Too hard, too dirty. I decided to make it simple and go back to the old ways – taking from those who do work. It's kinda a family tradition. Like my pop before me. I've been watching all the bars in Quint City. This is the best. Me and my buddies like taking the best. And we'll take good care of this place. And you." He stared down at Alixa, smiling again, this time showing how few front teeth he had.

She removed his hand. "Looks like you are the gang leader here. Can your buddies do any of this without you?"

"Never tried – don't know." Max put his hand back and let it drop a bit, adding some pressure.

"Thought so – bullies." Alixa mumbled, with what passed for a sigh, adding in her 'all-business' voice, "I'm warning you...you don't want to do this."

"And you are going to do what, hurt me? A little thing like you?" Max laughed.

"You might want to listen to her," Sev put in. "Bigger men than you have regretted not heeding that warning."

Max continued to laugh, and let his hand drop to caress her breast.

"Right," Alixa said.

"Left." Sev agreed. He tightened his grip on her hip to let her know he was ready. He brought his left hand forward, bending his elbow. He waited for her next move.

"Max, you've been warned. This is MY ---," and she moved.

Leaning against Sev and using his arm for balance, Alixa brought her legs up suddenly and forcibly planted the pointed toes of her shoes just below Max's knees. He went down, hard. At the same time, Sev swung with his left hand and decked Leander, who went down next to his friend. Alixa picked her way carefully around the now-moaning Max, who was writhing on the floor. She stood with her hands on her hips, glaring down at his face from above his head, her back to the rest of the room. She knew that Sev's trio of friends would keep the other intruders busy.

"Well, now. Looks like things have changed for the bully-boy."

"My knees – you broke my knees," he whined.

"Quite possibly."

Max tried to get up, but his hands were pinned to the floor. Alixa's foot was on his right hand. She increased the pressure on it, leaning in, so the heel of her shoe was now in the palm of his hand. And she slowly continued to lean on her left foot, bouncing down on it a bit as she did.

Max screamed. A few times. With each bounce. Loudly.

Alixa lifted her left foot off his palm and turned her attention to his right hand. It was pinned at the wrist by Sev's foot. She positioned her right foot in the palm of his hand, heel first.

"More?" she inquired.

"My place," he gasped. "Nyall owes it to me. Mine."

"Slow learner, this one," she commented to Sev. "When this is over, please remember that I did warn you," she added to Max.

She hopped on her right foot, using all her body weight. The heel of her shoe went through the hand to the floor.

Max didn't even scream. He just passed out.

She pulled her foot out of her shoe, and Sev helped her remove her shoe out of Max's hand.

"Time to put out the garbage?" She looked at Jerred and Sev, who signaled to Reive and Mako. "All of it, please, boys. Make the extras work, too."

The remaining two humans of Max's party came forward to drag him out to the street with one hand each. Leander staggered to his feet, rubbing his jaw, and Mako moved to steady him upright. It was obvious that without Mako, Leander wouldn't remain standing. The halvsie started to protest, but Jerred used a twist grip on his arm. The halvsie's choice was to go or get an arm broken. Reive was ensuring the goons went quietly by twisting one free arm behind a back. As they got to the door, it opened and Samson Rogg, one of the town's constables, entered. Everyone moved back into the room, dragging Max along.

"Someone reported hearing screams." He looked at Alixa. "I was afraid it was you."

"Not this time, Rogg."

Rogg looked at Leander, who seemed more out than conscious. "What did you hit him with?"

"Oh, that one wasn't mine. Sev decked him with a left hook. He must be tough if he's back up this soon." Alixa smiled the smile of innocence and nodded downwards. "Mine is the one still on the floor."

Max, now that he wasn't moving was back on the floor. His legs were bent at the knees. Rogg took in the damage with one glance.

"Both hands? Alixa, I'm sorry, but I'm gonna have to report this." Rogg shook his head. "You can't just maim people. Who are these guys?"

"I think I can explain, Constable. It was a defense of property and body."

The new voice came from a doorway above the bar in the seldom-used balcony. An old man with long, wiry white hair pulled back into a ponytail, grinned, showing yellowed teeth from a lifelong habit of tobacco use. Walking carefully, yet with a certain grace, Nyall Pyrsen descended the stairs from the balcony to join the party. He looked like a refined gentleman gone slightly to seed, but he still had presence.

Mako immediately let go of the barely conscious Leander, who promptly regained a restful posture face-down on the floor, in order to place a chair for the old man. Nyall Pyrsen sat down and looked around him, apparently amused.

"Pyrsen, we thought you was dead," mumbled Leander, rolling over to look up. "Max wasn't looking for you, he just wanted this place."

Rogg, his face showing confusion, stared at the old proprietor.

"Nyall, I thought you sold out to Alixa and went off-world. Back to Earth." The constable got out his datapad. "Would someone please tell me what the hell happened here? And keep it simple."

"Rogg, these guys, "Alixa indicated the five strangers, "came into the pub and announced they were waiting for someone to come in from the mine. They didn't order drinks, but these two," she continued, pointing to the men on the floor, "went to the facilities and cleaned up – a bit. When Sev and company came in, the ruckus started."

"Looks like a mighty one-sided ruckus from where I'm standing," mumbled Rogg.

"They are starting a protection scam," said Nyall. "They were waiting for Sev, as he got a large bonus today – it was announced officially. I guess they figured that the pub run by a woman was going to be the easiest to take over." The old man grinned, which was not an overly pleasant sight – the yellowed teeth looked sharp. "They, of course, figured wrong."

Pyrsen glanced at the two men on the floor. Maxfield was now sitting up, looking at his hands, one of which was still bleeding. Alixa reached behind the bar, grabbed a clean towel, and tossed it to him. It landed on his head.

"Quit dripping on my floor." She glanced at Pyrsen. "You know these guys?"

"Well, actually, I knew Max's father. He and my dad were partners once, and after Dad's death, Max's father edged me out, in a manner similar to what Max here was offering you. Extortion does run in that family. I got away with some money, call it creative bookkeeping, but I knew I had to disappear because they wouldn't be pleased when it was discovered. I came here, and built the bar." Nyall smiled at Alixa. "It wasn't a great life, but it beat what I had left behind. When I took you in, I saw you had the potential to run the place, and when the time came that I couldn't manage it anymore, I turned it over to you."

"Did you know that these idiots would come looking for you?" Sev asked. "Is that why you trained Alixa?"

"Sev, I trained Alixa so she could defend herself against cretins like these." The grin came back. "She learned quickly. You all did – I saw Jerred and Reive both use the arm-twist to great effect." He held up a hand as the constable started to say something, and continued. "No, I didn't know these particular goons would show up to molest her. I do know that this bar is a worthy target for any protection racket." The old man spoke to the constable. "I'll bet that if you do some checking, you'll find that Alixa isn't the only one who has been threatened."

"Hold on. Alixa, are you saying that these men threatened you?" Rogg was doing his best to listen and fill in a report at the same time.

"The one bleeding did more than threaten," she replied with a face. "And I did warn him."

"I'll testify to it. He was mauling her," Sev stated firmly. "If he presses charges, we'll all be happy to meet him in court."

Rogg looked down at Max, who was trying to wrap the towel around the bleeding hand with the badly bruised one.

"Molesting and threatening her? Big mistake. We don't have much of a town here, and some of the miners aren't very bright, but we run it clean," the constable said. "The Dancing Pegasus is home-away-from-home to a lot of workers because of Alixa. We'll take you to a doc, but I want all of you – including the halvsie – on the next transport out of here." He folded up his datapad. "Let's go."

Max started to protest. "I'm hurt!"

"Do you want to press charges against Alixa and have to admit, in court, that this tiny woman got the best of you?" Reive spoke for the first time. "Personally, I'd recommend against it. She has lots of friends who don't like to see her being harassed.

Mako nodded. "Take some advice: leave Gencoa."

The two goons picked their leader up off the floor and started dragging him to the door with the constable, who had Leander in tow, following. Mako shoved the halvsie out behind them as Alixa yelled, "Max, you can keep the towel as a souvenir!"

The four friends and two proprietors watched as the five culprits left.

"Sev, why don't you make Sun Wukongs for six," Alixa said. "See if you can do it as well as I can." She put her regular shoes on and frowned at the blood on the heels of her fighting shoes. "And remind me to give Rogg a drink on the house the next time he comes in."

"I must say, Alixa, those shoes are remarkable," Nyall commented as she cleaned the heels.

"Steel toes and heels make a great combination," she agreed as she put her special pair back behind the bar. "Even if I can't dance in them, they do give a new meaning to the phrase, 'spike heels.'"

Interlude

Sam 1701 stopped reading and gazed at the massive number of files before him wondering if it was even possible for a single man to go through such a volume. He was surprised to find that someone had placed food on his desk and that it must have been a while since they did for the meal was cold. *Ah well, a man has to eat anyway. Can't live on words alone.*

After his meal, he wandered the stacks around him again picking random files to review. When he sat with them before him, he realized he had a pile more substantial than the first. He inserted the first in the viewer and began again.

The Last Stand

by
Kimberly Richardson

If it weren't for my damned curiosity, I wouldn't be here. Then again, thank the spirits for my damned curiosity. When I say spirits, I don't mean the things that keep children from going to sleep at night. I mean the ones that I serve to people who want to forget it all, at least for one night. That is what keeps them coming back here, the poor bastards. Before I get ahead of myself, let me introduce myself. My name is Kylar Stand, owner of The Last Stand, a bar and sometimes place to rest your weary (drunk) head on Pluto. After many years of trial, tribulations, and travel, Pluto finally became livable to humans. The only problem was that once they finally arrived here, they discovered that the planet was inhabited by strange beings that were welcoming yet indifferent to them. Thus began the increased population of Pluto, the little planet that could.

Where do I fit in all of this, you may ask? Well, my grandparents were some of the ones who first traveled here and decided to stay among the Plutonians. They lived and thrived and had children who married Plutonians. They, in turn, had children and, well, that's where I come in. I'm a half-breed, although if you were to look at me, you wouldn't even consider me part human. My light blue skin and red hair clearly make me Plutonian yet my eyes are the only human part of me; while all Plutonians' eyes are a bright purple with no pupils, mine are brown with pupils. I also have the ability to cry, a trait that Plutonians do not have. Since they left me a substantial amount of money, I created my own place and named it The Last Stand and made it a place for all to come in and have a drink.

There are several major cities on Pluto, and each is ruled independent of each other as though they were small countries like on Earth. Within each major city are several zones for certain activities to keep peace and to make sure that all follow the rules. My bar is located in the Pleasure area of the major city of Styx, named after one of Pluto's moons. The Pleasure area consists of bars of every kind imaginable including carbon monoxide dens for those who want to, what they call, FLY. Strangely enough, human themed "parks": places that are simulated park areas like the ones I had heard about on Earth, complete with grass, trees, flowers, and even a simulated sun so that the effect is truly lifelike. Those places were made so that humans who lived on Pluto would be able to have a small piece of Earth if ever they needed a "quick fix." I've walked through some of those "parks" and felt both odd and comforted, probably due to the human in me.

The Last Stand, my bar, used to be a simple place for simple folk who just wanted to come in and enjoy a bit of drink, no matter how weird their request (I had it all), until SHE showed up. And that, dear readers of this strange story, is why I curse and bless my curiosity.

It was close to closing time, and I had just washed the last glass while my assistant, Nial, wiped down the tables with her long dark purple tongue, giving it the proper shine they were known for. Although she was older than me by several moon cycles, she acted like I was her big brother in many ways. As long as it made her happy, I had no reason to complain.

"Nial, don't forget that spill by the back," I said as I placed the last glass on the shelf behind me.

"Why didn't you make him clean up after himself?" asked Nial as she finished off another table with a flick of her tongue. "I don't care who he is, he's a customer just like everyone else and needs to respect this place just like everyone else!"

"Nial," I sighed, "for the last time; he is on the Pleasure Council. He decides if we stay open or not. You know how it goes." I ran a hand through my coarse hair then stared at my double-jointed hand. "They tell us to jump, we say how high and do it with a smile."

"But he ordered that special bottle of wine from Charon, knowing that even if a drop spilled, it would take days to clean it up." She pulled back several chairs to get a better look at the "spill." Charon wine is hard to make, hard to transport, and hard to drink, yet it is worth drinking it. I had a glass of the thick black liquid once, and it was enough to satisfy my curiosity and to order several bottles for my own place. "Shimak!"

"Hey, hey, where did you learn that word?"

Nial blushed, making her blue skin deeper in tone. "You don't remember the other day when you dropped that box on your foot?"

"Do you listen to everything I say around here?"

"Why do you think I carry a notepad with me?" Nial grinned, showing off her very white pointed teeth while I shook my head then resumed my closing duties. I was about to turn off the backlight when the front door transporter signaled that a customer was about to materialize inside. I returned to the bar and waited as the customer's form began to show in a shimmer of light within the transporter. Within a few seconds, a young human woman in a green dress appeared in the bar. She looked around several times as if wondering if she made it to the right place then stared at me with wide eyes.

"Is this The Last Stand?" she asked.

"That's what it says on the sign," said Nial with a bit of sarcasm in her voice. I coughed once, letting Nial know that now was not the time to serve up a slice of Plutonian sarcasm to the human.

"Yes, this is The Last Stand. I am Kylar. What can I get for you?" She took two steps then crumpled to the ground like a piece of paper. Both Nial and I rushed over to her to make sure we suddenly didn't have a corpse on our hands; that would not be good for us, especially with regards to the Pleasure Council. I placed a finger against her neck then blew a sigh of relief; she was alive. Nial lifted her up and dragged her to the nearest table then gently laid her on her back while her legs dangled from the edge. I stared at her face; she was very, very human. No special features to speak of. I took a closer look and suddenly, her eyes flew open, and she made as if to jump away. I quickly took several steps back with my hands in the air, showing peace.

"Relax, you're still at The Last Stand," I said in a calm tone. I glanced at Nial, whose eyes were focused on the human, then back at her. "Do you remember coming here?" She nodded yes slowly. "Are you okay?"

"I... think so," the young woman said as she struggled to sit up then began to rub the back of her head. "I don't feel anything different on me. What happened?"

"You came into our bar, took two steps then passed out," said Nial with a fresh touch of sarcasm. Nial was one of the Plutonians that did not care for humans too much; as far as she and others were concerned, as long as humans didn't try to upset the order too much, then there were no problems. "Anything else we need to know?"

"My name is Wendy. I'm from Vindal's. I'm one of his... girls." Vindal's was one of the "companion places" in the Pleasure area, a place to enjoy all sorts of desires, no matter how strange or unpleasant. The women were there for the whims of the clients. I looked at her face again and now noticed a faint hint of a Suction on her left cheek. Wendy saw where my eyes had landed and she placed a hand to cover her cheek.

"You've been used for Suction?" I had to ask no matter how blunt. She nodded yes and looked as if to cry. I quickly ran behind the bar and got her a glass of human brandy then carried it over to her. "Here, drink this. You need it." She greedily drank it down and handed the glass back to me. Instantly, the colour returned to her once pallid cheeks.

"Thank you."

"Don't thank me; why did you pass out like that?"

She sat down at the table and then both Nial, and I followed suit. I had a feeling this was going to be a story that I would regret hearing later.

"I left Vindal's. I had no other place to go to except here. I'd been told by some of the other girls that The Last Stand was one of the better bars to frequent." She looked around at my limited décor then at both Nial's blank face and my curious one. "We girls can leave Vindal's whenever we like; we are not slaves like at the other companion places. We can come and go as we desire. However, I want to leave for good. I want to go home."

"Well, where does your family live around here? I can at least take you there if you need help trying to get there." A single tear fell down her cheek and without thinking, I wiped it away with one of my fingers, much to Nial's surprise. I stared at my wet finger then sniffed it.

"Plutonians can't cry, right?" asked Wendy.

"True, but I can. I'm part human. I have only cried once in my life." I wiped my finger on my pants. "So, where does your family live here, or are they on one of the moons? You can easily take one of the shuttles. Just give me the address, and I can find out for you." Wendy stared at me in silence then soon more tears fell down her face. Nial took a clean rag from her belt and handed it to her.

"Thanks," she shakily said as she wiped her face. "My home, my family, they're all on Earth. I came here several moons ago."

"What did you used to do?" I asked.

"I was and still am an author. I lived in a city called Memphis, Tennessee in the United States of America." Nial frowned as I searched my memory for any kind of information about that place. Since I had never visited Earth, my knowledge was very hazy except for what the human side of my family had told me years ago. Yet, the Plutonian side of me was much stronger; since that was all I knew, I had no real reason to read about Earth as much as other Plutonians. We Plutonians are a funny lot; although we did not care too much one way or another about humans, we did care about Earth and what that planet had to offer our little home. Our planet encouraged trading with Earth, and their leaders were just as encouraging.

"Nial," I said as I turned to my partner, "ever hear of that place?"

"Yeah... actually, I have. The United States of America, connected with other countries known as Canada and Mexico." I turned back to Wendy, who was now smiling at me.

"Well, at least one of you has. So, that is what I used to do. I decided to come here as part of the research for a new book and wanted to immerse myself in Plutonian culture. Your ways of life, what you do for fun, how this planet could, after so many years of humans thinking that it was inhabitable, be habitable." She shrugged her shoulders then took the glass and began to roll it between her hands. "I guess I got too curious. I wanted to learn more about the Pleasure area and got myself signed on as a companion. I had no idea just what I had gotten myself in. Now, I want out. I want back home, but Vindal won't let me out of my contract. He said he liked me too much and that I needed to stay for my entire length of time as stated in the contract." Another tear fell down her face. "I want to go home."

"Well, why don't you just board a ship and leave? Happens all the time," said Nial. I cut her a look; I couldn't tell if she was being sarcastic or not.

"You don't understand." She then turned around and pulled down the back collar of her dress, revealing a raised square on her neck. I peered for a closer look; there were 6 numbers tattooed under the square: 5 8 2 7 4 6. Her companion numbers. I leaned back.

"Nial, lock the door, please." Nial did as told without question. She knew me and knew when a situation just got serious. Once she sat down again, I said in a calm voice, "So. You are the property of Vindal himself?" Wendy turned back to face us with a concerned look.

"He liked my looks and the way I was so 'human.' I wasn't like the others. He likes my brain as well, thinks I'm special. You know," she said while laughing and rubbing the back of her neck, "the thing is that I even told him about my life back on Earth; me being an author, my notes for my latest book, everything. Turns out I got more than I bargained for."

"When did he do that to you?" asked Nial, pointing a long finger at her neck.

"One night when I was taking a nap in between clients. It happened so suddenly that I barely had any time to react to it. All I felt was a slight pressure against my neck and then the scent of burning flowers. Next thing I knew, everyone was treating me differently because Vindal himself had marked me. At first, I thought everything would be okay, then I found out that he wanted me to be his own companion. I tried to let him know that I wanted to return to Earth but he wouldn't hear any of it. He said that I needed to complete my time on my contract: seven moons. According to Plutonian time, I've only completed one moon cycle."

"So you ran away and landed here," I said in a cold voice, my mind already thinking of the consequences that had yet to occur. Vindal. Shimak.

"Please. I could think of no other place to go to, plus... well, people talk."

"Yes, they do."

"I want to go home. I don't want to belong to Vindal." I got up and walked over to the bar to get the bottle of brandy for Wendy and two glasses of Charon wine for Nial and me. As I poured the glasses of wine, I glanced over at Nial just staring at Wendy, who looked beyond worn out. I sighed.

"Are you hungry?" I asked. "I don't have much here but what I do have is yours." Wendy's face lit into a tired grin as I placed the glasses of alcohol on the table then raced back to the small eating area behind the bar to fetch something close to decent for her. As I looked around and opened containers, my mind buzzed: what exactly did humans eat? Why did she come to my place? What would this mean for my business and my customers? I opened a large container, sniffed it and made sure it was edible, then plopped it all on a plate and walked back to the bar and set it before the human. Nial's eyes lit up with amusement as she watched Wendy sniff at the food while trying very hard to figure out just what it was.

"Before you even ask, it's edible," I said in a tired tone, then proceeded to take a small amount of it with my fingers and pop it in my mouth. I chewed and smiled then swallowed, letting Wendy know that it was indeed edible and quite tasty. She looked down at her plate then pulled off a piece of what looked like blue coloured meat and placed it in her mouth. Suddenly, her face went from unsure to happy as she chewed quickly and swallowed then reached for another piece.

"We never had food this good back at the place," she said between stuffing her face. "We usually got cheap knockoffs of human food, or what barely passed as such. This is from Pluto?"

"The finest. I pay a nice price for getting what I keep as mine here." Wendy tore off another piece and stuffed it in her mouth then took a long swig of brandy to wash it down.

"Thank you. I'm feeling much better. Look, if you don't mind me asking, how did you two learn English so well?" Nial cut me a look that said: "Is this human for real?" Yet I merely smiled and said, "For me, I learned through my human relations. We Plutonians learn languages rather quickly. English seemed too easy for us."

"It sounds guttural at times compare to our language," said Nial in an offhand way, "yet it is all part of our two worlds knowing each other better within reason."

"Most of the women in the companion place were human. Only three were Plutonian, and they only met with human males. The rest came for us and to explore a female human. Apparently, we are not built like you." She took another sip of her brandy. "The first Plutonian male I had spent more time touching my body than anything else. He would ask me questions about how certain body parts worked, and then he would touch them and see if they would react in different ways. He wasn't hurtful, just curious. Others, however, want to do Suction." She placed a hand on her cheek, not realizing what she had done. I gently removed her hand from her cheek then touched the spot with my fingers. It still burned deep down. Suction is quite the "pastime" for the Plutonian; our system can handle such an action.

"The client told me that I would not be affected in any way during Suction," said Wendy with a hint of anger in her voice. "He knew, however. In fact, I actually remembered him grinning like a child as he watched me go through the after effects. That, along with no longer wanting to be owned by Vindal, are my reasons for wanting to return to Earth. I never want to experience Suction ever again."

"What is it you humans say? One man's drink is another man's poison," said Nial. She then took a slow sip of her wine. Her eyes rolled back in their sockets as she allowed the emotional impact to overtake her. Truly amazing wine. I took a sip then set my glass down. I had more questions; this was not the time to allow anything to cloud my brains.

"So, you came to Pluto by yourself? Did none of your family want to come as well?"

Wendy looked down at her chewed fingernails then said in a low voice, " They were against me leaving Earth from the beginning. I wanted to prove to them that I could do anything I put my mind to. I wanted to write a new novel fueled by my experiences here. While I do have enough to write several novels, I'm just ready to get back to my world."

"But wasn't that the point behind having our cities reflect some of your human ways?" asked Nial as her eyes rolled back. "We welcomed your kind to our planet and created familiar things so that those who stayed would never be... what's the word again?" Lonal?"

"Lonely," said Wendy with a hint of a smile. "And yes, most of the humans here have forgotten Earth yet there are some who miss the blue sky and clouds. I miss my city, my friends, everything." She fell silent while I stared at her; she had spoken enough for the night.

"Nial," I said in a soft tone while my eyes focused on Wendy, "go home. I'll finish everything here." Nial was about to protest then fell silent as she got up and let herself out of the bar using the transporter without looking back, leaving me with the human. For several minutes, neither of us said anything but just stared: she stared at her hands, and I stared at her hair. Our hair feels like shards of glass when rubbed the wrong way; rub it the correct way, and it feels softer than the feathers on a bird. Without asking, I reached over to touch her hair. She did not move, only her eyes followed my hand then they focused on me.

"You are the first human whose hair I have touched," I said as my long fingers combed through it. It was curly and dense, and I felt myself wanting to become lost in it. Such a strange emotion.

"I take it you never go to the companion centers? Plenty of human women to choose from. All races, all sizes, all everything, for the discriminating Plutonian palate." I said nothing but continued to stroke her hair. "I had more Plutonians play with my hair than anything else."

"It is fascinating. Tell me, can you use it as a weapon like we can with ours?" She pulled back gently with a laugh.

"No. As far as I know, I have never used my hair as a weapon."

"Some of our finest warriors got that way due to how they styled their hair as weapons. We take pride in such matters." I let my Plutonian pride come through; even though I had human blood in me, I considered myself to be truly Plutonian. I shook my head, clearing it of what humans called "small talk" and returned to serious matters. "Where will you sleep tonight?" The look of fear returned to her eyes.

"I don't... know."

"Do you not know of anyone around here who can help you?"

Her eyes went wide. "No one. Everyone I know lives in the companion center. I took a chance on leaving, but I had to do it." She wiped her fresh set of tears with her arm. "Look, I'm not that big. Can I just stay in one of your storage boxes or something? I promise I won't touch anything here." She grabbed my arm with such force that I almost went into defense mode; as much as Plutonians love pleasure in all forms, we will defend ourselves if necessary. I blinked, allowing myself to calm down and force my blood to not boil, then sighed.

"You want to stay here?"

"Please, I have no other place tonight. Please?" She still gripped my arm, and I gently removed her hand. Suddenly, I had an idea. I got up and walked towards the back of the bar to our back entrance leading directly to my dwelling by a private transporter. It proved to be effective whenever I needed to leave my establishment for various reasons. I turned back to face her and said, " Come on." She got up without a word and walked towards what looked to a solid wall with a small console on the left. I flipped it open and punched in my code then stood back as the transporter came to life. Lights began to glow as the transporter hummed. I punched the final code in and suddenly, the door slid open to reveal a small bubble. We stepped in, and I slid the door closed.

"We'll be there within-" I began to say just as the transporter went into full effect and zoomed through a tunnel. Wendy leaned against the wall and braced herself, although it looked as though she was about to get sick. The transporter, once moving, was silent as it flew like liquid mercury. Then, before she got sick, the carrier came to a halt. The door slid open to my dwelling and none too soon. Wendy stepped out of the transporter, took two more steps then proceeded to get sick all over my floor. I sighed. Humans.

"You do not need to keep apologizing for getting sick on my floor," I repeated within the past several minutes as Wendy sat across from me wringing her hands.

"I can't help it. Call it human guilt," she said with a nervous laugh that I did not join in. I was beginning to wonder if perhaps me being kind to a human was worth the trouble. I sighed and looked at her; she couldn't seem to stay still.

"If you are nervous, walk around," I said with a wave of my hand. "You have more than enough room to walk, and you will not get in the way before you ask me." Wendy got up as I suggested then proceeded to walk in a circle in the main room. I watched her in silence, not really knowing what to do next. I had never had a human in my home dwelling, let alone a female at that. True, I did have other Plutonians here for recreational events and the like, yet all of the Plutonian women were acquaintances. I had never been... involved with anyone. Plutonians do not know the concept of love. We know how to enjoy pleasure in every form, yet to love one another is something very foreign to us. Those that are close to us we perform a blood bond in which we drink a cup of each other's blood. That would be as close to "loving" someone as the humans do. So, while I sat there watching Wendy pace back and forth, I wondered if I could ever have a human as a companion. Many Plutonians paid very high prices for human companions and used them as they saw fit, in every extreme. Some even marry humans, as did my family. I continued to look at Wendy and wondered about her family; what were her units like? Did they all worry about matters like she? Why didn't any of them travel with her to Pluto? Suddenly, she stopped and sat down next to me, jarring me out of my thoughts.

"For me to get on a shuttle undetected, I will need to get this.. thing out of my neck. How can I get it out?" I turned her around and lifted up her hair. There was the raised square in her neck along with her numbers. I touched it lightly, and she gave a little jump.

"Did I hurt you?"

"No, but it is connected to him. It's like an overloaded sensor. Vindal wanted that in me so that, no matter how I felt, he could always press the back of my neck and I would give out the appropriate sensation, and he would immediately feel it as well." I sighed then lowered her hair. She turned to face me and took my hands in her own. The act startled me, yet I willed myself to calm down. " Do you have a knife or something sharp?"

"To cut that thing out of you? No thanks. I said I would give you a place to stay, not create a reason for me to die swiftly at the hands of Vindal." She pressed my hands to her own and gave me a look that showed that she no longer cared about anything except to get home.

"Fine," she said as she dropped my hands and got up, "I'll cut the damn thing out myself." She began rummaging through several of my shelves then moved to my eating area. I jumped up and ran towards the room just as she raised a knife to her neck.

"Don't!" I screamed. Wendy held the knife high, ready to cut deeply. I walked over to her and took the knife from her, then slammed her down in a chair and said in a cold voice, "Lift your hair." She did as I instructed, revealing the square bump. I placed the tip of the knife against the square, and she shuddered. I pressed the tip a bit further and watched a thin trickle of blood slide down her neck.

"Your blood is red?" I asked, foolish for even asking such a question at a time like this.

"Will you just get on with it?" I pressed the knife a bit further, causing her to sigh deeply and shake even more. I then dug the tip right underneath a corner of the square then grabbed her head with my other hand to keep her steady.

"Do....you...see it?" she asked in a moaning tone. More blood flowed as I dug in even more then gasped with surprise as a hint of black appeared.

"I can see it!" Wendy moaned in response as I let go of her head then lifted the tiny flap of skin to reveal more of the black square. It was firmly attached to her, yet I was not about to stop now. I lifted the flap of skin even more then began to lift up the knife underneath it. The square made a sucking sound as I wormed my knife even further under the square. I blocked out Wendy's increasingly loud moans as the square gave up a good fight from her body. It did not want to come out. I then threw the knife on the floor, ignoring the blood splatter, then grabbed the black square and pulled with all of my might. I pulled and tugged as Wendy moaned and shook. I pulled and pulled until the black square began to slide out, little by little. I felt myself smiling as I pulled and pulled, not giving up at all.

"How are you?" I asked while pulling. Wendy only continued to moan; that was enough for me. Just as I had half of the square freed, I gathered all of my Plutonian strength that we are known for and pulled downward. Wendy screamed as the black square landed in my blood-covered hand. I placed it on a table then rushed to get healing supplies for her. When I returned, she was on the floor with blood still pumping out of her. I had to act quickly, or else I would soon need to come up with a reason for the authorities as to why I had a human body on my floor. I lifted her blood-soaked hair then placed five drops of pure Plutonian blood on the wound followed by a piece of white cloth. Our blood has many healing properties and can also suture a wound within seconds. The fabric was made out of a unique material that can absorb any liquid. After patching her up, I took a step back and waited. Two minutes later, I heard her cough as she struggled to sit up in her own blood. I helped her up then, with my own hand on the back of her neck, led her to my washing basin then sat her down on a small stool while I prepared a bowl of warm water. Her body was limp, yet it did respond to me moving it. I almost felt sorry for her. Almost. When I set her down on the stool, I could hear her breathing quite slowly. The blood would take some time to incorporate into her system, but for the most part, she would live.

"How do you feel?" I asked while the water ran into a small white bowl. I kept my back to her, not wanting to see her face just yet. It had been hidden under her matted hair and blood.

"Shit."

"What does that mean?"

She coughed a small laugh. "It means... shit."

"I do not know that word." I turned around with the bowl and a towel. "Please explain." She lifted her hair from her face; she looked paler than before with dark circles under her eyes. "The square is on the table outside, in case you wanted to look at it." I dipped the towel in the water then began to slowly wipe her face. Her eyes looked down at something far away from all of this. "You miss home."

"It means trouble, or something bad, or a situation that you can find no solution to."

"Pardon?"

"You... wanted to know what shit meant. I just... told you." She tried to smile yet it looked like a grimace. I washed her face in silence, not knowing what to say. "And yes, I miss home."

"Now, you can return."

"If Vindal doesn't find me first." Suddenly, I dropped the towel and raced to my main room and stared at the square. It seemed like such an ordinary piece of blackness and yet it was a source of many problems. How long would it take before he figured out that she was no longer connected to him?

"How far could you go without him noticing your presence with this thing?" I yelled.

"I don't know; that's why I want to go as soon as possible." I heard Wendy walk out of the washroom and up to my back. I could tell she was stronger than before and thanked the blood.

"We need to go back to the bar to get some items you'll need to leave without too much of a problem," I said as I turned to face her. "You'll need the fare for the trip plus do you have your identification cards with you?"

"I stowed them in my clothing in case I did," said Wendy as she patted her chest. "I do have some money as well."

"Stolen currency?"

"No, made myself with clients when Vindal was gone on an excursion on Cerebus."

"Is he still gone?"

"Actually," she said slowly, "I think he might still be gone. He never told me how long he would be up there." I grinned widely, showing off my filed teeth.

"Then that will work to our advantage," I said as I walked into the washroom to get the bowl and towel. "If Vindal could feel your every emotion when the square was pressed, could you also feel his?"

"He had it set as one way. I would never know what he was up to." Perhaps this catastrophe had a chance to turn into a bit of luck for not only me but for the human as well. Yet, in looking back at this tale in my life, I still shake my head with the incredulity of it all.

After cleaning her up, we made our way back to the bar through the transporter. This time, as we both stepped out of it, Wendy did not get sick. In fact, probably in thanks to the blood, she looked far stronger than ever. Before we walked back inside of the bar, I made a motion for her to keep silent while I took a quick scan of my bar just to make sure no surprises were waiting for us. I pressed my hand to the square that sat in my pocket, hoping that everything would be okay. I blinked and opened the door quickly.

Nothing. Only a small bar with tables and turned off lights. I blinked again, turning on my examiner vision, and scanned the bar again. Still nothing. Perhaps luck was on our side, as the humans would say. I took one step then another. Still nothing. I blinked, returning my vision to normal then turned on the switch for the lights. I waited until all of the lights were on before waving for Wendy to come in. She made her way to a table and sat down while I walked behind the bar to get what she needed.

"Can we talk?" she asked in a whisper.

"We are fine," I said while counting enough currency for her ticket. One-way trips were, of course, less expensive than a round trip. I knew that she would never return. I counted the stack of bills just to make sure that it was enough then got a bottle of Charon wine for us to enjoy if only for a brief moment. Every area of the major cities had a transport center for people to use when needing to take a shuttle to Earth or any other planet with which we had contact. I walked over to the table with items in my hands then sat down, handed her the currency, and then poured a glass of wine for us both. I had a feeling she would need it more so than I. She took her glass, raised it in a sad salute, and then downed it all in one gulp. I raised my glass to my lips, barely tasting the delicious wine.

"I don't know how I can ever thank you for doing this," she said in a shaking voice while taking the pile of currency from me. "I suppose I'll never see you again."

"Probably not. I don't think you'll want to come back here."

She smiled at me then a funny look passed her face. Suddenly, she slumped across the table, and I cursed my "good" luck. There was a thin arrow sticking out of her back. Just as I reached towards it,

I heard a cold voice next to my ear say, "The square. Now." Vindal. I turned around slowly to face one of the most feared and yet respected Plutonians standing right behind me. His blue skin shimmered under his black tunic as he held out his very long hand towards me. I reached into my pocket and handed him the square. He looked at the square in his hand then crumbled it like a piece of paper and blew the ashes away. Suddenly, I heard the transporter hum to life as several Plutonians materialized in the front door. One of them carried a Fantu, a deadly crossbow with arrows filled with a poison that kills anyone before they realize they have been hit.

"A Fantu," I said, not really sure of what to say at that moment. "A good weapon of choice."

"How long did you think it would take before I would kill the human?" asked Vindal in that same cold voice.

"Now what?"

"I beg your pardon?"

"Now that your precious human is dead, what will you do?" Vindal stroked his chin thoughtfully, making me more nervous than ever. "I suppose that you'll just choose another one to mark?"

"And why should my affairs be of any concern to you, half-blood?" His purple eyes stared deeply into my human brown ones. "She left without permission before her contract was up. She paid the price." He and his two associates walked to the front transporter while I sat there and watched them in stunned silence. Vindal touched the transporter control then stood back as it hummed to life. When it was ready to transport, the three stepped inside of it then left without another word to me. I stared at the transporter as it died down, leaving me with a dead human woman still seated at my table. He left without doing anything to me. Either he was very busy at the moment, or he knew that whatever he did would never be as bad as leaving a corpse in my bar. I finished my glass of wine then took hers from her hand and took the glasses to the bar. When I turned around, I screamed Shimak!

Wendy lifted her face to me while she reached around to pluck out the arrow.

"Careful," I said, not sure if my mind was playing tricks on me. She ignored me as she plucked out the arrow from her back with a grunt then threw it away. She rubbed her back as she tried to sit up. I raced over to her and checked her back. Thankfully, there was no blood on her clothing, yet I knew that the arrow had a serrated edge to it. She rubbed her back again then stretched her arms over her head.

"You were dead," I said in a stunned voice. No one survives an attack from a Fantu.

"All I remember is that I was talking with you then everything went black. I could hear voices, yet they sounded muddled. Then, I felt my nerves working overtime and, well, here I am."

"The blood!"

"I beg your pardon?"

"It was the blood! The drops I gave you penetrated your system and removed the poison, or at least killed it off." I stared at her in wonder. "You should have been dead."

"Was it-"

"Yes. He did not even want your body. Left it here for me to clean up." Wendy wiped away a single tear.

"My body's not even worth a burial." She then took the bottle of Charon wine, raised it to her lips and drank deeply. Once again, I was stunned; there was much more to this human woman than I had initially thought. When she finished, she wiped her lips with the back of her hand and grinned.

"Now what?" I had to ask.

"Seeing as how Vindal knows me to be dead, I can leave without any worry from him. Can I still use the money?" I gave her the blessing that Plutonians share: right hand, palm out while fingers wiggled.

"Go. Return to Earth. Write your novel." She took the currency in her fist and crumpled the notes then got up to leave. Suddenly, she raced towards me and kissed me fully on the lips. My human eyes stared at this human touching me in such a manner; I had no idea what to do. I could taste the wine on her soft lips. After a few minutes, she pulled away from me and said, "Thank you, Kylar, for everything." She then walked over to the transporter and, after punching in the coordinates of the shuttle, stepped in and disappeared from my life. I watched the transporter buzz with energy then quickly die as she reached her destination. I sighed deeply then began cleaning up from the "activities" of the day.

A while later, I opened the bar, ready for customers. My bar never really shuts down, only takes "breaks" to refresh and prepare for the next round of whatever. Nial appeared in the transporter, ready to earn her pay as always.

"Where's the human?" she asked.

"Gone."

"Gone, huh? Good." Nial smiled widely then began preparing the bar for our customers while I wandered to the back and sat down on a small stool. Although I had only known Wendy for such a short time, it was interesting to spend that time with her. She was different. I stroked my chin just like Vindal had done earlier and thought.

"Nial?"

"Yes, Kylar?" She appeared in the doorway with a small towel on her arm.

"How long have you worked here?"

"Many moons, why?"

"Can you do me a favour?"

"What?"

"Watch the place for me. There's... something I need to do."

"When will you be back?"

"I do not know." I refused to tell Nial any other details, yet the look I had on my face should have been enough. Nial knows when something is on my mind. She left me in peace while I gathered up what I needed then walked out of the room and towards the front door transporter. Setting the coordinates, I left before Nial pried any other answers from me. Within seconds, I had arrived... and just in time.

"Passengers for XR-1298, Earth Summer Cycle, now boarding!" The conductor waved for passengers to make their way towards the shuttle. I had never seen a shuttle close, only as they flew away. It was the shape of our gurfruit, or like a ball of foot, as they say on Earth, and glowed silver true. I made my way to the booth and purchased a ticket then raced to the line of passengers as they steadily made their way towards the shuttle. While I walked with a calm pace, my eyes darted everywhere for her. I had to find her. Suddenly, I saw her hair bouncing ahead of me, and I pushed past some older Plutonians to get closer to her. When I reached her, I grabbed her arm, causing her to turn around with a startled then surprised look as we made our way towards the shuttle. I said nothing but held her arm as we walked. I looked up and saw the ink black sky of space overhead. Soon I would be leaving all of this and facing a new world, one filled with the unknown. I glanced at the sky once more then at Wendy, who looked at me with a funny look.

Curse my curiosity...and bless it as well.

Thanum o'n Dhoul

by

R. L. Jones

2nd Bar On The Right, Drink On Till Morning

The Star-Crossed Rover was nested securely in the maintenance dock of Mandrake Cluster space station. The crew had been through the depths of space for nine months, scanning nomalies, anomalies, abnomalies all the while taking very particular particulate samples. It was a poor use of military power and equipment, but when the endless cycles of mankind on mankind, humanity against the alien world, wars had moved on to other sectors for a breather what is a WMD to do but adapt or rust. This left this little old but reliable hulk of a warship, forever being on the point of the Sol Exodus into new frontiers, out of a job, for now, that is. The ship and crew were not disbanded, dispersed, or discharged; they were on a temporary civilian commission to the highest bidder at least until a new war came along. Doctor Jack Bay was the highest bidder by a single credit flash. He was very proud of his genius hybrid partner who had nanoseconds faster speed than the other bidders. This got him the decorated ship he wanted. A crew disciplined enough not to murder each other, which they were very good at, and a tested fully operations military grade vessel in the bargain, two rare things when you plan to tame a dog of war to be a bloodhound.

"Mandrake Cluster! Godz, what a garbage dump! If there were a leg pit in the universe, it would be sent here for punishment. It's a cluster alright." Captain Henry Drake the third grumbled while entering the science lab to inform his civilian employer that they were ready to announce space leave. He had completed a full inspection of the crew, verified stasis shut down of the Hurl Drive, checked the latest military transmission updates in a vain hope their battle readiness would be reactivated. They traveled here to meet their civilian boss, clear the credits so everyone could scrape a little R&R, even out of this floating amalgamated garbage refuse of a space station.

Doctor Bay's Cybuddy was working the consoles. He wasn't bad for a hybrid. Hell, half of Drake's own people were implanted to one degree or another, still, this thing, er... person was another matter of degree. The inhuman eyes looked up, saw the Captain and spoke first.

"Indications are we are all ready to depart. You have completed the ritual with your crew? We are all clear here Captain." It wasn't really a question just another formality that he performed when working with common base humans. You see, Puck was human too, or at least nearly half of him. His implants were mostly internal except for a moderate pointing of the tips of his ears with specialized communication upgrades. These tended to radiate in the visible spectrum. All in all, it was a small price to pay for 360-degree perception. The whites of his eyes were not. They reflected black with luminescent seven-pointed star pupils giving him vision ranged into both the UV and IR edge of sight. The rest of his external appearance was fully human.

His classification was Hybrid. He took the name Puck as a nickname since Phase IV Unit Computational Kryptonic series was clumsy even for him to say. His original personality was lost during an incident involving being caught in the middle of a fight between two drunken space marines, an unlicensed neural blaster, and his own cerebral cortex. He wasn't fast enough to tell the two customers he was available for rent by both parties at a discount and wasn't fast enough to dodge the close range pulse that left his body in perfect condition but his grey matter just this side of Halo-pudding. Now, thanks to Doctor Bay's paid improvements to a brain-dead vegetable, Puck ranked among the most advanced civilian model hybrids in this sector, but human rights were now denied him due to his percentage of augmentations. He was property like any toaster; still, it was nice to have a mentor with significant credits. Even after the brain wipe, Puck didn't have to give up his night job. The Doctor had appetites that worked out well that way and no longer involved the risk of agitated space marines.

"Yes, Puck... You can inform the Doctor..."

"Inform me what? Captain." Doctor Bay entered from the secured bio lab chamber.

"We are at last ready to leave your fine ship. Me to secure another fortune with the successful finds from these last nine productive months, and you, your crew, to wreak havoc in typical military fashion on the unsuspecting local dock inhabitants." He said this smiling. The good doctor was just as happy to reach station as everyone else, well... Perhaps not Puck. Who really knew what that artificial cerebellum was thinking inside his near perfect body?

The Captain grinned back, something he only allowed himself the luxury to do with civilians, and he did like this odd couple.

"Indeed we are ready, and I suspect your assessment of my crew is a tad mild. I'm hoping the bonus bounty for this excursion will cover most of the damage they will do. If the place doesn't survive, then they need to build better way stations out here in Never-space." Never-space was a derogatory term used by spacers for areas mostly unexplored and lacking stars or planetary objects. It was not a pure vacuum by any means. Space was never entirely empty something was always swirling in the depths.

"Let's try and beat them through customs shall we Captain. One final bit of advice, the place you want to visit is the second bar on the right side of the station's central axis. Don't miss the glowing shamrock. You and your crew should avoid the opposite axis. This is an isolated way-station but it is still the only place for light years with press gangs, brute squads, and less than original humans, or worse, rumored to lurk unchecked on that wing. Oh, and the name of the best tavern is Finnegan's, hope you like old earth Irish atmosphere. Should your people find themselves on the wrong axis, never go into Mortimer's. You know the tales of more wretched hives and all that. In Mort's... the hive part is true. To this day I don't understand how bugs can make it into space with such success."

***

Wake Me In The Mourning

"Finn......Finnegan!" The voice carried through the crowded area of the tavern where patrons were making a ruckus with the band on stage. It was always packed in Finnegan's when the Clancy Clones were booked to perform. Penny whistling, bodhran banging, and flash fiddling made their own brand of chaos as a rule. If S.E.T.I. had picked up this rattling from the deep space two hundred years ago, we may have abandoned any hopes for intelligent life in the stars. As luck, Irish or otherwise, would have it only such a racket could only be exported by humanity and during the last potato famine of the Weather Wars of 2025, with the full force of a human exodus from earth.

Finnegan had a theory that the reason so few aliens were found, lots of life but not much intelligence, was because anything sane was moving away at Faster-Than-Jones speed, light speed being too slow, to avoid whatever was making such a gargantuan racket. Now the explored universe was filling with crazy life of all the good, and bad, mankind had to give. Finnegan didn't consider anything wrong with that, and here he was on the rim of the expansion with Jenny Rose heading in his direction. She had been following him from one new station to the next as he always stayed one step ahead of the first smell of civilization. There she was, her sable velvet ribbon keeping her waist length hair out of the drinks.

"Clear out your ears you dotty Irish giant." It was true. Finnegan was larger than life. He stood six foot eight, muscles on muscles, long blond hair to his shoulders. People thought of Thor when they first saw him. Up until he opened his mouth and then his Gaelic accent took that image away right fast.

She started to yell at him again, "Hush woman! You'll disturb the audience, I see ya!"

"You'll be doing more than see'n me if'n you don't lean down here. I have a message for you." Finn leaned down until he was fully cross the bar as his own personal she-devil of a waitress grabbed his ear and pull him even closer to whisper.

Rose was not a tall woman, think of a Pekinese challenging an Irish wolfhound and you got the picture. "The Doctor has docked."

"Double be damned, why can't space just be swallowing that Mephistopheles souled pain in my arse!" Finn gritted his teeth.

Rose nodded in understanding. This was becoming a habit. The Doctor showed up with things that Finn wanted plus one thing that he could not allow to be found with each and every visit. Finnegan turned his attention back to Rose.

"Make sure we have the cosmickey thingy ready. Make sure we

have more than enough for the next time too. Why couldn't there be a nice little war or supernova, or something nearby like a black hole or a whole billiards table of black eight ball holes to discourage this pest." He cursed.

"Look on the bright side Finn. Think of what new and wonderful favors he's found this time." Rose said trying to soften the mood.

"Yeah, there is always some honey with the hemlock. But... It ain't natural him finding new flavors of alcohol sifting through space like a gold miner. Why do I bother with brewing and barreling my stock? Maybe I should just do like him and get a galactic vacuum cleaner to suck up all the clouds of moonshine out there." Finn seemed to consider this option. "At least, he seems to be the only one playing this game. I don't have to be in more than one place in the galaxy at the same time. Speaking of time, he should be darkening the door. I should get him over into the private bar. He'll want to gloat over all the new tastes he's found."

His traditional bar rag was polishing an already gleaming surface of the ancient oak woodwork. Finn's overly large hands were making wax-on motions in his absent-minded Zen-like state. It came with long years of practice and was a mantra for the calm it brought him. Underneath was a much more turbulent range of feelings. This chamber of the tavern was empty until the door swung open being held by Rose motioning Doc Bay and his faithful companion Puck, carrying a sizeable metallic case with "Bio-Hazard" blazoned on the outside, into the comfortable and cozy chamber. Of all the areas of the space tavern, this one was styled traditional old earth, no tech, real bottles lined the shelves, a single mirror reflected from the back of the bar with angles letting the barkeep see everything even when his back was to the customers.

There was an age darkened baseball bat with signatures burned into the surface. Louisville Slugger was etched in bold print along its side as it rested on display. The bat was not a fake and probably worth more than the entire credit value of the tavern. On closer inspection, if you knew what to look for, there was a not-so-authentic strapping wrap on the grip and that strapping was dotted with micro patterns showing a faint glow of power and humming. Puck locked his eyes on the slugger as he came near the bar. His systems flashed a weapons alert, but then his own eyes met with Finn's. There was a moment of understanding. They were here for business and renewed friendship. No reason to question or report the presence of a quasi-legal weapon disguised as a sports bludgeon artifact. The Doctor had never considered programming him with government standards for ethics and morals. Come to think of it, Jack Bay operated on only one paradigm. Do whatever you want and harm none that do not seek to harm you or others. This simple code allowed him to reap all the joy the universe had to offer and meet out significant justice where needed.

"Finn! We meet again." Doc's genuine happiness at meeting his old friend came through. It was infectious as always, and Finnegan knew he was going to have to play the Doctor carefully; he too would try and enjoy this near yearly rendezvous.

Putting away his wiping without as much as a glance, Finn reached for two glasses and an ancient and special bottle. The same bottle he had tapped during the last visit of this adventurous duo. "Doc, you made it back! And Puck, you still haven't found a way to program your escape from this old pirate."

Puck knew this game and imitated his human counterparts with the proper and expected response. "Good to see you, Finn. Why would I ever want to leave the Doctor to be a victim of your larceny and corruption, after all, he knows I'm only staying around for his body."

"Damn it all Doc, what are you spiking his oil can with and can I trade you for some. Rose is costing me a fortune in legal and medical bills. I need a hybrid that will work off an AC/DC charge." Finn joked back.

"What's ailing Rose? Perhaps I can prescribe an analgesic to your wit." The Doc returned the folly.

"It ain't her that's hurting Doc, and you're not that kinda doctor. She just has a mean backhand to overly amorous customers. You could make a fortune here on station if'n you take up dentistry. I believe she's loosened so many teeth that they've started to refer to her as the satanic tooth fairy." He paused to fill the glasses and asked Puck, "You still on the wagon Puck? I'm gonna have to make a rule about allowing people who don't drink in my establishment. Something along the same line as those who try to talk religion in my Pub, had to use Old Lou just yesterday when a couple of Faboggian Cultist came in and didn't take to the first warning."

Puck replied neutrally. He was not fully sure if Finn were joking or serious. Sometimes his grasping of human nature was… how you say, lacking instinct. "Sorry, Master Finn. I have hoped to find a stabilizer that would allow me to imbibe your stock. Since I spend all my time working with complex hydrocarbons, my own curiosity on how to operate the JCE [Jones Complex Equations] for Hurl Drive operations remains a mystery to me. My inability to attain a significant degree of … What do you call it…? 'Buzz,' a critical component of advanced space drives makes me deficient in that area of science. I do not care for that limitation."

"Don't go putting yourself down, the little wizard here will probably find a concoction for you that will do the same thing." Finn chuckled, "You should do that for your friend here Doc. It ain't right leaving him sober and having to be spending all that time looking at you, being unlubricated and all, is all I'm a say'n."

"I never thought of that and Puck, you never mentioned a desire to get snookered much less wanting to learn JCE. It might be advantageous if we're caught with only you being conscious in the deep. But enough of that, are we here to drink or what!" The doctor was already reaching for his glass and signaling for Puck to crack the case to start the discoveries.

There were twenty-five individual filled glasses of varied colors and aromas set before the bar. All of the native samples were back on the shelf and Finn was here to find what the Doctor had discovered mining the Alcohol Belt. You see, for more than two hundred years, scientists have known that space contained vast regions with collections of hydrocarbons in the form of alcohols, what they had not known was the near infinite effect cosmic forces made to these chemical structures. The doctor had started his own unique enterprise by isolating and duplicating these effects. He was harvesting celestial liquors on a scale never considered, and Finn was his secret distributor. What the doctor didn't know was Finn's own secret and the subtle game that the two of them had been playing out over the last several decades. You see, it all started back in the 1850's in Dublin.

A small meteor had landed in the lush barley fields outside of Dublin. The contents of that falling star held micro strands of very special complex hydrocarbons. The harvesting of infected barley ended up in a batch of whiskey. That batch of whiskey ended up at a particular Irish wake where a corpse, one Timothy Finnegan, a six foot eight young blond was laid out after a fall with head trauma. In a fit of extreme grief, two ladies and one childhood friend began a quarrel over giving the dead lad a send-off with the first corking-o-the-jug. His childhood friend, Michael Maloney snatched the jar of whiskey from the women and poured a double jigger down poor dead Tim's open mouth. There was an immediate reaction to the event. Tim started vibrating and twitching. His eyes sprung open, and he sat up flush with life sputtering. Maloney sat down shocked flat on the floor with the cork in one hand and the jug between his legs. The two women, a Molly and Mary they were, both fainted dead away. Some of the party fled the house screaming of demons and others dropped to their knees praying it was a miracle.

Over time, the story was almost forgotten as just a case of mistaken diagnosis, or deep coma, and soon after, Tim and Michael left Ireland for the wilds of America. Michael Maloney faded from the records, but oddly enough, where ever there was a point in history making a difference for mankind, there was a tall blond bartender with a sweet Irish brogue giving sound advice to customers. That bartender spent some time in the late 1920's serving drinks and advice to students, future leaders, and writers around Annapolis. A certain bar outside of Cape Canaveral, often frequented by men destined to reach the stars in the 1960's, a pub outside of the Caltech in 2213, leaps of mankind's future always seemed preambled by swaying ambulatory retreats from such places of cheer, like the inhalation of the breath of life, before a jump into the great unknown.

Finnegan knew the truth. It took him hundreds of years to understand on that day he died and lived, he was given a second chance by this quirky, weird universe. Somebody had to be immortal, and he was it. Of course, there was that Jew fellow that Italian, and that Romanian prince, and ... Well, those were just stories as opposed to other real immortals out there. Here he was. Three hundred plus years and going strong, not looking a day older than when he died, only now this doctor and his tinker toy, with his new ship and crew, were giving him a headache. The last two visits, Finn fixed.

The doctor's discovery he fixed by giving him a......Cosmickey Finn and was prepared to do it again but this Pucky creature could be a real problem. In fact, Finn was already wondering why Puck had not questioned the odd behavior of his mentor after the last visit. It had to be evident that Bay was returning with the same discovery over and over again, and not remembering it. Ok, Finn thought, I'm going to have to spend some quality time with the droidling. It wasn't his favorite thought. Having been considered a third class, or lower, citizen by the Brits in his homeland, then the Americans, thanks to JFK, that nonsense was over there, he never felt good about the dehumanization of anyone, but these hybrids made him twitch. Finn was beginning to think he just might be getting old and set in his ways.

Before he could deal with Puck, here were all the new taste to explore and yes Doc was holding the last one off to the side. The same game as last time keeping the Uisce Beatha hidden until the end. The samples where much better than expected with flavors and bouquets never before experienced. Two were going to be marketable beyond expectation. He would send one back to the Sol system, maybe have its premiere in the Martian Dejah Thoris Cosmoplex. That was now the cultural and arts center for the inner planets. The other, perhaps he would send it to the 4S City (Seventh Son of the Seventh Samurai) on Suribachi IV. It had a sake flavor after all. The others were good but nothing more exceptional than could be found from using new species of wood to barrel age a decent whiskey. Now we are down to the wire, the last sample.

Doctor Jack Bay was nearly quivering with eagerness to present his triumphant find. The ultimate drink, "Try this, barkeep." He smiled like a Cheshire cat in heat, "It's going to knock your magnoslippers off."

Finn reached for the last shot. He swirled the golden liquor around letting the molecules slowly drift up his senses, all the time hoping it would not be the aqua vitae. No such luck, there it was. The distinct scent and nostril back taste that pulled his life back from the long sleep three centuries and a half or more. Doc had yet once again found nature's own treasure of treasures. The Spanish had searched the new world for it. Alchemist had sold their souls for it. Big Bang Pharma ran quixotic experiments down endless false leads. Botanist's combed the rainforest of the worlds. Yet this cute spoiled rich kid with multiple degrees, too much IQ, and a techno Tonto for a half-life partner could not help but find the cosmic rarity, not once, not twice, but every damn time he wandered into the deep dark nowhere of deep space. It was enough to drive you to drink. At least, we are already in a bar.

After extolling the virtues of the previous amber elixir, Finn suggested that the Doc take a tour of the tavern and enjoy the band. He said that he would like to speak with Puck over trying a new faux-beer. It was a lab creation from the Jupiter Lunar Legion where large numbers of people settled from cultures frowning on the use of alcohol. Personally, Finn thought that it was a celestial blessing, those people could not safely operate Hurl Drives. FTL engineering by the use of Hurl Drive was as much quantum state perception and state of mind as technology.

The chosen poison defaulted back to man's ancient secret and familiar formula of yeast, sugar, and patience. Sure, some said the use of other chemicals could create the proper state of mind to activate and direct the Jones Equations, but the results often proved less reliable. Several Jamaican based transports who tried ended up coming back from destinations before they left. Hurl Drive was mostly quantum engineering with a sense of the absurd generating a perception field for consistent and safe transition.

Finn, who had spent most of his three centuries around engineers, never met a competent one that didn't drink like a fish. Those that didn't weren't much more than out of work mathematicians wearing grease-stained overalls and developing calluses on their fingers. Hence, he came to the conclusion that the faster than light propulsion was a discovery destined to be. If religion had not occupied the Irish for centuries, he believed Emerald Isle would have conquered space long before the Americans and Russians and finally the Chinese fumbled their way through it.

"Were you serious about wanting to be able to operate space drives Puck?" The hybrid watched as his friend exited the private bar, the sound of the Clancy's "No, Nay, Never-space, No more" were cut off by the closing door. He turned to Finn giving him one hundred percent of his attention, which was a disturbing skill.

He responded, "I do not feel it is rational to depend on the limitation of baseline humans when in uncharted and negligibly populated expanses of space. On more than one occasion, the engineers, even on such a notable vessel as the Rover, have been subjected to excessive null states. May I be perfectly honest with you Master Finn?"

"Always Puck, if you please."

"You standard humans do well in a universe that operates on complex mathematical principles, what is disturbing is those principles are minor moments of rationality surrounded and mutilated by chaos variables. This means you are a perfect match. I, on the other hand, only operate on logic and rational functions. This is my failure. A long time ago I realized that my analytical abilities are unmatched by any biological, but, I will never be more than an infant. You, pure humans, make leaps beyond my ability to calculate." He ended his comment and looked down showing despondence in the silence.

With a quick wipe of the bar and the clinking sound of shot glasses going back into the sink, Finn took a moment to think before responding. "Mister Hybrid... You have made a clear and correct guess there, but, like my old school marm use to say... Tiny, she used to call me that because I wasn't, being the biggest in my class,... Tiny she said, I've got to pass you cause you got the answers right, but you don't get an A cause you never show your work. I know you didn't cheat because your classmates did the opposite. They showed their work but got the wrong answers.

That's what you are doing Puck. Showing your work but the universe doesn't do things that way, not since Einstein anyway; you need to consider leaving the hardware behind and requisition some good old bio-ware. Try moving some of those Nano-chips from your skull, put them in that pretty wee arse o yours as back-up. I'm sure Jack won't notice if'n you keep the padding. Get some top of the line real human brains inserted in that Jack-o-Lantern noggin of your'n and you'll be writing poetry in no time."

He understood Finn, mostly, the tendency to drift from normal speaking to old home style was disturbing, but Puck had calculated when Finn did it he was saying something worth hearing. The idea of going bio was something he never considered as a solution. More of that "not showing your work" kind of irrational thinking, biology was fragile, less dependable, harder to replace, and limited, but here it was. The solution to his dilemma on a silver platter over a round of drinks he could never appreciate. It was time to broach the other question he had for Finn.

"Since you asked me to stay behind; I must consider that it is over your performance with my companion and his repetitive discovery plus your interference with the use of that discovery." Puck noticed that Finn started to reach for the baseball bat, but stopped himself. He also knew that was no ordinary stick of wood, historical references or not, he could perceive the cloaked energy signatures leaking out of the normal human vision range.

"I've decided to come clean with you on that score. We can't be dancing to this same tune every year. Doc must know just what he's found and why he canna ever be marketing that particular brew or... the good doctor will have to have an unfortunate accident." He saw the tightening of artificial muscles, so very human-like, and so much more. "I don't want that last option any more than you do my good fellow so let me tell you why."

The story of the Fountain of Youth and all the consequences of such a discovery were ever to be known poured out over the next several minutes, the logic of what a destabilizing effect on human culture it would have to grant one never-ending generation a stranglehold on the vitality of an entire species youth. The horror that only limited quantities of elixir would ever be available and who decided just who was worthy. Finn told him of his winning and losing of enormous fortunes, the pain of seeing friends fade to dust, the unbelievable beauty of seeing humanity reborn better each generation always a little better than the one before. He told of the nightmare of cultures that became frozen in their fundamentally rigid views. Then, he told of the joy being on the expanding edge of mankind's march through the galaxy, he asked if the hybrid, who also had much more extended life potential, if there was any fault perceived in keeping this secret locked away at least until evolution granted the human species the wisdom to go with it.

Puck never said a word until the end. Then, "In all this time you have been the sole keeper of the cup. Have you ever tried granting immortality to others?"

"Of course, soon after my discovery, years after my recovery from death, I started a small select group through a dummy corporation under the disguise of a philanthropist interested in people that lived exceptionally long and healthy lives. They were the first to take an exodus from the world. I doubt anyone will find them. They suffered a lot of hardship in the pre-space years when discovered. The public never fully knew about them, but governments went crazy trying to seek them out and force their "long life" secret into the laps of the powerful. Uisce Beatha is not a cure-all by any means Puck. Human minds are not impervious to mental illness, such are acerbated by the rapid changes going past them while all the time they remain the same as they were when first consuming it. Accidents are all too common a solution to immortality, war, famine…we seem to be somewhat protected from the general health ills, at least we are spared that. Radiation still kills cells, poison works, bullets and blasters and any proper application of smackdown will end a life just like mortals.

My best friend Michael Maloney, who was responsible for my resurrection, went the hardest. He became so afraid of his own shadow he hid away from everything. He became so deluded and paranoid that he wouldn't even eat or drink. It was a hunger strike that would make Gandhi look like Fatty Arbuckle… Nevermind, the other downside is no one knows what you mean when you pull up old idioms."

"You seem to have weathered these traumas in good condition." Puck observed.

"The scars are like your augmentations, they all are on the inside, but you are right. I have the real luck of the Irish. The question now is what are we to do about Doc? I have a special strain of nano-complex devices that allow me to affect short-term memory and implant suggestions. It's a twisty little beastie I tell ya. Inactive it looks like a faintly green shamrock all open and innocent under the microscope, but charge it with the right sequence, and the thing knots up, turns black like a hangman's knot. You have seen the results of it working, but I'm willing to consider a different solution if'n you have one." Finn was honestly concerned. He had become quite impressed with the doctor and his skills. In many ways, his cavalier approach to life was much like his own. There had to be a way out of this conundrum that didn't involve mayhem.

"Why not just tell him what you have told me. I can tell you he is not interested in fame and glory. The discovery of the molecular alcohol structure was his real prize. He will probably be more agitated over having been caught in an endless rerun. He's not interested in more credits. That caryatid's stone was lifted long ago, and he would need this Uisce to live long enough just to put a dent in the principle his own family and personal wealth have amassed. Chances are Bay will be glad to know why he's not going to be aging, however." Puck pleaded.

The bartender took a moment to consider that. Of course, the Doctor would have sampled the finding, even from the first time it was discovered; he was not the type to risk others on an untested chemical concoction.

"Let's go get him. I hope this is the right decision. I'll lock up the samples later; you program the tanks on your ship for transfer to the usual storage location here on station."

***

Me Father, He was Orangutan, and Me Mother Sidhe was Green

The two exited the old style bar behind and entered the main tavern. The Clancy's were on break for the station's second shift, and there was the third member of the bar staff standing, honest to Godz, on a real soapbox at the mic. Finn never missed a chance to bring back forgotten bits of nostalgic junk. A real stage microphone acquired when the Apollo was excavated after the 2025 revolution. The internals were replaced. No more wires and such, but the raspy quality of the audio was authentically duplicated.

Standing on the soapbox was one Jamie Seamus O'Flaherty. All of five foot two, the regular patrons called him Chaun, short for leprechaun. He was just beginning his oration of the house rules. A custom which started when the bar first opened and now generated as much audience participation as any sing-a-long with performing bands. O'Flaherty took a deep breath which expanded him to look most froglike. His own color tinted a shade green which Finn was sure a trick Rose did with the house lights just for effect and to match the horrid green outfit he wore. It had to have been gleaned from some Cthulhuian universe intent on driving men insane.

"Now be listern'n hear ye swaths of drunknaids, dealertaints, and missbegothams! His voice reached every ear in the place even though the words didn't rightly make much sense. That was O'Flaherty's distinctive trait, the unabashed ability to mangle any language he spoke. It was rumored that when he spoke Chinese, they would literally drive chopsticks into their ears to stop the pain.

"Now quiet down I say. We be hayv'n many a nude face out dar in der odd-ye-ants. Ye all be need'n to learn'n the rules. Rule one…

No Relick'n Allowed!"

That was the audience's clue, and in a unified voice from all but the newcomers they responded, <NO RELIGION!>

Seemed even the Chaun didn't stand by his own rule. Some would say it was his own fluid brand of phony edits. O'Flaherty returned the echo, "That's right…No Relark'n in dis here bar. That means no Fruitkin Buttkiss's."

The crowd, <NO BUDDIST!>

"I say'ed that… And… no Methadroidlist…"

<NO METHODIST!> They cheered back.

"Cursin right, just what I say… No Meet-a-Hemorrhoidist "We ain't be gotten nanny room fur Protestiesrunts nor Luciferians too!"

<NO PROTESTANTS, NO LUTHERANS, NO, NAY, NEVER!> The tables vibrated with fist poundings and foot stompings and gales of snickering.

The Chaun was on a roll now, and his use of proper nouns had become a dealer's choice of chaos. "Kayyyywreckeded! No Praytooteroots, nare Laid-Utter-Grunts, nether more! We ain't gonna be toolerattan'n any Late-You-Are-Morons."

<MORMONS!>

He was on a roll, "Must-be-Thems!"

<MUSLIMS!>

"He-be-You's!"

<HEBREWS!>

"Annnnnd! No damn Sainted-Froggy-Lust!

<SCIENTOLOGIST?!> Some of the crowd was not too sure of that one.

"Cat-a-holics"

<CATHOLICS!>

"We shore haint be gonna putt'n up with no Ain't-Ye-Piss'd!"

<NO ATHEIST!>

The audience was on a roll, and Jamie Seamus O'Flaherty was riding high on the wave. He took another deep breath. The audience knew something "Chauntastic" was coming. "We done with all misty-cool briefs and now we be on to da other fourbody'n topic, now ain't we."

<YES!>

"And that be the toolpricks of POLETICKS." His eyes insanely sparkled at the very thought. "No, dish cuss'n from Dumberats,

Creepubicons, Lumberterrorunts…"

The crowd jumped in and interrupted. <DEMOCRATS, REPUBLICANS, LIBERTARIANS!>

"Right Oh, me felleroots… and no Common-Newts.!"

<COMMUNIST>

"Scrotum-Lost"

<SOCIALIST!>

O'Flaherty's was winding down as the crowd rose to their feet and cheer the last one, "And we nayders ah gonna be bowl'n down to no doomed Monkeyarsed!" They were waving and dancing.

<NO MORE MONARCHIST! LONG LIVE THE QUEEN!> The glasses and mugs were clinking, and toasts were going round.

Finn and Puck caught up with the doctor at the edge of the crowd now dispersing into the wings of the tavern.

"Hey ya, Doc. Enjoy the show?" Finn said while wiping his hands still holding his totem bar rag.

Doc replied, "It was great as usual, always different. I'm a little disappointed in not hearing a warning about Anarchistic Jehovah Witnesses, however."

The smile on Finn's face was infectious. "You mean the Ancient Cursed Jello-Witless don't you."

Doc looked like he had swallowed day old bourbon. "Don't you start! I may have to do a full diagnostic on poor Puck here. I'm not sure his logic circuits survived listened to that oratory without suffering some overload."

Keeping a straight a face as normal when responding he rejoined, "My systems are intact and fully functional Doctor. However… you may have to reboot my galactic thesaurus. I believe it has gone extinct."

"What did you do to my android back in the bar Finn? I didn't know you served senses of humor with all that other swill." He was really smiling an equally infectious grin, and Finn was feeling guilty that he had not planned to come clean with the good professor long ago.

Doc inquired further, "Oh, I have always meant to ask but never did before…… where did you find O'Flaherty?"

"Actually," Finn began all smiles, "He found me. I was caught in a tropical storm back on old earth some seven years ago. As much as I hate civilization, they have made a real fanatic attempt at rebuilding some old lost areas and allowed real weather to hammer a set of islands in the Pacific. I was making a tour of some of the ancient cultures trying to reinvent their lost concoctions. That's when I found myself on Borneo, lost in the new and improved jungle, having turned wrong off a beach trail. I heard this horrid sound coming from deeper within the foliage and followed it to a clearing. There, dressed in, honest to Saint Bridget, a grass skirt and wearing a coconut shell for a skull cap was this creature dancing and singing about Noah, the flood, and unicorns. He was utterly crazed drunk as a skunk. When seeing me he froze, for no more than a second, and started caterwauling how his mother was Danu, Celtic Goddess of War and the sacred Shamrock, and his father was The Old Man of The Forest.

Years later, I found he was referring to Old Tom Willow from the Tolkien histories, but considering where we were at the time, I thought he was talking about one of the local primates that had been genetically reintroduced to the wild. Never the less, he sobered up, kinda-sorta, and attached himself to me saying it was divine providence that brought us together and since, I'm not kidding there really was one there…a rainbow, rainbows are so rare with weather control in full operation, he said he could'na find his pot of gold and was destined, though I believed he said cursed, to be my companion. That is how I inherited Mr. J. S. O'Flaherty leprechaun extraordinaire." His two companions just shook their heads in disbelief sure that Finnegan was pulling their leg again.

The trio was being jostled by the patrons in a ritual dance of finding good seats for the return of the band, fresh rounds, and by those who existed in a state of paranoia looking for tables with their backs to the walls. In all of this organized confusion, the Doc spotted his shipmates from the Rover and caught their attention. Finn managed, like a ringmaster of this, his circus, to herd the group into a corner of the bar still unclaimed with good acoustics. Finn's idea of good acoustics meant a clear view of the band with an extremely limited hearing of their product. He genuinely liked Celtic music. It came somewhere below wild sex in a field of clover, much lower than a smooth whiskey or a perfect beer, and the Clancy Clones were just about the best. The problem was, after a tri-century of critical indulgence, which means he noticed every rhythmic miss of the bodhran or edgy screech of a penny whistle, he felt every mistake in his bones. Now that the friends were all gathered, Doc opened the introductions, "Finnegan... This is Captain Henry Drake the third of the good ship Star-Crossed Rover and his infamous crew. Captain... I'm glad you found the right bar. This giant in the apron here is the right honorable Timothy Finnegan, owner, operator, distributor of celestial ambrosia from the best tavern in all of known space."

"Damn glad to meet you Timothy, and I can assure you my crew here feel the same, they would say so if words could get passed their guzzling anything put in front of them." The captain thrust out his hand and two strong grips tested each other without going over the line into rudeness. He continued the introduction. "This is my ship's engineer, Gary MacAmber, and his second, Ilia Mercutio. Half Japanese, half Scot him and half Ukrainian, half Sicilian her, and all that makes for a scary experience trying to make sense of anything they may say or do." Gary was short and tight with eyes that gleamed mischief and where the Scot was hidden in his gene pool was a good guess. Ilia was tall blond and harshly handsome. You would never consider her beautiful, but when she moved, pretty flashed out of every motion. "That hulk looming behind them nursing a tankard is Smith. If he has a first name, origin, or parentage, no one has dared to step forward and claim responsibility or guilt. If a fight breaks out, I suggest you stand behind him and shout encouragement, so there is no mistaking who he' going to be doing devastation upon."

Responding to the introductions, he said. "Please everyone call me Finn or Finnegan. Only my exes and lawyers call me Timothy, and it's easier to remember after a night of bacchanalia since the name is over the joint." He paused for a moment after moving around to his own side of the bar. "And now the first fresh round is on the house."

"Cheers!"

Being the barkeep extraordinaire, Finn asked the covey of new friends if they would indulge him in a game he liked to play with new customers. He would stare deep into the eyes of each person there for a few moments then individually make a selection from his massive stock selecting what he felt was a perfect choice. The Captain received a tumbler of T&T. In the old days that was Tanqueray and tonic but the current gin mix was now branded Tachyon & Toxic. It was a strange brew with snapping crystals that tickled across the palate, bitter at first but transitioning into smoothness often found only in aged high-end liquors. The good thing about a T&T was you had to work extra hard at getting really drunk, but it gave you a controlled fuzzy feeling on the first sip. Perfect for those who never liked to lose control and Captain Drake was positively captivated by the selection.

The engineers were oddly matched. Finn served up MacAmber, the Chief, with a pint of the old Black and Tan. No frills, nothing special other than Harps and Guinness which were like liquid gold expensive imported from old earth to the rim. His second, Mercutio got a novelty Suntan & Eclipse; still, an excellent stock of ale but the mixture was kinetic in nature. You could watch the lighter half swirl in constant motion in the glass. The two halves never thoroughly blended due to a slight polarization of ion-charged ingredients in the fermentation. Sometimes it was more fun to just watch it than drink it. However, once consumed the action didn't stop. You could feel the dance continue once the two parts had been swallowed.

The last of his new customers was waiting like a statue; Finn stared for nearly a full minute into the deep violet eyes of one Sargent Major "Tank" Smith. His nickname had dropped in a side conversation earlier. Glancing back for a second time, as if to make sure of the feeling, Finn pulled out several devices and props from under the bar to begin his magic. It took another full minute to set up the stage for this last act of alchemy. Every eye was on the master now as a bottle in the shape of a crystal skull was uncorked and precise, measured shots were poured. This was followed by a ceramic jug with three XXX's etched into the brown body of the antique, a tablespoon from an unlabeled container of clear white liquid was decanted from what had to be a mason jar. Doctor Bay was certain he saw the metal tablespoon begin to sizzle and dissolve before that measure was added to the mix.

Finn then said to the audience, "That's the primer...now for the explosive." He pulled a red bottle with a Skull and Cross Bones blazoned on the label, a similar bottle all white with a Bio-Hazard label in red, followed by a blue one with, honestly... the universal symbol for Danger High Radiation clearly printed on the outside. Three equal generous doses were added to a metal mixing cylinder followed by what looked like two cubes of dry ice still smoking. He capped the top, donned thick insulated gloves, and began shaking the contents. Some edged away from the bar thinking that this could go badly. The serious look on Finn's face as he shook and listened to the rattling inside the cylinder didn't improve their apprehensions. There was a sudden popping sound which made everyone around jump in their seats. Opening the canister, Finn quickly poured the icy mixture into a ceramic glass shaped like a fat Buddha. He placed a tiny bamboo umbrella speared on the bottom with a cherry, olive, and onion plus a straw in the top then handed the thing to Smith.

Not a word was spoken; faces were frozen in shock, as Smith wrapped his massive hand around the figurine glass. The Captain had the feeling the grip was something like what Hercules must have made when strangling the serpents sent by Hera to slay him. Smith slowly raised the object up feeling every eye on him, and he took a sip. The smile blossomed across his granite face. There was an optical illusion that the Buddha actually winked.

He uttered one thunderous subsonic sound. "Perfect!"

When far enough away, and in whispers, the group would snicker a comment or two about Smith's liking girly drinks and would ponder if he had other dainty leanings, perhaps non-regulation lacy undergarments, but even with the libations of drinks flowing freely, none were so sodden as to openly test any theories near enough where the "Tank" could hear. Suddenly, the building joy of the gathering was tempered by two simultaneous events. The Clancy's began tuning up for their next set and Smith got a seriously sober look about him while glancing at his universal wrist comm.

"Captain!" Smith signaled to the Captain, "We have a situation."

"What's the problem Sergeant Major?" Drake demanded.

"I've just gotten an alert from Tech Jones 347 and 349." Smith replied, "The location is triangulated well in the area you declared off limits, sir."

"Are you telling me those Welshmen have gone and wandered into the one part of the whole space station that I personally forbade access prior to debarkation?" The captain's tone was sending a sobering effect through all those within hearing. Even the Doc and Puck were taking measure to come to terms with this announcement. The Doc was first to respond followed by a steady nodding of agreement from Finnegan.

"Captain, you don't need be wasting time. People don't stay traceable very long once the tentacles of creatures that find comfort on that side of the tracks get a good grip. There is no authority on this station that will help. We should act now." The seriousness of Docs tone was matched by a steady return of all the drinks to the bar and Finn saying, "Head for the door gentlemen and lady, I'll guide you through the station, but I need to get Lou first." Finn was already moving back into the private bar as some of the others were asking who was this "Lou." He returned with a low strung quiver strapped to his back and the grip of the Louisville Slugger baseball bat extending out the top making it easy to swing into action. As Finn was meeting his friends at the exit to the bar, the tuning of Clancy's had finished followed with a clear voice coming over the audio.

"Hey! Finn! Are you gonna be leav'n far a mite?" It was the lead tenor of the Clones, Epsilon Clancy, eyeing the group from the stage.

Finn responded. "I'll be back, need'n sum fresh air with my friends."

The Clone yelled back, "Excellent… Now All you Drunknaids, Spacenicks, and Scallywankers… here is a song you only get to be hear'n when Finn is out of the house. So get ready for the Irish Legend of…"

As the door was closing behind him, Finn heard the first notes and lyrics seeping through, and he groaned.

"(Tim Finnegan lived in Watling Street. A gentle Irishman, mighty odd…)"

Leading the crew of the Rover through the twist and turns of the jingo designed station until the lights turned into a murky sputtering of unwelcomeness, they were on the forbidden wing and oddly enough the fading signal of the lost crewmen was still flickering active. The destination was Mortimer's. In an odd turn of design, this dive was a polar opposite of Finnegan's on the station schematics. It was certainly opposite in appeal and attractiveness.

"They are somewhere inside." Smith indicated, and Finn finished with, "Let me try the first rounds of negotiations, shall we?"

The décor was black. Black floors, ceilings, tables, chairs, walls, even the bar was a smut black metal. It left you with a chill and a feeling you should have a canary in a cage with you here. The lights were low to cavernous with just enough illumination to keep the mind from entering a state of coma. At the center of the bar was a tall figure, tall as Finn but lean to the point of skeletal, that seemed so due to his actually wearing a black velvet top hat, a stovepipe, severe tuxedo. Not to be finished there, he kept his left hand, wearing a thin leather glove with white lace lining; solidly gripping a silver skull ruby eyed walking cane. It gave an impression he would collapse into a pile of bones if the grip were lost. His right hand was delicately tapping a shot glass of something. Finn got closer and could actually smell the hint of the drink. It was absinthe. The original formula, not the novelties that had resurfaced over time, with green ichors dancing in the glass like temptations from a grave.

"Hello, Mortimer. We would like you to return a couple of our missing friends, or else!" The tone was not pleasant.

Gary leaned over to Smith and said, "That was diplomatic?"

Smith replied. "My kind at least," As he moved his hand closer to his weapon.

"Tisk, tisk,… You charge into MY establishment, disturbing MY clientele, and make demands… Where have your manners gone, or has old age finally gotten the better of you Timothy?" Mortimer focused his sunken eyes on the party standing united in the center of the bar as they looked around wondering who in the darkness must qualify as clientele.

"We,… I am not here for games, Mortimer. You, or that which passes for your friends, have mistakenly retained at least two of MY clientele's crew. You are on notice that they are free spacemen, under contract, and military. I'm sure your scavengers can find replacements from the dregs that stumble in here for a final fix of Toxidrone or whatever last rites you serve to the mostly dead humanity that are your customers."

"Very well, Old… and I do mean that in the kindest of terms, Old Friend. Let me let you discuss this with those who laid claim to the two lambs your sheepdogs have let go missing." He said that while tapping a signal into a device panel near his drinking hand, a side door opened and several heavily armed mercenaries came out saying. "Mort, what do you want? We just about have the two noobchicks trussed up and ready for transport. We have to get moving. I think they might be military and…..." That was when they notice the room was not empty and that lack of emptiness was filled with many people wearing distinct uniforms similar to their captives.

Mortimer was unmoving, but the crew of the Rover had started to go for the mercenaries. Finn pulled "Lou" from over his shoulder and tapped a sequence on the digital wrappings. A blue pulse fired out of the top of the bat and sent the merky's into temporary convulsions. Finn then turned his attention to Mortimer, who simply raised his hand in a casual gesture that he was not participating in the show any longer. "Tank" reached the mercenaries first and had them disarmed and strap locked before the others move into the back exit from the direction they had entered. Ilia took the chance to groin kick one of the merky's on her way by. Finn stayed with Mortimer as the battle ensued in the other room, he knew the reputation of his opposite number here at space dock and was not going to give him a shot at anyone's back.

From another entrance behind the bar came one of Mortimer's own bartenders, he was holding the paraphernalia to concoct a refresher shot of absinthe, like nothing unusual was going on. The boy was dressed, more undressed, in faux-leather. He was anorexic with short stubby hair dyed in swirls of color; at least some color was evident in this pit. The leather consisted of a flight hat cocked to one side, straps of crossing bands, short shorts with a spike-studded codpiece, and, honest to Godz, thigh top high boots. All the leather was shinily polished, he would have been cute twenty pounds heavier and with visible eyes, not the sunken pits of someone who had seen too much, done too much, been done unto much, and none of it right. Finn had learned more than two hundred years ago that he couldn't save everyone. He even learned he was damn lucky to save anyone. The rescue of two crewmen going on in the back would do for today and putting any dent in Mortimer's operation was a cherry on top. This kid was a lost soul if there was even a soul left in that shell of a human.

Finn knew there were more mysteries out there in the universe. His whiskey miracle was one. Whatever Mortimer had consumed, and when, was another, but it was really not a miracle. It was a curse, and a cosmic joke that two immortals of Life and Death would be serving drinks in the deep dark of space was the punch line. A screeching of the door to Mortimer's meant someone had come in behind Finn. Faster than should have been possible for such a giant, Finn maneuvered where he could see both Mort and the new disturbance. Oh, this was not good!

Standing in the doorway was another strikingly tall man. He honestly wore an Aussie hat with long style bush coat, and knee-high cavalry boots, all dust brown tan and well worn. He cocked his head up and violet piercing ancient eyes bore forward. He nodded once.

"Finn. You're in the wrong bar. Mort, don't you be moving an inch!" Here was another immortal. One Cassidy R. Longstroke, stood perfectly still waiting for a response.

"I didn't know you were in this area of space Cass. What brings you to paradise?" Finn asked this, but he knew the reputation of one of the oldest immortals. Cassius didn't show up unless something needed killing. He was a self-appointed safety valve for his kind. That included Finn, Mortimer, and now Doc when they got to have a come-to-jaysus conversation if they had the chance. Finn saw a line of sweat rolling down Mort's neck. This was going to be fun.

Cass replied, "Nothing you have done Finn, but Morty here has been spawning some Zombie-boys. I believe he's looking for a source of the fountain of youth since he can't find the Tree of Death anymore; he has been using a half-mix of ju-ju juice from leaves of the Immortalitree. It has questionable effects. I think he wants your source of the Tree of Life to compensate. Hope you are not here making a deal. That would be very... unfortunate indeed for both of you."

"Nope, I'm here to rescue a couple of customers who got lost. I don't deal with the devil or his butt boy experiment here." Finn responded."

"How rude, and I thought we were going to be friends..."

Cass cut Mortimer short, "You can shut up now, or we see how much of you we need to leave in one piece to reanimate. Alive is not accurate for what you are now, an intact corpsuckle."

"Just so we are upfront here," Finn started, "There is a new member of the Uisce Beatha side of the brotherhood."

Cassidy's frown got deeper, "Not you too, Tim. We had an understanding about the dangers."

"I've been keeping control on this one, but there is an exceptional scientist just in the other room, and I'm going to bring him into the game." Finn was still holding "Lou" with his fingers just over the controls. "He's one in a billion Cass. And... I'll take responsibility for his education and termination if need be should it go wrong. Deal with the Wart here as you will."

"I think not." Mortimer made a finger light motion over his cane, and the very floor opened up beneath him. Cass had his unique, custom made pistol out and discharged, but the wraith Mortimer had slipped into the oubliette portal under his feet. It wasn't a perfect escape. The shot fired by Cass obliterated the top hat at least. The only problem was the shot continued on and splattered leather boy into the diorama on the back bar.

"Damn, bad luck that!" Cass muttered as he dropped the weapon back into his duster.

"Not really, that kid was dead inside the moment he crossed Mortimer's sensors sweep. I gave him maybe a month, and Toxidronic poisoning doesn't end well. It's the nuclear equivalent of the DT's with no coming back. You did him a favor. I noticed the tremors already starting when he first walked in. Are you going after Mort?

"Certainly, He is on my Dead to be Offed List. Jumping in a hole and Jonesing out of the system is not going to end this." He offered.

"I hope you get him soon, the station has developed a distinctive odor since he arrived. I think it needed fumigating long ago. Of course, civilization will certainly follow soon." Finn predicted.

"And that is both our sign to push farther out to the edge. I really hope we don't see each other soon Finnegan. The idea that three immortals could find themselves in one spot in the whole known galaxy is too unhealthy for the probability Godz to justify." Sounds began to come from the back room, and Cass took that opportunity to spin and exit with one last Parthian comment, "Say Hello and Goodbye to Mom and Dad for me when you get back to your bar…" And he was gone leaving Finn more puzzled than before.

The crew reentered as the last flash of a tan duster slipped out of site. Finn gathered the troops and led them back through the maze of the station to his oasis. There he set up the Jones boys and their fellow rescuer's with a fresh round of happiness and was surprised to find those boys were actual descendants of the inventor who discovered FTL space travel. He asked to steal the Doctor Bay and Puck for a while and placed O'Flaherty on table duty to ensure these friends were not neglected. Rose would have been his first choice, but she had not loosened her normal count of dentures this evening and Finn was not too sure his new collection of space adventurer friends would recognize their danger and not set off the two-legged dynamite. He was pretty sure no one had twisted enough taste to try and proposition Jamie Seamus O'Flaherty but gave a glance at Smith pondering, but the image gladly would not stay in his brain. There would be Shillelagh Law in full rage if they did, but you can't open a bar without a little risk.

"Let's adjourn to my office in the back shall we." Directing the Doc and his partner through the drawbridge slab of dark oak separating the back bar from customers. It was then that he saw Rose heading straight to him, the band in her hair streaming behind her like a kite's tail, or maybe it was a dragon's, she reached Finn as his hand began to turn the brass doorknob.

"You have company," Rose said this, her hand on top of his, with all the weight of someone just announcing the bomb was detached and falling from the belly of Enola Gay.

Finn cocked an eyebrow and didn't have to ask who before Rose offered, " I saw Longstroke pass the bar a few minutes after you left with your friends and the two in your office came in here moments after that."

"I spoke with Cassidy. Who's in my office? Cause nobody goes in my office without my permission." Rose glared at Finn's face like he had been sipping vacuum when he said that and got this ... You are about to get your karma kicked look... for hinting that she was responsible for what happens in the universe. She actually sniffed as if she smelled something bad, turned and stalked back to her customers. Lord help them. Finn opened the door, and before he could signal the two behind him to fade, three faces were looking into the room's mystery. A man was sitting behind Finn's own desk with his feet resting crossed and relaxed on the top of it. The feet were covered in leather suede moccasins with standard issue magnoslip strips attached to the bottom. The legs and torso were covered in worn Levi denim overalls, all that covered by a leather jacket with streamers of fringe, all this was decorated with beads and turquoise, and at the top of a face so old and wrinkled it looked like a flesh-colored fractured lunar map of Titan. Above it, all was another top hat. Finn first thought, "What is it with top hats today," first Mortimer and now this, the difference being that the one on this head was worn leather and decorated with beads, a feather, and what looked to be a dream catcher attached.

"Whatcha staring at Boy?" The voice was familiar but scarier like an echo from some primordial cave. "Yer mama taught you better manners. I know'd cuz I taught yo grandpappy those manners with enough tail switch'n to see that they got learnt." Then it dawned on him like a cathedral bell ringing doom. This was Medsyn Joe. He was the oldest of all the immortals. Finn met him as a child, minus a thousand wrinkles or so, long before his own whiskey event. Seeing Cass was improbable. Seeing MJ was impossible. As his head was still spinning and trying to get a feel for the implications, he caught a flicker of another. She was lying casually over to the side on his office couch and making it look like Goddess Bast had decreed this was her throne and proceeded to purr with satisfaction. Finn recognized her in an instant.

Long ago, when Finn had met Cassidy for the first time, Finn was extracting a number of lead slugs from that immortal's chest, Cassidy happened to show Finn a photograph, non-perforated, of this very lady. They both had exchanged histories of their longevity; Cass said that there were two unknowably ancient of ancients. One was Medsyn Joe, and the other was Lady Lil. Here they were.

While Finn's jaw was working up and down, the words kept being swallowed causing him some degree of indigestion.

Joe continued, "You there, Tin Man, take a seat next to Miss Lilly cuz these other poor fools will lose all blood flow above thar neeks if'n she gets too close." The Doc was raising his hand to protest that he was immune until Lil looked directly into his eyes, he decided he wasn't nearly as immune as he believed. Medsyn Joe gave a smile of wise understanding as he watched the impact she was having. "Don't feel bad thar buttercup, you all get back to normal when she's not around slinking up the joint. Down to business, Timmy me boy... You are about to give the Doc here the bad news bout his medical condition. We are here to be tell'n ya to quit sweating the problem. We all came here to let you be know'n there's a new game afoot. Some folks with your medical affliction, but poor judgment, like Mortimer, are being put on the T0-Be-Dead-Soon List. To accomplish this as quickly as possible, we are forming the Methuselah's League.

You, the Doc here, and to some degree, Cassidy will be responsible judge, jury, and executioner when long-lifers go bad. With the expansion of humanity to the stars, immortality is not going to be the hazard it was when we was confined to our own neck of the woods but thar has to be a rational human guide to the species and certainly a force to contend with bad seed like the Mort. Ya'll going to be that force for this quadrant of the expansion."

The Doc looked back and forth at Finn and Joe. He was trying to figure out what this whole show was aside from some tomfoolery being pulled when Puck whispered. "Doc... Finn was going to tell you before this party began. You have discovered an immortality elixir in that last sample and have so multiple times. You've stopped aging, and your base DNA code has been mutated to be regenerative. It seems these two are suggesting you join their fraternity, but you're going to have to stomp on some malignant immortals as dues."

Doc responded, "How did you figure all this out?"

"Finn told me when we were alone. He's not supposed to create any new immortals, but this, as you can see, has taken him by surprise as much as it has you." He confessed.

Then Finn took a moment longer to interrupt the pause, "I'm a bartender, not a space ranger! Why me?"

Medsyn Joe looked at him like he was a child. "Cause yo jess happen to be here. Simple as that. More so, we don't need no warriors, we need ordinary folk, people skills, with a good dose of morals, ethics, and grit to do what is right. You've proven that much without interference from us. Now haven't ya? Given the right circumstances, you probably would have ended Mort's leech'n career. Cassidy lacks some of those skills which means you get to boss the group. Doc here will be ya'lls tracker, Cassidy will be the hammer. We clean up space. Keep Truth, Justice, and Humanity going forward! The Bad get de-immortalized with prejudice. Say you're in?"

Lady Lil now straightened up and leaned forward. Her eyes were piercing and evaluating, each and every one of them felt like a mouse trying to decide if the cobra was hungry and there was little doubt she expected unanimous and committed agreement or they would be considered a threat.

In unison, both Finn and the Doc nodded assent. Puck was considered a part of anything Doctor Bay decided, so the five were now the first of the Methuselah prodigies. Lady Lil spoke for the first time. Her voice was like a siren's melody. "You have made me very happy boys." At that moment any one of the new League knew they would do anything to keep her feeling happy and she handed each a comm-slip. "In case you ever need to reach me. You had better seriously NEED me... Understand?" The communication-slip said:

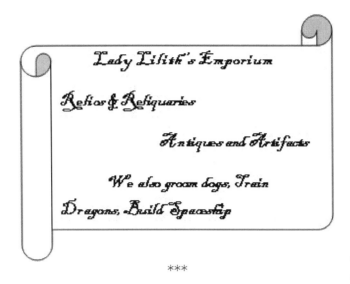

Lady Lilith's Emporium

Relics & Reliquaries

Antiques and Artifacts

We also groom dogs, Train

Dragons, Build Spaceship

***

Thanum o'n Dhoul

For Tim Finnegan, this had turned out to be one of the longer days of his tri-centennial career. The Immortals had departed, if not the station, at least his tavern. The Doc was back on board the Rover and was negotiating a new contract with captain and crew. Doc had decided to try and keep them and together use them for the "Police Action" he had been drafted into doing. Puck was researching biological options to his humanity. Finn had received a comm-link code from Cass saying he was in hot pursuit and would keep him informed when Mortimer was cashiered. Rose had gone to her quarters, alone as was her nature, and the bar was spotless. The Clones had left him in the bliss of silence. Medsyn Joe had left a guide for the Methuselah League, a sort of Articles of Actions. Basically, immortals would be created and recruited if they met some pretty severe guidelines and no nay votes of the League. Finn was good with that.

He headed to the back tavern to secure the samples Doc had left when to his shock and surprise he realized the door to the back tavern was unlocked. Damn, he had rushed to get "Lou" from the cradle and failed to secure it. Opening the door, the horror hit him. There splayed unconscious to the world was the horrid lime colored form of Jamie Seamus O'Flaherty. Sprawled out on the top of the bar with the sample case open and empty, surrounding him like

Lilliputians around Gulliver were empty shot glasses and not a single drop untouched, most importantly number 25. He was dreaming the rapture of the Emerald Isle, and the Uisce Beatha was working its transformation.

A grumble like the first tremor of a quake began vibrating in Finn's chest. His face began to infuse with alarming red, his hair was picking up a static charge of rage and blood vessels were standing out on his brow and neck like bolts of liquid lightening and then the sound came out echoing through the bar, down the halls vibrating through bulkheads and quatranteun plating of the entire Mandrake station.

"CCCHHAAAUUUNNN!"

Critters

by
Herika Raymer

It had been a slow couple of days at the Ursa Minor Pub, but Eddie did not mind. After the rush of activity due to the recent science freighter explosion and the resulting clean-up, he could use the breather. The common room needed a massive clean and disinfect, and the stock was running a bit low. Not enough to be alarming, not yet. Good thing the supply freighter was due at the end of the week. He just had to make it until then. If nothing else, he could start making his infamous Testers, a chaotic mix-up of available stock to placate the barflies until their regular drinks could be served again.

He looked up as a few space skimmers set off the proximity alarms. As they neared, the scanner on the window identified them as runners from the clean-up crew. Glancing at the time-keep, he realized it was close to mid-meal. Not that there was a set schedule out here in the Vast, but sometimes the feeling of a routine was comforting amid the eternal black.

"Patch!"

A head popped up from underneath one of the tables. Her mop of curly hair bounced happily as she jumped up from where she had been cleaning. Even from here he could see her mismatched eyes - one green and one blue. A genetic anomaly even in these times. A mere slip of a thing, she had wandered into his bar one day and never left. No one had ever come asking after her, no family and - thankfully - no authorities. She wore the usual thermal suits to help regulate body temperature in deep space, but her favorite jacket seemed to be a patchwork of materials. Hence her nickname. He was glad for the company and even more so for the help. Steady workers were hard to find at nexus points like the one his bar was stationed at. Made most Terrans feel off because there was no set point of gravity. The bar did not orbit - it stayed in place. Only things did not always work as they should, and the atmosphere did not always feel right. Someone once described the atmosphere as being adrift in the middle of the ocean and never knowing what the weather would be. Patch never seemed to mind though, or at least she hadn't complained. He did not know much about her but never pried. He figured she would talk to him when she was ready.

"Customers coming!" He thumbed to the ships approaching the landing. "Best get the range fired up."

She nodded and quickly made her way to the kitchen behind the bar. In her wake, he noticed she had done short work of the common room. It was in order: the old-fashioned wooden tables gleamed from polish, the cushioned chairs looked inviting, the windows were grime-free, and the decorations on the wall were dusted. The Ursa Major Pub might not look like other space bars, but Eddie prided himself on offering "an old-fashioned feeling of home" to his patrons. Apparently, Patch shared his pride in the bar and made sure to keep the place presentable and have a welcoming atmosphere. It amazed him how much she could do in so little time. He had been sure it would take them days to straighten the mess after the clean-up crews left, depositing space junk as they went. Each time, though, she had everything in order in a matter of hours. He did not know how she did it but was grateful for it.

"Whew!" one of the men exclaimed as he removed his helmet after crossing the threshold. He breathed in deeply and smiled. "Nice to breathe something other than recycled air."

A second man joined him, also breathing deep. "Hey, yeah." He looked over at Eddie. "How you do that?"

The bartender smiled. He had forgotten that the air pumped into the bar had a cool tinge that tickled the nostrils thanks to its source, something missing from the almost metallic taste of the recycled air of space ships and space stations. Coupled with the gentle cleansers just used, there was a nice clean scent floating about. "Have one of the ice converters below," he said simply. "Helps push fresh air into my little bubble here."

"Nice," a third said as the trio made their way to a table. "Where you get the ice from?"

"Mostly from ice moons," he answered as he met them there and set down some drinks in front of them. Something general and light, since he was not sure they were on duty. No one objected. They just grabbed the glasses and took a long draw. "Never sure about comet ice, never know what's in them," he finished with a wink.

The men laughed as he returned to the bar.

Patch came out from the kitchen and approached them. She stood silently as she passed their menus to them. Her face was friendly, but she did not say anything. The men seemed confused for a moment and looked about to say something.

"Sorry about the relics, guys," Eddie interrupted them. Patch was not much of a talker and did not like being forced to talk, even for the sake of good manners. "But the less energy I use on the small stuff, the more I can spare in case of an emergency."

"Is this paper?" the first man asked, holding up his menu.

"Yup," he said with pride. "Passed down through generations. Notice the lamination is still intact. That was not easy, even in storage."

"Man, you must be a walking museum," the first guy went on. "Haven't seen stuff like this outside of one."

"Some of the older treasures still have use here in the Vast," he replied almost defensively. "Especially near nexus points, where electronics don't always work like they should."

"Wait." The third peered at his menu. "Does this say 'cooked'? Not 'replicated?'"

Eddie nodded and grinned again. "Another relic in the back, boys, a range. Modified to use materials that cannot be recycled as fuel. Granted, the foodstuffs may have a different flavor than you might expect, but we cook here, boys. So enjoy."

Excited at the idea of fresh food, the trio made their orders. Patch took the menus and returned with regular drinks. The teasers he had provided on arrival were customary to give a taste of what he had. If they wanted more, they would have to order it, and the cost would be added to their bill. It was not long before the aroma of cooking drifted forward from the back.

The three inhaled as one, and the bartender could swear he saw them drool.

A few more runners arrived, depositing crews of three each. They were not dressed in clean-up crew uniforms, so he guessed they were the assessors sent in to find out what happened to the science freighter that blew up. Eddie greeted each group personally and walked them to a table, then was sure to place the teasers before returning to the bar. Patch was kept busy serving the tables. Sandwiches were especially popular since they were tasty and quick, though the other dishes which took longer were just as delicious. A couple of the tables ordered more alcohol, which he provided. As he poured and mixed the drinks, he caught snippets of conversation.

"... so odd, no readings before it happened..."

"... everything seems to have been going according to plan..."

"... no reason for the thing to blow..."

It was troubling, he had to admit, for a space freighter to explode this close to a nexus point, a place normally considered to be safe because of the lack of typical space physics. If the cause could not be determined, people might stop coming here. That would not be good for business. Unlike other bartenders, he had chosen to build close to a nexus point because there was no set gravity and it seemed the usual laws of the Vast did not hold. Nexus points were not the typical vacuums of other areas of space, and it was easier to build here. The only problem was that electrical and digital were not entirely reliable, hence the use of "relics" he had inherited. Until now, they had all sat in storage. Now furniture and tapestries, old paintings, dishes, cutlery, and other items adorned his new home. It was kinda nice, not relying completely on electronics. However, the recent disruption might prompt authorities to order him to vacate for safety's sake.

Science freighters like the Destiny had been sent to further map out and examine different regions of the galaxy. Even though space travel through the Laniakea super-cluster had been shortened by the use of Jones' Hurl Drives, it was still smart to know how to navigate. Asteroids drifted, comets flew, stars collapsed or formed, moons coalesced, sometimes planets were destroyed, and with the expanse of Terran settlements, sometimes space trash was a problem. In many cases, mapping out interstellar bodies helped scientists figure out patterns of space movements and even have a chance to catalog new celestial bodies and space life forms. For one to blow up with no apparent cause was alarming.

Another proximity alarm, but he was busy serving the drinks ordered to pay it too close attention. He returned to the bar, collecting the sample glasses as he did. Once there, he began to wash them.

It took a moment for Eddie to realize a silence had fallen in the bar. Looking up, he saw that attention was directed to the threshold. Patch was the only one looking at the door, but he could tell his customers were aware of whoever was there.

Standing there, alone, was a bedraggled man. His science uniform was dirty and looked worn, though not torn. He did not pause but walked directly to the bar. Patch abandoned the common room and brushed gently past Eddie to pour the man a drink.

No, she poured him two drinks.

She set one directly in front of him, and the other in front of the empty seat next to him.

"Long day?" she asked.

Eddie slowed but did not pause completely. She spoke so rarely, he had learned that it was important when she did. Best he paid attention.

The man wrapped his hands around the glass and stared blankly into the liquid.

She waited and idly wiped at the countertop beside him.

"They didn't listen to me," he rasped after a moment.

She reached under the bar, grabbed some clean glasses and began to "dry" them. Eddie noticed her fingers brushed again Old Faithful, the projectile rifle stored there. He was not sure if that was a good sign or not.

"I told the navigator they were headed towards a cluster of critters, that they were swarming the nexus," he went on. "He didn't believe me. Said I read too much old fiction..." He lapsed into silence.

"Critters?" she prompted.

"My ancestor warned people about them," he continued. "Was called a crackpot and ignored. He tried to show them pictures but was told there was nothing there. The ones who listened were mocked like he was. But they're real, the critters..." The man sat in a miserable silence for a moment. "It was not intentional. They just drift around, and sometimes they interfere with the working of space vessels. They just drifted through a sensitive part of the ship, disrupted the signal, and set off a chain reaction."

"That must be TJ, one of the few survivors," Eddie heard one of the patrons say.

"What is he talking about?" someone asked.

"You're new," the first responded.

"Yeah."

He nodded towards the troubled man at the bar. "TJ Constantine was one of the crew of the Destiny. He's supposed to be a great cartographer, helped map out most of the areas of the Laniakea super-cluster, especially around other nexus points. Has a knack for it really, and has helped several freighters navigate those points without incident."

"Until now," the second one groused.

"But what's he talking about?"

"Amoebae constablea," Eddie heard the second mutter derisively.

"He still going on about those things?" his companion asked doubtfully.

"Yeah, says they were responsible for the Destiny exploding."

If TJ heard them, he gave no sign. The silence that followed was thick. Eddie could feel the mounting tension. It began to press upon him like a palatable force. In almost all unfortunate situations, there were those who looked for a scapegoat, someone to blame for a seemingly unnecessary tragedy. He did not like the idea of TJ becoming that target.

Patch reached over and refilled the second glass.

"The Destiny just got too close," the man in front of her said, his drink still untouched. "I tried to warn them, told them the critters were right in front of them. But the sensors didn't pick up anything, so they told me I was imagining things. If they had just listened."

This matched up with the snippets he heard earlier, about there being no evidence of foul play and no recordings of any readings. However, judging from the souring expressions on the seated group's faces, he doubted they would take that into consideration.

"Usually they just float around, absorbing whatever it is they need," TJ was saying, his voice heavy. "Normally I could help the navigator cut a path around a cluster of them and not really get into why. Only this time, this nexus was full of them, and the navigator was tired of moving around what he thought was clear areas. But there were more than I had ever seen before. They gather at a nexus... maybe it is a breeding ground... maybe it is their home... I don't know, but there are always more at the nexus points..."

"What about here?" Patch asked.

"Yeah, they're here," he said, looking around as if seeing things for the first time. "You're smart though, not much electronics around. You'll be alright."

"Good to know," she rejoined as she filled the half-full second glass.

"What is she doing?" he heard a patron say.

"Filling the glass, stupid."

"But no one is drinking out of it."

"TJ must be, otherwise why would she fill it?"

"His hands have not left his glass, and look - his is still full."

Eddie stole a glance over as he placed some empty glasses under the bar. Sure enough, TJ's hands were still wrapped around his full glass, and the one beside his was sweating but also already half-full again.

Seeing motion in his peripheral vision, he noticed one of the boys holding up his sensor array reader. He had it directed towards TJ and was adjusting it. "Nothing. Nothing on any of the settings. There is nothing there but him."

"Then who or what is drinking?"

They all looked at the second glass, and again it was empty. No one saw it move, and nothing could be seen to consume it. Patch just refilled it again.

""So you can see them?" she asked.

"Yeah," TJ answered miserably. "Guess I inherited it. Now they call me crazy."

"Why would they do that?"

"Because they can't see them!" he growled. "If they can't see it, then it must not exist."

"A lot of things exist that we can't see," she pointed out.

"Yeah, but if they can't pick it up on their stupid sensor machines, then they don't believe it's out there. At least not until it is right up on them."

"The critters can't be read on a sensor?"

He looked at her as if she had said something painfully obvious. "Sensors are only made to detect what we measure. And those measurements are arbitrary. Do we really know a pound is a pound, a decibel is a decibel, or a pulsar is a pulsar? No, we just agree it is. Those are energy readings that can be seen, felt, heard, and in some cases smelled. They need to stop being so stubborn and realize that their measured world is only part of a bigger universe, and those parts unexplored just might not show up on their machines."

The tension got thicker. Whether TJ intended to or not, he had just insulted everyone else in the room. Maybe he had meant to, but it was not smart, given how badly he was outnumbered. Eddie did not want a fight in his bar, but he could almost taste one building.

"Think about it. The mapped galaxy is akin to a sphere about 100 light years in diameter. In that vast space, there are over 500 G-type stars. What constitutes 'G-type' but a set of criteria terra-formers have agreed on? How is a 'light year' really measured, except on the accepted equation as proposed in history? Since A.D. 2213, we have interstellar flight made possible by Hurl drives by Dr. Richard Jones. For over 200 years, we have been using these engines that were built using formulas used on faith."

Eddie listened with interest. There was some truth to what the boy was saying. All the equations taught and used were never really questioned, but that was because they had been proven in use before and given the same results each time. The proof was enough to have future generations continue to use the original on faith that the result would always be the same. Granted though, who decided what measurements were? He knew the answer, as did anyone else. It was in the name. Usually, measurements were named after those who determined them. In fact, there was a rumor that Dr. Jones had been aided by his local bartender in the Hurl drive creation. It is also rumored that the drive doesn't work unless the operator is at least two sheets to the wind. This rumor helped the joke of the name "Hurl," given that most people could not hold their liquor too well.

"Is there a way to detect these critters?" Patch asked.

TJ shrugged, looking more miserable.

"Maybe you can find a way."

He looked at her oddly, as if he did not believe she had said that.

"It's going to happen again, isn't it," she asked.

TJ paled. "Yes. Unless they can find a way to help ships detect the critters, it will happen again. They are still out there, and the ships are still examining the nexus points."

"Can't you be there?"

"Not on all the ships, and even if I'm not, I will probably be blamed. After all, I've cartographed most of these sectors. If a ship runs into a problem, it will be my fault for not noting it."

"Maybe they won't."

TJ slumped in his chair. "They will. Whether I am there or not, they will. Their angry voices joining with the memories of the screams. I can't take it. I just can't."

"So then do something."

He looked at her, lost.

"Your family can see them, right?"

"I guess," he agreed dubiously.

"Then you can find a way," she said encouragingly. "Find a way to stop the voices."

"You don't know what you're saying." His face tightened in anger. "My ancestor tried. He used what he had and couldn't convince anyone. What chance do I have now? I have been trying with the equipment we have now. That's how I know the critters cannot be seen. No matter what setting I have tried - infrared, dark matter, sound, ultraviolet, heat sensor - nothing registers."

"Not by agreed parameters, huh?"

He nodded.

"Too bad there are no new parameters."

"What do you mean?"

She shrugged and poured more into the second glass.

He looked at it, seeing there was no one there for the first time. Or was no one there? Eddie could not see anyone, but Patch had been refilling that glass consistently. So something must be there. The tension in the air changed, it was no longer menacing but more curious and anxious.

He smirked. "You see it."

"Nope."

"But..."

She just smiled at him.

He looked at the glass again, which was missing a small portion of the drink. He took the glass and looked inside. Looking at her, his eyes seemed to gleam. "Can I take this?"

"Why?"

"I want to measure the absence."

"Pardon?"

"Old scientists proved their guesses, or hypotheses, by trying to disprove it. Like reverse-psychology. They would try to disprove to prove, and the more something existed, the more it became measurable. After a while, the guess became fact - it became a theory. You gave me a way to prove I'm not crazy. I never thought to measure the absence. I have a way."

Eddie watched as TJ straightened from his slumped sitting position to sitting straight. He was holding the glass like it was precious. Grinning, he made his way out of the bar.

There were scattered mutterings in the room.

"... think he will do it?"

"... still, think he is crazy..."

"... what does he plan to do..."

"Look at that!"

Attention turned to the threshold.

Beside it was a discoloration in the adjoining wall. It had not been there before and was in the form of a large blob. As they watched, it dissipated.

Outside, TJ's skimmer launched and flew off to new possibilities.

Interlude 2

The room had grown cool around Sam 1701 giving him the idea that evening must have arrived. He had dug through most of his second selection of records. He eyed the remaining few and decided that he could finish them without it taking all night. Besides the one hint, he needed to find might be in the next file he tried. *Just these few and I'll call it done for the day. Then, I can get some food and sleep.*

He opened a small green box and pushed the play point to begin the file playback.

All Hallows' Eve at Midnight Absinthe

by
J. H. Fleming

He knew the party was a bad idea. He could feel it, deep in his gut. Or perhaps it was the bad cheese he'd eaten the other night. Either way, it wouldn't end well.

"C'mon, Jake, it'll be great!" his bartender said. "Think of all the customers we'll draw to the bar. Everyone likes a little culture and history. Add in some spirits, and we're gold!"

"I can help," Dera, one of the regulars, offered. He still couldn't figure out why she bothered. She was young, early twenties, fair-skinned and sweet. Never drank anything but old world soda, and always wore flower print dresses. She seemed to belong in a library, or a school, not a backwater bar on a forgotten planet.

"What do you say, Jake?" his only employee asked again. Haze was in her thirties, with short red hair and her signature camo pants and black tank. Not to mention her combat boots and old world tattoos. In the five years, she'd worked for him, she'd never once shown the slightest interest in anything but acquiring new "toys." But times, apparently, were changing.

"If I agree to this, I'm not lifting a finger to help. This is your baby."

"Understood," Haze said.

"Does that mean the party's on?" Dera asked.

"It does," he conceded. "May the forces help me," he added to himself.

Haze smirked at him while Dera clapped her hands and squealed. He shook his head and continued wiping down the bar. It was early morning, and he was normally in bed at that time, but Haze had dragged out her request by detailing everything she had learned about the holiday, as well as all the advantages the bar would enjoy by celebrating it. Honestly, he didn't much care, so long as it wasn't his to plan and didn't cause any problems.

Haze and Dera left, still absorbed in their conversation, with only an absent-minded wave in his direction. That left only him and Theodore, who was just finishing his final drink of the night.

"If you indulge them, they'll want to do other holidays. Then it will turn into tea parties, charities, fundraisers. The bar will become the social hub of the star system."

Jake chuckled. "I doubt that. Have you ever witnessed Haze's decorating skills?"

"True, but she's got Dera helping her."

Jake threw his rag in the basket under the bar in response.

Theodore drained his glass and stood. He was a tall, thin man, with lank black hair and pale skin. He always wore a long black coat and boots, no matter the weather. He drank heavily, and often, and he'd been a regular since Jake had first opened the bar.

"Don't suppose you'll give me one for the road."

"You know better than to ask."

Theodore nodded as he headed out the door. "Till next time then."

Once the door had shut behind him, Jake sighed and grabbed the glass from his table. Business wasn't bad, but it had been slow lately. Maybe a party was just what they needed.

***

That week Haze and Dera began buying decorations. Jake wouldn't let them put anything up yet. He had a mood in the bar that he'd carefully crafted over the year, and if it was to be changed, he wanted it to be as brief as possible.

"I need some advice," Haze said one evening when she had a free moment.

"I'm always willing to share my wisdom."

"Pumpkins. They've been extinct for a while, and I'm not sure what to use as a substitute."

"Squash? Tomatoes?"

"No, I need something bigger."

"Why not—"

"Oh! I've got it. Thanks, Jake."

She hurried to the back room, leaving the bar to him. "You're welcome?" he called after her.

Dera approached then, smiling as she sat. "The usual," she said.

He poured her a glass of Frosty, the newest soft drink created that year. He didn't know why she never ordered alcohol, and he didn't ask. Not his business.

"So tell me, Jake," she said, "when are you going to get hitched and have some little ones? Surely you've done all the roaming you can stomach?"

Jake chuckled. "No one would marry me. At least, no woman with an ounce of sense in her head."

"I'd marry you. Under the right circumstances, of course."

"And what would those be?"

"Are you proposing?"

He glared at her in response.

Finally, she laughed and said, "Oh, you know — unconditional love, complete faithfulness, constant doting on me, presents ... Great sex, too. I'm afraid that's a must."

"And what would I get out of it?"

"The pleasure of my company, of course. And did I mention the great sex?"

Jake laughed as he moved to the other side of the bar to help a different customer.

"We'd make a fine pair," Dera called after him.

"Keep dreamin', babe," he answered. "This one's not the settling kind."

"Had to try."

More people came in, and he lost track of time as he took orders and mixed drinks. At times he wondered what the heck Haze was doing, but the thought was pushed back as the night drew on. Finally, just as things were dying down again, she reappeared through the back door.

"Where've you been?" he asked. "I'm not paying you to not work."

"I was working. I bought the decorations."

"That's not in your job description."

"Neither is putting up with your grumpy ass, but I do it anyway."

"Burn," said Theodore, who was just taking a seat at the bar. "You two are like an old married couple."

"Is everyone intent on talking about marriage tonight?"

"Why, who else brought it up?" Haze asked.

"It doesn't matter. So where are these decorations? Don't I at least get a look at what I'm paying for?"

"They're out in the ranger. Too heavy to carry all at once, and I'd prefer to wait till everyone's gone."

"Fair enough."

It was another couple of hours before the last customer left, leaving Jake, Haze, and the regulars. With only a silent nod, they moved as a group to retrieve the decorations.

***

"One minute until arrival," the W.I.T.C.H. said.

Althea lowered the speed on her inter-planet ship and flicked the various gauges that would prepare her craft for docking. After adjusting her angle of descent to a more parallel course, she flicked the autopilot switch and hurried to the back compartment to change. Years of travel and research was about to pay off, and she wanted to look her best. She would need a bath, and a costume for sure, and possibly an alias. Or perhaps not. Her real name was old world, and fit the persona she intended to convey. It was just a bit risky if things ended up going south.

Her wardrobe already consisted of several black dresses and slacks, so she added the star necklace she'd recently acquired and a bracelet of smooth black stones. She was still new to studying the old world religions, so it still felt like playing dress up. At least she wouldn't have to completely fake it, though. This was her moment, and she was going to be sure to enjoy it.

***

The bar looked like the autumn days of old had come in for a drink, got wasted, and threw up all over the place. Nowadays the weather went from scorching to freezing with no in-between, but he'd heard the transitions seasons had been quite nice.

Near the bar and along the back wall were Haze's holiday decorations, which she had researched extensively to make sure she got it right. There were spiders the size of dogs in every corner, three

W.I.T.C.H.'s around a large black tub, and even a Scarey Crow, looking down on all of them from a tall post.

"Farmers used to stick them in fields," she said, catching him staring. "They were supposed to frighten people and animals from the crops."

"Impressive," he said. "I didn't realize W.I.T.C.H.'s were invented so long ago. Surely they're still fairly young?"

"I couldn't find a lot about them, so the modern version was all I had to go on. Can't imagine they would've needed space travel communicators back then, but better than nothing."

"I still can't get over the watermelons," he teased. "They don't look anything like pumpkins if the pictures are accurate."

"Yeah, well, they're big enough to carve. And we can paint them orange, so problem solved."

"So long as you don't make a mess."

"Me, messy? Please. I'm practically an artiste. I could do this in my sleep."

Jake didn't argue, simply went back toward the office as Haze started in on the first "pumpkin." He remained there the rest of the day, updating the books and going over the bills. They'd been a bit low last month, so he hoped Haze's party would help to make up for it. Perhaps he'd move into the bar, after all, cut out his personal bills to save some money. He'd thought of it a time or two, but something always stopped him. This time he might not have a choice. Either way, the party was a temporary fix; he needed some long-term ideas.

He spent the next couple hours jotting in an old notepad since a digital transcriber was just one more item on a long list of things he couldn't afford. He was so engrossed that when there was a knock at the door, he jumped.

"Opening time," Haze called. Wearily he closed and put away his books and followed Haze to the front of the bar. The planning could wait.

***

"Remind me why I agreed to this?"

"Because you love me. And it will be fun. Plus, it will bring in customers, just you wait."

Haze had wrangled him into carving the "pumpkins," and so far there'd been nothing fun about it. The bar would open in another couple hours, and they only had one more day to prepare for the party.

"I don't see Dera here helping."

"She'll be by later, just like always. You should know better than to rely on her for anything."

He couldn't argue with that. He stuck his knife in the watermelon and carved out another rectangular eye and lopsided smile. He couldn't fathom why anyone thought them scary, or even fun. They were just a pain in the ass.

"I can't so much as look at another," he told Haze as he added his newest to the group. "This was—" A knock at the door cut him off. They looked at each other for a moment, then he walked toward the door. "Any distraction will work," he mumbled. "Sorry, we're …"

But he never finished. Once he'd gotten the door open, he saw that it wasn't a local patron as he'd expected, but someone from a past he'd buried deep. He stared open-mouthed and speechless until she said, "May I come in?" And he knew it wasn't her.

"Y-yes," he stammered, still reeling from the whirlwind of his emotions.

"Thank you."

She was a willowy creature, with a slender frame and limbs and long black hair, curling all down her back. Her eyes were the same almond shape and shade of brown, her skin the same creamy tone. They could've been clones of one another. Only the voice was different. The woman's was deep and smooth, not high and airy as he'd expected.

"How can I help you?" he asked, staying near the door so she wouldn't venture too far in.

But she ignored him and approached Haze. "How inventive," she said, eying the watermelons. "I wonder if anyone will appreciate the effort? It's hard to tell on the lesser planets. So many things are lost with time."

"I never caught your name," Jake said.

"Althea," she said, turning to him again with a smile. "And you're Jake Lorens. I've been anxious to meet you."

He glanced at Haze, who had raised an eyebrow at him.

"Well, you found me," he said. "What can I do for you?"

"Is there somewhere we can speak privately? What I have to say is somewhat delicate."

"Haze can overhear anything you say to me. I'll simply tell her once you're gone anyway."

Althea nodded. "Very well. I'll begin by saying that I am a wanderer. I arrived this morning from Beldessa and intend to stay only a few days. I am also what the ancient world would call a prophet. The things I dream come to pass, always."

She ignored the snort from Haze.

"A couple days ago I dreamed of your bar. There was a fight, with smoke and blood and death. The worst I've experienced in quite some time. Since your planet was on my way, I decided to stop and warn you."

"Oh, come on," Haze said. "You don't believe this, do you, Jake?"

"I'm not asking for money," Althea quickly said as he turned toward her again. "Just came to give a warning. You can do with it what you will."

She headed to the door then before he could respond. He looked at Haze, who was shaking her head.

"What a nutjob," she said as she stabbed her knife into the next watermelon.

***

Not half bad, Althea thought as she went back to her ship. She hadn't lied, exactly. The dream part was mostly true. It was what had led her to the Path in the first place. But it wasn't the only reason she was there. She'd made a note of every piece of furniture and all the doors. Jake had had a green table brought in, complete with antique game balls and hitting sticks. Most of the green had peeled away over the years, and in many spots it was black. He probably couldn't afford the modern holographic ones. She supposed it added to the charm.

He'd also added an old music box, though she doubted he'd figured out how to use it. It had sat silently in a corner while a rock station played over the sound amplifier, so it was likely decoration only. Not bad for the only alcoholic establishment for a radius of one hundred miles. There were only three doors, the front, the washrooms, and the one leading to the back rooms, and probably a back door.

Neither of them would be too hard to handle if events turned nasty. It was apparent the woman was military, probably NCSO, or maybe even League. And Jake carried an old world pistol if she read him correctly. Likely something under the bar too, but it might not come to that.

When she got back to the ship, she activated her receiver and switched it to Solitary. A micro symphony began to play as she entered her notes from her first encounter.

"Some military experience, old-world technology, risk: minimal. Did not note item as a decoration, so back storage highly likely."

She paused, considering simply asking him about the artifact … But no, it never worked that way. She would stick to the plan, and with any luck, she'd be gone in a few days with the item in hand. If she played her cards right, they might not even notice it was gone.

***

They finally took a break from decorating and passed a normal night, or as normal as it could be with orange watermelon carvings staring at you. The general crowd was gone by one a.m., leaving only Dera, Theodore, Haze, and him for the final hour.

"Dera, why don't you ever drink anything but old world soda?" Theodore asked. His words were starting to slur, and he was having to lean against the bar to keep from falling over, but Dera took it as a serious question.

"I actually like the taste," she said. "Besides, they're a part of our history. I like thinking that my ancient ancestor once drank the exact same thing."

"Alcohol was around back then, too," Jake put in.

"True, but then I'd end up like Trippy Slurs-a-lot over here, and I can't count on any of you to make sure I keep my clothes on."

Haze snorted. "I'm sure not a babysitter, so I'll attest to that."

"Well, I mean what do you do when you're not here?" Theodore continued. "Do you have a life, or do you just drink soda all day?"

Jake stifled a laugh as Dera answered. "I guess it's personal history night. All right, I'll play along. I'm originally from Beldessa. I had a scholarship and good grades, but I felt restless, so I moved here. Now I spend my days typing numbers and my nights chugging soda. End of story. Jake?"

"What, my turn?"

"Yeah, spill it."

"Well, there's not much to say. I was an army brat, lived all over the galaxy when I was a kid. No siblings. Moved out on my own when I was eighteen, haven't seen my folks since. Oh, and I used to want to be a musician."

"Get out of here," Haze said. "What, you're a Romanova now? Did you play an old world instrument too?"

"I did. Piano. I think the old styles evoke something the modern music lacks."

"So, you are a teenager?" Theodore asked, looking at Dera through a haze of confusion.

Jake laughed and clapped him on the back. "It's bedtime for you, friend. Haze, can you lock up? I'm going to take him home."

"You got it. But can I make a suggestion?"

"Sure."

"Let's get a piano in here. A big old world one. Then you can croon to our customers and word will spread, and before we know it, you'll be touring the galaxy."

Jake chuckled as he dragged Theodore out the door. "I never said I was good."

***

"You're out of your mind," Jake said.

Haze and Dera were standing before him with a bright red outfit. His costume for the party.

"C'mon, Jake, it's a tradition!" Haze protested. "I want everything to be perfect, and this will help more than you know. Besides, it's either you or Theodore."

"Hell, no," Theodore said from his booth, not looking up from the papers spread out before him.

"See?" she continued. "That leaves you."

"It'll bring good luck," Dera added.

Haze reverted to pouting, her lip protruding comically.

"All right!" he said. "I'll wear the damn thing. But if I get so much as one snicker, it's coming off."

"Nude works for me," Dera said.

"Gross. Please bring a change of clothes, Jake."

While the women fussed over last-minute decoration changes, Jake sat down across from Theodore.

"How do you always get out of everything?" Jake asked.

"I helped carry things. And I don't work here. Not my responsibility."

"Ah, that's what it is."

Theodore sighed and looked up from his papers, resting his chin against his folded hands.

"I may have to cut out early tonight."

"You wouldn't dare."

"I've got work, and this one could be a big one. You know how often those come around."

"It's just one night. Couldn't you make it up tomorrow?"

"Sometimes one day makes all the difference."

Jake sighed. The bar looked like a black, orange, and yellow candy store, the women were making him dress up, and now Theodore wouldn't be around to make it bearable. He was tempted more and more to dip into the cider early. It was going to be a long night.

**

Imagining yourself as a disembodied spirit was a lot easier said than done. Althea had been at it for at least two hours, and she still hadn't reached that peaceful state necessary for high-level casting. This was why she stuck to old-fashioned manipulation and persuasion. She was too impatient.

"Try again," she commanded herself, doing her best impression of her master. Obediently, she drew a deep breath and closed her eyes again. She had tried every method there was to ascend quickly, but she had failed at all of them. After another ten minutes of nothing but her temper rising, she gave up and settled for a modern alternative. Her land scanner was on the other side of the bed, so she rolled over, reached, and grasped it. The plant she'd left during her first visit could only do so much. She would just do a quick fly-over, use the scanner, and then focus on more important things. Like her outfit for that night. Doing anything half-assed just wasn't her style.

She adjusted the coordinates on the ship's control panel and rummaged through her small closet as the ship sped off toward

Midnight Absinthe. Slinky black dress or elegant black dress? Tight fit, or flowing? And what would she do with her hair?

"You're too obsessed with the material," she said in her master's voice. "True happiness will only come when you focus only on the spiritual."

"Yes, master," she mumbled. "I'll get right on that. Right after I steal this artifact. You understand."

She chose the elegant dress, which fit her well enough to accentuate curves, but was free-flowing enough to be comfortable. With that decided, she clasped her rowan necklace around her throat and slipped her black beads around her wrist. She bet she'd fit right in if she lived a millennium before. The ship's panel beeped to let her know it was close to its destination, so she grabbed her scanner and prepared it to receive data.

It started right as the ship beeped again and she quickly typed in new coordinates. It wouldn't do to sit around and be noticed. Her timing couldn't have been more perfect. The scanner began processing as the ship turned and set off for its new destination. She'd have a 3D blueprint of the bar by the time it arrived, and by morning the next day, she'd be on her way home with a new pretty. It was almost too easy.

***

When they opened, and the customers poured inside wearing all manner of costumes, Jake didn't feel quite so ridiculous. But just quite. All the other men wore black capes and fangs, or horrifying masks and sporting bloody weapons. None of the others were dressed as Bob the Apple. Haze just smiled when he glared at her across the room. She wore a form-fitting black suit with black ears and a tail, and Dera had painted whiskers across her cheeks. Dera herself wore a short fluffy dress covered in fake blood, and fake wounds were covering her from head to toe. A bloody knife completed her outfit, though he wasn't sure exactly what she was supposed to be.

He almost didn't recognize Theodore. The man wore an ancient suit, older even than the old world style, with cuff links and a cane and top hat. He actually bowed when Jake approached him. "What are you?"

"A gentleman," Theodore said matter-of-factly.

Haze turned up the music then, which made further conversation difficult. Jake wandered around, thanking everyone for coming and complimenting them on their costumes. Then Haze gave him "the look" to signal she was swamped and he went to help behind the bar. He barely looked up as the music played and time wore on.

"I like your costume. It's very … cute."

Jake looked up to see Althea across the bar. She was dressed in black, with long flowing sleeves and skirt, and a pointed black hat. She smiled as he fumbled to put his bottle down. "I didn't expect to see you again," he said.

"Well, I figured, I'm here, I may as well have a good time."

"You certainly came to the right place. You want a drink?"

"You're not going to run me off?"

"Why would I do that?"

She shrugged. "It's what people do, once they know about me."

"Well, not this guy. Have a drink and enjoy yourself."

He lost sight of her as the customer flow picked up again. Then Dera started the costume contest, and he had a short break to simply watch and enjoy himself. As Dera rattled off names and costumes, the contestants turned and posed. Just as he began to relax there was some muted shouting near the door. People were shoved in both directions as a group of men pushed their way forward.

All of them wore old world dress pants and shirts, along with bowler hats and sunglasses. Jake moved quickly, getting around the bar and in front of them in seconds. "Can I help you, gentlemen?"

"Beat it, appleman. We're busy."

"I'm the owner, and I don't appreciate you jostling my customers. Now, you can calm down, or I can help you find the door."

"We're not leaving till we find that witch," another man said.

"Soon as we find her we'll be on our way."

"You want a W.I.T.C.H.? Why?"

"Old world, jackass. That psychic bitch. We've been tracking her since Argentin."

"There are no witches here," Jake said. "You're welcome to join the party, but I won't hesitate to throw you out if you cause trouble." He could feel the eyes of everyone in the room and belatedly realized the music had stopped.

One man drew a laser blade and stepped forward. A loud click behind him told Jake Haze had pulled out his shotgun.

"I think you should leave now," Jake said. "I won't ask again."

The men looked back and forth between him and Haze, then the frontman put his weapon away. "You just made yourself an enemy," he said. As they turned to leave, he added, "This isn't over."

Jake stood his ground until the door closed behind them, then he turned back to the party. "Carry on," he said as he went back to the bar. Haze wouldn't let him hear the end of it if he sent everyone home.

It took a while, but the mood eventually returned to normal. But it wasn't until the early hours when the place was clearing out that he saw Althea again.

"We need to talk," he said.

She nodded. "I'm sorry for causing trouble. But thank you for not turning me over to them."

"I could ask why they're after you, but the chances of you tell me the truth are small. You can hide here overnight if you like unless you have somewhere better to stay, but tomorrow you're gone. Understood?"

She nodded quickly. "Yes. And thank you."

***

Those stupid witch hunters had nearly ruined everything, but in the end, they actually helped her. She had spent most of the night trying to figure out a way into the back rooms, but Haze had watched the entrance like a hawk. Once when the bartender was busy, she had almost managed to sneak past, but then a tall man wearing an ancient world suit was standing in front of her.

"Afraid I can't let you go back there. The bathrooms are that way if that's what you're looking for."

"Oh, silly me. Thank you."

After that, she tried going around outside, but it was secured by not only an old world lock but a modern high-dollar sensor that would alert every badge within fifty miles that there was a break-in. He couldn't afford the modern range weapons, but he didn't skimp on security.

Reprogramming the sensor's codes would take time, and time was what she didn't have. So she'd wandered back in, thinking she'd have to resort to seduction when the witch hunters had barged in. They hadn't been on her radar for a couple weeks, so she'd hoped she'd lost them. Looked like she'd thought wrong.

She'd quickly ducked behind the bar when she saw them, hoping they hadn't seen her in that split second. Forcing herself to focus, she sought to calm her mind and find her center. She smiled wryly when she succeeded. Why was she only talented under pressure?

As subtly as she could, she whispered chants of aversion and repelling. She threw in illusion for good measure, just in case. She'd never actually seen the chants work, but her master claimed more than fifty percent of magic was belief. So if it worked, she chose to chalk it up to her chants, because that would build her belief for the next time.

Once they'd gone, she'd stayed hidden for a few more minutes, to be on the safe side. Who cared if other partiers gave her funny looks? And then there Jake was, offering her his bar for the night, as though he'd read her mind. She could almost believe he was the witch.

As soon as the last customer had gone, Jake sat at the bar with Althea. "Start talking," he said.

She grinned sheepishly. "They hate me because of my gift. It happens wherever I go. Interest in the old world and the old ways has risen to new heights. It's only fair that the hunters rise with the gifted."

"Is that what you call it?" Haze asked as she gathered the leftover glasses.

Althea looked down at the countertop. "I'm sorry for causing trouble. I'll be gone in the morning, I promise. I would hate for anything to happen because of me."

Dera and Theodore joined them then, sitting on the other side of Jake. They didn't seem quite sure what to make of his guest.

"So you're... what? A magician? Is that the right word?" Dera asked.

"A witch," Theodore offered. "The old world kind."

"Where was this knowledge when I was decorating?" Haze demanded.

Theodore shrugged. "I liked your version."

Haze just scowled as Jake said, "So these guys are witch hunters. Do they think you'll curse everyone or something? I mean, none of that's real. No offense."

"None taken. And yes, they do believe that. To be honest, I'm not very skilled. My dreams are real enough, but the rest is more of a lifestyle. But they want to erase even that."

"Why not just go to the authorities? You haven't committed any crimes, so they should offer protection," Dera said.

"They don't care," Althea said, a note of resentment creeping into her voice. "The hate and prejudice were supposed to die with the old world, but some traditions run too deep. I get by. And all the traveling gives me a chance to see the universe, make new friends."

"And enemies," Theodore said. He stood and made for the door. "I'm calling it a night. Good luck to you."

"You can sleep in my office," Jake said. "I've got an old sofa. Not the most comfortable, but it's better than the floor."

"Too true," she agreed.

"I'll finish locking up," Haze said.

Althea followed Jake to the office, smiling as she passed through the entranceway. She was finally here, and so was the artifact. She thought she could sense it. Or that could just be her excitement, but she chose to believe there was a magical connection. It recognized something in her and responded.

The office was exactly what she expected of a forgotten planet bar office. Small window, gray walls, small desk, filing cabinet, a couple chairs. He'd squeezed a couch against one wall, but it was covered in paper, clothing, and trash.

"I'll get that," Jake said, grabbing a large pile and placing it on the floor near the desk. "Don't usually have customers in here."

"Don't fret on my account. I'm just grateful to be here."

"Well, I'll leave you to it then. There's another bathroom back here, just down the hall. I'll be back in the morning to let you out."

She thanked him again as he left and sat on the couch listening to his footsteps walk away with her eyes closed. When all was quiet again, she stood and cracked her knuckles. If she were lucky, she'd be gone in an hour.

***

Haze was locking the door behind Dera when Jake returned to the bar.

"I don't like it," Haze said without looking at him. "We should send her away. Since when do we let crazy people sleep in the office?"

"You expect me to send her away with those men looking for her? I'm not cruel, Haze."

"Never said you were. But there's a difference in being kind and being stupid. She's trouble."

"You're probably right," Jake said. But he wouldn't listen. Every time he looked at Althea he remembered, and all logic fled his mind. It was all he could do to resolve to send her away in the morning.

Haze brushed past him and gathered her belongings from the storage bin in the hallway. "It was a good party, Jake," she said. "Thanks."

As the back door shut behind her, he poured himself another drink. The decorations didn't look quite so festive anymore to his tired eyes. More dark, maybe. Ghoulish. He'd have Haze take them down first thing the next night. It had been a good party. The place hadn't been so full since its opening, and the profit was outstanding, from what Haze had hinted. But he was ready for things to return to normal. More than anything he wanted to get out of the damn apple suit.

He gulped the last of his drink, turned off the lights, and stumbled for the back bathroom where he'd stashed his change of clothes. When he reemerged, his mind was already thinking of bed, until he noticed the bright blue light coming from under the office door.

***

Althea had emptied nearly every drawer, looked under every piece of furniture, but the artifact wasn't there. She'd even attempted a seeking chant, and one for revealing lost objects, but neither had proved useful. It had to be here. She'd planned so carefully, double-checked all her references. Unless he kept it at home, which she wasn't willing to contemplate. She sensed he thought she was attractive, but there was no time for proper seduction, not with the witch hunters so close. Besides, he spent more time at the bar than home, and all his money was put into its improvement. This was where he'd hide it.

So she continued her search, determined to spend the entire night looking if need be. In the end, it was sheer luck that brought it to her hands. She had been searching a drawer for the tenth time and shoved it a bit harder in her frustration. The wood hit loudly and stopped, still open. She pushed and realized it had caught on the inside. It wouldn't budge until she pulled the drawer out and looked for the problem. There, stuck to the underside of the drawer above it, was the artifact.

Somehow she managed to refrain from crying out in delight. Barely. With trembling fingers, she gripped its edges and pulled it free. It came easily. Adhesive blocks had been made for easy placing and removal and worked on any surface.

The artifact was everything it was supposed to be: a small black dagger, made entirely of some ancient stone. No light reflected on its surface, but as she held it, it began to emit soft blue light, growing stronger with every second. It was a shame she couldn't put it down to a magical connection; the stone was supposed to do that when it contacted heat, or so the writings said. Some sort of biological mutation. Which meant she'd have to seal it away tight if she wanted to get away unnoticed.

She had just dropped the dagger into her hat when Jake opened the door. "What are you doing?" he asked. "What was that light?"

"S-sorry," she said. "It's just a little trick I learned. Nothing dangerous. I was using it as a nightlight. Sorry if I frightened you."

"It's fine. Just startled me is all. I'll be out of your way then. Unless you need something else?"

"Oh, no, I'm fine."

It was all she could do to not hide the hat behind her back, or push past him and make for the door. Thank the forces the thing had stopped glowing when she'd dropped it.

"Well, good night, then," he said.

"Good night."

As soon as he shut the door, she scrambled for her few belongings and again checked that the dagger was securely tucked away. The getaway was all that mattered. Althea tiptoed to the door and pressed her ear against it, hoping to hear Jake's footsteps receding. Nothing. So either he'd already left, or he was waiting. There was nothing for it. She pulled open the door and looked both ways. The small hallway was empty. She closed the door softly behind her and made for the back door.

***

Something wasn't sitting right. Jake couldn't put his finger on it, but he believed Althea was hiding something. Considering he'd just met her, there were likely many things she was hiding, everyday secrets that everyone carried. He just hoped they weren't going to affect him. He was a sucker for brunettes, especially those with darker shades because they all reminded him of her. But with Althea, it was a double blast because her features were similar too. That was partly why he was struggling with wanting to help and wanting to keep an eye on her. He didn't want to be blindsided again.

When he shut the door, he went back to the bar, just to double check that all the doors were locked and there wasn't anything else he'd forgotten. The ritual was so ingrained in him that he almost didn't have to think about it. His mind wandered to Althea and that blue light, so it took him a moment to realize that something wasn't right.

Bright light shone through one of the front windows, revealing the dust motes in the air. He had the presence of mind to drop to the floor just before the first round of fire broke the glass. He couldn't tell if they were shooting old world bullets or laser blasts, but both would hurt if he didn't avoid them.

The emergency trigger was under the bar, so he crawled as fast as he could in that direction as more glass broke. Luckily that was also where he kept his shotgun, which would tide him over till a Responder could arrive. Before he could press the trigger, someone grabbed his leg and yanked him back. In a flash, he rolled over and prepared to kick, but stopped short when he recognized Althea.

"What are you doing?" he whispered. "Someone's attacking!"

"You can't bring a Responder here. Not yet. Trust me on this, I've dealt with these guys before."

More glass broke so she urged him up and pulled. He quickly grabbed his shotgun and followed. Men's voices echoed through the room, coming closer.

"It's those men from before, isn't it?" he asked as she pulled him down the hallway.

"Yes, but—"

Something banged against the back door, blocking their exit.

"The ceiling. Hurry!" He pulled her into the storage closet and shut the door. She produced a soft light from some small device, not blue, he noted. "We need to get to the crawlspace. See the trapdoor up there? I'll climb up and then pull you up after. Okay?"

She nodded, and he started climbing the shelves. Thank the forces he'd packed so much stuff on the shelves. The last thing he needed was the whole thing falling on top of him and letting them know where they were. The trapdoor opened easily at his touch, and he climbed inside. As soon as he felt stable, he reached down to pull Althea up. She was surprisingly light. When she was safe, he put the trapdoor back in place and motioned her to follow him.

There was a vent in one outer wall and a ladder that led to the roof. He would wait on trying to leave that way, make sure the coast was clear. He peered through the vent and saw two land rangers out front, the lights still on. A few men lingered around them, spaced out to keep an eye on all possible exits. All of them were armed.

"All right," he whispered, turning back to Althea. "Start talking."

"I don't know what you mean."

"Don't play stupid. Why did you stop me from pressing the trigger? A Responder would be here by now!"

"Exactly. The last thing I want is getting involved with the Authorities. It's better if they don't know I'm here."

"Just why are those guys after you? It's not just the religion thing, is it? No one is this fervent anymore."

"If I knew—"

"Stop the act. You're obviously hiding something, and I've half a mind to turn you over to them if you don't start talking."

"You wouldn't."

"Try me."

She regarded him a moment, probably trying to decide if he was bluffing. Finally, she sighed. "All right. It wasn't just a vision that brought me here. I've been looking for something. An ancient artifact that is said to have old world powers. The witch hunters not only want to destroy all of us but every trace that we existed, especially if it's something powerful. They caught word of my mission and made it their personal objective to stop me."

"So it's chance that they're here at all? If you left, they would too?"

"Not necessarily. They're after the artifact too, so they'd probably be here anyway."

"Why? I don't have any witch artifacts."

Althea bit her lower lip, then opened the small bag at her side. "Does this look familiar?" she asked. She produced a black dagger, which began to glow a bright blue as she held it. She quickly set it down, and the glow disappeared.

Jake swallowed. "It's Lilia's dagger. The only thing she left behind."

"Someone special to you?"

"She was my fiancé."

Althea carefully put the dagger away again, saying, "What happened to her?"

"I ask myself that every day. She simply didn't come home one day. All of her clothes and books, just gone. All except the dagger. It looked so ... I don't know, important I guess, I thought for sure she'd come back for it. So I hid it away. It never glowed like that for me."

"Huh. Cold-natured or something?"

"Maybe."

"So why'd you hide it away? And how did she get it in the first place?"

"I have no idea. But hiding it seemed like a good idea at the time. I mean, I remember she'd always kept it in a certain wooden box, so I figured maybe it was something special. I don't really know what to tell you. It was mostly a whim. I hadn't thought of it in years."

Althea nodded and looked through the vent again. They could hear shouting coming from below, hopefully relaying the message that the bar was empty. Maybe the hunters would leave, and Jake could call a Responder.

"They'll be able to tell I didn't leave," Althea said. "They've got some fancy new tracking unit. They're not going anywhere."

"Are you a mind reader now?"

"Excuse me?"

"Never mind. Look, we can't just sit up here all night. If they don't leave, what happens when my bartender shows up for her shift? We need a Responder. Now."

"No. Let me try something first."

Althea pulled the dagger out again and set it on the floor. It glowed briefly at her touch, then resumed its normal appearance.

Althea placed her hands on either side of it and began to whisper softly so Jake couldn't make out the words. He had always been a skeptic, so he wasn't surprised when nothing happened. Althea swore and began again, closing her eyes with her head slightly raised. Nothing. When she began a third time, Jake lost his patience and grabbed the dagger.

"This isn't working. I think we should take our chances with the roof."

Althea swiped at the dagger, but he held it just out of reach. "Yesterday you didn't even remember it was there. Don't act like it means something to you now."

"Doesn't matter. It's still not yours. And considering you're the reason we're in this mess, I've half a mind to turn you over to them and go home."

Her eyes could've cut. "They won't let you. You know of the dagger so you may try to use it. They'll kill you too."

"You're bluffing."

"Try me."

They glared at each other until he finally shook his head.

"I should've just nixed the whole party idea. I just knew something would go wrong."

"I would've shown up with or without the party. At least this way you got to have a good time first."

Jake glanced through the vent again then stood. "I'm trying the roof. You can join me or continue hiding here. I don't really care."

"My hero."

She ended up following him, but he bet it was only because he'd taken the dagger. He'd only been on the roof a handful of times, so it took him a minute to find the ladder again. He had to tuck the dagger through his belt loop and shimmy up with the gun propped under one arm. There was no way he could trust Althea with it.

At the top, he paused and listened, but he couldn't hear anything.

"If we die, I'm haunting you," Althea said.

"The dead can't haunt each other."

Slowly he pushed the trapdoor open and peeked out. There was no one that he could see. He opened it the rest of the way and climbed further up. "Looks like the coast is clear," he whispered.

Althea came up behind him, looking all around. "We should wait," she said. "We're not safe."

"Should've listened to your girlfriend."

Jake whirled around at the new voice. One of the men had appeared from behind an air unit and had a short laser pointed their way. Quick as a flash, Althea grabbed the trapdoor and fell back into the crawlspace. When the man attempted to follow her, he found it locked from the inside.

"Stupid witch! You, open it!" He shoved Jake at the door, but he raised his hands and shrugged.

"I don't have a key for this. It's an old world latch, no keys."

The man punched him, and he fell on his side. "We'll just use you for leverage then. That will make her come running." Before he could explain, the man grabbed Jake by the back of his collar and dragged him to the edge of the roof. "Hey, boss! I caught the owner!"

While the man was distracted, Jake fumbled for the knife but found only an empty belt loop. Althea must have nicked it when he wasn't looking. And he'd dropped his gun by the trapdoor. It was enough to make a man curse women forever. But there was no way he'd die this way. When the man reached for him again, Jake grabbed his arm and propelled himself into him, knocking them both to the ground. They rolled for a moment, struggling for the gun until Jake slammed his head into the man's nose. They guy abruptly let go, and Jake fought the bile that rose in his throat and pulled the gun free. Then he climbed on top of the man and held the weapon just under his chin. The man's nose was bleeding and swollen.

"Don't move," Jake warned.

"They'll shoot you down before you can blink," the man rasped.

"Then at least I'll take you with me. What are you after? Why are you chasing Althea?"

"She's a witch," the man said as if that explained everything. "She deserves death."

"And who gave you the right to make that decision?"

Without waiting for an answer Jake slammed the gun hard into the guy's head, knocking him out. Then he crawled back to the edge of the roof and peeked over again. Some more men were gathering, preparing to climb the ladder. He ducked back out of sight and considered. He could try to pick them off or hide the way the man had. As a last ditch effort, he moved back to the trapdoor and pulled, but it stuck fast. Althea didn't answer when he knocked. Not that he could blame her. She had told him they should stay put.

He scooped up his shotgun and hurried back to the edge. The men were already ascending. He wasn't a killer, but he wouldn't just sit back and let them come either. He made sure there was a shell in the chamber and took aim, but the first guy fell before Jake could pull the trigger. The shot came from elsewhere and caused the top man to hit into the ones below him and knock them all onto the ground.

Jake scanned for the source of the shot and spotted a ranger in the distance, parked near the hillside. Haze. Eve from that distance he could recognize her. He quickly took aim again while the men were down and shot the one who was just starting to get up again. Just a leg shot, nothing the guy couldn't recover from. Haze fired again too, and then a third shot rang out, and a fourth, both from different directions. The men still around the Rangers took cover and returned fire, forcing him to duck. But no matter how they hid they were always exposed on one side, so it wasn't long before all were indisposed. That just left those inside.

Jake quickly descended the ladder as Haze pulled closer. Theodore and Dera appeared a moment later, both armed and back in their normal attire. Haze still wore her catsuit.

"What are you all doing here?"

"I warned you that woman would be trouble," Haze said. "I noticed the goons on my way home. Thought they were sneaky, but not sneaky enough. So I rounded up the troops and came to your rescue."

"Why didn't you call a Responder?" Dera asked. "They're sending someone over now, but it was news to them."

"I was interrupted. Look, Althea's still in there and who knows how long it will take the Responder."

"Bad idea," Theodore said. "There are still a lot of them, and they're aware of us coming now. We'll be slaughtered."

"I'm not going to sit back and let them kill her."

One of the wounded men began to laugh, and Jake turned in just enough time to avoid being shot. He wrenched the gun from the man and pushed him back. Haze and Theodore began to search for the rest of the guns.

"You can't save her," the laughing man said. "She'll die now, or die later."

"Shut up," Jake said. "I'm going in."

He walked up to the door, Haze hot on his trail.

"At least be smart about it."

She took one side of the door while he took the other. Dera and Theodore stood on either side, out of the line of fire. Haze counted down on her fingers, and Jake swung the door open. Dozens of bullets immediately rained through the entranceway. They stopped for a moment as the men recharged and the four quickly fired their own shots. They managed to hit a few if the cries were any indication, but there were still too many.

"I'm going around back," Jake said. "Cover me."

Dera went with him while Haze and Theodore held the front. Thank goodness there aren't any side windows, he thought. The back door was slightly ajar, so they entered cautiously, but didn't see anyone. Jake checked his office, but there was no sign of Althea; the shots continued to rain, but they were slowing down.

"Keep close," Jake whispered as they crept down the hallway.

One of the men turned and saw him, so Jake pulled Dera to the floor just before the man could shoot. Jake returned fire a moment later, hitting the man's leg. After that their attention was split between the front and the back. Jake counted seven of them and hoped he hadn't overlooked any. This needed to end. Minutes passed, and two more men went down. Someone outside cried out as Jake fired again. He was nearly empty.

"We yield!" one of the men called out between shots. "Just give us the witch, and we'll leave."

"Not a chance," Jake said. "You can leave after you've laid down your weapons, but Althea stays."

The men whispered a moment, then the leader answered, "Very well. We'll go. But our weapons we'll keep, thank you. You have my word no shots will be fired."

"Not good enough," Jake said. "I've had just about enough of you, so if you don't lay down your weapons and get the hell out of my bar, I'll instruct my crew to reopen fire."

A second later they heard the clatter of metal hitting the floor, and Jake peeked into the bar, barrel extended. The men were all empty-handed.

"I want you to leave now. If you return, it won't be your legs I aim for."

The leader ushered his men out the door, where Haze and Theodore kept their weapons aimed. A trail of blood dripped from a hole in Theodore's shoulder, but he stood his ground.

"Tell the witch we'll see her soon," the leader said as they entered their rangers. Before they could pull away a dozen Rangers came speeding in, sirens wailing.

Jake lowered his weapon and the others followed. "You okay, Theodore?"

"I'll be fine."

"We'll get you fixed up, don't worry," Haze said.

Jake was relieved he could finally breathe easy. He didn't think he'd have to worry about looking for Althea. It didn't look like any of the men had gone out the back, and the door hadn't opened itself. She was probably already miles away.

***

Althea had fled to her ship as soon as she'd gotten a chance. She felt bad for abandoning Jake, but she figured he could take care of himself. The trek had taken a bit longer, what with her looking over her shoulder every few feet, but she'd reached it at last. She was still proud of the way she'd swiped the dagger. She'd been sure he'd notice, but her luck had prevailed. Once inside, she changed into sweats and a shirt and hid the blade in her secret storage space. No way she'd risk anything happening to it. As she took flight, she activated the plant she'd left in the bar. There'd been no time to retrieve it during her escape, but at least she could discover how it turned out.

For a while, it was just back and forth between the Responders and Jake. She had to give him credit, he didn't once mention the dagger.

"They said Theodore should be out tomorrow," a woman's voice said. The bartender?

"Good. It could've been a lot worse." That was Jake.

"You really need to change your taste in women," a different woman said.

"You can't blame it all on her."

"Right. Half of it was yours for being an idiot." The first woman again.

"We're all alive, aren't we?"

"We are. Same time next year, then?"

Gardner's Hole

by
Tommy Hancock

Light sliced into the cavernous barroom like a sun itself dawning in the massive structure. The barkeep's husky but rumpled form barely registered movement as the crudely cut metal doors flew open, handmade hinges squealing like rudely awakened children. From half-lidded eyes, the bartender watched as the first body through the entrance flew head first, tossed apparently by at least one of the ten figures that walked in behind it. As the airborne customer broke the bar's threshold, the man behind the crystalloid and chrome serving counter did little to acknowledge his first customer of the day. The crowd behind the nearly unconscious man, potentially customers two-through eleven, at least coaxed him to speak.

"The usual?"

His guttural rattle and gravel voice provoked a mixture of whoops, hollers, and expletives from the throng that stood in the middle of the bar. Entering in a huddle, they now spread themselves out in a sort of crudely crafted semi-circle, the moaning body of the first man in at their feet. At the center of the circle, which coincidentally lined up with where the bartender was, stood the largest of the ten. Even if the keep hadn't known the more than motley crew occupying the only thing he owned in the world, he'd have known that the other nine revolved around the crimson-tinged giant currently in his line of vision.

The blood-skinned man ran a brawny hand over the top of his bald head, shined to a glisten even in the dim lights of the bar. Bright hot red like the barrel of a recently and well-used laser pistol. "'Course, Gardner," wheezed the nearly eight-foot-tall being, his voice like noxious gas escaping from a busted hose. "It's always the usual. The boys like to get worked up," he kicked the man on the floor with a black steel boot, "when we have guests."

The man moaned and coughed as the boot crashed into his side. He rolled over, throwing up bile and blood, then casting his eyes at the enormous man who had kicked him.

His body bulged obscenely with strength, muscles and veins dominating everywhere his scarlet skin showed, like thick, hungry snakes atop one another. He and the men with him all wore the same black pants and steel encased boots. The lower half of the uniform of at least three dozen armies across the galaxy. Above the waist, however, the leader sported something other than the reinforced starmatter flak jackets or ragtag shirts his men wore.

The skin of a creature hung about his log thick neck, its front legs dangling over his shoulders and down his overly defined chest. It was a grandeen, a creature native to the piddly planet they all stood on, a rather savage large beast with features both canine and feline. Its orange and green mottled fur contrasted blindingly with the man's skin and the hindquarters of the hide trailed behind him like a cape.

The bartender watched as the other nine men, at least six of them from varying parts of the galaxy, took their swipes at the man on the floor. As the symphony of kicks accompanied by cries of pain played on, he reached under the counter and pulled out glasses, three in each hand. His face showed nothing as he scooped out another four. No interest. No concern. Nothing. But his eyes, tiny orbs of silver, never left the crowd before him.

"Frakus," the downed man spat, pushing himself up to his knees, "Make this easy on yourself." The words brought snickers and chuckles from the men looming above him, but he ignored them. "Don't make this any more difficult for you or your men. I wouldn't come all this way alone. You know the Patrol better than that!"

Each word he said seemed to pick him up that much farther off the bar floor. The bartender watched the beaten man try to stand, clutching at his side as he did. He was young, probably less than thirty earth years. He stood in profile to the bar and its keeper, but Gardner saw enough to know, if not who, what the man before him was.

Close-cropped scalp gripping blonde hair. A standard issue gray and black uniform handed out to every new recruit their first day on the job with Galactic Patrol, the largest private security agency for the last century, employed by most planets as a police force. The gaudy emblem of the spiraling Milky Way with crossed laser pistols emblazoned over it showed on the slender, almost wiry officer's left shoulder and left pants leg. The one over his heart hung loose, ripped by one of his current hosts most likely. Fresh blood and new bruises peppered the side of his face the bartender could see, plenty of siblings to the injuries hidden under the uniform.

What was missing explained why the officer now stood alone facing ten of the most skilled, deadly criminals for hire any planet or race could boast. Standard issue weapons for Galactic Patrol officers on the outer edges of the Galaxy usually included the traditional law issue laser pistol, but also at least one other gun, a laser baton, and a standard Diamondite dagger, replete with sheath. All of this normally hung from a thick leather belt dotted with other pouches and pockets hiding all sorts of toys. This officer, this walking dead man Gardner solemnly mused to himself, looked naked without his weapon belt.

Frakus grinned broadly, rows of sharpened lily white teeth showing between ebony lips. His men all laughed as the officer stood straight up. Two moved forward, their gloved hands raised to slap the idiot down again, but they stopped. Frakus had his right hand out to his side, palm out, holding them back without a word.

"You're right, Teddy," Frakus said, his whisper of a voice disturbingly relaxed, almost friendly, "I know your masters very well. More than one of them has eaten their badge while I fed it to them as they died."

Frakus' followers all laughed uproariously. The officer's neck tightened suddenly, a vein popping up prominently. Rage soothed whatever pain he felt as he roared and jumped forward, his hands clenched into fists. Both aimed at Frakus.

His punches crossed less than six inches of air before Frakus raised his own arms suddenly. A hideous hiss ripped from his throat as his boulder-like red hands wrapped around the officer's wrists, fingers like iron nearly breaking them. Frakus yanked hard, ripping the smaller man from his feet and flinging him across the bar. The officer yelped in shock and then groaned in agony as his body crashed into one of the twelve tables dotting the bar floor. The table, soldered to the metal floor, didn't tremble as the man's body slammed into it. The cracking of bone ricocheted off the black metal walls.

Peeling off like scales from a snake, Frakus' cronies fanned out, each one heading to take their piece of what remained of the patrol officer. Frakus stood his ground, his obsidian eyes cutting after his men, a pleased smile tattooing his face.

"Back up to the bar, boys," Gardner invited loudly. "The rocket fuel in this crap is gonna eat up my good glasses!"

Frakus' black glare shifted sharply, his eyes sparking with fury as they stared down the bartender. Gardner showed no reaction to the gaze that barflies said killed some in a matter of seconds. He simply nodded at Frakus, held up a heavyset chromium mug, vaulting it above the heads of Frakus' entourage who, at the mention of drink, forgot the injured plaything by the table.

Frakus reached out and latched onto the last two of his men dashing for the bar. Jerking on them, then gesturing with his bald head toward the officer, Frakus shoved them that direction. They responded without a sound, shuffling off quickly. They leaned over, grabbing the fallen man like a sack of laundry, and harshly forced him up. He screamed painfully, biting into his lower lip to cut off any other sounds. The two thugs dragged him toward the bar where Frakus now stood, just two feet from the bartender.

The two escorts pushed their cargo before them, banging him up against the others at the bar. With each bump or rub, someone shoved an elbow or dropped a shoulder or fist hard into the officer's side, trying to make him squeal. Blood trickled from his mouth as his teeth cut into his own lip, but not one murmur left his throat.

As his captors hoisted him against the bar roughly, Frakus reached out and took the officer by the chin. He raised the blonde head to look at him, the human's slumped over height only reaching the giant's waist. Frakus said, "Let me tell you what else I know, Teddy." He pulled his fingers from the man's chin, letting his head bob up and down like a ball. "I know that you're an eager new recruit. Probably the top of whatever academy class or military training service you were hatched out of. You want to make a name for yourself, maybe even get promoted, add a comet or two to your epaulet." Frakus dug a long-nailed finger into a rip in the officer's uniformed left shoulder, where insignia once had been. Teddy squirmed, his legs giving way slightly. Grinning, Frakus continued, "You went looking for the biggest capture you could make, an arrest that they would write holosongs about. And you came here. Rookie. You've been in the suit, what? Two years?"

"Not even one, " Gardner offered. "Haircut's too short. Uniform still has remnants of pleats and pressing." He raised his head, this time his eyes locking with Frakus'. "Even though you've done your best to beat them all out."

The blond officer turned his head slowly to look across the bar. His hazel eyes narrowed as they encountered the gaze of the bartender. Silver eyes, a slight sparkle in them of something undetermined, but mostly clouded with boredom and resignation. "How…" stammered Officer Theodore Rexner, "How do you know that? Were you a…part of the patrol?"

Gardner didn't say a word. The guffaws and growls of Frakus' entourage provided answer enough. "Gardner?" Frakus belched. "A Patrolman? Kid, he can barely stay in that Interplanetary Bartenders Group he's in, much less put on a badge."

"Guild."

The single word was hard and sharp like the Diamondite dagger Rexner no longer had. Strong enough to silence every single thug and criminal in the room and to cause Frakus to seethe, "What did you say?"

"Guild," Gardner said, a little more levity behind the gruff tone."It's an Intergalactic Guild of Bartenders."

"Guild," Frakus chuckled, slapping Teddy Rexner viciously on his injured shoulder, mimicking a friendly tap from a drinking buddy. "Whatever fuels your rocket pack. None of it means anything here." He reached out, wrapping Rexner's uniform lapel in his thick fingers, yanking the man up into the air for effect. "Just like your stinking badge and fancy toys, Teddy. None of that means anything. Not on Tyxos."

"Wrong…" Rexner spat, the words coating Frakus' upturned face. "You're wanted on ten different planets, Frakus. You can't run far enough…to get away from me. Not even here."

Veins popped up like steel chords on the outlaw leader's neck. He lowered Rexner close to him and leaned his face against the man's belly. Wiping back and forth, cleaning Rexner's spittle from him, Frakus then flung him again, throwing him away like a used towel. Rexner yelped as he fell against another table, this one also unforgiving. The crack of bone ricocheted off the metallic walls of the bar as he crumpled to the floor.

Frakus, grabbing up a glass of whatever Gardner had poured,

crossed the distance between the bar and Rexner in two steps. "You don't get it, Teddy," the scarlet-hued criminal barked. "Didn't they tell you in Cop School what Tyxos means? How it's the only world the little blue people who used to run across this rock knew? The single word in their primitive language?" As he talked, he drew a blade from a sheath on his hip with his free hand. It was slender, tendrils of yellow energy swirling around it. He leaned forward and slashed the knife across Rexner's exposed right cheek.

The officer barely flinched, still unconscious. "It stood for everything to them," Frakus said, sounding almost like a teacher now. "If they needed food, they said Tyxos. If they wanted to screw their buddy's girl, they cooed Tyxos. But when all the great minds finally studied the little blue jerks- after the corporations had killed them all. Who knew they'd make such great appetizers?- do you know what they discovered." He bent over, almost as to whisper to Rexner. "They learned that Tyxos actually means only one thing." He reached around with the hand holding the glass. Tipping it just above Rexner's new wound, Frakus said, "'Sanctuary.'"

The verdant green liquor poured from the glass in a steady stream, disappearing into the gash on Rexner's cheek. Vapor rose when alcohol mingled with blood, sending a ribbon of pain through the officer's body. He spasmed, his head popping up, his eyes wide in agony. The scream ripped through every ear in the bar and beyond, causing people in the street to stop and look. Then move on when they realized it came from Gardner's place. The bartender, though, didn't slow down his glass cleaning. He simply stood and watched, his silver eyes half closed.

"Damn...you!" Theodore Rexner screamed, his body quaking. "By...the authority..of..." the next few words were lost to sobs and slurred words..."I arrest you..."

Frakus' left boot collided with the officer's chin as his mouth worked, trying to deliver the last few words he'd practiced since setting out for Tyxos. Rexner's head lobbed over, almost as if his neck had been broken. It lolled back the other way, though, as blood, teeth, and saliva crowded on his lips, trying to escape as he lost consciousness again.

"You know the rules," Gardner said from the bar. Frakus turned, cocking his head to make sure he heard right.

"Rules?" the giant mocked as he spun on his heel, stomping

toward the bartender. His gaggle of goons followed behind like little-depraved ducklings after their ugly mother. Slamming his right fist into the chromium bar top, leaving a new dent to join all the others, Frakus roared, "What rules? Whose bar do you think this is, Gardner?"

"Mine." Gardner's hand shot out suddenly, wrapping itself around the top of Frakus' fist. The red behemoth started to yank free but was startled to find he couldn't. Strength like the pull of gravity itself held Frakus' hand still. The two beings exchanged glances for only a moment, hate and a touch of fear in Frakus' eyes, nothing at all in Gardner's. The human relaxed his hold, flattening his hand out on top of Frakus' fist. "Yours to use of course. As long as you remember the rules."

Frakus didn't speak. He didn't nod. He didn't acknowledge Gardner's statement. He pulled his hand off the bar and threw his shoulders back. His chest jutted out, and his arms bowed out at his side. The bull preening for his herd.

But every one of them understood what Gardner had meant. Frakus' gang was only the most recent victor in what had become sort of a contest between factions on Tyxos since Gardner had made the planet that welcomed everyone his home. The tiny ball of mud and crystal was replete with bars, brothels, and other purveyors of ill repute. But for a time that no one cared to recount, Gardner's Bar had been both the worst of the lot, but a shining jewel of sorts. Although the human played host to whoever had enough credits to buy the swill he poured, it was no secret that Gardner's could belong to someone, much like children claiming a clubhouse. Several had done just that. Murderers, gamblers, smugglers, even for a period sex traders. Even though Frakus' was the latest, others had come, and gone-vanishing from Tyxos like itinerant bands of criminals tend to. They'd all put their mark on Gardner's at one point or another, the roughest and vilest of gangs. Each one called its base, headquarters, its home on Sanctuary. But unlike the rest of the planet that had no laws, there were rules in Gardner's.

They were simple and unspoken-most of the time. And although no one could clearly recall ever seeing him enforce the rules, it was believed by most on Tyxos that the primary rule, other than no killing and no wasting of drinks in Gardner's, was that you didn't piss off Gardner.

"Frakus…"

The voice cracked, rising out of pain that would have killed most people. But it carried just enough strength to turn every head away from the awkward scene at the bar.

Officer Theodore Rexner no longer lay against the table. He was up on one knee, his head raised. The open wound on his right cheek frothed, pink foam rising and falling from it. A giggle from one of Frakus' men broke the silence, inviting his cohorts to snicker as well. Frakus smiled, his row of white fangs fully showing. He walked toward the quivering officer, his men moving with him, all gathering about Rexner like predators to prey.

"Yes?" Frakus said in a lilting, sarcastic voice. "What is it, Teddy?"

Rexner took a deep, rattling breath, his shoulders slumping forward suddenly. He pulled himself back up quickly, his craned upward, his eyes on Frakus. "You…" his voice scratched like metal on metal, "are…under arrest."

The peals of laughter and insults to Rexner's maternal heritage erupted before the officer ever finished his last word. Two of Frakus' men slapped each other on the shoulders as if they'd just heard the funniest joke ever. Others shook their heads or turned away, unable to control the giggles and sneers. Frakus put his hands on his hips and flung himself back, the sound rumbling from his throat ringing like raucous thunder.

And Gardner watched from the bar as Theodore Rexner proved what it took to be an officer for Galactic Patrol.

Ducking his head, Rexner leaned slightly to the left and jumped from his knelt position. The top of his skull connected with the belly of the figure just to the left of Frakus. The squat fuchsia colored alien with four tiny horns protruding from his forehead squawked in surprise as the human slammed into him. The two bodies dropped to the floor, the arms and legs of the outlaw flailing, strange clicking shrieking from its lips. But Rexner's limbs, they didn't flail.

As they fell to the floor, the officer wrapped his legs around the lower body of his victim. As they tumbled left and right, Rexner's hands found what he'd gone after. Not a desperate move to die fighting. He wanted the guns the fat little thug brazenly wore on his hips.

Stripping the weapons from the holsters, Rexner threw himself backward, letting loose with his legs. He crashed hard against the floor, already squeezing both triggers as he fell. One concentrated blast sliced through the figure he'd tackled, freeing its left arm from its shoulder. The second shot went wild, marking the wall just behind Gardner with a charred scar.

Chaos reigned for but a moment, but it would have to be enough for Theodore Rexner. Most of the gang crowded around Frakus instinctively, either expecting him to protect them or hoping to impress by taking a shot for him. Three of them advanced directly on Rexner, unafraid of the last desperate act of a dying man.

One shot creased the shoulder of the lead attacker. He squealed, like a mouse in the clutches of a cat, and grabbed at his new wound. The two behind him pushed him down and walked over him, nothing going to keep them from showing off to Frakus. The officer fired again as he struggled to his feet. The shots missed their mark and no time was given for another try as his two foes struck simultaneously. One flung a spike-covered fist into Rexner's face, blinding the officer, as the other slid to the ground, slicing out with its feet.

Rexner fell, his grip loosening on the guns. As they flew skyward, he slapped the metal floor again. This time, however, he ignored the throbbing ache his body had become and, his back flat on the floor, kicked out with both legs.

His left boot collided with someone's skull, the breaking of bone echoing around the room. His right leg struck nothing, and as he pulled back to kick again, something snatched his right ankle. A red hand.

Frakus snarled like a mad animal, jerking Rexner off the floor. Men fanned out around him as he spun, swinging the officer like a child's toy. Rexner groaned as his body smashed against a chair, then another immovable table. Frakus' men watched, some with insane glee painted on their faces, but all silently. They had never seen their leader torture a body like this. Nor had they ever seen someone take such abuse and live.

A blast rumbled suddenly throughout the bar. A brilliant flash of light blinded all open eyes for a second as a thick green beam struck one of the tables closest to Frakus. The metal piece of furniture glowed bright orange for only a moment, then melted to the floor, a slow flowing pool of slag.

Gardner stood where he'd always been, but there was no glass in his hand this time. In its place rested a large black and silver large barreled laser rifle, heat shimmering off the weapon's massive mouth.

"I said," Gardner intoned, his voice barely louder than before. "No killing in the bar."

For a half-second, Frakus considered tearing across the barely lit hull of metal Gardner called a bar and eviscerating the human with one hand. Everyone knew this, saw it in the twisted tangle of rage dancing across his features. His large hands clenching together into huge fists, each knuckle lined with a pointed bony protrusion. But, something stopped him. Maybe Gardner's finger tensing at the trigger of the laser rifle he held. Or possibly simply the look in Gardner's silver eyes. Like cold steel.

No killing," Frakus spat, ruthless sarcasm dripping from every letter. "Fine. We'll just beat him some more, then turn him out. " A few of his followers growled and harrumphed in support of this. "Then he can die anywhere he wants to."

The throng of cutthroats and ruffians seemed to come back alive with Frakus' last word, throwing up a motley cheer of expletives and roars. They turned around their backs all to Gardner, slithering in and out of the tables, like some disjointed serpent, all moving toward the still crumpled officer. Frakus stalked calmly forward, the head of the odd beast, coming to a halt in front of his quarry. Bending, he tucked one thick finger under Rexner's chin and lifted slightly. The man exhaled, more moan than breath, his entire body wincing as if in pain.

"Well, Teddy," Frakus said, like a disapproving parent speaking down to a child, "Anything else you'd like to say before we continue."

Rexner's jaw worked up and down, no sound leaving his lips initially. As if his mouth moved to work the words out, to coax his voice back to life. "You..." he finally managed..."are under arrest for... assaulting an officer...of... a certified private police...agency...and other...crimes..."

Laughter might have ensued from Frakus' men again had their leader not stood up, jerking Rexner's head savagely backward as he did, and roared. Not a grumble or an angry shout, but a true savage, guttural howl rising like an angry storm from deep inside Frakus' colossal form.

"Crimes?" Frakus shouted, glaring down at the man on the floor, ready to kill him, Gardner or not. "Do you think what I've done to you today even touches my list of crimes, boy? You're out here because, for all I've done, the Patrol or any other two-bit law club hasn't had one thing on me! Not from when I robbed the Orion Exploration Payroll ship en route from Granisy 1, not the hijacking of Yeket's own presidential spaceliner! Not even the murder of those hundred or so people in that backwater colony on Pluto! Nothing!"

Rexner raised his head fully now, looking straight into the black pit of Frakus' eyes. "One hundred and thirty-four," he said, his voice suddenly strong.

Fury gripped Frakus like a vengeful lover. Reaching instinctively to his hip, he drew a laser pistol and fired point blank into Rexner's forehead. The energy beam canoed through the top of the officer's head, flinging him back against the table.

"Add yourself," Frakus seethed, 'to the list."

"Armstrong."

Frakus tilted his head to the left at Gardner's voice. His fingers gripped the pistol lightly. A lift and pivot of his shoulder and then he and his crew would really own the bar. "What did you say?"

Green laser fired all around Frakus. Three of his men screamed out, each one falling as the beam struck them. The others spun suddenly, drawing their own weapons. Frakus turned and, without thinking, fired his laser pistol as he leaped across the bar. The blast went wild, smashing a stack of glasses behind Gardner. As Frakus landed with a thud, his face planted itself against the mouth of Gardner's raised rifle.

"I said," Gardner replied through gritted teeth. "the name of the colony. Armstrong." He pressed the hot barrel against Frakus' face, forcing the alien to grunt and step back from it. Cocking his chin into the air and raising his voice, Gardner asked, "You did get all of that, right?"

"Every word."

Frakus swore angrily as he turned, his men doing the same. Silence struck each one at what they saw.

Galactic Patrol Officer Theodore Rexner stood up. On his own feet. An open wound on his cheek. His uniform in shreds, blood, and bone showing through the rips and tears. A furrow dug out of the top of his head. And yet, there he stood, straight up and in full voice. Except, when he opened his lips, his wasn't the voice anyone heard.

"'You're out here because, for all I've done, the Patrol or any other two-bit law club hasn't had one thing on me!' Frakus' words poured from Rexner's lips sounding as they had moments before. Clear, crisp. And in Frakus' voice. "Not from when I robbed the Orion Exploration Payroll ship en route from Granisy 1, not the hijacking of Yeket's own presidential spaceliner! Not even the murder of those hundred or so people in that backwater colony on Pluto! Nothing!'"

Frakus' men stood, looking at the officer using his voice, then back at him, utterly stunned. Confused himself, the alien outlaw leader reacted the only way he knew. Growling, he lashed around with his left arm, knocking Gardner's gun away. The bartender, expecting the attack, fell back, but there was not enough room to maneuver behind the bar. Frakus' hand knocked the laser rifle out of Gardner's grips, sending it skittering across the bar top. Coming fully around, Frakus snatched Gardner by the neck, his fingers squeezing like deep space clamps on docking stations.

"What," Frakus boiled, fangs nearly taking Gardner's nose off, "is going on?"

Gardner's face showed no fear. No emotion. Nothing. Neither did his words. "Like the kid said, you're under arrest."

"Why?" Frakus asked incredulously, still trying to make sense of it all. "He your kid or something? You're just a waste of sperm and flesh! You're a damned bartender!"

Something happened then that no one in the bar currently had ever seen. Or heard of. Because the others who had seen it had all disappeared, gone off planet. Frakus and his cronies though just moved on like criminals do.

Gardner smiled. His seemingly permanent somber granite expression cracked and shattered as a broad grin crossed his face.

"Look around, Frakus," he said, his head still dangerously close to being popped like a ripe fruit if Frakus chose to. "Look closer at where you're standing."

"Hey," one of Frakus' thugs wheezed, "He's...He's right. Look, over here. On the wall."

Light from the fixtures along with a little glow filtering in over and under the rough cut batwing doors into the bar fell in strands across the wall to the right. The speaker and two other criminals stood there, looking up. Frakus turned, his eyes narrowing. On the wall, nearly faded away and hidden in intentional shadows, was an image. An insignia.

A gaudy emblem of the spiraling Milky Way with crossed laser pistols emblazoned over it.

"A ship." Frakus finally understood. He'd been on one long ago when he was a young thief, nabbed at some floating outpost near Uranus. "It's a Galactic Patrol transport ship."

"Yep," Gardner said, his hands sliding down to the rim of the bar while Frakus looked away. "Crashed here back when most of the governments elsewhere decided to turn a blind eye on Tyxos. I buried it deep when I crashed it, turned it into a bar, and waited."

"Waited?" Frakus shrieked, looking back at Gardner. "Waited for what?"

"You," Gardner said, his hands already gripping the bar's edge, his thumbs under it. "And all the others like you. You weren't around then, Frakus, but things were bad all over. Giving murderers, rapists, and world killers a place they could go to be free, could live if they wanted to, was a strange, but popular idea. And Tyxos was perfect for it, a way to get the bad seeds planted elsewhere." The smile broadened. "The lie about the little blue people who lived here and their one-word language helped, too."

"So," someone piped up from behind Frakus, "this whole damned planet is a trap??"

"Not intentionally," Gardner said, his words coming faster now as Frakus unconsciously relaxed his hold, "But it occurred to the Patrol and other agencies as well as some planet governments that it might not be a bad idea to have someone here. Someone who fits in, blended, was even ignored. Someone they could tap when the bad guys got too bad to be allowed off Tyxos out of energy cuffs. So, they sent me."

"But," Frakus insisted, "This is Tyxos. Anything goes! You can't arrest me!

This is Sanctuary!"

Gardner's grin seemed to encircle his head. "Go tell a cop."

Gardner pressed the two buttons his thumbs rested on and then flung his head forward. His forehead crashed into Frakus' face, causing more surprise than pain. Enough that the outlaw cursed and opened the hand around Gardner's neck. As Gardner fell to the floor behind the bar, the light fixtures dotting the room began to hum. Jagged bolts of energy fired from each one of them, some of them hitting nothing but the bare floor, but a pair struck flesh. Two of Frakus' men cried out, nearly simultaneously dropping to the floor, paralyzed and unconscious. Every Patrol Transport carried Tranquilizer Discharge Units.

"Kill them!" Frakus shouted to his four still conscious allies as he filled his empty hand with his second pistol. "Kill them both and melt this ship to the ground!"

Laser fire ripped through the air as Frakus and his men blasted any and everything. Officer Rexner dodged a blast by dropping to his knee and rolling backward, bending impossibly nearly in two at the waist. Flipping his legs over his head, Rexner swiveled his hips, his legs spinning at an odd angle to avoid another laser.

"Rexner!" Gardner shouted, sounding more like a commanding officer than a bartender as he jumped from behind the bar, turning in the air. Both of his hands clutched two sleek black pistols. Standard high-grade inexhaustible ground war laser pistols, eternal batteries included. "Door duty!"

"Affirmative!" On his feet again, Rexner bolted for the door, just steps ahead of one of Frakus' men. As the two faced off, Rexner held his hands up and palms out as he commanded, "Stop by order of the Galactic Patrol!" The light from beyond the door reflected oddly off the deep ditch running through the top of his head.

"I ain't," the average sized blue-skinned goon yammered, "goin' to jail! And ain't no freak like-"

White light danced around Rexner's fingers, emanating from the center of his hands outward. Two waves of energy shot from him, crashing over the man before him. Blue flesh glowed brightly as rivulets of smoke began to rise from his arms and face. He opened his mouth to scream, to beg, to say anything, but nothing came out. His face frozen in shock, he fell backward, his entire central nervous system disrupted.

Gardner hit the floor by the wall, dropping behind a table onto one knee. The man who'd discovered the Patrol logo on the wall giggled insanely, standing only a few feet from Gardner. A laser blade sparkled in his hand, tentacles of searing light dancing around a thin filament sprouting from a handle. Without looking at him, Gardner extended his right arm and fired one of his pistols, the other dancing about in front of him, seeking a target. A yelp later, the curious criminal lay across the table Gardner knelt behind, adding more cover for him. The blade slipped from his now limp hand, the energy and filament retreating into the hilt as it fell.

Frakus, still standing where he'd held Gardner, fired wildly. His head thrust back, a sound somewhere between thunder and breaking glass exploded from his throat. He no longer cared that his men fell around him like empty shot glasses. They did not matter in the long run. Weak because they needed to follow someone. But in the heat of unexpected battle, he knew he was different. And no two-bit Patrolman and whatever the Helios Rexner was would stop him. Frakus slung laser fire like philanthropists threw credits at the poor. Just biding his time.

The two of Frakus' sidekicks still standing pressed their backs together, able to see all sides that way. Gardner stood up suddenly, his eyes looking across the room at Rexner. Rexner nodded once and swung his right arm around. Both of the wanted men faced one of the officers. And both swore in their native languages as they turned their guns to fire. And both were too late.

Gardner's shot landed dead center in the chest of the one looking at him. Rexner's disruptor wave slammed into the other one, causing his body to spasm. The two fell against each other, awkwardly supporting one another for a few seconds, an odd tableau, before tumbling over like broken toys.

"Gardner!" Frakus screamed, holding his two pistols high in the air. "I will bathe in your blood and sleep in your guts!" As if to punctuate his declaration, the crimson-skinned fugitive tossed his guns behind him and, his now empty hands bared into fists, jumped flatfooted from where he stood. Aimed right at Gardner.

Gardner squeezed off a shot from each gun, one searing the top of Frakus' bald head, the other nicking his left fist. Neither slowed the juggernaut hurtling toward him. Dropping the guns, Gardner dove to the left and very nearly made it.

Frakus' punch landed before he did, pummeling Gardner in the right shoulder. Gardner folded, crushed into the wall. Frakus, landing on his knees, raised one fist and lowered it hard into the man he pressed against the hull of the crashed ship. As crimson skin bruised white flesh, another blow dropped like a planet from the sky. Rexner stood his ground at the door, although his eyes drifted to the horrible punishment Gardner now received. Yet he did not move to help. He could not.

Curled up into a ball against the metal wall, Gardner let his left side take most the punishment. He'd been here before, he told himself in those frantic, agonizing seconds Frakus pounded him. Every single time, there was one moment. One single solitary point where the tide could be turned. That came in this fight when Frakus took a breath, raising both fists at the same time. Exposing his body.

Gardner's left leg shot out, his reinforced boot burying itself in Frakus' abdomen. The criminal bawled a mix of curses and breath as his lungs emptied. Pulling his left leg back, Gardner pushed off of it and launched himself upward. His fingers threaded together. The two-handed fist clipped Frakus under the chin, knocking him back, thick arms flailing.

Finding his feet, Gardner returned what Frakus had given him, unmercifully delivering blow after blow. Frakus tried to defend, utterly unaware of the literally inhuman strength Gardner packed into each punch. Throwing his arms up to shield, Frakus' balance shifted enough that Gardner's last punch of his volley knocked the wanted criminal to the floor of the ship.

As Frakus timbered, Gardner, straddled him, his left hand reaching behind his back. Tugging at the hem of his pants, he pulled a transparent strip off his belt. Frakus, still unwilling to be beaten, threw a punch with his left hand. His face fell slack in awe as Gardner, with only his empty right hand, caught the fist in mid-swing. Frakus bellowed in frustration. His other arm lay helpless under him, trapped by his own weight, and Gardner stalled his fist. Muscles bulged on Frakus' arm, veins showing clearly on his neck as he strained against the human holding him back. But Gardner's body tensed as well, muscles seemingly sprouting from hiding like thick roots rising from the ground.

"But..but," Frakus stammered, "You're...just a bartender!"

"No one in the Guild," Gardner replied as he snapped the strip he held around Frakus' wrist like a whip, "is just a bartender."

As the nearly invisible strip struck Frakus' arm, an odd smell like ozone burning instantly filled the bar. Frakus tried to pull away, to shake Gardner off of him, but his body trembled, as if suddenly very cold. His eyelids fluttered like dying insects, first quickly, desperately, then slowing until closed. His head tossed back and forth for a few seconds until finally lolling to the left, his tongue embarrassingly hanging out between his gaping fangs.

Gardner lowered the red fist clenched in his hand, placing Frakus' arm across his own chest. As he stood slowly, his body screaming every inch, he looked toward the door. "Rexner," he groaned. "Assist."

"Affirmative." Rexner lowered his arms and sprinted to Gardner's side. Offering both arms, Rexner waited as Gardner took hold, then lifted the man slowly, until he was standing.

"Sorry," Gardner said, craning his neck one way, then the other, letting it crack, "you took such a beating this time around. After we clean up the mess, I'll put you in stasis for your new face and repair."

"Not an issue," Rexner said, his youthful voice deeper now and less human. More mechanical. "It's why synthetic droids are issued to Patrolmen with the right clearance. To be the partner no one sees."

Yeah," Gardner said, "but you're more than that. I don't think you were created to be bait for a trap."

"In fact," Rexner countered, "I was. 'Whatever purpose the Patrolman sees fit, the Synthofficer will provide.'"

"Hm," Gardner laughed, "Then I wish they'd made you a woman."

Synthetic droids in the Galactic Patrol numbered less than a hundred when initially created. Now that number, Gardner knew, was at least half. Built to mimic human physiology, even down to having synthetically produced skeletal structures and plumbing that pumped a blood-like substance, synthetic droids could be overwritten, both their physical appearances and their personalities. Rexner was this particular droid's seventieth personality and face. A new one each time a planet's government demanded the Patrol snatch a criminal from Tyxos without disrupting the false belief that no law existed there.

That was what made Gardner so successful as possibly the deepest undercover officer the Patrol had. When a criminal, the worst of the worst, needed to be removed from circulation, they called on Gardner.

As he chuckled alone, Rexner now in full synthetic mode, his temporary personality application no longer necessary, Gardner surveyed their latest capture.

All ten men lay unmoving, each of them at the least unconscious, some of them paralyzed and immobilized for many days to come. But, no dead. Gardner prided himself on his one rule. No killing allowed in the bar.

"We'll get these below," Gardner said, unconsciously gesturing to the door beyond the bar. "and teleported to Prison Central. Red Hot here," he motioned at Frakus, "needs to go first. That molecular destabilization band comes in handy, but it won't keep him out too long."

"I know," Rexner said as he leaned over to take ahold of Frakus' exposed arm, "that I probably ask this every time and forget it because you do a new personality overlay, but" he ducked his head under Frakus' arm and without effort hoisted the giant alien off the ground, his legs dragging the floor, "you talked about being here when Tyxos was settled. That was-"

"Too long ago," Gardner interrupted.

Rexner nodded, able to determine the unspoken command his superior had just issued. "And then there's your strength. Just how old…"Rexner hesitated, looking into Gardner's eyes, "and just what are you?"

Gardner sighed. "Yeah, I'm going to have to make sure your next personality has a lower curiosity quotient. Come on," he said, stepping over to another prone body, "let's get this cleaned up. Moons rise in three hours. Night crowd will be coming in."

Roxy Socksy

by
Robert J. Krog

At about noon on a Saturday, Boris Feldon stormed into the Brain Nova saloon, slammed his credits down on the bar, looked Adolf in the eye and said, "I can't pilot sober; this bastard," he hooked a thumb at the green-skinned alien beside him, "won't drink, and I don't drink alone."

Adolf just smiled and asked, "What'll you have?"

Boris held up a hand. "Slow down. What's your name, barkeep?"

"Adolf."

An expression of disgust crossed Boris's face. "I can't call you Adolf. I'll call you Sam, and I'll have whiskey."

As Adolf gave him a shot, he said, "and one for you, too."

Adolf smiled, "I try not to drink on duty."

"And I don't drink alone, Sam, so have something with me."

Obligingly, he poured himself a glass of wine and took a sip.

Boris raised an eyebrow, shrugged, and examined his shot glass.

Boris turned to the alien. "Get you anything?"

"I do not drink alcohol," the alien explained.

"Not a problem. There's water, fruit and vegetable juices of human and Sladen origin, merca, soft drinks, alovil, tea, even milk."

"Water," said the alien, taking a stool.

Boris had taken a sip of his whiskey and was mulling it over. "That'll do," he said, and he slammed it back. "Give me another, Sam."

Adolf gave the co-pilot a glass of water and Boris another shot.

"So you don't fly sober?" he prompted, drinking from his wine glass.

"Only an insane man pilots a Hurl drive sober," Boris declared. Adolf was familiar with the claim. Most Hurl drive pilots made it.

"You're a long distance pilot then. We usually only get folks moving about the system, here. Come from far off?"

"I started this run at Earth," said Boris, "but that was three years ago, according to the ship's clock."

"Holy mackerel!" said Adolf, "you've been to the homeworld!"

"Yeah, it's pretty nice, or so I hear, I only saw it from orbit."

"You're fooling."

"Nope, I isn't."

"You didn't stop in to see the pyramids or the Statue of Liberty, look at live elephants, or eat a pizza made in New York, or anything?"

"It's just another place, only older. I was busy."

Adolf shook his head and took another sip of his wine.

A young woman, pretty enough, but tired looking and carrying a suitcase, stepped into the otherwise empty place and came almost diffidently up to the bar. She placed her luggage by a stool and took a seat, uncertainly, straightening her jacket and smoothing her auburn hair. She had a nice figure; full without being plump, but not skinny or bony.

"It doesn't like unfiltered air," explained the green alien, hooking a thumb at Boris. Boris stood and swirled the whiskey around in his glass, giving it the eye for a bit.

Adolf raised an eyebrow at the alien as he stepped over to his third customer of the day. She seemed worried, maybe sad. He couldn't tell yet. "What may I do for you, ma'am?"

"I thought all Sladen's were drinkers," Boris declared in an outraged voice. The woman turned, startled by the outburst.

"So you have repeated for six weeks," said the alien, "but it is not so."

"Every damn one I ever knew before you."

"Don't mind him, he's a deep space pilot," Adolf explained to the woman.

"Um, okay," she said. Her voice was pleasant, slightly raspy, no, slightly furry. "I'll have a cola with a splash of rum, please."

So she wasn't used to bars, he assumed. He smiled, "Sure thing. Have a preference on the rum?"

"Um, the usual, I guess," she said, her blue eyes avoiding his. No, she wasn't used to bars or drinks.

"Of course," he said, and mixed her drink.

"Every damn one but you, Mexl, every damn one is a drinker. I had my pick; I had my choice. I picked a sure drinker for a co-pilot because I can't pilot sober. Who the hell can? Do you know I was barely buzzed when I set the course for Smith's World?"

"Yes," said Mexl, mildly.

"Did you notice that we almost crashed?"

"I made the necessary corrections with the maneuvering drive when the Hurl drive disengaged. We made a standard orbit around this planetoid."

"Well, it was damned poor form!"

The woman actually shook and spilled her drink at the volume of Boris's voice.

Adolf stepped over and replaced her drink. "I'm sorry," he said, "He's a deep space pilot."

"Of course," she said, testing the beverage. She sipped and made a face.

"If you just want a cola," he whispered, "I won't let them in on the secret."

"Please!"

"Did you notice," Boris asked his co-pilot, just as loudly, "That this isn't Smith's world?"

"Yes, I did. But we are in the same system. This is Jones's World. We can make Smith's World in two days, using the maneuvering drive."

"You're fired," said Boris.

"Thank you," said Mexl, "I'll stay with the ship until a replacement can be found. There must be some way to let us both out of the contract."

"Must be," said Boris, downing another.

Adolf made to refill the glass, and Boris nodded, slapping more credits on the bar. "Thanks, Sam," he said.

"Is Adolf going to be here, today?" the woman asked.

"That's me. What may I do for you?" said Adolf, easing back over to her.

"But?" She looked pointedly at Boris.

"He likes to call me Sam, so I let him. It sort of comes with the job."

"Oh, right." She smiled, relieved.

"So, what may I do for you?"

She gave a sidelong glance at Mexl and Boris, who were discussing their contract, leaned in, and whispered, "I'm friends with Andrea, and she said you might know someone who could take me off planet without asking to see a passport."

He nodded knowingly and wondered who Andrea was. A lot of people came in and out of Brain Nova. A lot of them made assumptions about his connections, too. The first thought that came to mind was, I have no idea, little lady. The next thought was, Those are the loveliest eyes I've ever looked into.

She held his gaze with hers. Her shy, unsure, needy eyes pleaded with him, and he felt his blood stir. He breathed deeply and said, "I don't know for sure, but I probably know someone who knows, if you catch my drift."

She nodded, swallowing hard, and asked softly, "How soon do you think you'd be able to find out? I'm in a dreadful hurry."

"Well, I have to go carefully," he whispered, "this isn't a company affiliated saloon, but almost all the pilots who come through the door are company affiliated, and none of them would want to risk their jobs taking an undocumented passenger."

"I can pay for passage; I can pay double or triple the regular fare if someone will have me," she said.

"That'll probably help. Give me a few minutes to wrack my brains over this, okay? It's not a favor I get asked every day."

"I can pay you, too," she offered.

He patted her hand and stepped away for a bit. She nervously sipped her cola.

"I don't actually give a damn what the contract says," roared Boris, suddenly. The woman jerked in surprise again, dropping her glass on the floor. It shattered. Boris went on, not noticing. "Who cares? Not me. Do I look like I care? Nope, don't care. Will the quadrant manager care? Maybe, but he'll have to talk to next guy up the chain, who will have to talk to the next guy up the chain. By the time they decide how to mark my file and let me know my fate; I may be ready to retire."

Mexl said, "You exaggerate."

"Not much. Here, Sam, give me another." But Sam had already replaced the woman's drink and was on the other side of the bar cleaning up the mess with his handy vacuum. He smiled over at the pilot and said, "Be just a moment."

Boris appraised the situation and muttered, "Got butterfingers, lady?"

She shook her head, then nodded, then shook her head again.

Boris laughed, "Can't make up your mind?" Mexl looked her way and waved a sympathetic, vestigial antenna at her from atop his hairless head.

"Shouts make me nervous," she admitted.

Boris looked at her, perplexed. "Who's shouting," he asked.

She stared for a moment then laughed a short, nervous, tittering laugh. Beside Boris, Adolf appeared and dropped off another shot of whiskey. Boris took it in hand without looking at it and smiled a crooked smile at her. "You're cute, miss. What's your name?"

Her nervous smile faded, and she said softly, looking at her feet, "Roxanne."

"Here's to you, Butterfingers Roxy," he said and threw back the shot.

Between them, and completely overlooked during the exchange, Mexl sighed and sipped his water. He said to her, "He's a deep space pilot."

"Well, he's the first man to ever toast me," she said as Adolf appeared and refilled the shot glass, "and that's pretty typical for me, actually." She sighed and looked away. Mexl turned back to Boris. "You'd be away and in charge of a ship, but I'd be dumped somewhere with no prospects of legally hiring on anywhere else. They'll let you slide a while because you're making them money. My prospects won't be so good. We have to do it via the contract."

"But I can't fly with you, Mexlplexlshmexl," said Boris, after downing another shot.

Stiffly, Mexl, responded, "That is not my name."

Boris shrugged, "Well, for me, it's just as good, because I can't pronounce it the way it really sounds. Damn, this is good whiskey." He turned to Adolf and said, "Do you know?"

Adolf shook his head, "I don't. What do you mean?"

"Do you know?" he repeated, "I've been sober for six weeks in hyper Hurl sub etha space."

Stiffly, Mexl said, "That is not what it's called."

"Don't give a damn, chap," said Boris.

Adolf turned away from them and risked a look at Roxanne. Her pleading eyes were following him. He smiled to comfort her and kept wracking his brains. Every pilot whose name came to mind was a company man. The whole system was taken up by company ships. He stepped over to her and asked, "Where are you looking to go, anyhow?"

She shrugged, "Off-world is good. I mean, I just have to get off this rock. I'd like it to be somewhere with its own atmosphere for a change. That'd be nice, but really, it just needs to be not here."

"If you could tell me where you were going, I might be able to come up with someone or someway. Smith's world?"

"That's as good as anywhere."

"Okay, I'll think some more." He turned away then turned back, "How soon do you need to go?"

"The sooner, the better, today if I can."

"Wow. That's soon. Let me think. No promises, okay?"

She nodded. He retreated to the other end of the bar past the arguing pilots. There was one guy he knew, a devil may care guy kind of like this Boris fellow, but sober. O'Kelley, or something, was his name. He glanced at his calendar. O'Kelley's regular run brought him to Jones's world that very night.

"You can actually recite the contract?" Boris was amazed.

"I can recite it, but unfortunately, it is difficult to interpret. The language of the contract is not like the rest of your language."

"Well, it's legalese, isn't it," said Boris.

"I do not understand."

"Neither do I," admitted Boris, noting that his glass was empty. He rapped it on the bar. Adolf was there in a flash. "Here you are," he said with a smile.

"It's damn good whiskey, friend," said Boris.

"It's a good label. They make it on Smith's world using barley, just like back in Scotland on the Home World. The barley is of the same genetic stock, though of course, the ground it's planted in on Smith's world isn't the same."

"I'll have some more, Sam," said Boris, wiping his mouth.

Adolf refilled the glass and slid on down the bar to Roxanne. She gave him that nervous smile. "Got any ideas?"

"I'm still mulling it over. Tell me, are you running from something or toward something?"

She gave a wan smile. "It's a little of both. No, it's a lot of from and only a little of to, but I wish it were all to if you know what I mean." Her smile became wistful. He felt hot looking at it.

"I don't quite understand," he admitted, and he patted her hand, "Look, I might know someone who can help you. He comes in here every time he's in port. He's due tonight, so if you just hang around, we'll see him before the sunrise, anyhow."

She glanced at her watch. "It's not even one in the afternoon."

"They say patience is a virtue."

"I'm not even sure what virtue is, but I guess I haven't got a choice but to wait."

He refilled her glass with a smile, wishing he didn't want to stretch over the bar, take her face in his hands, and pull her lips to his. He retreated to the other end, pretending to clean something.

Boris's voice rose in volume again. He proclaimed, "Mexl, it just isn't right for you to be so stiff. God knows you're a stick in the mud, even if you don't know what that means. Just have a drink."

"No," said Mexl.

"Just take a sip."

"No, thank you."

"Just one, damn sip."

"No, and thank you, and no."

The bell on the door jingled. Adolf looked up. Roxanne glanced at the door and turned her back on it just as soon as she did. Her face lost color. Two blocky men entered and took a careful look around the bar. The one on the right, who was older, perhaps in his forties, with early graying hair and scars on his face, called across the room, "This is the Brain Nova Saloon, right?" He had to be loud to be heard over Boris.

Adolf smiled his welcoming smile and said easily, "That's what the sign says."

Scarface called back, "The sign's turned off and covered with dust."

He just nodded, still smiling, and asked, "What may I do you for?"

The younger guy, blonde and twenty-ish, said, "Couple of beers'll do fine, Gus."

They gave Roxanne a significant look and then took seats in a booth. Adolf nodded and went to the keg.

Boris was still at it, "Your problem… your problem is that you have no sense of beauty. A lovely lady is sitting beside you, and you haven't so much as winked at her as anything."

Mexl's perplexity was eloquent in his raised eyebrows and drooping lips, "She is not a member of my species."

"I'm not asking you to mate with her. I'm asking you to appreciate beauty, man!"

Roxanne gave the two a horrified look and shook her head.

Adolf carried two beers across to the heavies and set them down on coasters. "Do you want to pay now or run a tab?" he asked, knowing, of course, that they'd be around a while.

"We'll run a tab, Gus," said Scarface.

Blondie lifted his glass and said, "Thanks."

"Who thought you up?" asked Boris, "Your people… your people are photosykinetic."

"Photosynthetic," corrected Mexl.

"Photosyn… your half tree for God's sake."

"It's true, we have traits common to both fauna and flora. As for who 'thought us up,' that would surely be the creator of whom you speak."

"He was drunk that day."

"I hardly think so." Mexl's tone was slowly relaxing from it's earlier, rising indignity. He seemed to be resigning himself to a lost cause.

"Gus," said Blondie.

Adolf paused, halfway between the booth and the bar.

"Yeah, Gus, mightn't we have a word?" asked Scarface.

"Sure, what may I do for you?" He casually returned to them.

"Could I get some peanuts?" asked Blondie.

"I'll bring a bowl."

"That girl," said Scarface, "that girl at the bar."

He avoided the temptation to point her out and clarify whether or not it was she they wanted in the otherwise empty bar.

"Yep," he said, nodding and waiting.

"We'd like to extend her a polite, a very polite, invitation to come over here and discuss matters with us. Would you be so kind as to carry that invitation for us, so as we don't seem too… well, too pushy, if you know what I mean?"

Somehow, he knew exactly what was meant.

"I'll pass it along gentlemen. Just keep it polite and non-pushy in my bar, if you please."

Scarface smiled, showing teeth. If he meant it to be reassuring, he failed. Adolf crossed over to Roxanne, leaned in and said, "Those two want to talk to you. I'm only passing the message, and if you want me to help you get out of here, I will."

She whispered back to him, trying to appear matter-of-fact, but unable to keep the tremble from her tones, "There's no place on this rock for me to go. I might as well stay at the bar."

"Fair enough. I won't let them take you out of here with anything less than an official arrest warrant."

"What about them?" she asked.

"Hold on," shouted Boris, "what about that paragraph three, stuff?"

Mexl explained, "Article four, paragraph three won't work, because I don't require the transplant of a vital organ."

"Why can't we arrange it that you do?" asked Boris, spinning his empty glass on the bar.

"I think not."

Adolf was glad that Boris's noise was covering his conversation with Roxanne. He answered her, "They're union heavies, right? They work for Chief Vic, the man who runs the mine worker's local, 317, and owns the whorehouses?" She nodded. "You don't have to talk to them if you don't want to."

"I don't."

"That's fine." He went behind the bar and refilled Boris's glass. From their booth, Scarface and Blondie waved him over. When he approached, Scarface raised an eyebrow.

"So, you delivered the message or held a conference?" he asked Adolf

"The lady says she's not interested in talking." He shrugged, nonchalantly.

"We were afraid of that. We figured she came in here because it's a guild establishment and all. She asked for sanctuary?"

"The lady's business is her own," said Adolf, adopting his put-everyone-at-ease smile.

"You didn't answer the question," noted Blondie through a

mouthful of peanuts.

He shrugged and walked away.

"Hey, I'm talking to you!" shouted Blondie. Adolf turned to see Blondie out of his seat, but Scarface's hand had caught his wrist.

"Sit down, Jeff," Scarface ordered, "Like I said, guild establishment. If we make a fuss here and bust this place up, hurt Gus, or shut this place down, the guild won't allow anyone else to come here, and The Boss'll never have another properly mixed Pan Fried Champaign Salad again. Isn't nobody else knows how to make that around here, except Gus, here."

Jeff wavered on the verge of violence. Adolf stood his ground, mildly. He noted the presence of a plasma pistol tucked into Jeff's waistband. Behind him, Boris and Mexl continued to argue, apparently oblivious.

Scarface urged, "You louse this up and deprive The Boss of his favorite drink without trying a little more diplomacy first, you'll regret it. Sit down."

Jeff sat, his eyes staring holes in Adolf who approached the table again, "Please do remember that this is a guild establishment, and I reserve the right to serve whom I please and kick out whom I please. If you want to drink, eat, talk, sing, or in any other way enjoy yourself or even conduct business of your own, that's all well and good, but if you molest one of my customers who's not offending anyone else, I draw the line. Get it?"

Scarface smiled that non-reassuring smile and said, "There's no trouble here, none at all. There won't be any molesting coming from us."

He smiled back, "Very good. Let me bring you, gentlemen, a pitcher, shall I?"

"That'll be fine," said Scarface.

He left them to go get a pitcher of beer and passed by Boris, who was pounding his head slowly on the bar. Mexl was merely watching. It was hard to tell if the alien was consternated or amused. He took a moment to use his phone to find O'Kelley's number and send him a message.

It's Adolf at the Brain Nova. If you will be in, tonight, we need to talk. Got a friend in trouble. You could help. She can pay. No questions asked.

He refilled Roxanne's glass with a solemn nod. Her hand shook as she took the glass. When he was passing back by with the pitcher, Boris was saying, "All personality conflicts must first go to arbitration before reassignment can be considered? Really?"

"That is what the contract states," said Mexl.

"It's insane," said Boris.

"But it is what you say the contract states."

"What if we crash into a star next time because you don't drink? Will we need an arbiter then?"

"I'm not sure that the contract addresses such concerns in such an instance. I believe it addresses fault, damages, insurance, credits owed to the company and heirs, and so forth. You must know we would be dead, in any case?"

"I don't want to crash into a star, Mexl."

"Neither do I."

"Then you have to start drinking!"

"I will not."

Adolf set the pitcher on the table in front of the heavies and said with the same put-them-at-ease smile, "It's on the house, gentlemen."

"You're mighty kind," said Scarface, "mighty kind. I'm going to pour myself one and-"

"Allow me," said Adolf, pouring.

"Thank you, thank you. And I'm going to go have a talk with little, Miss Roxy Socksy over there, all pleasant, and non-pushy. You don't need to worry about a thing."

"Okay, Roxy Socksy? I'll bite."

"Well, before she was The Boss's girl, you know-"

Adolf gave a start.

"You didn't know she was Chief Vic's girl? She is. Well, before then, when she worked in Madame Preston's, she never let her gentlemen callers see her feet. She might not wear anything else, but she always wore her socks. She was funny that way. She once cut a man with a straight razor for trying to take her socks off; Nearly killed him, damn near. The Boss got her out of the trouble, but after that, she was his girl. He took a liking to her, to the mystery of all. He's never seen her feet either. Says he respects her too much. He wants to know the mystery, but only if she's willing to reveal it. Roxy Socksy. Yep, he likes her a lot. He's really hurt she wants to leave him, what without even saying goodbye."

Adolf stood there a moment, absorbing that, realizing what he was getting into and feeling pretty stupid about it. I should have seen this coming a light year away. Wow.

Scarface and Jeff watched his face for a bit, smiling, then Scarface got up, beer glass in hand, and sauntered over to sit beside Roxanne. Adolf tried to remain impassive as he returned behind the bar. He tried to imagine the shy, uncertain, gentle, beautiful woman at the bar cutting a man up. He tried to imagine her as a prostitute. He had trouble with both images.

"So Roxy," said Scarface, "You mind a few, polite words?"

"You can talk as long as you want, but I'm not going back," she said. The tremble was gone from her voice.

"Vic's hurt you left that way, stuff packed up and gone, no note, no call, or message, no warning. You took that painting he likes off the wall."

"It was mine," she said, "I painted it."

"Well, he's fond of it, but that's not really the point."

"What is the point?"

Adolf observed from his spot at the end, straining to hear over Boris, who was getting loud again. He had to admire her spunk once she was facing the enemy.

"The point is," Scarface said, "he misses you. The painting is only a reminder of you and what it is he cares so much about."

"I thought it was fair enough to him when I left him that red dress he likes so much."

"Now, I didn't know about the red dress. You are quite the looker in that red dress, some men say you look better in it even than in just your socks."

She blushed at that but maintained her cool. Adolf approved.

"However," said Scarface, "even the red dress isn't the point. The point is, he cares about you. He wants you to stay. He sent me to ask, nicely, to ask nicely. Will you stay, Roxy?"

"I know you want to have a job, plant boy," roared Boris, "but a job won't do a dead man any good will it? I can't pilot sober, and I can't drink alone!"

"Please," asked Scarface, "could you keep it down, we're trying to have a polite conversation here."

Boris looked the big man over and asked, perplexed, "Who's being loud?"

Adolf stepped over and explained, "He's a deep space pilot."

Scarface sighed in recognition of the fact and said, "Oh."

"I know he cares," said Roxanne, "after all, he did have my fingers reattached, and the plastic surgery to fix my face after the burns didn't leave a sign of the injury. He cares a lot about my looks." The tremble was back in her voice. Adolf felt himself go cold at what he heard.

"Now, Roxy, you can't blame the man for that. He's under a lot of pressure, and, considering the circumstances, you could almost call those incidents accidents. Anyway, he didn't mean it, and, as you can see, he was awfully sorry." He directed her attention to her own reflection in the mirror behind the bar. "He made up to you about it. He made good. He almost made better. Just look at that face. You're sixteen again."

"Yeah, sure, but who wants to be sixteen again? I'm leaving."

"Oh, Roxy. Say it isn't so."

"It is so, George. I'm leaving, or I'm dying, but I'm not staying any other way."

Adolf eased over to refill her glass, though it was mostly full.

"A little space, eh, Gus?" asked George.

Adolf said, "Roxanne, you have guild sanctuary here if you want it. You can stay as long as you like, hours, days, years."

Her face was inscrutable, but George's was tense. He said, "Your guild immunity will only get you so far, here, Gus. Trust me, you don't want in on this."

He looked the old enforcer in the face and said, "Yes, I do."

"You see," said Roxanne, "when a man is still a man and not a drone, like you, men like The Boss, the things he does, it touches off a chord in real men."

He was surprisingly calm at what she said when he responded, after a moment's pause, "I've seen the good their outrage does men who don't like The Boss and his ways, and I've made a tidy profit at making their outrage out to be what it is, just noise. I've got the off switch to other men's noises, right here." He patted his waistband, where, Adolf did not doubt, there was a plasma pistol.

Plasma pistols didn't worry him much, he had a plasma rifle of his own, under the bar. It was usually set on stun, but it had the full lethal range of settings. Ignoring George, he said, "If you want guild sanctuary, you've got it."

George said, "Gus, The Boss is fond of his Pan Fried Champagne Salad, but he's fonder of Roxy Socksy. You can bet your life on it. In fact, you are betting your life on it."

"It wouldn't be the first time I bet my life," he said, pulling the plasma rifle out and aiming it at George's chest. "I no longer wish to serve you drinks, pal, so beat it."

In his peripheral vision, he saw Jeff belatedly realize what was going on and jump up, pulling his pistol. He whirled and fired off a stunning shot with the rifle. It knocked Jeff back onto the table, out cold. He had the rifle trained back on George before George could get his hand on his pistol. Slowly and easily, George put his hands on the bar.

"Now, see," said Boris, "there was a perfect chance for you to get injured and taken off active duty, with pay. I could be calling in for a slovenly drunkard of a co-pilot right now."

"Forgive my slow reflexes," said Mexl, dryly.

"All right," said George, "All right. I'll collect my friend, and we'll leave. No trouble. Word of honor."

He rose and crossed the bar. He hefted Jeff up on a shoulder and carried him to the door. He paused there to say, "You're pretty fast and accurate with that rifle there, Gus, but Vic's the best there is with a pistol. That's how he got to be boss if you follow me. I'll send flowers to your funeral because I sure will miss having a guild bar around. I was kinda fond of drinking Brain Novas from time to time."

"It's Adolf."

"I'll be sure they get it right on your headstone." He carried Jeff out the door.

"You shouldn't have done that," said Roxanne, quietly. She was very pale.

Adolf set the rifle on the top of the bar, pointed past her at the door. "Well, it's too late now, but I don't mind having done it."

"Some attention here, Sam," said Boris, tapping his glass on the bar, "Our negotiations need lubrication."

Adolf obliged, keeping the rifle close and his eyes on the door.

Roxanne leaned over the bar and said to him, "I don't want anyone to get hurt on my account. I'll go. They'll let it all slide then."

He said, "You'll get hurt."

"He always fixes me up, after." She was terrified, he could tell. It made something in his guts twist, knot, and pound in silent, raging fury. "I won't let you do that. I'll keep them at bay until I can get O'Kelley to get you off world."

"They know where I am. I'll never get to the ship."

She was probably right. He knew it. "We'll think of something."

"Now see," said Boris, swaying a little as he stood. He leaned on the bar for support, "Now see," he repeated.

"My eyes are in working order," said Mexl, "do continue your sentence to the end, if you can."

"If they can find a solution to their conundrum, we can find one for ours."

"I'm not familiar with that word. Are you able to define it?"

"Which one?"

"Never mind," said the alien, "you obviously mean a problem. Do go on."

"Where was I?"

The door opened and a short, fit looking, little man stepped in. He was flanked by George and a revived, angry, but shaky Jeff. Adolf had seen him often enough to know him on sight. He was the union chief of the mineworkers and the owner of the whorehouses. He was Chief Vic, The Boss, and he was clearly angry by his pose, for his face was obscured in shadow. He left enough room for his men to spread out on either side of him, but he stayed where he was, backlit by the light coming through the door, a shadow of a man.

"Roxy," he said in a tone that commanded.

She turned but did not go to him, for Adolf put a hand on her shoulder. He didn't restrain her, but he said, "Don't," and she hesitated. He pointed the rifle at the specter in the doorway at the same time.

"Gus, isn't it?" asked The Boss, his hand hovering over his pistol grip.

"Adolf."

"This isn't your concern. The lady won't be harmed, but she belongs to me, and she's going home with me. You let her go. You keep to your own business of mixing the best drinks in the system, and we'll call it pax, nice like. No hard feelings."

"I've offered this lady sanctuary according to guild rules," said

Adolf, calmly, "You need to forget she's here, and you need to leave." This is stupid, he thought, I'm about to die.

"You fellas at the bar might want to slide down to the other end and then move on out the back door," suggested The Boss.

Boris looked at the shadow in the doorway and said, "Your problem is, you have no appreciation of beauty."

"What?" asked The Boss, momentarily at a loss.

A whiskey glass flew across the room with surprising accuracy for Boris's state of intoxication. It shattered on the doorframe, inches above The Boss's head. Guns leapt to hands, and plasma blazed around the room. A shot from George had shattered the mirror directly behind where Boris had been standing before he fell to the floor. Jeff, who had gone for his gun first, had been stunned again by Adolf. Adolf's rifle had been knocked from his hand by a shot fired by The Boss. All the while, Roxanne shrieked in terror.

"I fell over," stated Boris, slightly outraged, but unheard over Roxanne's weeping pleas.

"Please," she said, "I'll go, just don't hurt anyone."

"Damn right, you will," said The Boss, standing calmly in the doorway,

"You're messing with the guild," said Adolf, nursing a stinging, but fortunately undamaged hand.

"Screw the guild," said The Boss, "what're they going to do except close up shop and go somewhere else? Hell, I might not let you leave. I might insist you stay."

Adolf knew he was probably right.

"You, Sladen," The Boss snapped, "pick up your drunk friend and carry him out before I forget to be mannerly about this affair."

Mexl slid off his barstool and stood facing him.

"Who's drunk?" asked Boris, from the floor.

Adolf noticed, for the first time, that Mexl had a plasma pistol.

"You can't be serious," said The Boss, aiming his pistol at Mexl's tentacle adorned head.

"But I am," said the alien.

"Please," said Roxanne, "There's no need. I'm going with you. All I really needed was a drink to clear my head." She started to walk to The Boss. George chuckled. His pistol was also still in his hand, and it was aimed at Mexl.

"Get off it," said The Boss, eyes trained on Mexl.

Faster than Adolf's eyes could follow, the alien's hand moved. Two plasma blasts exploded from the tip of his pistol, and two holes appeared, one in The Boss's head and one in George's. They fell over without changes in their expressions. Mexl replaced the pistol in its holster without a glance at his kills and reached over to help Boris up.

"So, that being over," said the pilot, "where were we?"

"Back on section one, paragraph one," said Mexl.

Adolf let his breath out slowly, realizing he had been holding it. He hopped up, slid over the bar, and went to Roxanne, who was standing halfway between the bar and the door, her hand over her mouth. He put his arms around her and guided her back to her stool.

"It's okay, he can't hurt you anymore."

She nodded, not trusting herself to speak yet. He circled around, poured her a rum and cola, and passed it to her. "Drink this fast," he suggested. She did, then gasped and set the glass down with a bang. He checked his rifle, but it was ruined. He checked one of the front windows and saw that just one guy was standing guard out near the dome entrance beside The Boss's car. He checked out the back door and saw another probable heavy out there.

Back at the bar, he interrupted pilot and co-pilot to shake Mexl's green hand and say, "I can't thank you enough, and I think you should know that there're still two out there, one at each door."

"It will not be a problem," said Mexl.

"All the same, you guys should probably get back to your ship immediately." He eyed Boris who was clearly two sheets to the wind, maybe three.

"We still have unfinished business here," explained Mexl, "but I expect we will be on our way, soon."

"I'm really grateful to you," he said, "but I can only wait so long before I call the police, and they probably won't look kindly on this. The Boss being dead, they'll let me off, even though he had them in his pocket, but you'll be toast if you stay. Roxanne here will be all right, now, I think."

She looked over, her face flushed, her expression strangely lost. He wanted to kiss her worries away. He really did.

Mexl nodded politely to him and said, "It will only take a moment." He stood and bowed to her, and said, "I see that you're a drinker."

"Not really, this was my first one, but it seems to help."

He nodded, "I have a proposition for you that will solve your problems and ours." His gesture took in himself and Boris only, Adolf noted with a sinking feeling.

"Yes," said Roxanne, "Yes, I'd love to go with you."

"It is not allowed for in the contract," said the Alien, "But it will keep this one happy if you drink with him. I'll be able to stay on the freighter amicably doing my job, and by the time the manager chain figures it out and decides on a course of action, as Boris has somewhat accurately stated, I may be retired or reassigned. In any event, I'll be making money for them, which will cause them to look at me more favorably." He was placing his pistol on a stunning setting as he spoke. He picked up her suitcase, gave her the same arm, and led the way around the corpses and out of the bar, his free hand near his pistol.

Boris said to Adolf, "You, sir, have a sense of beauty." He tossed more credits on the bar and weaved out after them, a happy expression on his drunken face. Over her shoulder, a stunned Roxanne called out to Adolf, "Thanks for everything."

He waved and following to the door, his insides echoing the lost expression she had worn moments before. He watched Mexl casually dispatch the guard at The Boss's car. The starport was in the next building. They could be away in five minutes. He looked down at Jeff's comatose body. Without artificial reviving, he'd be out for an hour or two. Adolf went back behind the bar and checked his messages. O'Kelley had responded, Sure thing, pal. I'll be in at eighteen hundred hours, your time. He picked up his wine glass and downed the rest of it. After a moment, he poured himself a shot of whiskey in the same glass and downed it, too. He looked at the clock. It was one in the afternoon. He refilled his glass and called the police.

The Saga Of Snagnar Jim

By

Terry Alexander

Mercy Melancholy gazed at the door waiting for the next customer to appear, or the slow-moving clock hands to roll over to closing time. Tuesday nights were always slow at McRuffian's Bar at the far edge of the Galaxy.

Her upper hand brushed an unruly lock of hair from her eyes. She gazed at her new hairstyle in the mirror. A four-armed Merurican beauty stared back at her. She took great pride in her appearance, and her hair was her passion. It maintained its natural green shade on the sides, the top cut into the new Fiery Lava Glow style.

She turned, as the door opened, hoping a party would walk in and breathe some life into the empty tavern. Her hopes dropped to the floor as Snagnar Jim appeared.

"Mercy, good to see you." He walked up to the bar, leaning his four elbows on the slick surface. "It's been a long time."

"What are you doing here, Snagnar?" Her eyes narrowed. "How did you find me?"

"Ran into a fella on Belknap Four, weird guy, curly hair, black hat and the longest scarf I've ever seen." A smile touched his face. "He told me you were working here."

"My friend has a big mouth." She placed her upper hands on the bar, her lower hands reached for a glass and a bottle from the cooler. "Glasgow Ale, on the house." She popped the top from the bottle and filled the glass with orange liquid.

"See you're still pissed at me." Snagnar lifted the glass to his lips. "I'm not the same guy I used to be."

"Those smugglers nearly killed me." She brushed at her hair again. "Besides, an Oxnar doesn't change its spots."

"Hairstyle suits you." Snagnar nodded. "Never figured you for the flame look though."

"It cost me thirty rens." Her eyes fastened on his face. "What do you want? I know you didn't track me down to talk about old times."

Snagnar drained the glass and slammed it on the bar. "I've turned my life around. Got a job and I'm rolling in rens."

"Really?" Mercy feigned surprise.

"I'm with the Supreme Fighting Conglomerate, challenging Bebop Saloub for the Intergalactic Heavyweight title this weekend." His finger tapped the glass. "Got another one of these?"

"That's ten rens." Mercy popped the top and filled the glass.

Snagnar pulled a roll of bills from his pocket and tossed it on the bar. "I've got money. That should square up my debt."

Mercy counted through the stack of mixed currency. "This is more than twice what you owe me." She pulled ten rens from the stack for the cash register and stuffed the remainder in a zip-pouch in her side. "Now, what do you want?"

"Who said I want anything?" He sipped at the ale.

"Snagnar." Her yellow eyes fastened on his face. "You don't throw money around. What's going on?"

"I need a place to hide until the match."

"Spill it." She pulled a cold Glasgow from the cooler, popped the top, and drank it straight from the bottle.

"You should let that breathe. Tastes a lot better when it hits the air."

"I said spill it."

He took another drink, licking orange fizz from his lips. "Rosebud Salen is after me. He wants me to throw the match. He's betting everything on Bebop."

"Salen, you're tied in with Salen! He's the biggest thug in this part of the galaxy. What's he got on you?" She drained the bottle, wiping the excess from her mouth.

"I was passing through the Redrum District, ran into Akbar the Magnificent. I was down on my luck and didn't know he was working for Salen. He bought me a meal and gave me some spending money."

"Get to the point?"

Snagnar frowned. "The IGP (Intergalactic Police) busted Akbar." He shrugged. "Salen thinks I gave him up. After that, I put on a mask and started fighting. It was the perfect hideout."

"Now it's not perfect." Mercy shook her head. "How did Salen find out about you?"

"One of the jobbers on the circuit turned me in. Fella named Blue Midnight had trouble with the law and needed money. He heard that Salen was after me, and made a few calls."

"How much did Salen lose when Akbar was bagged?"

"Seven million rens." Snagnar glanced toward the door. "Did you hear something?"

"Damn, that must have really pissed him off." Mercy shook her head, her lavender eyebrows arched. "You need a bodyguard."

"Yeah." He glanced toward the door. "Did you hear that?"

Mercy squeezed his forearm. "Who did Salen send after you?"

"Me, I'm afraid." A rock-like figure moved through the door. His skin was marked off in squares like building blocks. Thick wires ran from his shoulders to his wrists and from his hips to his ankles. A circular wire ran around the center of his face, disappearing behind his head. "Nothing personal, Snagnar, I need money, got all those little Blagers to feed." He pulled an odd pistol from a holster at his waist. Once free of the scabbard, it snapped open into a multi-barreled weapon. "You can come with me and let Salen deal with you, or you can die right here. Your choice."

"Put the blaster down, Zzbot." A metallic snap followed Mercy's voice.

His colorless eyes shifted to Mercy and widened in fear. "Where did you get an Imperial Disruptor?"

"You know what this baby can do. You're a Blacmar. It can reduce you to pulverized ash. You might skrag Snagnar before I dust you, but are you willing to take that chance?" Mercy smiled.

"You don't want to get involved in this. It doesn't pay to mess with Rosebud Salen." A tremor ran through Zzbot's fingers.

"Your time is running. Either make your play or back down," Mercy growled.

"What's it gonna be, Zzbot?" Snagnar taunted. "You got the squares to try Mercy. I've known her for a long time. She doesn't bluff, and she doesn't back down."

"Next time, Snagnar, next time." Zzbot pointed the weapon toward the ceiling.

"Leave the blaster. Put it on the table and scoot your butt out of here."

"We'll meet again, lady, and it won't be a nice experience." He tossed the blaster to the table. Keeping his hands in sight, he backed toward the door and slipped outside.

"He'll be back. You should have skragged him." Snagnar reached over the counter and pulled a cold Glasgow from the box.

"With what?" Mercy brushed the pesky lock of hair from her face. She tossed the disruptor on the counter.

The color drained from Snagnar's face, leaving it pale and drawn. "That's not a real disruptor. He could have killed me." He drained the bottle in two gigantic gulps.

"Don't get your pelops in a wad. I knew he wouldn't try anything." She glanced at the clock over her head. "It's nearly closing time, want one for the road?"

"What about my offer? Are you going to help me?" He glanced at the blaster on the table. "Do you hear that?"

Mercy glanced up suddenly. "What did you say?"

"Ticking, I hear ticking."

Her hands fisted in Snagnar's collar and yanked him over the counter. She slammed him to the floor covering his body with her own as an explosion rocked the building.

Dust and debris pelted Mercy's back. The bar shielded them from harm, projecting the force of the blast toward the ceiling. She rolled to a sitting position, brushing the dust from her new hairdo.

"Would you mind getting up?" Snagnar mumbled. "It's hard for a guy to breathe down here."

"Sorry." Mercy struggled to her feet. "Damn." The blast had reduced everything in the bar to jagged rubble. She glanced at the missing roof and saw stars twinkling in the heavens.

"What the hell was that?" Snagnar rolled to his feet, brushing trash and dirt from his expensive clothes.

"A bomb in the pistol grip." Mercy nodded. "Zzbot activated it before he put it on the table. Knew he gave in too easy. There's more to this than throwing a fight, and I don't believe that crap about Akbar the Magnificent."

"When Akbar was busted, I uh...I sort of cleaned out his safe."

"You stole from Salen? Are you out of your mind?" She grabbed Snagnar by the lapels and yanked him close. "Why did you involve me in this?"

"The guy with the curly hair said you'd help me."

"Come on, we've got to get out of here." Mercy pushed him

against the scorched wall. "I know a guy who can hide us out for a few days."

Snagnar grabbed two bottles of Glasgow and followed her to a section of standing wall. "Where are we going?" He shoved the bottles in his coat pocket.

"Don't ask stupid questions," Mercy snapped. "We're leaving before Zzbot comes back to check his handiwork." Her lower hand hit a cleverly disguised switch. With a whirl on pneumatic gears, a section of floor dropped and slid to the side.

"Where does that go?"

She shoved Snagnar into the opening. "A friend of mine lives in the lower tunnels." She dropped down behind him, felt along the wall, and flipped a switch. The section of floor slid back into place.

"Damn, it's dark down here." Snagnar's voice held an uncertain tone. "Guess we can feel our way along. Hopefully, we won't fall into a pit."

"Shut up and follow me." Mercy scraped a polytrlene flair against the wall. It sputtered once and caught, turning a twenty-foot circle into bright daylight. "Shorty lives under the garment district."

"That's five miles from here."

"Yeah." Mercy nodded. "And three miles under. Stay in the light. There's Boogers down here."

"What?"

"Boogers, tunnel gang. They beat the hell out of anyone they find, break arms and legs, and leave them laying for the Dusters."

"Dusters, you didn't say anything about Dusters. I thought the military killed them all."

"The Dusters adapted fast. They moved into the tunnels to avoid the soldiers. The Boogers cripple their victims, and the Dusters eat them. You don't want to end up as Duster crap. So be quiet and keep up."

Mercy jogged along the wide path. Snagnar matched her pace.

"Why does your friend live down here?" he whispered.

"IGP is after him. They think he killed Venom George." Mercy paused at a fork in the smooth-walled tunnel. "This way."

She raced down the smooth worn trail for nearly a mile. She stopped, as the tunnel narrowed. Snagnar stood by her side, his hands on his knees, gasping for air.

"Let me catch my breath," he panted.

"We'll have to go slower now. It's tight in there. Keep the torch in sight. Don't make any noise. We've got to get through the narrows without being spotted."

"Okay, I'm ready." Snagnar exhaled a deep breath.

The rough walls scraped against her back as she wedged herself into the narrow opening.

"These walls are like sandpaper. I'm leaving hide behind." Snagnar palmed the rock walls and inched forward.

"Shut up," Mercy whispered. "Sounds carry a long way in here." She eased to a stop, dropping the torch to the gritty floor and smothering the flame with her boot.

"What's going on?"

"Shhh, I heard something."

The silence stretched for several minutes. Mercy gnawed her bottom lip Sweat formed on her brow and threaded down her cheeks. The sound of scuffling feet on a gritty floor caught her ears. That's got to be Boogers, Dusters would smell us and attack.

She froze in position, drawing shallow breaths, lest her harsh breathing give their position away. She felt a tap on her shoulder. Her lower arm reached out and clamped over Snagnar's mouth.

"We've got company." She leaned to his ear and whispered. "Back up, we've got to go around." She felt his head bob through her hand. The pressure eased as Snagnar moved away.

Moving at a snail's pace, the pair retreated from the narrows into the wide corridor.

Harsh lights cut through the darkness. "Mercy Melancholy and Snagnar Jim. Nice to see you." A high-pitched voice came from the void behind the lights.

Mercy held her hand over her eyes to break the glare. She caught glimpses of figures moving toward them.

"Zzbot said you might come this way."

A figure stepped into the light. Mercy couldn't make out the face, but she recognized the stance and build. "Glimmer."

"The one and only. I owe you for busting my arm a few months ago. Nobody hurts one of us and lives to brag about it." He turned his head offering a glimpse of his profile. Scales covered his reptilian face, his eyes wide-spaced over a wide snout, while a long serpentine tongue licked along long dagger-sharp teeth.

"I hate dealing with surface pukes, but when Zzbot said that you were involved in this mess, I gave a shout out to the boys. Knew they'd want to pay their respects." Five hulking figures moved from the shadows into the light.

"Can you really do all those moves I've seen on the Vid?" A hulking blue-skinned thug stared at the fighter.

Snagnar grinned. "You bet." His feet moved to shoulder width, knees slightly bent, and his hands doubled into fists. "Care to see?"

"Mercy." Glimmer licked his brutish eyebrows. "I've got two guys back there with Dracolian pistols, and they know how to use them."

She raised her arms in the air. "Come on, Snagnar. They've got us."

"I'd rather go down fighting," he snarled.

"Talk sense into your boyfriend." Glimmer smiled. "We're going to turn you over to Zzbot, and he'll deliver you to Salen. You never know, he might let you live."

"Damn, boss. That's a good one." A hood laughed. "Salen's never been a nice easy-going guy."

"Shut up and pat them down," Glimmer ordered. "Check Mercy's crotch good. She's been known to carry a tap explosive."

"Can't a girl have any modesty?" Keeping her remaining arms in the air, her lower right hand disappeared inside her skirt. She withdrew a pebble-sized ball and tossed it to Glimmer. "There you go."

"Snap the bracelets on them. We don't want them to get lost." Glimmer leaned against the wall, as the thin metal band snapped on Mercy's left wrist. "You know what these things can do. Joemag is packing a dead switch. If he goes down, it's all over for you." Glimmer chuckled as a bracelet was fitted on Snagnar. "Get moving. Zzbot's waiting for us on the Main Drag."

"You like to live dangerously." Mercy stared at the bracelet, a small green light blinked from in its center. "There's a lot of Dusters between here and Main Drag."

"Shut up, sweet cheeks." A burly thug with a wide flaring gorilla nose shoved her from behind. "We've got this covered." He glanced toward Snagnar. "I wish you would have tried something. I'd beat you into hammered Duster slep."

Snagnar pursed his lips. "I'll give you a chance later. I haven't whipped a Klenn in a long time."

"Quit the gab and move out. Take the lead, Pitchy. Straight through the Spews." Glimmer pulled the brute to one side.

"You're in a hurry." Mercy moved into position behind Pitchy.

"Sooner we deliver you, the sooner we get paid." Glimmer's long slender tongue flickered into each nostril, cleaning dirt and grit away. "Take the rear, Joemag. I want you far away from those two. If they try anything, drop the switch."

"All that humidity is going to ruin my new do," Mercy mumbled.

"Don't worry your pretty head about it. You won't be alive much longer." Glimmer prodded Snagnar in the back with the nasty end of a Dracolian. "Get moving." He struck a flare against the floor, lighting the chamber. "Kill the lights."

"Glimmer, get up here," Pitchy stammered. He held the flare high above his head. A pale green glow came from the pools dotting the wide area at the end of a slight decline. A thick mist swirled, carried by tunnel winds.

"What the splok is wrong with you?" Glimmer stomped to the front of the line.

"Something's moving out in the mist." Pitchy nodded. "Could be Dusters."

"Sounds like your man is losing his nerve," Mercy taunted. "Maybe I should go first."

Glimmer pressed a stud on the side of the Dracolian. "Heat 'em up boys," he ordered. "Just in case Pitchy's right." He moved to the front of the line, following the slight depression into a wide cavern.

"I wouldn't rush into that mess," Mercy said. "Look to the right, two Dusters are hiding in the shadows."

"Those are rocks." Glimmer moved forward slowly, the oversized pistol gripped tightly in his fists.

"Damned idiot." Mercy edged to Snagnar's side. "Get ready. Things are going to get interesting," she whispered.

"What's going on?"

"Glimmer's careless. Be ready, we've got to protect Joemag. We can't let him drop the switch."

Snagnar nodded.

"One more thing, don't get killed."

"You two shut up and get moving," Joemag ordered.

"We're moving." Mercy nodded.

"We've got fifteen milars to get through this mess." Glimmer stepped around a green pool of fetid liquid. Pitchy followed, placing his feet in the same tracks. The Klenn's head turned a complete rotation, glancing in all directions. Heavy sweat formed on his sloped head cascading down his face.

"Nervous." Mercy stepped in the old tracks.

"Be quiet. You don't want the Dusters to find us." Pitchy's head snapped to the front.

Mercy stumbled at the edge of the pool, falling flat on her stomach, splashing the stagnant water.

"Get her up," Glimmer hissed.

Snagnar's multiple hands lifted her upright. "What are you doing?" he whispered.

"Buying us a few seconds. Keep your eyes on Joemag." She resumed her place in the line. A coating of slimy mud covered her arms. She rubbed the slime around the bracelet.

"Glimmer, I don't like this. Place makes my skin crawl." Pitchy's head completed another rotation. "What are you doing?" His eyes fastened on Mercy.

"Wiping mud off."

"Damn it, why don't you two talk louder so we can attract all the Dusters?" Glimmer shook his head in disgust. "Keep it down."

"Boss, this bitch is up to something." Pitchy aimed the blaster at her head.

"Put the gun down. No shooting unless we have to." Glimmer circled the next pool. "Joemag, keep your eyes on Mercy. She's one slick female."

"Gotcha, Boss," Joemag stuttered.

"There's something moving in the mist." Pitchy's voice cracked.

"We're nearly out of this mess. Don't lose your nerve." Glimmer turned toward his captives. A huge dark creature leaped from the swirling fog.

Sharp claws buried in Glimmer's back, slicing through muscle and sinew. It slammed him to the rough floor, clawing at his chest. He triggered three shots into the air. The second hit Pitchy in the chest, burning a fist-sized hole in his chest. The enormous Duster dragged Glimmer into the darkness.

"Get Joemag." Mercy ripped the blaster from Pitchy's hand. "Don't let him drop the switch."

Three Dusters charged Pitchy's body. The green glow of the

water reflected off sleek interlocking scales. Long savage claws hooked into the thug's flesh. Roundheads dipped to the ground. Mouth tentacles wrapped around the body, pulling it toward the huge dismembering beak.

Snagnar spun and leaped on Joemag. His greater weight bore the smaller man down. The hands on his lower arms wrapped around Joemag's smaller hands, squeezing them together. The larger upper arms wrapped around the small hood and squeezed.

"Get off me, you bastard." Joemag drove a knee straight into Snagnar's groin.

A burning pain exploded in the fighter's privates and raced through his belly. Tears misted his eyes. He squeezed Joemag's hands tighter.

Mercy lined the blaster on the nearest Duster. The weapon bucked in her hands as she pulled the trigger. The creature's head exploded in a fountain of yellow goo. It collapsed to the ground, kicking at the air. The two smaller beasts backed away, dragging Pitchy's body.

"Come on, we've got to save the boss." Two hoods at the rear ran toward the carnage.

Mercy dropped to the ground. She triggered two off-balance shots. The lead tough staggered, as the blast took him in the stomach. Blue intestines plopped onto the gritty surface. His eyes rolled back in his head as he dropped into the rancid pool. The second was much more fortunate. The blast took him square in the face, reducing it to bloody mush.

"Grab a weapon. We've got to get out of here." She jumped over the pool and sprinted through the thick pea soup.

Snagnar tucked the smaller man under his right arm, his lower hands wrapped tightly around Joemag's hands, squeezing the fingers together. He scooped up Glimmer's Dracolian and raced after Mercy.

"Why are we running?" he panted.

"This place will be packed with Dusters before you know it. Don't forget the Boogers, they're thick down here." She glanced down at the wide-eyed man, struggling to break Snagnar's grip. "Don't lose that little guy."

She turned left at a large bubbling puddle. "This way, that one's about to blow." The water boiled. Steam rose from the center. A putrid stench filled the air as each bubble burst. "We've got to get to get to the Caspar refinery before that thing pops."

"The sewer refinery." Snagnar adjusted his grip on Joemag. "That place has been abandoned for years."

"We've got to find cover before we're boiled alive." She glanced over her shoulder. A small fountain of scalding liquid lifted in the air and settled back to earth. "It's got to be close."

"It's straight ahead. I can see the outline." Joemag pushed against Snagnar's forearm.

"He's lying. I can't see anything."

"If you two do-gooders get boiled, what do you think will happen to me?"

"He may be telling the truth. These Polaris turds have excellent eyesight." Mercy held her blaster under the small man's chin. "Can you see the door?"

"No, just ladders leading to the roof. When this place was active, the owners ran advertisements for their products on holo-signs. The ladders were for the workmen."

A steady hiss sounded behind them, growing louder with each passing second. "You need to hurry. When that hot goop erupts, it'll melt the meat from our bones."

Snagnar shifted the little man to his shoulders. Joemag looped his arms around his neck, his hands gripping the switch tightly. "Don't drop that."

"I'm not crazy," Joemag shouted. "If you die, so do I."

"I see the ladders." Mercy sprinted forward. She leaped into the air, her hands catching the steel supports. Her feet landed on the rungs. "Come on."

Snagnar jumped. His upper arms closed on the ladder, and his feet found purchase on the corroded metal. Within seconds, he drew even with Mercy.

"Look for a window. We have to find a way inside." She glanced toward the bubbling pool. A sickening glow painted the mist in dark emerald hues.

"There's a door on the roof," Joemag screamed. "Hurry, we're running out of time."

Powerful muscles bunched as the pair took the rungs three at a time. Gravel and dirt crunched under Mercy's feet, as she leaped to the roof. Years of neglect had treated the old building poorly. The flat roof sloped oddly toward the center and creaked at her every step.

"Be careful. It could collapse at any second," she warned.

"I see the door." Snagnar moved forward. The roof groaned under his feet. "Gotta take this slow."

"We don't have time for slow." Joemag kicked his chest. "Hear that hissing. It's getting ready to spew."

"We have to chance it." Mercy shrugged. "Make a run for it. We might get lucky."

"Oh, Slep!" Joemag screamed.

Mercy and Snagnar raced across the roof. A thunderous crack sounded beneath them. A section broke away behind them, crashing to the floor. Mercy grabbed the rust-pitted door handle. The lock held fast.

The spews erupted, like a giant exhaling a huge gust of air. "Hurry up, we've only got a second to live." Joemag's voice verged on panic.

"Shut up, little man." The tendons stood out on Mercy's arms. The ancient handle crumbled under her grip along with a section of the lock. Snagnar's heavy foot lashed out. The door flew open, slapping the inside wall.

"Get inside quick."

The first drops of scalding mud and water smacked the ancient roof and smoldered. The trio darted inside. "Brace the door. We don't want that slep flowing in on top of us," Mercy shouted.

Snagnar nodded. He slammed the door and wedged his back against it. "This thing's getting hot. How long will this last?"

"Not long." Joemag nodded. "It should be easing off soon."

"Easy for you to say. This door is burning through my clothes."

"Hang on, Snagnar." Mercy walked to the edge of the catwalk, staring down into the abyss below. "We've got to get to that cross beam. Once we cross that, it'll take us into the bowels of this building. Then it's a straight shot to Shorty's place."

"Shorty McCoy, the guy that killed Venom George?" Joemag's eyes widened. "You know him? Glimmer gave that guy a wide berth."

"Good friend of mine." Mercy peeled a layer of rust from the metal stairs. "These things are corroded, but if we go slow, we should make it."

"The door's cooling off. Pressure's easing up." Snagnar climbed to his feet. "Can you walk?" He turned to Joemag. "Or do you want me to carry you?"

"He can walk down the stairs." Mercy brushed the hair from her face. "Wish I had a pair of scissors." She blew an exasperated breath toward her forehead.

Snagnar went first, easing his massive weight on each stair. The metal creaked and swayed at each step.

"Maybe you should let me go first. The big guy's liable to break it down," Joemag said.

"And give you a chance to run off and drop the switch?" Mercy shook her head.

"In case you guys haven't figured it out yet, our fates are tied together now. If you die, so do I. Get it."

A blaster shot glanced off the handrail next to Joemag's head. "What the hell?" Mercy spun. The blaster bucked in her hand. "Grab the runt. We've got to get out of here."

"How did anyone survive out there?" Snagnar slung the smaller man over his shoulder and sprinted down the stairs.

"Don't worry about that, run!" Joemag yelled in his ear.

The blast pulverized a section of the wall, turning it to dust. A large figure leaped into the opening. The firing tube of his multi-shot zap blaster glowed. A beam shot from the fluted tip. The metal handrail near Mercy's head glowed briefly and melted to slag.

"You forgot about me. Pretty careless."

"Zzbot, how did you follow us down here?" She ducked as a second blast zinged past her head.

"My little secret." He ducked behind the wall.

Mercy fired three quick blasts, turned, and raced down the stairs. She caught Snagnar easily. "What is wrong with you? Can't you run any faster than this?"

"Almost lost Joemag when the shooting started. If he hit the floor, you know what would happen." Snagnar jumped onto the beam and hurried across to the next tunnel.

"Yeah, I know." Mercy paused and triggered a half-aimed shot at a shadowy figure at the top of the stairs. "I don't get it, he's not following us."

"Maybe he doesn't need to." Snagnar exhaled a deep breath. "Maybe he knows where we're going."

She grabbed Joemag's shirt and lifted the little man to eye level.

"How did Glimmer know where to find us in the tunnels?" She shook him for greater effect. "How?"

"I don't know." Joemag squirmed. "He got a message about a job, rounded up a crew, and went to the narrows. He had some guys stationed inside for an ambush, while the rest of us waited outside."

"Don't lie to me, you little turd. I'll wring your neck and shove it up your dying ass." Spittle flew from her mouth, covering Joemag's face.

"I ain't lying. Glimmer never gave us any details." Joemag's eyes widened. "He just said the money was good."

"Ease up on him, Mercy." Snagnar shrugged. "I think the little puke is telling the truth."

Her rage-filled eyes softened. "You might be right." She loosened her grip on Joemag. "Come on, we need to get out of here."

Their footsteps echoed from the narrow walls as they made their way down the steep corridor. Mercy paused at a heavy metal door. Her hand closed on the handle and pulled. "Why are all the doors locked down here."

"Any other way to the lower tunnels?" Snagnar licked his lips anxiously.

"This is the only access from here, and I'm not going across the spews again." She braced her foot against the wall and pulled. The door creaked. Thick sheet metal buckled, but the door held fast.

"Blast the damn lock off." Joemag met the woman's eyes. "My hands are getting tired, and I need a bathroom break."

"Can't risk the noise."

"Here, maybe both of us can get the damn thing open." Snagnar's hands closed on the handle. Mercy braced her foot against the wall a second time.

"Okay, now." She closed her eyes and pulled. The tendons stood out in her arms and shoulders, crawling up to her neck. Metal shrieked. The framework around the lock shattered, showering debris on the floor.

"Come on, let's get a move on." Snagnar stepped into a narrow stairway, leading down into darkness. "Damn, wish we had Pitchy's flare right now."

"Let me lead. I can see in the dark." Joemag elbowed past the four-armed giant.

"Don't try anything shifty. I can see well enough to drop you,"

Mercy warned.

"I can't believe it. You're the most ungrateful woman I've ever seen. I've saved your ass twice, and you still don't trust me."

"Hard to trust a Booger," she said.

"I wasn't a willing member." The short man walked confidently down the steps. "It was either die or do what Glimmer ordered. Which one would you choose?"

"I know which one I'd take," Mercy snapped.

"Whatever." Joemag shook his head. "I wasn't kidding about the bathroom break. I've got to go."

He hurried down the stairway. Snagnar and Mercy were hard-pressed to keep up.

"Guys, we've got a problem here."

"What now?" Mercy whispered. A high-powered round splattered the wall. "Forget I asked." She dropped to the metal steps and returned fire.

"No wonder Zzbot didn't follow. He knew these guys were waiting." Snagnar triggered two quick shots at the unseen assailants. "Any idea who they are?"

"Boogers. I recognized Slack-Jaw Slim." Joemag huddled against a support beam.

"Damn, Slack-Jaw is a torturer. These guys really want you bad." She lifted her head and fired blindly into the darkness below.

"You're wasting ammunition," Joemag mumbled. "Wait until they fire. Shoot at the flash. You might get lucky and hit one."

"How were they able to find us?" Snagnar asked.

"You haven't figured it out yet," Mercy whispered. "These damn bracelets are sending a signal. As long as we're wearing them, the Boogers will know exactly where we are. Joemag, is there any way to get these things off without dying?"

A white-hot plasma blast zinged off the decayed stairway. Snagnar returned fire. "Did I hit anything?"

"No, but you scared the hell out of him. Couldn't tell for sure who that was. Looked a little like Digger." Joemag's voice trembled. "What are we going to do? We can't go down, and Zzbot's waiting for us up top."

"Focus. Can you get these bracelets off?" Snagnar repeated.

"Sure, if I didn't have my hands full, and if I didn't have to go, bad."

"Don't look at me. I'm not touching your junk," Mercy said.

"It's the other one," Joemag groaned.

"Oh hell, all we need is for you to mess yourself, so everyone can smell us coming," Snagnar quipped.

"You don't understand. Polarans have a ritual we must perform when we have a body function. It requires the hands. Our religion decrees that we perform the ritual whenever we relieve ourselves. If our internal pressure builds to a certain level, we vent the excess gas."

"How much gas are we talking about here?" Mercy fired at a blaster flare. A loud groan and a flat whump rewarded her efforts.

"You nailed that one," Joemag whispered.

"What about the gas?" Snagnar interrupted.

"More than enough to kill us all," he answered.

"Death by a giant fart." Snagnar laughed. "Never thought I'd go out that way."

"Mercy Melancholy, we need to talk." Zzbot's voice rang from the upper levels. "Let's make a deal. I don't want to kill you, Mercy. Throw down your weapons and walk away. My business is with Snagnar and the turd."

"He's lying," Joemag whispered. "He'll kill us all."

"She knows," Snagnar replied.

"Why do you want the turd? That doesn't make any sense." Mercy transferred the weapon to her lower hand and wiped sweat from her palm.

"He's a present for Slack-Jaw." Zzbot grew silent for several seconds. "Well, do we have a deal?"

"I'm mulling it over. The turd is holding a kill switch that controls these bracelets. If I agree he'll just toss the thing over the side, and Snagnar and I are history."

"Snagnar is bought and paid for. Salen isn't very happy with him. Still, it is a vexing problem." The silence stretched for nearly a minute. "The bracelets have different signals. I can block yours long enough for you to go downstairs. One of the Boogers has the key."

"Anyone got any ideas?" Mercy whispered.

"I've got to go. I'm almost at the venting point."

"Snagnar, take him up the stairs. Find a good spot and let him take care of his business."

"You've got to be joking." He jumped to his feet. "There's no way I'm helping Joemag relieve himself."

"We're going to die if you don't," Joemag whined.

"Go. Give me a minute to think." Mercy stared upward into the stygian blackness, hoping to spot a glimpse of Zzbot. "The turd has to go. He's about to vent some poisonous gas."

"Polarians have some unique physiology. He can go, but you're in crossfire, so don't try anything."

Mercy listened to a buzz of whispers behind her as Snagnar and Joemag moved away. "Why not kill us all now and be done with it?"

"Oh, my God." Snagnar gagged. "Hurry up, please hurry up." He hacked several times.

"Sounds like Snagnar doesn't like his current job. When Salen gets through with him, he'll beg to wipe the turd's ass every day," Zzbot chuckled. "My God, the Polarian is rank today."

Snagnar crept to Mercy's side and whispered in her ear, "Get ready to start shooting."

"What happened to the runt?"

"He's back there saying his prayers. Said I couldn't stick around for that. We crammed the switch inside the dung. Joemag said it'll buy us a little time."

"My God, that is foul!" Mercy pulled the collar of her shirt over her nose. "Where is he?"

"He'll be here in a second. Give the stench an opportunity to drift up the stairwell. Then pop off a shot at Zzbot." He passed her the Dracolian and took the blaster from her hands. "More firepower."

"What good will that do?" The collar muffled Mercy's voice. "I don't know where he is."

"I'm ready." Joemag appeared at their side. "We should hurry. We have to get those bracelets off before my leavings lose consistency."

"Oh, crud." Mercy gritted her teeth.

"Take the shot. I'm gonna blast away at the Boogers. Maybe I'll get lucky and hit something." Snagnar lifted Joemag and settled the small man on his shoulders. "Let's go." He triggered the blaster three times in rapid succession, then jumped to his feet and bolted down the stairs.

Mercy fired the Dracolian straight up. The air between her and Zzbot ignited into a mini fireball. The flaming gas highlighted the Blacmar for an instant. Mercy quickly triggered a second shot. Zzbot staggered and disappeared from sight. She turned and, using the light from dwindling flames, raced after her companions.

Snagnar blasted his way down the stairs, firing into the shadows. Two of the Boogers lay dead at his feet. The others turned and disappeared into the darkness.

"Quick, check the bodies. See if one of them is carrying the key to your bracelets." Joemag's voice rattled. "We don't have much time."

"Check them out. I'll keep watch." Mercy lifted the Dracolian in a two-handed grip.

"Found a flare." Snagnar ripped the pockets open. "No key."

"Check Loop-eared Benny. He was Glimmer's most trusted lieutenant," Joemag stammered.

"Don't lose the flare. We'll need it later." Mercy licked her lips anxiously.

"If there is a later. We're dead when the bombs explode." He searched inside each pocket for the key. "I can't find anything. I'm going to ignite the flare, get some more light down here."

"We've got Boogers out there waiting for us to do something stupid," Mercy warned.

"If we don't find that key, we're soup anyway." Snagnar scraped the flare against the rough floor. A tiny flame sprang to life, growing larger, bathing the area with light. "Look at this. He was wearing the key as an earring."

"Get these damn things off." Mercy glanced down the shadowy tunnel.

"Here, Joemag." Snagnar tossed the Polarian the key. "Do the honors."

Snagnar held out his arm. The small man fitted the small key into the bracelet lock and twisted. The shiny metal fell to the floor. He hurried to Mercy's side and quickly completed the operation. "We've got to move."

Snagnar lifted Joemag to his shoulders and picked his way along the tunnel.

"Faster, faster." Joemag's heels drummed along his sides.

"Why, we're out of danger now?" Mercy asked.

"The switch will grow hot before it triggers the explosions. Polarian dung is very flammable!" Joemag shouted. "Now do you understand?"

"Oh hell." Snagnar raced down the tunnel, holding the flare high. "Just hope we don't run into anymore Boogers or Dusters."

"The Dusters are filling up on the dead," Mercy said. The trio rounded a blind curve. "The access to the lower tunnels should be close." A large explosion shook the walls. Dust and bits of rock rained down on their heads as they hit the rough floor. A wave of flame passed over their heads, scorching the air.

"Damn, that was the bracelets?" Snagnar climbed to his feet, rubbing his ears.

"Aided by a little Polarian dung." Mercy brushed a coating of dust from her hairdo.

"It's not my fault. I told both of you I had to go." Joemag lifted the torch from the floor. It sputtered weakly and sprang back to life.

"Who in the hell is making all the noise?" a heavy gruff voice demanded. An enormous bald man stomped into sight, his huge hands cradled around an ancient-looking weapon.

"It's me, Shorty." Mercy stepped forward. "I see you're still carrying that old Beckman single shot."

"It gets the job done." He patted the wooden stock. "They don't make them like this anymore. This thing can stop a runaway Plazer Beast." He looked up into the tall woman's eyes. "Why are you here, Mercy?"

"Looking for you." She turned to her two companions. "Guys, this is Shorty McCoy. Shorty, this is Snagnar Jim and Joemag."

"Snagnar Jim. You're fighting Bebop Saloub for the title this weekend." He looked at the short man. "Aren't you one of the Boogers?"

"Not anymore. They tried to kill me." Joemag nodded.

"The three I ran into won't be trying to kill anyone anymore." He turned to Mercy. "Nailed them with one shot." A smile touched his face. "Now, how can I help you?"

"Rosebud Salen is after me," Snagnar answered.

"When you piss somebody off, you go right for the big guy, don't you?" Shorty shook his head. He turned to Mercy. "You want me to hide him out until the match."

Mercy nodded. "I'm going topside. I've got business with Rosebud."

"I can do that." He turned to Snagnar. "Bebop is tough. Have you ever fought a Galvaran before?"

"Once, got my butt kicked." Snagnar cast his eyes to the floor. "I'm going to counter everything he tries, match him punch for punch, and see if I can catch a break."

"That strategy is going to get you beat." Shorty winked at Mercy. "Don't worry your pretty head. I'll take good care of them." He motioned Snagar and Joemag to follow him. "You've got to be aggressive to beat a Galvaran. They have one weakness, and you've got to focus on it and pound him hard."

Snagnar's eyes brightened. "What weakness?"

"Long muscle running along their ..."

Mercy smiled. "Better listen to him," she mumbled. "He can get you the title." She checked the Dracolian's charge and retraced her steps through the tunnel. An access port to the surface lay just beyond the staircase ruins. The flames from Joemag's dung gave her just enough light to see across the opening. Dozens of hungry Dusters pawed through the crumpled steel and rubble searching for tender morsels.

I've got to do this slow. Dusters love carrion. Hope they don't decide to give up a cold meal for a warm one. She tiptoed along the smooth rock wall. Her hand gripped the pistol grip tightly. A young pup lifted its gore-covered tentacles from one of the Boogers. It sniffed the air and resumed its feast.

Mercy wiped sweat from her brow. That was close. The darkened tunnel mouth swallowed her. She felt along the wall, searching for the circular latch that would provide her access to the world above.

Damn it, where's the latch? Her hands patted the stone wall fruitlessly. Just as she was about to abandon her quest to find the latch, her lower hands felt the lever.

Her hands closed on the rusted circle and twisted. The tendons in her arms stood out as she struggled with the latch. With a loud squeal, it turned in her hands. She swung the door open and stepped inside.

Feeling secure, she pulled a flare from her boot top and struck it to life on the rock wall. The machine-cut tunnel led upward at a gentle angle, the narrow walls scarcely ten feet across. Her hair brushed the ceiling.

Bad place to get into a tussle, no room to fight. Holding the torch away from her body, she began the ascent. Dust clung to her sweaty forehead after the first few minutes. Mercy longed for a drink of water or a cold Glasgow Ale.

The first intersection should be just ahead. She licked her lips and kept moving upward.

A hint of cool air touched her cheek. Her right hand circled the Dracolian's grip. A narrow pinpoint of light loomed ahead, growing larger as she approached.

Perfect place for an ambush. If Zzbot survived, he's waiting for me. Mercy hugged the wall, peering down the tunnel.

The Blacmar's not an idiot. If he's there, he's seen the reflection of the torch. Her mind replayed the staircase shootout. She had hit Zzbot with a hurried shot, saw him fall. Doesn't mean he's dead. It's ten steps across. Then I have to go through another hatch to get topside.

She stepped back, positioning herself in the center of the tunnel. She drew a deep breath into her lungs and tossed the flare into the tunnel entrance across the way. Two hasty blaster shots scorched the walls. Mercy ducked low, drawing the Dracolian, and leaped across the empty space.

A blaster shot sizzled above her head. She rolled across the uneven floor, firing the large pistol at the blaster flashes. She caught a glimpse of Zzbot, lying in a crumpled heap, against the tunnel wall. A thick fluid leaked from a gaping hole in his blackened chest.

Zzbot struggled to lift the blaster. Mercy fired the Dracolian. The blast struck his elbow, burning it to slag. Black foam bubbled from Zzbot's lips as he reached for his backup weapon.

She closed the distance fast and snatched the small blaster from his hand. She stuck it in her belt. "Looks like the mighty have fallen." She aimed the oversized pistol at his head. "Where's Salen?"

"Go to Bleek." Bubbles burst on his lips. Black ooze covered his chin, dribbling down his neck. "I won't tell you anything."

"I think you will." Mercy smiled. "The Dusters are below snacking on your hired help. They'll follow the sound of blaster fire, and you know Dusters. They're always hungry."

The dark eyes closed briefly. "I'm not gonna tell you anything."

"Imagine what it's like. You can't defend yourself. When they find you, they'll start at your wound, nibbling away. I've seen them eat. That beak will strip the flesh from your bones." She paused for a moment. "You'll be in agony until you draw your last breath."

"I'm not talking."

"Have it your way." She nodded. "I'll find Salen on my own."

"Kill me before you leave."

She shook her head. "Don't think so. I'll find a nice hiding place so I can watch the Dusters feast. Hearing you scream and blubber will be a wonderful thing."

"I'm begging you, kill me."

"Where is Salen?" she repeated. "I'm gonna find him with or without your help. Tell me what I want to know, and I'll put you out of your misery."

Zzbot closed his eyes. His teeth gnashed together. "He's at Dragon-Fang, having a party. Waiting for me to bring Snagnar. He's gonna torture your boy. It gets the working girls in the mood, to see some poor jerk die slowly." He glanced up at Mercy. "Now, keep your part of the bargain."

"You wanted Snagnar to go through the same death you're trying to avoid." She shook her head. "You really are a piece of slep."

"I told you what you wanted to know. Now kill me."

"My pleasure." She pulled the mini-blaster from her belt, placed it in the center of his forehead and pressed the trigger. His hot blood coated the walls. She trotted to the intersection. The door stood open. A bitter smile touched Mercy's lips. She raced up the tunnel toward the surface.

The double sun rose over the northern horizon as she emerged into the sunlight. Mercy glanced at the rundown surroundings and knew she was in Skiz Town, a collection of derelict structures, abandoned due to the constant sandstorms that ravaged this section of the planet.

"Hey, Cutie, what's a nice-looking thing like you doing here?" A triple-eyed Zylatrope stepped from a lopsided doorway. The early morning sun reflected from his translucent skin. "Don't see too many of your kind in Skiz."

She turned and placed her lower hands on her hips and folded the upper arms across her chest. "Do you know the Dragon-Fang Lounge?"

"Cutie." He smiled, showing a mouthful of double teeth. "You need to stay away from Dragon-Fang. There're some bad boys in that playground."

"I'm in a hurry. Can you give me directions?"

"You got any money?"

She pulled the wad of bills from the side-skin flap. Peeling a single from the stack, she held it between her fingers. "One for directions, more if you can get me there."

He eyed her warily. "How much more?"

"Three."

"That's more money than I've seen since the third moon exploded." His elongated fingers scratched a black growth on his ear. "What do you think, Herbert?"

The lump unfolded into a prominent nose and white eyes. It rattled off a series of buzzes and clicks.

"We'll get you there." He smiled. "But it'll cost you five."

"Done." Mercy passed him three bills. "You get the rest after we get there."

"Shrewd woman. I appreciate that." He nodded. "I'm Skully O, this is Herbert Seven. Pleasure to do business with you."

"What exactly is Herbert?" She asked.

"Herb's an Avaran Slug. His original host had passed on, and he was near dead himself. I was sleeping in an alley one night, and he attached to my ear. After I got used to him, we became friends." He glanced up at the sky. His eyes focused on the amber clouds racing toward them.

"We'd best get inside. There's a storm coming, and that sand will shred your flesh."

Mercy shook her head. "I've going to Dragon-Fang, quick as possible. We can make it before the storm hits."

Skully O grunted a laugh. "That thing will be on top of us in a flash. Believe me, you don't want to be in the open when it hits." He turned and walked inside a nearby building. The slug buzzed with excitement. "Yeah, I know Herb, but what can you do? City people think they know everything."

The first grains of sand stung her face. Mercy fingered the spot and noticed a drop of blood staining her fingertips. "Wait for me." She hurried after her strange companions and followed them inside the swaying structure.

"This is a quick hitter." Skully O blockaded the entryway with a huge slab of wood and braced it shut. "They blow themselves out pretty fast. Soon as it's safe, I'll get the sloop, and we'll get started."

"How many people live in Skiz Town?"

"Not really sure. We were a thriving little community at one time, then the hot air mass settled over our heads and the town started dying." He brushed sand from his hands. "We can't get good jobs in the city. So most of us stay here, hoping things will get better."

"What did you do before the third moon exploded?"

A long buzz came from the parasite.

"What did he say?"

"He thinks you ask a lot of questions." Skully O grinned. "I owned a little store before things went to hell. I catered in hard-to-find items. If I didn't have what you were looking for, I'd find it."

She listened intently as the sand scrubbed the building, eating away at its crumbling surface. "How often do these things blow through?"

"Five or six times a day." Skully O peeked through a sliver in the makeshift door. "It's easing off, should be able to start out shortly."

"Great, I've got an appointment at Dragon-Fang." She rubbed a hand across her dry mouth. "You got anything to drink? I'm dry as a bone."

"Not here." Skully O shook his head. "Come on, we can make it to the sloop. Best get started while we can."

An intense buzz came from the slug.

"What's he talking about?"

"Said there's a Koloff brew in the sloop." He lifted the brace and tossed it aside, and removed the barricide. "Stay close. Don't want you getting lost." Skully O raced outside. Mercy jumped to her feet and followed rapidly.

Bits of sand, driven by the dying wind, stung her face and arms. She squinted her eyes, keeping Skully O in sight. The odd man turned into a tall building. She stopped at the entrance, staring into the darkness.

Could be a trap. He's seen my money roll. "Skully, where are you?" she shouted.

The loud clatter of an ancient motor echoed from the building. A huge tracked machine rolled toward her. It clattered, banged, and wheezed as it came to a stop. Skully O opened the side hatch. "Climb aboard, we need to get moving. We need to reach the safe zone before another storm blows up."

"What the hell is this thing?" Mercy caught the handhold and climbed aboard.

"Mining sloop. Long time ago, Kerlock Mining and Speculation had one of the biggest mines on the whole planet. When the climate went to hell, they closed down, didn't even take their equipment." He nudged two levers forward. The rusted vehicle rattled and groaned as it gained speed. "Settle in. It'll take us a little while to get there."

Mercy nodded. "Long as we get there." She opened the Koloff brew and drained the bottle in two gulps.

"You look familiar. I've seen you somewhere before."

"You ever been to McRuffians Bar?" She glanced out the filthy side window. A dark shape moved at the corner of her vision. "Was that a Duster?"

"That's Matilda. She's got a litter in my old store. When they get older, she'll take them down to the tunnels." He leaned forward, glancing through the dirt-smeared glass. "Another storm building up. We need to get past that signpost yonder."

"Can this thing go any faster?"

A rumbling buzz came from Herbert 7.

"What?"

"I've got it floored now. The old sloop ain't made for speed, but she's got plenty of power and endurance." Skully O grinned. "Don't worry. We'll make it."

"What if we don't?"

"Then you better hope the sand doesn't plug the intake on this old rust-bucket or we're dead."

"Is that one a, what did you call it, a quick hitter?"

"Nope, that's a spreader."

"A spreader?"

"All day storm."

Her eyes returned to the signpost ahead. A sour knot grew in her stomach. "It's going to be tight."

Herbert 7 chuckled.

"He said you worry too much." Skully O laughed.

Fine sand splattered on the windshield, growing in intensity and volume. The grains grew larger, pinging on the thick glass and ringing on the metal sides of the sloop.

"Good thing we're close." Skully glanced through the side glass. "That one's shaping up to be a real steamer."

Mercy glimpsed the Duster through the rearview mirror. The large animal gathered her brood and ushered them into a large hole under the building. "You know it's bad when a Duster seeks cover."

"Don't get your panties in a wad. We'll be there in two shakes." Skully showed a lop-sided grin.

A blaster shot ricocheted from the roof of the sloop.

"By Upert's beard." Skully flinched. "Who's shooting at us?"

"One of the Boogers." Mercy pulled the Dracolian from her belt. "Can't tell where he's at."

"Why?" Skully swung the control stick, the sloop turned at a sharp angle. "Why would a tunnel rat shoot at us?"

"They want to kill me." Mercy answered.

A second shot careened from the tailgate. "Damn, we've got to find some cover." He pushed the left stick forward, the tracked vehicle pivoted sharply.

Mercy held the pistol to his head. "Go for the sign."

"Are you crazy. If he hits the motor or the air scrubbers, that storm will finish us."

"Ten bills."

Skully licked his lips. The parasite chirped in his ear. "I know, but we need the money." He turned to Mercy. "What do you want me to do?"

"Get us out of the storm."

"How good can you shoot?"

"Fair." She cast him a sideways glance. "Why?"

"Pop that rear glass out and climb in the back. You've got to find the shooter and nail him."

A frenzied buzz came from the slug.

"It's ten bills." Skully pushed the right lever forward and yanked back on the left. The sloop turned on a dime and sped toward the sign. "Get back there. I don't want my noggin blowed off."

Mercy squirmed around, her back pressing on the dash. Bracing her feet on the rear glass, she marshaled all of her strength and pushed.

A third shot careened off the roof. "Hurry up, he's finding the range."

"Nearly there," Mercy said in a gruff voice. A series of web-like cracks spread across the thick glass. A fourth shot bounced off the steel-reinforced bumper.

"He's gonna nail us if you don't stop him."

A loud groan came from Mercy's lips. The cracks widened. With a final burst of energy, the glass burst free and landed in the bed.

Mercy quickly crawled through the window. Bracing her elbows on the roof, the Dracolian gripped tightly in her fists, she waited for the next shot.

Bits of sand and gravel pelted her face, filling her mouth and nose. "Hard right," she screamed.

Skully hit the lever. The vehicle turned sharply. The abruptness of the maneuver nearly threw Mercy from her perch. A blast sizzled into the dry dirt.

"I've got you now." Mercy spied the flash from a rooftop beyond the sign. She sighted down the barrel and squeezed the trigger. The round fell short. It slammed the side of the concrete structure, punching a gaping hole through the outside wall. She readjusted her angle and fired twice in rapid succession.

The top floor disappeared in a fiery explosion. Flaming debris and chunks of concrete rained to the ground. "Get us out of here before the storm hits," Mercy shouted. She huddled against the cab as the wind grew stronger, small particles stung her exposed skin.

She glanced through the fingers covering her eyes. The sandstorm swirled over her head, gathering strength. Get this damn thing moving.

Skully straightened the vehicle. The engine coughed and strained, as it approached the corroded post. They passed the marker as the storm unleashed its fury.

The force of the grit striking her lessened. Mercy brushed the sand from her eyes and stared at the maelstrom behind them. "Snagnar owes me big for this." She climbed into the cab, sand cascaded from her hair. "How long before we get to Dragon-Fang?"

"We're rolling good now." A half grin creased Skully's face. "Be there before you know it."

"Wake me when we arrive." She closed her eyes and snuggled into the cushion.

Mercy woke with a start at a violent jostling on her shoulder. She blinked her eyes several times, as she regained her senses.

"We're here."

"So I see." She studied the layout of the Dragon Fang Lounge. "Lot of guards."

"They're expecting you."

"I expect they are. What the hell is an armored unit doing here?"

"They took some fellas inside before I woke you." Skully nodded.

"A Mercurian like you, a human, and some short guy, not really sure what he was."

"Damn it, you sat here while they took them inside." Mercy's eyes narrowed. She grabbed the handle and kicked the side door open. "Those are the people I'm trying to save."

She stuffed the large Dracolian in her belt, hoping it wasn't too noticeable and darted into a nearby alley. Gotta find a way inside. A brief movement at the far end of the alley caught her attention. A small child ran down the alley and disappeared seemingly into the concrete.

Mercy raced through the garbage-filled passageway, She paused at a narrow door. The entrance was clearly built for someone nearer Joemag's size. Tight squeeze, maybe I can make it.

The door opened easily, she hunkered down and forced her body into the narrow confines. Hope none of the baddies show up now.

An interior ladder stretched toward the roof. Her back scraped against the rough wall as she climbed. Mercy reached an opening into a crude air tunnel and crawled to a side window. Don't know who built this, must have been constructed for the people of Quonset 4. She stared at a bank of windows on the third floor of the Dragon-Fang Lounge.

Her three companions were bound and kneeling before Rosebud Salen. A large Booger, a blood-crusted bandage wrapped around his head, held a blaster to Snagnar Jim's temple. Although she couldn't hear any words, the message was unmistakable. The crime lord approached his prisoners, grabbed Snagnar by the hair, and spit in his face.

Mercy had to find a way across the alley. She had to save her friends. Backing to the far wall of the ventilation chamber, she pushed off with her feet, hands scuttling across the floor. Her upper arms shattered the thin barrier. Her lower hands grabbed the window ledge propelling her into space.

The Booger shifted the weapon, drawing a bead on the flying figure. The blast destroyed the window and burned the air above her head. Her upper arms stretched out, strong hands caught the edge of the window sill. Her feet slapped the wall. Leg muscles bunched on contact with the rough surface. She kicked back with all her strength. The force of her swing carried her in a wide arch.

"Get that bitch!" Salen screamed. "Kill them all."

Mercy yanked the Dracolian from her waist as she landed. She triggered a quick shot at the injured Booger. He slumped forward, half his chest missing. "Find cover!" she shouted.

Her friends scurried behind an Oxnard table. A huge Bulber waddled toward her. The tuberous creature held a viper lance in his pudgy hands. His species were famous for their skill with the weapon.

He threw the lance with all his strength. Blue energy crackled around the tip. A sulphur smell filled the chamber. Mercy dropped to the floor. It sailed over her head. The edge sank into the far wall. The concrete bubbled, turning to a melted magma as energy leeched into the material.

"Go on, Boss." The Bulber spoke in a thick, moist voice. He placed his body between Mercy and Salen. "Get out of here."

She rolled to her feet. The Dracolian bucked in her hand. Dust rained down on Salen's head as his bodyguards shoved him through the sagging door.

Mercy lined the heavy pistol on the Bulber and squeezed the trigger. It clicked empty, the charge exhausted. Tossing the worthless weapon to the floor, she raced forward and landed a hard right and left with her upper arms. The spongy flesh gave under her fist. A yellow tongue licked at the clear fluid running from its cavernous mouth.

"You've got to do better than that." The Bulber's stomach quivered.

"What are you, some sort of radish?" Mercy lashed out, landing punch after punch.

"Racist. I'm a turnip." A back-handed blow caught Mercy on the jaw and sent her sailing to the molten wall.

"You can't fight him toe to toe," Snagnar yelled. "That's Leon Rapa, Salen's second in command. He's never been beaten in a fistfight."

"Good thing for you punks I'm not on the circuit. None of you losers could beat me." His beady eyes fastened on Mercy. He shuffled toward her, his bare feet covered with feeder roots, scraping along the floor. "You killed a lot of good men today. I gonna enjoy crushing your skull."

A thunderous crash echoed from the lower floors, followed by the sound of blaster fire. Rapa turned toward the ruckus. A flustered

Rosebud Salen ran into the room, minus his two bodyguards. A short-barreled blaster was gripped tightly in his fist.

"There's a nut in a mining sloop downstairs, yelling about ten bills," the mobster shouted. "Kill the lot. We've got to get out of here before the IGP show up."

A freakish smile spread across Rapa's face. "My thoughts exactly." He turned to Mercy.

The bartender yanked the viper lance from the wall, the tip glowed a violet hue. "Hey Shorty, don't earth people eat turnips?"

"Yeah," a gruff voice answered. "Ate them myself on occasion."

Rapa backed away on clumsy feet. "Put that down." His hand reached for the blaster on the bar. Stubby fingers circled the grip as the hot lance seared through his mid-section, the tip protruding from his back.

Mercy snatched the blaster from his limp fingers. She trained it on Salen. "You've got a choice, Rosebud. Drop the pistol or die."

The hood glanced at the dead Bulber. He dropped the blaster to the floor and lifted his hands above his head. "You win."

Skully O paused at the crumbled doorway, hands resting on his knees. "You forgot to pay us," he gasped.

"You earned every bit of it." Mercy pulled the wad of bills from her skin flap and tossed it to Skully. "Call the IGP. Tell them we have Rosebud Salen at the Dragon-Fang Lounge."

"Let me catch my breath." Skully nodded.

"Could you and Herb handle a regular job?"

"What kind of job?"

"I'm going to open a new bar, provided that Snagnar Jim wins the title this weekend." She glanced at the three men rising from cover. "Think you can handle that?"

"I'll win. Shorty told me where to concentrate my attack. The title is as good as mine."

"Good thing." She nodded. "You're gonna build us a bar, real classy place."

"I get to work in this bar?" Skully asked.

"You and the whole crowd." She answered.

"I'm in."

"Great. Now call the IGP."

"Excuse me, I'm leaving before the cops show up. We're not on good terms of late." Shorty winked at Snagnar. "Remember what I told you. Keep pounding on Beboop, and you'll get the title." His hands fell on Joemag's shoulders. "Come on, little man. I can use the company."

He nodded. "When the heat is off, we'll take you up on your offer."

Mercy pursed her lips. "The door is always open."

"Ol' Jake"

By
Bobby Nash

Ol' Jake was not unique in the galaxy.

Stop by any bar at any of the planets along the galactic arm the locals referred to as the Antares Beltway and you'll find Ol' Jake there. He'll be the one behind the bar, slinging drinks and entertaining the guests. He might not always look the same-- and sometimes he might actually be a she or an it depending on your destination-- but at the core, each and every one of them is 'Ol Jake.

Ol' Jake was an android barkeep.

Designed and mass-produced by the J-Acme Corporation of Laganos Prime, the Bartender Jake series was designed to offer a stable and reliable means of service to establishments along the Beltway, where the units were first marketed. So far, the program was a rousing success and rumor had it that the line would soon expand to other arms of the galaxy. The Ol' Jake nickname came when the advertisements pasted the zero one model as 01' too close to the word Jake in a less than flattering font. Most consumers thought it read "Ol' Jake" and the term stuck, much to the chagrin of the manufacturer, who had long since given up trying to correct their loyal customers. As long as they kept buying the units, the J-Acme Company could care less what they called them.

Ol' Jake was a standard model C7 android with a multi-phasic polycarbonite duraplast shell that housed a Trojan A-27 holo-emitter that allowed Ol' Jake to assume various shapes loaded within its database. Depending on the clientele, Ol' Jake matched to fit the occasion. On ladies night, Jake took the form of a well-built muscular man wearing tight jeans and an even tighter t-shirt over his chiseled frame. During Happy Hour, the image was generally that of a statuesque, leggy brunette wearing a short black skirt and a tight black top that showed off ample cleavage. There were multiple hair and skin colors that could be tailored to a number of species that populated the galaxy. There was no end to the outer shell Ol' Jake could take. There was even a custom setting for the more advanced users who knew how to program the android to their own specifications.

Twenty years ago, Durlan Koth opened a small bar just off Main Street in Crater Quay, the largest city on a burgeoning back world planet called Sharlotte Beta. He'd called that first bar Koth's, which, while unimaginative, was the first bar open in the city. Business boomed, and eventually, Koth expanded his operation.

On that day, the Olde Star Tavern was born.

Now, twenty years later, there was at least one Olde Star Tavern on every planet along the Antares Beltway. In some cases, there were more than one, especially on the larger core worlds where civilization thrived. Durlan Koth had turned his small neighborhood bar into a profitable enterprise, one that made him a wealthy man.

The original bar in Crater Quay was still around, although these days it was more of a historic landmark than anything else, including a profitable bar. Koth couldn't bring himself to shut down the old place, even though it brought in fewer credits than any of his bars. To save money, he had purchased an Ol' Jake to run the bar there. Not only did he save money on paying multiple flesh and blood employees to run things, Ol' Jake was an instant hit with the populace. Surprisingly, profits doubled, then later tripled.

Being a smart businessman, Durlan Koth soon had an Ol' Jake model in place behind the bar in every one of his establishments. As in Crater Quay, profits rose, and Koth expanded again. Last year, he joined the elite list of business owners earning over ten billion credits a year. Koth's fame continued to rise. He could have stopped there and basked in his successes, but he wanted more.

Although he no longer ran the day to day operations inside his bar, Durlan Koth liked to keep involved. He made it a point to visit each of his establishments on a regular basis, which kept him traveling across the breadth and width of the Antares Beltway in his private starcraft. This week, his tour brought him to Antax Prime, a bustling commerce world in the heart of the Beltway. Antax was one of a handful of planets that made up the centers of power for The Confederacy, an alliance of worlds that had banded together over a century earlier for mutual protection and expansion. The Alliance had become the Confederacy almost one hundred years ago. The centennial anniversary of the signing of the Declaration of Confederacy was only a few weeks away, and celebrations were planned on all of the planets along the Beltway. Antax housed the seat of the Confederacy.

Each of the Olde Star Tavern locations were planning to throw a bash to celebrate. It was going to be the biggest party the citizens of the Confederacy had ever seen.

The shift started off like any other shift.

Durlan Koth's driver dropped him off at the entrance of the main Antax City location. There were three Olde Star Taverns on Antax, each of them profitable, although none so much as the one he was visiting that morning.

"Good morning, Ol' Jake," he said as he turned on the lights.

"Good morning, Mr. Koth," Ol' Jake said in a robotic monotone as he powered up. The unit was in sleep mode until the lights came on. With his holo-emitters turned off, a power-saving feature that extended the life of the emitters when Ol' Jake powered down for the night, the robotic bartender looked very much out of place behind the polished wood veneer. Although he had seen the robots in this form many times before, it never failed to look odd to him.

"How're tricks, Jake?"

"Tricks are good, sir," Jake said, his voice morphing from an electronic timbre to a silky smooth voice as the unit reverted to its primary holo-shell. At the customer's request, the units were fitted with a default holographic shell. All of Durlan Koth's robots defaulted to this same look. The brunette was tall with long bare legs stretching away from a short skirt to the strapped high heels she wore. Her shirt was black with the Olde Star Tavern logo emblazoned on the front. Not only was this look a favorite of Koth's, but it seemed to be popular with most of the clientele on many worlds along the Beltway.

Not for the first time, Koth wondered if she had been patterned on a real woman. And if so, what had happened to her.

Koth took a seat at the bar and pulled several sheets of paper from his briefcase. He powered up the computer interface tablet as well. A holographic screen flared to life above the tiny device.

"Will you be joining us for the full day, sir?" Jake asked. She had started to wipe down the bar, despite the fact, there were no customers. Koth assumed that was one of the robots pre-programmed tasks.

"I'm afraid not. I'm neck deep in planning this centennial celebration thing. I've already rented out the vacant warehouse next door and have workers coming in to get it fixed up nice as an overflow to handle the crowds."

"A great idea, sir. That should accommodate the crowds nicely," Jake said. "Are you going to bring in extra help as well?"

"Yes. I've hired on some locals to serve," Koth said. "I'm also thinking about bringing in a few more Ol' Jake models to help out."

The bartender said nothing, kept wiping down the bar.

Koth noticed the lull in the conversation. It was unusual for Ol' Jake to drift off from such a discussion. "Does that bother you?" he asked, curious.

"Why would that bother me, sir?" Jake said. "It is a sensible precaution considering the number of patrons we are expecting for the celebration."

"You just seemed... I don't know, distracted."

"Not at all, sir. I am merely running through the day's schedule." Jake snapped her fingers. "Where are my manners, Mr. Koth. "I forgot to ask you if you wanted a drink." She smiled. "Not very smart for a bartender, eh?"

"It's a little early for me yet, Jake, but I wouldn't say no to a cup of coffee."

"You got it, boss." Jake moved off to start a pot of coffee brewing.

When the door chime sounded, Koth was surprised. He hadn't been expecting visitors. "I'm sorry. We're not open for business yet," he said as he turned to face the early morning customers.

There were five of them, four men and one woman. Each was dressed in a fine business suit that looked for all the world like it was freshly tailored and never been worn before. Two of the men remained outside but took positions near the door. The other three entered, lead by a man with a big smile and an outstretched hand.

"That's okay, Mr. Koth," the lead gentleman said. "My name is Tollok Bey. And we're not here to drink."

***

Durlan Koth wasn't sure he'd heard correctly.

"Let me get this straight," he said. "You want to rent out my bar on the centennial celebration day?"

"That is correct, yes."

"Are you crazy? That's probably the busiest day we've got coming up. This place will be packed. I can't afford to turn away business like that."

"I assure you, we can make it worth your while, Mr. Koth," Bey said.

"May I ask why?"

"My card," Bey said, handing over a thin plasticard. As soon as Koth's thumb touched the card, a holographic heads-up display hovered above the card. A head scan of Tollok Bey was there, rotating back and forth as if he were on a turntable. Koth read the man's information and couldn't believe it, so he reread it.

"Is this for real?"

"Yes," Bey said. "I work for Alvi Stinston."

Koth deactivated the card's hologram. "What does the top aide to the President of the Confederate Alliance want with my bar?"

"It's simple, Mr. Koth. President Stinston is a fan of this establishment. He spent quite a bit of time in here... before he was elected to office, of course."

"I had no idea."

"Of course not," Bey said around a disarming smile. "It was a long time ago. With the centennial celebration coming up, my boss wanted to give something back to the community. It was his idea to hold a party here. In addition to the credits you'll be paid to suspend your normal business for the night, you'll gain a good deal of exposure for your establishment from the media coverage the President's live address will garner."

"He would give the centennial address here?"

"That's the plan," Bey said. "All you have to do is say yes."

Koth's smile spread. "How could I say no, Mr. Bey? You've got yourself a deal."

"Excellent. There's a lot to do to secure the area before the President arrives."

"Of course," Koth said. "My bar is your bar."

"Very well, Mr. Koth. Someone from my office will be in touch today."

Durlan Koth was still floating on air after Tollok Bey left.

"Did you hear that, Jake?" he said.

"I did indeed, sir. May I be the first to offer you my congratulations?" Ol' Jake said as she placed a fresh drink in front of the jovial bar owner.

"This could be big for me," Koth continued. "The President of the Confederate Alliance is going to talk live to the entire Antares Beltway, maybe even to star systems beyond, and he's going to do it from this bar."

"It's one for the history books, sir," Jake said.

Koth's eyes widened. "You're right. I hadn't even considered that. For years, when school children learn about the centennial celebration address, my name will be associated with it. Long after I'm gone, my legacy will live on. If only they..." his voice caught. "If only my parents had lived to see my success."

"I'm sure they would be very proud, sir," Jake said before wandering back to work.

"You bet they would," Koth said.

***

The leader went over the plan again.

He had worked out contingencies for every possible scenario. His group was determined to have their message heard. They were going to ignite a fire that would spread across the entirety of The Beltway and beyond. He prepared a speech and stood before the recorder in the tiny apartment he had rented under an assumed name in Antax City.

"People of The Confederacy," he started. "I address you today as a patriot. For far too long I have sat back and watched as the confederation that I love slowly slipped away, only to be replaced by greed and corruption. No longer are we a coalition of planets and peoples joined together for a common cause. No, now we are a group of systems out to take what we can for ourselves while our neighbors starve to death in filth and squalor. We have become a nation of predators."

He paused, let out a small resigned sigh.

"No longer are we an alliance. That term no longer applies. In an alliance, all are equal under the eyes of the law as well as the Most Holy. Look around you, my friends. Do you honestly believe that The Confederacy remains an alliance? Can you recall the last time any of our leaders worked together for the greater cause of the citizens instead of lining their own pockets at the expense of the common man?"

The leader's expression hardened.

"I, and others like me, can no longer stand by and watch as the Confederacy that we love is torn apart by the misguided few who have seized power for themselves. No longer will we stay silent. We are legion, and our voices shall be heard. You never know who among you feels as we do."

The camera zoomed in closer.

"To those of you out there, brothers and sisters, husbands and wives, children of a system of government that has betrayed you, I implore you to rise up against those who have led us down this path toward destruction. Rise up and let your voices be heard. Rise up and prove your loyalty to The Confederacy and everything the alliance stands for. It's time to rise up and take back that which is rightfully ours."

The camera zoomed in even closer.

"We are patriots--

--and we are everywhere."

The recording ended. He watched the playback and smiled. It had gone better than he had expected. Truly, the spirit had gotten into him as he spoke. A feeling of excitement flowed through him. For too many years, this plan was little more than a dream, one that he hoped would come, but also one that he wasn't sure would ever arrive.

"I think we're ready," he told the small group standing nearby. His people. Never had he been so proud of them as he was at that moment. There was a lot to do and so little time.

"We're on the clock," he said, checking his chronometer. "Are you ready?"

A chorus of shouts filled the small apartment. The time had come.

"Showtime," he said.

***

When celebration day arrived, the city went wild.

Everyone in the capital took to the streets in a wild frenzy of song, food, drink, dancing, and music. Finding anyone not celebrating in some form or fashion was impossible. Even those in the service industry, who had to work, found ways to make the most of the event.

The Olde Star Tavern was a flurry of activity as the crowds poured in. It was standing room only as Ol' Jake flitted back and forth from one patron to the next, filling and mixing drinks as fast as the orders were placed. For the busiest day of the year, Durlan Koth had opted to go with Ol' Jake's leggy brunette look. She seemed to be a favorite of the customers, her tips always more than any of the other holographic bartender images the robot had at its disposal. Since Ol' Jake was basically an appliance to the owner, not much different than a blender, all tips went to the house. After all, what did a robot need with money?

It was an hour before the President's scheduled arrival and Alliance Secret Service was already on hand. All patrons of the bar were screened prior to entry, an extra security measure when hosting a VIP of President Stinston's stature. Despite a few grumblings about the wait to get in, there were not any major complaints. Everyone understood the need for heightened security.

Agent Bressler of the Confederate Secret Service stood at the end of the bar, his eyes darting about the room, always looking for dangers, always on guard against those who would threaten his president's safety. As the agent in charge, he was responsible for keeping his boss, the President, safe. With crowds filling the streets in joyous celebration, he would be hard-pressed to adequately secure any space on the planet.

Ol' Jake sidled up next to him. "Would you care for a drink, Agent Bressler?"

"I can't," he said. "I'm on duty."

"We do serve water," Jake reminded him as she handed over a cold glass.

The agent almost cracked a smile as he accepted the frosty glass. "Thank you."

"My pleasure. Let me know if you need another."

One of the bartender's primary functions, beyond serving drinks, was to recognize the customer's needs. This skill had served others in the same industry since the invention of alcohol. Your friendly neighborhood bartender was your server, a sympathetic ear to bend, and sometimes part psychiatrist. You would be amazed at the things people will tell their bartender that they wouldn't tell their best friend. Through a series of algorithms and data gathered from multiple surveys from across the Beltway. Ol' Jake was programmed to pick up on emotions ranging from anger to despair, happiness to shy. The unit was also equipped to predict dangers.

The first hint of something being amiss came early. Even as she continued to pour drinks, Ol' Jake replayed the memory files to see if she could find what had tripped the danger alarm. She considered alerting Agent Bressler or even the bar's owner, but without evidence, all she had was a... feeling.

But that is impossible, isn't it?

With the increased traffic in the bar, Koth had brought on extra bar-backs to keep the taps running, and the bottles replenished. There was a steady stream of muscular men carrying boxes in and out. Ol' Jake stepped aside as the latest box of Antarian Rum was unpacked, the bottles slid onto the shelf beneath the bar for easy access. The rum was a popular choice, especially in the capital city. It was also a favorite drink of President Stinston.

"Is everything okay?" Koth asked as he stopped by the bar.

"Everything is good, sir," Ol' Jake said without interrupting the flow. "Drink orders have already passed by this establishment's previous record. I would call tonight a success."

"As would I," Koth said. "Keep up the good work."

"I shall."

***

The leader shook his head once he stepped inside the Olde Star Tavern.

The workday had barely begun, and already citizens had come out to get an early start on the day's festivities. It was shameful. The people of The Confederacy had lost their way, and it broke his heart. No longer did the people work for the betterment of their homes. Now, it was all about me.

It was time to change that.

Once he learned that Confederate President Alvi Stinston was going to address the people of The Confederacy from the Olde Star Tavern, he put his plan into action. He applied for a job with the owner, a slovenly sort who was hiring those with strong backs and willing to work for poverty-level wages for a single day, maybe two if the party spilled over. With unemployment levels at an all-time high, there were plenty to choose from who would work for such a paltry sum.

The leader hated taking work from those who needed it more than him, but it was imperative that he be on site to put his plan into motion. He would donate his salary, meager though it would be, to charity when all was said and done.

Provided, of course, he survived it.

That was an outcome he could not guarantee.

Steeling himself for the task at hand, he opened the door and walk inside. The bartender was wiping down the bar, even though it didn't seem dirty to him. "Good morning," he said.

"Good morning," the attractive woman behind the bar said. "How can I help you?"

"I'm looking for Durlan Koth," he said. "I'm scheduled to start work today. I'm a little early." He smiled.

"Of course. Please have a seat, and I'll get him," the bartender said.

"Thank you, ma'am," the leader said.

The brunette walked off and headed through a swinging door at the far end of the bar that led to a back room where the owner no doubt kept an office.

The leader popped a handful of peanuts from a dish on the bar into his mouth. He hated nuts but loved the salt. Plus, he wanted to make sure he blended into the crowd. He was on his second handful of nuts when the owner arrived, followed by the bartender,

"I'm Durlan Koth. Thank you for joining us," he said.

The leader pasted on a practiced smile. "My pleasure, sir. I can't think of any other place I'd rather be today."

"Then let's get to work."

"Yes, sir. It's going to be a busy day."

***

Something was bothering Ol' Jake.

As an android, the bartender wasn't programmed with emotions of his own, but the unit's programming did include a multitude of scenarios that someone working behind the bar might encounter. Ol' Jake had algorithms for romantic questions, tending to a customer with a broken heart, offering a friendly, if not rhetorical, shoulder to cry on, unhappy patrons complaining about their boss, their job, their spouse, children, friends, relatives, and the like, and so many more.

Ol' Jake had yet to run across a situation that he had not been prepared to face.

Unlike living, breathing bartenders, Ol' Jake didn't get gut feelings. He had no hunches to play. He would simply interpret the accumulated data in his processors and determine the best response.

Today, however, something was off, but he couldn't explain it.

It wasn't one thing, one definitive issue that was causing this concern.

While Ol' Jake continued working, a part of him reviewed the data collected over the past few hours.

If there were something wrong, he would find it.

***

The President arrived an hour later than scheduled.

By then, the party was already in full swing. Revelers from all over the Antares Beltway had descended on the capital city, packing every bar, restaurant, park, and venue to capacity. Like all of the others, the Olde Star Tavern was packed to the rafters.

The president's motorcade took the only unoccupied street in the city to the side entrance of the additional space Durlan Koth had rented for the event. A special, highly guarded entrance was used to escort President Stinston backstage.

Koth was there to meet the leader of the free worlds.

"You have my deepest thanks for hosting this tonight, Mr. Koth," Stinston said as they shook hands. "Looks like you've got quite the turnout."

"It's a special day, Mr. President," Koth said. "If you need anything, just let me know, and we'll make it happen."

"I appreciate that, sir."

After a few minutes of pleasantries, Agent Bressler appeared at the president's side and whispered something in his ear.

"Thank you," Stinston said. "If you'll excuse me, Mr. Koth. A couple matters of state to deal with before we get started."

"Of course," Koth said. "We'll get started as soon as you're ready."

As the president and his secret service detail walked away, Tollok Bey, Stinston's aide, approached. "A pleasure to see you again, Mr. Koth. You've done a great job with the place."

"Thank you, Mr. Bey. I'm happy with how everything is working out."

Bey passed a small piece of paper to the bar owner. "Here is a list of what the president and his staff would like to drink. If you could see to that?"

"Of course," Koth said.

"Make sure you send the bill to my office," Bey said.

"Of course," Koth said with a smile. He had been wondering how he was going to broach the subject of payment. Now he was glad he didn't have to do so. "I'll have them delivered to you shortly."

"Thank you."

Bey left to catch up with his party as a smiling Koth went back to the bar to place his order. It's turning out to be a great day, he thought.

Pushing through the crowd, he finally made it back to the bar where Ol' Jake was holding things steady. "How's it going?" he asked.

"Everything's great," Jake said though holographic lips. "Do you need something, sir?"

He passed across the list of drinks. "Here's another order for you. It's for our guests."

"Give me a minute," she said and went to work.

Watching Ol' Jake work was always a sight, no matter what holographic form the robot took. Today was no exception. Holographic hands mixed drinks with smooth efficiency, spilling nary a drop. Each drink would be perfect, too. Ol' Jake was nothing if not consistent on that score.

There were more drinks than Koth could carry alone, so he called over two of the bar backs he'd hired for the day to help him. Each of them took a tray of drinks and followed the owner to the back.

As Ol' Jake watched them go, that uneasy sensation returned.

***

President Stinston was a natural politician.

He was instantly likable by those who voted for him as well as those who had not. His administration had been referred to as the greatest in decades. So far, President Stinston had not been involved in a single scandal, had very few negative headlines, and presided over one of the most peaceful eras the Confederacy had ever seen. They were going to celebrate the one-hundredth anniversary of the Confederacy during a time of peace and prosperity.

After spending an hour meeting and speaking with his constituents, the president made his way slowly to the stage where he would give a special State of the Confederacy address. His aide and security detail had tried repeatedly to speed the process along, but their charge was not cooperating. The stage was a secure area. On the floor, surrounded by thousands of revelers, the President was at risk.

The President, like so many others who held the position before him, had no intention of making their jobs easy. He was fond of saying "a president cannot live inside a protective bunker. A true leader has to be out there among the people."

It made for a good president.

It made for a bad protectee.

Despite Agent Bressler's urgings, it took another hour for his boss to finally make it to the staging area. With a wave to the crowd, the president was whisked behind a curtain into a waiting area behind the stage.

"Great crowd," Stinston said as he accepted a drink from Durlan Koth.

"We are honored to have you here, Mr. President," the Olde Star Tavern's owner said, offering a slight bow.

"The honor is mine, Mr. Koth," Stinston said before downing the glass of water. On his own orders, he wasn't allowed anything stronger than spring water before a speech. After his political obligations were fulfilled, he had already placed an order for an Altarren Whiskey, neat.

On the other side of the curtain, Tollok Bey had started addressing the crowd, getting them ready before the president came out to make his speech.

"He's really good," Koth said, listening to Bey's banter with the audience.

"Yes. I've never met a more natural formal speaker," Stinston said. "He certainly makes my job easier."

"I look forward to your speech, sir. If you'll excuse me," Koth said, offering a slight nod before heading off to check on bar business.

Suddenly alone for the first time since his arrival, President Alvi Stinston relaxed. His job was demanding, to say the least, but he had known what to expect going in. Thinking back on it, he had come a long way from the eager young man who had petitioned to become an elected official on his homeworld of Traxxol V, but yet he still felt there was still a longer road ahead of him. There was more he had to do yet.

Bey made a joke, which worked up the crowd. Once the laughter died down, Stinston signaled one of the many functionaries that followed along in his wake that he was ready. The aide ran onto the stage and whispered the message into Bey's ear.

Tollok Bey smiled. "Ladies and gentlemen of Antax, and to those of you watching from across the Antares Beltway, in honor of the one-hundredth anniversary of the founding of the Confederacy, it is my honor to present to you, the President of the Confederacy, Alvi Stinston."

A roar of applause exploded across the great hall, echoing through the streets as the president's address was broadcast to every planet within the Confederacy and on the worlds allied with the great state. The only way anyone would miss this broadcast is if they were trying hard.

Stinston blew out a breath, took another sip of water, and pasted on his best presidential smile before heading out to the stage.

The crowd went wild the moment he walked out onto the raised dais overlooking a crowd of thousands. Monitor screens mounted around the room allowed him to see as the broadcast showed images from multiple planets along the Beltway as Celebration Day was in full bloom.

Stinston waved to the crowds.

They loved him, and he loved them.

It took several minutes for the applause to die down. As he waited, the president waved, pointing out a select few in attendance who either contributed to his campaign, held an important position within the government, or could be of use at a later date.

"Good evening," Stinston said once the roar subsided to a loud murmur. "It is my honor and privilege to stand before you today on this most special of occasions," he said. "One hundred years. It seems so long ago, but yet not so long at the same time. One hundred years. They have not always been easy years, but from adversity grows strength."

The crowd roared.

"And our confederacy is indeed powerful. We have overcome a great many obstacles in our brief hundred year history, my friends. There have been wars, scandal, illness, and hundreds of other words to describe the trials and tribulations that brought us to this moment."

The crowd cheered.

"One hundred years," he said and smiled. "And we're just getting started."

Nearby, the leader watched and waited.

Soon, he thought. Soon.

***

"Excuse me a moment."

With a polite excuse to the customers at the bar, Ol' Jake stepped out from behind the polished veneer, calling over one of the extra staff on hand to help with the high capacity crowd. Normally, Ol' Jake would be the only barkeep on hand, but not even an android of Ol' Jake's skill could handle this crowd alone.

"Where are you going?" the young woman asked as she stepped into her spot behind the bar.

"I'll be back in a minute. Hold down the fort until I get back."

"Oh-okay," the back up said. Her voice was unsure. "Hurry back, okay?"

"I'll be back as quickly as possible."

Something was wrong. Ol' Jake was certain of it. There was a hint of danger with Durlan Koth, and the other two men had been at the bar. That sense of dread had only increased since the president's address had begun. Like the rest of the bar's patrons, Ol' Jake's attention was on one of the many monitors that lined the walls of the Olde Star Tavern. The president was in the middle of his speech, and the crowd was enthralled. The android had heard words such as charismatic, charming, and smooth to describe President Stinston. From the footage he had seen, Ol' Jake understood why. The man was a fantastic speaker. His words struck a chord in the emotions of his constituents and made them feel better. Of course, Ol' Jake was immune to such things. As an android, he was not programmed to feel anything.

And yet...

Something was causing the android's warning bells to go off. What Ol' Jake didn't know, was why.

He planned to find out.

To better replicate the humanoid form, the Ol' Jake android was built as close to the most common life form in the galaxy. That meant two arms, two legs, one head, and opposable thumbs. Granted, this wasn't the only configuration available in the unit's holomatrix, but it was the one purchased most often. The unit's holographic outer shell could change its appearance, but beneath its outward appearance was a fully autonomous and mobile machine.

And surprisingly, quiet on its feet for all the weight packed into Ol' Jake's thin frame.

Ol' Jake was halfway through the crown when the first shot was fired.

***

The crowd didn't react at first.

Fireworks and party poppers had been going off all day. One more POP in the middle of hundreds of others went by all but unnoticed by everyone.

--Unless they had an android hearing.

Ol' Jake recognized the sound immediately as a Kinski Auger pistol. The Kinski Auger was a powerful handgun, favored by criminals all up and down the Beltway. They were fairly inexpensive weapons, small enough to easily conceal on a person beneath a jacket or a loose shirt, and it packed a punch. They were available for purchase pretty much everywhere, including less than reputable sellers who did not bother with those pesky laws concerning waiting periods or background checks.

"Pardon me. Coming through" 'Ol Jake picked up the pace,

pushing her way through the crowd. Several patrons tried to stop her to chat or to inquire about another drink, but the android bartender ignored them.

As a member of the League of Intergalactic Bartenders, there were certain guild rules that Ol' Jake had to follow just as any flesh and blood bartender would. It was a short list, but an important one. Bartenders throughout the guild were taught these rules from their first day on the job. For Ol' Jake, they came preinstalled standard on each unit.

A bartender shall listen to his customer though he may charge a price. That price is not necessarily monetary.

The confessional of a customer to bartender shall be considered sacrosanct.

A bartender shall, at his or her discretion, serve the drink the customer needs, not necessarily the one the customer orders.

A bartender shall not leave the bar until the last customer is gone.

As an artificial life form, Ol' Jake had a few additional laws pre-programmed into his circuits. One of those, and the one he considered the most important, was to keep the customers safe. It was a sacred oath.

Ol' Jake's holographic form shimmered as he switched to one of his male personas. Patrons moved out of the way when they saw this form coming their way for fear of being bowled over. As the Ol' Jake android body was rather heavy, barreling through the crowd wasn't much of a problem, but as he wasn't interested in hurting anyone that was not an option.

"One side, please," Ol' Jake said. "Step aside."

The going was slower than it should have been. When the second shot was fired, Ol' Jake had only made it halfway to the staging area.

He quickened his pace.

With the third shot, some of the patrons must have realized that it was more than a simple party favors popping and exploding. Someone screamed, and a drink hit the floor, shattering the glass. Then came a shove, an innocent bump. Then another shove as the herd of revelers started to move away from the perceived danger.

By the fourth shot, pandemonium reigned.

***

Nothing was going according to plan.

The leader and one of his lieutenants had made his way within striking distance of his target. All they had to do was bide their time until the proper hour. It was perfect.

And then his lieutenant jumped the gun.

He had been serving drinks to Tollok Bey, the aide de camp to the president after he cleared the stage for President Stinston to take over. The aide took his drink with a smile and tried to engage the lieutenant in small talk. It was not a skill at which the leader's young friend excelled, which Bey noticed--

--and questioned.

"Stay cool," the leader whispered, even though his young friend couldn't hear him across the room. Even had he shouted, the president's address blaring through the room's speakers would have drowned him out. He hoped that pure force of will might be enough to reach his comrade.

It wasn't.

The lieutenant, that was the only name he knew him by because, for security reasons, none of them had shared their real names, panicked. He pushed the presidential aide backward, sending glasses filled with top-shelf alcoholic beverages crashing to the duracrete floor where they shattered into dozens of tiny shards.

Suddenly, the room's din died down, and all eyes were trained on the center of the disturbance. The lieutenant went for his weapon, and the leader cursed silently. That little fool is going to ruin things!

The moment one of the Secret Service Agents saw the weapon, he lunged for the gunman in an attempt to subdue or disarm him. In the panicked confusion of the room, it was hard to tell.

The lieutenant was faster.

The first shot went wild, missing the agent and hitting the ceiling where a newly formed hole rained dust down on the crowd. It was all the time the agent needed to get in close. He slammed into the lieutenant, each of them sprawling to the floor, wrestling for control of the gun.

The second shot caught the agent square in the chest. At close ranger, the Kinski Auger was deadly, especially when placed on its highest setting as it was then. The close impact blew a gaping hole through the area where the agent's heart had been only seconds before, killing him instantly.

The lieutenant pushed the corpse off of him and scrambled backward as the dead man's companions rushed forward, their own weapons drawn. He was outnumbered, outgunned, and assumed he was about to die.

Hands shaking, he raised his weapon.

One of the Secret Service Agent's was faster on the draw.

The lieutenant was dead before he could squeeze the trigger.

Already, the other agents were on the move, securing the area and moving the stunned president from the stage to safety. It was earlier than the plan called for, but the leader knew if he didn't act at that moment, he might never get another chance. He pulled his own weapon and fired twice, putting down the two agents near his fallen comrade.

The crowd, already spooked, exploded into a full-bore frenzy. The party all but forgotten, the patrons were now only content with one thing: escape. They pushed at one another as they clogged the exits. Some fell and were trampled as the throng surged forward. The bar's owner and security tried to settle them down, but their cries for calm fell on deaf ears.

For the leader, the pandemonium worked in his favor. With the crowds surging toward the exits, the president's escape route had been compromised. That meant they had to revert to their back up plan. The leader had been prepared for that, had been counting on it in fact.

Agent Bressler and his team had secured an anteroom off from the main hall. It was cramped compared to the area where he had been sitting.

"What's happening?" Stinston demanded.

"Trouble, sir," Bressler said. "We're cut off from the exit. "Go over there to the corner and sit tight. We'll keep you safe."

"Where's Tollok?"

"I don't know, Mr. President," Bressler said. "He's not my detail. You are."

"Someone needs to check up on him, Agent Bressler," the president started.

"Someone is, sir. Now, please, let us do our job."

***

Ol' Jake pushed through the crowd into the room just in time to see the Secret Service Agents take down the shooter. He recognized the man as one of the additional bar backs brought on to help with the crowds.

He had not been alone.

Sensitive scanners searched the room in search of the shooter's partner. Ol' Jake deduced that the two men he had seen with Durlan Koth were probably partners. If one of them had hostile intentions, then it was a safe bet that his friend had similar plans.

Ol' Jake was not built for combat. The designers of the android bartender had at one time considered the units for potential military application, but their plans had to be scrapped when the android's proved unable to effectively fight in a war. The skills were there, but at its heart, the android was an artificial life form and was subject to the core laws of A.I. manufacture. One of those immutable laws was preserving the sanctity of biological life. No matter how hard they tried to bypass it, the androids would not indiscriminately kill the opposing army's troops.

A war fought by soldiers who would not kill didn't seem like much of a war to those who commanded the battle plans so the project was scrapped and the androids put down their guns and picked up bottles and glasses.

Not that any of the Ol' Jake androids couldn't defend themselves.

They simply chose non-lethal alternatives.

Biologics, on the other hand, were not so thoughtful. Ol' Jake watched as the shooter fell to the floor, his life essence draining from him. He was no longer a threat, but his friend was still there. Ol' Jake scanned the room.

He found the other one off to the side, trying to blend into the crowd, but moving against the flow toward the partitioned off area, which was one of three places where he deduced that the president would be taken in case of an emergency.

Ol' Jake plotted the fasted route to the man he believed was the cause of the disturbance and pushed his way forward, cleaving a path through the panicked crowd. "One side! Coming through! Step aside, please!"

Reviewing the options open to him, Ol' Jake devised a plan.

***

Everything had gone to blazes.

The carefully laid plan of the leader had disintegrated into nothingness due to the actions of one man. One blunder had unraveled all of his meticulous planning. All was not lost, however. The leader had plans within plans. There were contingencies in place for every possible scenario he and his benefactor could account for and a few that seemed so outlandish on the face of it. Even if the leader fell, there were others poised to take his place.

They were prepared for anything.

Or so he thought.

Four Secret Service Agents were guarding President Stinston. He was outnumbered, but thankfully, he was not alone. The lieutenant had been only one of his men embedded in the event. The sergeant, the colonel, and the insider were all in the area. That evened the odds considerably, but he only had eyes on the colonel. The other two were nowhere in sight. He hoped they had not fouled up as the lieutenant had done.

He signaled the colonel, who nodded his understanding. They moved toward the stage's edges, each taking a different route to the staging area. With any luck, they would be able to catch then unaware.

The colonel pulled his sidearm from a hidden pocket and moved forward.

The leader kept his weapon hidden until he was closer. He didn't want to risk being spotted.

It was a smart plan.

The colonel took up his position and waited for the leader's signal. The insider showed up, better late than never, and pulled a pack from the container of glasses he was delivering. The leader was well aware of the contents of the pack. That was the final solution. If they couldn't convince the president that they were serious, then the package would be used.

Inside was enough explosive to take out an entire city block when detonated.

The leader was just about to slide behind the stage when he heard a new commotion nearby. He turned just in time to see the sergeant fighting with a man he had not seen before.

Whoever the new arrival was, he wouldn't be able to stop them in time.

The leader nodded to the insider.

And the bomb was armed.

***

Ol' Jake saw the man pull a gun.

His database identified the weapon as a Kinski Auger, a handgun favored by criminals across the entire Beltway after government policy made it illegal to own the weapon, which was capable of mass casualties due to it firing not only projectiles but also energy beams and bursts. All energy emitting weaponry had been outlawed in the Confederacy a few years earlier. It was one of the first laws initiated under President Stinston's administration.

The gunman pulled the Kinski Auger from a hidden pocket inside his work suit. Like the man who had triggered Ol' Jake's need to investigate further, the gunman was dressed as a bar worker, one of the temporary employees brought on to help with the extra crowds.

"What are you doing with that gun?" Ol' Jake asked him.

The gunman spun around and faced Jake, who wore the form of a handsome, muscular male native to the city. In this persona, Ol' Jake even spoke with a slight local accent.

"Hold it right there," the gunman said.

"I can't do that, sir."

The gunman was known as the sergeant to his group. Ol' Jake had no way to know that. All the android knew was that this man was a threat to the bar and its patrons. It was his duty as a bartender to protect not only his customers but the bar as well.

"Stand down," Ol' Jake said.

The sergeant pointed the Kinski Auger directly at Ol' Jake's holographic face. "I told you to stay back."

"And I told you that I cannot do that."

To Ol' Jake's precision sensors, most humans moved in slow motion. Before the gunman could pull the trigger, the android detected the tightening of tendons in his hand as his finger twitched against the trigger. It was all the time he needed to analyze the situation and take action.

Ol' Jake swiped the gun away with a flick of his hand, sending the bolt of energy toward the ceiling where it blew a small hole. Dust fell to the floor from the disintegrated duracrete. With his other hand, Ol' Jake grabbed the man by the front of his shirt and lifted him off the floor.

Startled by his strength, the gunman panicked and dropped his gun.

Ol' Jake carried the man over toward the wall where a temporary bar had been set up to collect and refill empty glasses. He lowered the gunman back to the floor next to the bar.

"Stay here," Ol' Jake said.

Then he bent the metal railing and twisted it around the man's hand.

He was trapped.

Ol' Jake had to hurry. His sensors detected the man's partners moving in on the area behind the stage. Whatever their plan, it went beyond simply disrupting the president's speech.

Jake sprinted across the room, covering the distance within seconds. He grabbed the man next to the stage and incapacitated him quickly with a non-lethal nerve pinch. The man dropped to the floor in a heap, his gun clattering to the floor.

It was just loud enough to alert the president's detail. An agent ran toward him.

"Agent Redding. Secret Service. Who are you?" the agent asked.

"I'm just the bartender," Ol' Jake said. He pointed to the two men he had disarmed. "These men were armed, and I believe have hostile intent toward the president."

"There was an attempt on his life. We don't know how many were in on it," the agent explained.

Jake pointed to the man on the stage and the other one at the far end. "I believe there are at least two more involved. Those two men are also armed."

The agent ran toward the stage, and Ol' Jake followed suit.

"Hold it right there!" the agent shouted to the man on the stage.

The colonel turned and fired his weapon without hesitation.

Ol' Jake slammed against the agent, knocking him out of harm's way just as the energy blast passed him. "Are you damaged?" Ol' Jake asked.

"I'll live," the agent said with a grunt as he got to his feet. "You hit like a mule, man."

"Thank you," Ol' Jake said, not understanding the comment.

The Colonel fired again, but this time Agent Redding was prepared. He sidestepped the blast and fired his own weapon twice, dropping the would-be assassin to the stage.

"That leaves only one," Ol' Jake said.

"Warn the president!" Agent Redding shouted, pointing toward the stage as he ran to catch up with the leader. "Go!"

Ol' Jake did as he was instructed. He leapt onto the stage and ran to the rear exit. He burst through the curtain and found himself facing another gun pointed in his direction.

This time it was held by Agent Bressler.

"Don't even think about it," Bressler said.

"Oh, good. Agent Bressler, it's you."

"Do I know you?"

"I've come to warn you," Ol' Jake said. "Oh, wait, you did not meet me in this configuration." The android's holo-emitter flared to life, and Ol' Jake resumed the shell of an attractive brunette bartender.

"Holy..."

"One of your agents, Agent Redding, and I stopped three of them, but there's one more armed intruder coming." She pointed toward the direction where Agent Redding had chased the last gunman. "Unless they double back, I believe they will enter through there."

The agents moved into position, putting themselves between President Stinston and the entrance. They didn't have to wait long. The leader burst through the entrance with his gun blazing. One agent took a hit and dropped.

The others opened fire. The leader took one hit, then another. He dropped to the floor, still alive, but barely.

The president pushed his way through the agents, despite Bressler's warning that he keep back. "Why did you do this?" he asked the dying man. "What did you hope to gain?"

"Freedom," the leader croaked. "All I wanted was to... free my... my people..."

"Free them from whom?"

"From you," the leader said around a cough. "The Confederacy is... is broken. It has been for... long time. We... it must be... fixed."

"Broken how?" the president asked. "I need to understand. I can't help you if I don't know what you want."

"Doesn't..." another cough. "Doesn't matter. Still, have one... one last card... to play." The leader looked toward the stage before his body sagged in death.

All eyes turned toward the stage.

"The pack!" Redding shouted.

Agent Bressler pushed the president back, covering him with his own body even as Redding took off toward the stage.

Ol' Jake was faster. Moving quickly, the android leapt up onto the stage and landed next to the pack. Not bothering with the zipper, he ripped open the bag and scanned the device inside.

"What is it?" Redding asked, slightly out of breath.

"I believe it is a bomb, Agent Redding," Ol' Jake said matter-of-factly.

"Can you disarm it?"

"I am uncertain. My programming does not include military applications. All I know is what it takes to successfully run a bar."

"Oh, great. Any idea how long we've got?"

"A matter of seconds," Ol' Jake said. "Maybe a minute."

Redding turned and saw Bressler and his men clear the president out of the building now that the crowd had dispersed. The sound of squealing tires told him that his team would get the president to safety. That was good, but it did nothing to safeguard the several thousand people nearby who would be caught in the blast radius. There was no time to evacuate all of them.

"I'm open to suggestion," Redding said.

"You should run," Ol' Jake said. "I do not know if this will work."

Redding shook his head. "If it doesn't, there's nowhere for me to run. Do it."

Ol' Jake reached into the bag, clamped the explosive device in his powerful hands--

--and squeezed.

Metal bent and plastic shattered as the device was reduced to nothing more than a bag full of spare parts, but the danger was not past. Electric energy sparked and popped, igniting the synthetic polymers of the bag.

"The bomb's range has been severely limited, but it will still explode," Ol' Jake told Agent Redding. "I'd suggest you run."

The Secret Service Agent did as he was told. He leapt off the stage seconds ahead of the blast. He hit the floor hard and covered the back of his head with his hands.

After a moment, he realized that the worst was behind him. He rolled over and looked back to the stage that was all but destroyed. Small fires dotted the area as pieces of the stage had been scattered about the room.

Ol' Jake stood there, his holographic shell flickering in and out of existence.

"Are you okay?" Redding asked.

"Aside from some physical damage, I appear to be undamaged, thank you, Agent Redding."

"No. Thank you. You saved my life."

"Just doing my job," Ol' Jake said.

The agent blew out a breath. "I need a drink," he said.

"Now that can be arranged," Ol' Jake said and headed back toward the bar.

***

In the week since the failed assassination attempt on the president, The Confederacy had been on high alert. Despite President Stinston's call for calm and order in response to the attempt on his life, the people demanded that someone pay for this act. The Confederate Assembly agreed and began drawing up attack plans against any enemy that they could tie to the assassination plot.

It had been a tense week, but things at the Olde Star Tavern had finally started to return to normal. The place had been a beehive of activity since the day of the Centennial Celebration. Secret Service, local and federal police, city engineers, the military, and of course, the press had been on site. Business had been steady, mostly those lookee loos who stopped by to get a peek at the investigation or out of simple curiosity.

Whatever the reason, Durlan Koth's profits were up, which made him happy.

Repairs to the Ol' Jake unit had been costly, but worth it. The android bartender was one of the heroes of the hour, and so many patrons had stopped in to buy him a drink, despite the obvious fact that the android didn't drink. The star treatment was all but lost on Ol' Jake. No matter what was asked of him, the android bartender's answer was consistent, "I was just doing my job."

It was a reasonably normal day when Agents Redding and Bressler returned to the Olde Star Tavern.

"Welcome, gentlemen," Ol' Jake said when he saw them. Once again, the android wore the holographic skin he'd been wearing on the day of the attack. It was at the request of Durlan Koth, an attempt to play up the hero angle. Once things settled down, he would no doubt return to his leggy brunette skin.

"What can I get you?" he asked the two agents.

"I'm afraid this isn't a social call," Agent Bressler said.

"Yeah. Just water," Agent Redding said. "We're still on duty."

"Have you not yet completed your investigation?" Ol' Jake asked.

"For the most part," Bressler said. "The case is still open and ongoing, but we're finished with our work here. Your boss can reopen the overflow area at his convenience."

"I'm sure Mr. Koth will be happy to hear that."

"We did have a proposition for you, however," Agent Redding said.

"For me? I'm afraid I don't understand."

"We would like to offer you a job, Jake," Bressler said.

"I'm flattered, gentlemen, but I highly doubt the Secret Service requires a bartender," Ol' Jake said. "At any rate, Mr. Koth purchased me from the J-Acme Corporation of Laganos Prime. He would have to sell me into your employ."

"You let us worry about that," Bressler said.

Ol' Jake leaned his elbows on the bar and listened.

"Agent Redding has suggested, and I agree, that you showed remarkable skill during the assassination attempt. When we see someone with your skills, we try to recruit them."

"As I'm sure you are aware, my programming is not compatible with military applications. It has been tried before."

"We don't want to turn you into a soldier," Redding said. "We want you to be an investigator. As a bartender, you've been trained to see things, anticipate needs, and pick up on visual and auditory clues, right?"

"That is a fair, if not simplistic, explanation of my abilities."

"And that holographic skin of yours allows you to blend in, go undercover," Bressler added.

"Come on, Jake. What do you say?"

The android took a moment as if to think it over.

He smiled and said, "Gentlemen, I think I'd like to hear more about this offer of yours."

***

Ol' Jake was not unique in the galaxy.

Stop by any bar at any of the planets along the galactic arm the locals referred to as the Antares Beltway and you'll find Ol' Jake there. He'll be the one behind the bar, slinging drinks and entertaining the guests. He might not always look the same-- and sometimes he might actually be a she or an it depending on your destination-- but at the core, each and every one of them is 'Ol Jake.

Ol' Jake was an android barkeep.

And now, thanks to the efforts of one model's quick thinking, Ol' Jake was The Confederacy's spy network.

What are you drinking tonight?

What Do You Have For A Rebellion?

By

Phillip Drayer Duncan

A rebel, a scoundrel, and bounty hunter walk into a bar…

"I'm having a dinner party, and I must choose the right wine," the woman pleaded. "I'm told you're the best."

Kap looked up from the glass he was shining. He could've let the machine do it, but there was something about drying by hand that just felt right. Plus, it added to the aesthetics. People didn't come to Kap's for cheap frills. Some came for the cheap drinks. Others came for the exotic drinks. Some came for the privacy of dark corner booths. Some came to socialize around the bar. Some came for the karaoke, though he'd rather some didn't. And some came for wisdom.

He smiled at the woman. She was a wealthy type. Probably staying at the casino on the other end of the station.

Kap wiped a hand across his blue face and asked, "What are you serving at this dinner party?"

"A steamed Flussan."

"What are the side dishes?"

"Does it matter?"

"Yes," he replied, ignoring the haughtiness of her tone.

"Buttered kauch and steamed veenier."

"Hmm," he said.

"What's wrong with that?" she asked, raising an eyebrow.

He shook his head. "Nothing."

"As though I could expect a bartender in a dismal place like this to have refined taste. Perhaps I'm wasting my time."

"You want a Quintarian red. Barrel aged for at least one hundred years. Avoid the mid-range and go top shelf. Personally, I'd recommend Yin-Lan, but then, I'd also recommend something other than veenier to go with my Flussan."

"A Quintarian?" she asked. "But that's not—"

Kap turned and pressed a few buttons on his order screen. A bottle of Yin-Lan came out of the drop slot behind him. He scooped it up and handed it to her. "I'm sure you're having a test run, right?"

"Several," she admitted. "I told the cooking staff they were going to continue making Flussan until I was sure I had the right wine."

"Then take this with you and see how you like it."

"And if I do?"

"Then place an order. I have enough on hand for a dinner party."

"And if I don't?"

He shrugged. "Then don't come back."

She turned and headed for the door.

A burly corporate type walked up and took the bar seat where the woman had stood. It was a busy night. Newcomers were having to wait for the room to clear.

"Are you Kap?"

"I am."

"They say you have something for everything."

Kap chuckled. His reputation was growing. He wasn't sure how he felt about that.

"What do you have for a bitch of an ex-wife? Particularly one who takes all your money, leaves you in debt, and sleeps with your friend?"

"Best friend?"

"Yup."

Kap turned again and pressed a few buttons on his order screen. Another bottle appeared. He produced a short glass, tossed in some ice, and filled it to the top with an amber liquid from the new bottle. He set the glass down in front of the newcomer and said, "It's called whiskey. Comes from an old, dead planet called Earth. It's where you humans originally came from."

"Thanks," the man replied, sniffing the drink. "Wow. Smells strong."

"Legend has it whiskey was invented to cure the ails of a love life."

The man took a sip, puckered, and asked, "Do you think that's true?"

Kap shrugged. "You tell me."

The man thanked him and moved away.

Kap let his gaze drift to the next man down. He was trouble. Kap always knew. It wasn't the casually worn flight gear which screamed smuggler. Nor was it the slight bulge under his jacket which clearly was a blaster. It was the man's demeanor. All swagger and confidence on the surface, but when one knew how to look a bit deeper, as Kap did, he saw a man on the run. The way his eyes shifted, carefully assessing the other patrons.

The man noticed Kap watching him and gave a slight nod. "Does everyone come here seeking a magic cure?"

"Keeps me in business."

"Nothing wrong with that," the man replied. "The galaxy could use a few more sagely bartenders. Not enough of that anymore. Most places have robot servers."

"That's why people like my bar, I guess."

Before the conversation could continue a nervous, young, green-skinned humanoid approached the bar.

Kap turned his attention on the newcomer. "What can I do for you?"

"Are you Kap?"

"I am."

The kid fidgeted. "I was told you could help me."

Kap smiled. "Let's hear it."

"Well, the thing is…" The kid paused to gather his thoughts. "I want to propose to my girlfriend."

"And?" Kap asked.

"And, well, I'm too nervous."

The smuggler chuckled and threw his arm around the kid's shoulder. "Young and in love. You ought to be scared."

Kap chuckled. "I have just the thing."

This time he produced a vial of green liquid. Before he handed it to the young man, he said, "Drink this about half an hour before you plan to ask her."

"Thank you," the young man said, taking the vial and dropping it into a pocket. "You think it will work?"

"I know it will."

Apparently feeling a little better, the kid paid and made his way out.

Kap turned back to the smuggler. "Your turn?"

"I don't think you have anything that can solve my problems."

"Try me," Kap said. A little quieter he added, "You're aren't the first man on the run to show up here."

The smuggler's eyes went hard. "You know who I am?"

Kap shook his head. "No, but I know a man on the run when I see one. This station is about as far from the center of the Imperium's control as one can get without going into dead space. And, it's a giant casino, resort, and travel hub. The kind of place where a traveler doesn't need much of a cover story. You'd be surprised how many outlaws hide here."

"Yeah," the man said, "well, aside from dead space, there's no place safe from the Imperium, and only a fool would try their luck outside the galaxy."

Kap opened his hands and shrugged in a solitary gesture. "I'm afraid I can't argue."

"The goddamned Imperium," the man muttered. "They rule the galaxy with an iron fist, and there's not a damned thing anyone can do about it. Best thing is to just keep moving. Never get in their sights."

"Especially when you've ended up on their bad side."

The smuggler chuckled. "All right, Kap. My name is Fussell Halloran."

"Ah," Kap replied. Everyone had heard of the famous smuggler. "I see."

"So, what do you have for a smuggler running from the Imperium?"

Kap took a few steps behind the bar and produced a tall glass. He added ice and then filled it with a clear liquid, before setting it in front of Fussell.

"Thanks," the smuggler replied, taking a sip. He raised an eyebrow and asked, "Is this water?"

Kap nodded. "Best you lay off the alcohol and keep your reflexes sharp."

"I was planning on drinking myself into oblivion."

"I know, but you asked what I had for a man in your position, and given the circumstances, water is the best thing."

"What makes you so sure about that?"

"Because of him," Kap said, motioning toward the other side of the room.

Fussell looked where Kap pointed then turned back to the bartender. His features drained of color, he said, "Damn."

Kap glanced back toward the figure who sat alone in the back booth. There was no mistaking who he was. The only reason half of Kap's customers hadn't fled was because either they hadn't noticed him, or thought it was an imitator. What would the most infamous bounty hunter in the galaxy be doing in a dive bar like Kap's? But there was no mistaking the war-beaten armor or the emotionless visor. It was Vaden Mandordor, and there was no question who he was there to see.

"I thought I'd shook him," Fussell said.

"Mandordor? There's no shaking him. Once he sets his gaze on a target—"

"I'm aware of the stories," Fussell said, glancing over his shoulder.

Vaden offered him a small nod in reply.

"I don't understand," Fussell said. "Why isn't he dragging me out of here?"

"Because Kap's is neutral ground. Everyone knows that."

"But he's working for the Imperium, and the Imperium doesn't have neutral ground."

"No," Kap agreed, "but even men like Vaden know neutral ground is necessary. He'll abide by the rules."

"So, you think I'm safe while I'm here?"

"Yeah."

"Do you need a dishwasher? I may never leave."

Kap chuckled. "Of course you will, but for the moment, you're safe. You have plenty of time to work out a plan."

"Yeah, and he's got plenty of time to work out a plan for every plan I might think up."

"Then I suppose the game is on," Kap said, shrugging. He moved down the line to help another customer.

There was always another customer.

One had just lost years' worth of savings in the casino. Kap had something for that.

Another had just lost his job. Kap had something for that.

A customer, whose face looked somewhat like a fish, had just been diagnosed with a terminal form of cancer Kap had never even heard of, but he had something for that. Not a cure for cancer, but a cure for the news. That's what he dealt in—the short-term solution.

Kap sighed. His reputation was becoming that of a cure-all, but the truth, the real truth, was that nothing he had behind the bar offered real solutions. At best, alcohol served as little more than a band-aid for the problems of the universe. And shilling out band-aids for problems of the heart was the act of a charlatan.

And who was he to cast judgment on the scoundrel? It hadn't been that long ago that he was in a similar situation. Perhaps that was what had concerned him about the man. Seeing his own reflection looking back at him.

Kap pushed these thoughts away and moved back down the bar toward Fussell. The smuggler was lost in his own thoughts and still working on his water, so Kap continued past him to the next customer.

Another newcomer, she was young and had a fierce look in her eyes. Kap noticed because her fiery eyes were staring into his own.

He paused, an uncomfortable feeling in his gut. What was it? It had been a long time since a customer made him feel uneasy, yet, there was something about the girl.

She was human. Early twenties. Attractive by the human species' standards, but that wasn't it. Kap had always found humans to be rather ugly creatures.

So, what was it then?

Did she look familiar?

One thing he was sure about was she wasn't dressed right. She bore the clothing of a lower-class traveler, perhaps looking for work, but her eyes told a different story. And the way she held herself spoke of an upper class. Another on the run, perhaps? Maybe that was it. Perhaps he was just seeing another reflection of himself.

He realized he was staring and asked, "What can I do for you?"

"Are you Kap?" she asked. "I've heard you have a cure for everything."

"Oh, boy, does he," Fussell said, his mopey eyes still pointed at his glass.

Kap grinned. "Let's hear it."

The girl replied with a shark-like grin of her own, her eyes still fastened on his. "What do you have for a rebellion?"

Kap stared at her for a few seconds, his unease growing. It wasn't often a customer stunned him to silence. He feared she might go on but still couldn't think of an appropriate response. The Imperium had ears everywhere. In public, such talk would get you strung up, tortured, and publicly executed.

Fortunately, Fussell came to the rescue.

"I don't think they make a drink for that," he said, giving her a once over. "Then again, if you're some rich kid trying to piss off mommy and daddy, just about anything he serves will do the trick. Am I right, Kap?"

Kap nodded.

The girl's stare didn't waver. "It's not my parents I'm rebelling from."

"Careful, kid," Fussell said. "That kind of talk isn't smart. Not even on a backwater casino station."

"He's right," Kap said. "If you'd like a drink, I think I can help. For the other... Well, you can take that to a different bar."

"I'm not afraid," the girl said, her eyes still locked on Kap's.

"Then you're an idiot," Fussell said, giving her a sideways glance. "Surely you've seen the vids. There are public executions every hour on the hour, and many of those folks aren't guilty of half the treason you just committed." He lowered his voice. "Even uttering the word rebellion in public is considered treason. Hell, everyone in here could be executed for what you just said."

"That may be true," she agreed. "But that doesn't make it right."

"Right?" Fussell asked. "What does right have to do with anything? It's the way it is."

"Not for everyone," the girl said. "Some people fight."

Fussell chuckled. "Yeah, the shadowy rebellion. A lot of good they've done. Most people doubt they're even still out there."

"They're still out there. I can assure you."

"Well," Fussell said, "if they're recruiting foolish young things like you, then they aren't worth much. Not anymore, at least."

The girl looked like she was about to respond, but paused to gather her thoughts. Her eyes shifted back to Kap. "You're right. They aren't worth much anymore, but they were, once."

"That was a long time ago," Fussell said. "Heroes like Ward Dicero don't exist anymore."

"Maybe they should."

"And maybe you should take this talk somewhere else," Kap said, crossing his arms. "I won't have it in my bar."

"He's right," Fussell said. "My apologies."

Kap kept his gaze on the girl, "Do you want to order something, or not?"

"I already did."

"And I already told you, we don't serve that here."

"I think you do," she replied. "Check in the back. It might be covered in dust, but I think you have it. Or, at least, you once did."

"I can assure you it's not something this bar has ever carried."

She stared at the countertop for a moment, then asked, "Do you recognize me?"

Kap shook his head. It was a lie, or, at least, a partial lie. There was something about her that was familiar.

"My name is Indra Hildebrand. My mother was Warana Hildebrand."

"The rebel leader who was publicly executed?" Fussell asked, jumping back into the conversation.

Kap was thankful for his interjection, as he knew his own face must have given him away.

Warana. It had been years. And, Indra. She'd been but a child.

"Yes," Indra replied, glancing at Fussell.

"Then you're an even bigger fool than I thought," he replied. "You know what happened to your mother. Hell, I'm surprised the Imperium hasn't executed you for just being her daughter."

"They've tried," she said. "They're still trying."

Fussell turned to Kap. "I'm suddenly not feeling as safe in your bar as I was a few minutes ago."

Kap ignored the comment and stared at Indra.

Indra stared back. "My mother believed in the cause. As did her best friend and comrade. Her leader. The great big hero, Ward Dicero. Champion of the rebellion. But when the rebellion fell, he disappeared. My mother died publicly, cursing the Imperium with her last breath. But Ward Dicero was nowhere to be found. And the rebellion has been in shambles ever since."

Fussell started to reply, then paused, his gaze moving between the girl and Kap, until finally planting on Kap. It was as if the smuggler was seeing the bartender's blue face in a whole new light. Kap didn't particularly like the feeling.

"Oh," Fussell said. "Oh, wow."

Kap gave him a sideways glance and said, "C'mon Fussell, you're not silly enough to believe that."

Fussell didn't reply.

"And you," he said, turning toward Indra. "I'm sorry about what happened to your mother. I'm not sure who you think I am or what you thought I might do for you, but I'm afraid I'll be of no help. I'm just a bartender." Indra started, but Kap put up his hand. "No. I'll have no more of this talk in my bar. It's dangerous and foolish."

Indra paused for a moment, then said, "The man my mother knew wouldn't have been afraid."

"Then perhaps he was a fool and not the hero you believed him to be," Kap replied, giving her a hard look. "And that's the end of the discussion."

Indra reluctantly stepped away from the bar but didn't leave. Instead, she claimed a small table in the back, gave Kap a glare, then sat, staring at her own hands.

Kap turned toward Fussell who was still watching him. "What?"

Fussell shook his head. "You made the right call. I don't blame you."

Kap stared at him for a moment and then moved away. "I have other customers to help."

***

"Commander Varanis," the Lieutenant said, offering a slight bow.

The Commander looked up from his desk, ensuring he showed the slightest hint of annoyance. In truth, he'd been eagerly awaiting the Lieutenant's arrival, hoping for good news.

The Lieutenant stood at attention, rigid, back straight with his hands clutched behind him as decorum demanded. He wouldn't move until Varanis acknowledged him. Like a statue, he would wait until he was called upon, even if the Commander made him wait for hours. At times, Varanis was known for making his subordinates stand at attention until their will broke and they crumbled. A truly disciplined Imperium soldier would stand quietly until they passed out from exhaustion. The weak would give in sooner, either begging his audience or pushing their weak minds to the breaking point, and falling to the floor crying. These were removed from his service immediately. Varanis had no time for weak minds.

This new Lieutenant had an arrogance about him Varanis

approved of, yet needed to break. The young man had all the makings of a fine officer, but Varanis needed to ensure his individual loyalty. If he ever wanted to promote from Fleet Commander to Planetary Duke, he needed the best around him.

And he would have enjoyed watching the smug tit stand until he fainted from exhaustion. Even more, he would enjoy taking the whip to him afterward. But, he was impatient for news.

"What is it, Lieutenant?"

"Our sources have confirmed," the young man said, grinning. "The girl is Indra Hildebrand. Daughter of Warana Hildebrand."

"How confident?"

"Almost certain."

"Almost?"

The Lieutenant faltered, but only for a moment. "Yes, sir. They have eyes on her now."

"By camera or in person?"

"Camera. Facial recognition software also confirms," he said, foolishly allowing a hint of excitement in his voice.

Varanis fixed him with a glare, and the Lieutenant's smile dropped away.

"Good," Varanis said. "Do we have a team in place?"

"Yes, sir."

"Something better than standard station security, I hope." Varanis gauged him carefully for a reaction. "I'd hardly trust the operational efficiency of Imperium soldiers assigned to a backwater station."

"Yes, sir. I checked the travel records. Ezell Squad recently landed on the station."

"Ezell Squad," Varanis repeated. "They're part of Thamopolis's Division, no?"

"Yes, sir."

"Why are they on the station?" he asked, not allowing any sign of concern. Inwardly, he was worried that his competitor might be honing in on his prize.

"Mandatory R&R, sir."

Varanis laughed. "Rest and Relaxation. Such nonsense. Thamopolis is a fool."

The Lieutenant didn't reply. Wise. If he had, Varanis would've taken him to the whip. As much as he despised his competing Fleet

Commander, it would be inappropriate for his subordinate to speak poorly of a higher ranking officer. Varanis had no tolerance for insolence.

"Good enough," Varanis said. "We'll use his vacationing Special Forces team. It will only make him look that much more the fool. Reach out to them."

"I took the liberty of doing so already."

Varanis fixed him with another glare but didn't respond. There was something to be said for taking the initiative, but it was important that the Lieutenant understood his place. This was Varanis's operation, and in the end, Varanis would get the credit for engaging his fellow Fleet Commander's team. Not some brash underling.

"Order them to engage," Varanis said. "I want the girl alive. Coordinate the fleet with their strike time. I want us dropping out of hyperspace as they're engaging. I'll take no chance of our prisoner ending up with another fleet. Understood?"

"Yes, sir."

"That will be all."

Varanis turned back to his desk, but from his peripherals noticed that the Lieutenant remained. He allowed an audible sigh and asked, "Is there something else, Lieutenant?"

For the first time since entering his office, the Lieutenant fidgeted. "The bar she's hiding in, sir."

"Yes?"

"Well, sir, among the lower class it's said to be a neutral zone."

"I see," Varanis replied, looking back up at him. "Tell me, Lieutenant, are we of the lower class?"

"No, sir. We're the Imperium."

"Then don't bother me with nonsense."

"Yes, sir," the Lieutenant replied, saluting, and marched from the office.

Once he was gone, Varanis sat back in his chair and clapped his hands together. Not only had they found the child of a famous rebel, but he was going to use his competitor's team to bring her in, and to top it all off, the young Lieutenant slipped up. When this was done, Varanis would have him whipped for the 'neutral zone' nonsense.

He smiled. It was going to be a good day.

**

Kap moved around the bar, still taking requests and offering drink wisdom. He would've liked to forget the earlier conversation, but Indra was still sitting at a table in the back.

At least that meant one of his waitresses, and not Kap himself, was refilling her drink orders. Kap worked the bar. When all the stools were full, it was all he could do to keep up, so he had two girls on staff to work the tables.

The only problem with working the bar was that Fussell was still present as well, and he'd taken to eyeing Kap with a mixture of curiosity and awe.

Kap eased his way back toward the smuggler.

"Need another drink?"

"Of water?" Fussell asked. "I'm not even buzzed yet."

Kap chuckled. "If you'd prefer booze I can fix you up."

"No," Fussell said, groaning. "You made the right call."

"Good, because we may have trouble."

"Huh?"

"Don't look," Kap said. "Keep your eyes on me."

"Okay," the smuggler said, eyeing him suspiciously.

Kap leaned a little closer. "In the past fifteen minutes, fourteen new customers have entered the bar."

"That's good."

"One would think. But there's one man sitting at the other end of the bar in casual clothing who came in alone. He looks like a vacationer who just strolled in to check the place out, but his face is lined with scars, his eyes are periodically scanning the room, and he hasn't touched his drink."

"Okay," Fussell said, then leaned back and laughed, as though the bartender had said something funny. As he leaned back in, he said, "Saw him. You're right, he doesn't fit, but that doesn't mean he's trouble."

"He's not the only one," Kap said. "A few minutes after he came in, two more rough looking men entered. They're sitting in the back at a table, also not touching their drinks, and barely speaking to one another. A few minutes after they came in, another man came in by himself who is much the same. And a few minutes after that, another group of three came in and positioned themselves in the other back corner."

"Seven."

Kap nodded.

"You're sure?"

Kap nodded again.

"You seem to know an awful lot about these things for just a bartender."

Kap didn't reply.

"So, you think they're here for me?"

"Perhaps," Kap said, absently wiping the top of the bar with his towel. "Or perhaps they're here because of a loud mouth kid."

"What are you going to do?"

"Me? I'm just a bartender. I'm not going to do anything."

"So why are you telling me?" Fussell's eyes hardened. "If you think I'm about to throw my life away to save some punk kid with a big mouth, you aren't half as smart as these folks seem to think you are."

"Maybe not." Kap shrugged. "But I've been bartending for a long time, and I know people. I can tell when a man needs redemption. When he just needs a reason to take a stand."

"And I suppose I'm that sort of man?" Fussell chuckled. "And what about you, Kap? What kind of man are you?"

Kap stared back at the smuggler for a few moments and finally said, "A coward."

Fussell peeled his eyes from the bartender and took a drink of his water.

Kap continued, "And that, more than anything, is how I can tell the difference."

The conversation over, Kap moved down the bar and took drink orders, ignoring the truth of his own words and hopeful he was right about the scoundrel. Of course, if the men respected Kap's neutral zone rule, it wouldn't matter. They'd simply wait until the girl left and follow her out.

And if they made their move in the bar, there was always his waitresses, but like him, they might be more inclined to not get involved. If he got a chance to warn them, he would, but they were staying busy with their customers for the moment.

Stupid girl, he thought. Why had she come here? This could, and likely would end badly. He'd just have to wait and see.

He didn't have to wait long.

The man at the bar paid his meager tab to the nearby kiosk, then started toward the back of the room, in Indra's direction.

Another of the lone men started easing his way in that direction as well. They hoped to catch her off guard.

His glance fell on Indra. She wasn't even looking up. She had no idea the danger she was in.

His heartbeat quickened. Fussell was armed, but he didn't know if he'd intervene, and it was too late to warn his girls. His bar was known to all as a neutral zone. He'd even hung a sign over the door and over the bar to serve as reminders. Even the lowest scum of the galaxy wouldn't dare start violence in a place posted with the galactic symbol for neutral zone. The Imperium though, they didn't care. In a few moments, a young woman was going to be assaulted, subdued, and dragged from his bar to be tortured, then executed.

But maybe he was wrong. Maybe he was just being a silly fool. Maybe the conversation with Indra had caused his imagination to overwork.

He scanned the room once more, his eyes stopping on the dark visor of the bounty hunter. Kap could feel the hunter's gaze staring back at him. It wasn't a pleasant feeling. Vaden Mandordor's dark visor turned and gave the room a once-over, then he turned back to Kap and offered a little nod.

The bounty hunter saw it too. It wasn't his imagination. Not that he expected the bounty hunter to get involved, and surely if he did, he'd side with the Imperium. But his silent message spoke loud enough. There was about to be a show.

Kap turned back toward where Indra sat. The first man was closing in, the second only paces behind him, and still, her eyes didn't lift from the table.

Just before the first man reached her table one of Kap's waitresses, Vera, stepped in his way with a drink tray. Vera and Venias were both shapely creatures and despite being Klem, a green-skinned species, they tended to catch eyes of human men. The sheer dresses and heels didn't hurt, either. They both made bank on tips.

Vera stopped in front of the plain-clothed Imperium soldier, offered him a seductive smile, and said, "Hey there, cutie. Can I get you a drink?"

"No, thanks," he said. "Excuse me."

He stepped past her and moved to stand in front of Indra. Finally, she looked up from the table, and while Kap couldn't see the soldier's face from where he stood, he could see Indra's. He could see her fear.

Vera looked to Kap for confirmation.

The other soldier was almost to her as well. She stood in between them.

He had less than a second to decide. It felt like the whole of reality slowed down while he made his decision. He could leave it alone. He could choose to not get involved. The soldiers would haul the girl away, and he could go back to running his bar in peace. But if he got involved, he would be a culprit. He'd be executed too, and he'd be dragging his loyal girls down with him.

In the end, there was only one thing he could do.

He gave her the nod.

Vera moved with incredible speed. She went for the soldier standing in front of Indra first, kicking him in the back of the knee. Before he had time to crumple forward, her other leg kicked out at the soldier approaching from the other side, catching him in the crotch. And before he could double over, she was back on the first, using her free hand to slam his head against the table. In her other hand, she still held her drink tray, and none spilled.

The man's head bounced off the table with a thump, but much to Kap's surprise, he still managed to go for the gun concealed beneath his jacket. Vera moved first, whirling her drink tray around and slamming it into his throat, crushing his Adam's apple. Then she spun her body around and kicked a sharp heel into the throat of the second man, repeating the same effect.

It happened incredibly fast, but the other soldiers didn't falter, and instead picked up the pace, moving in and going for their guns. These weren't everyday grunts, Kap realized. These were Imperium Special Forces.

On the other side of the room, Venias tripped one as he rushed past her, then spun and kicked the blaster pistol out of the hand of a second man. Unfazed by the loss of his weapon, the man grabbed a glass and smashed it against the table, shattering the end into a sharp point. He jabbed at Venias, but she side-stepped, grabbed his arm, pulled him toward her, and snapped his neck. The first man was already rising as she snapped the second's neck. The connection between his brain and nervous system broken, the glass slipped from his grip, but Venias snatched it out of the air, turned on the first man, and rammed the broken glass through his eye.

Four down. Three remaining. That was more than half, but the others were closing in, weapons bared and pointing at Vera. There was no way she could avoid being shot.

Then the closest to Vera fell as a blaster bolt took him in the back. Without even bothering to stand up, Fussell had spun around on the bar stool, took aim, and fired. The other two soldiers took aim on him, but Fussell managed to shoot once more, hitting one of them in the chest, before the final man returned fire.

Fussell hit the ground as a red laser bolt seared into the front of the bar. Despite the first miss, there was nothing Fussell could do to avoid a second shot.

Again, time slowed down.

Kap allowed an inward sigh, then hurled the glass he'd been polishing across the room. It hit the final soldier between the eyes, shattered, and knocked him to the ground.

There was a moment of stunned silence, and then people started screaming. Then they started running. Half of the bar bolted for the door, but before they could make an exit an energy shield popped up between the bar's entrance and the rest of the station.

The Imperium.

Kap was only surprised for a moment. Of course, they'd been monitoring. It was entirely possible that they still had someone on the inside. Just about any one of his patrons could be an Imperium spy. Or perhaps they were using the station's cameras from the hall. It wasn't a real surprise either way.

On the other side of the room, Vera took Indra by the hand and brought her toward the bar. Venias stepped in line beside them and glared at anyone who dared look in their direction.

As they approached Kap asked, "Are you all right?"

Indra nodded. "Yeah, I'm okay. Thank you." She looked between the two waitresses. "Thank you, as well."

From where he still sat on the floor Fussell said, "Hey, don't forget about me."

"Right," Indra said, glancing down at him. "Thank you."

Fussell pulled himself up from the ground and glanced toward the barrier blocking the front door. "I've got the feeling we aren't out of this yet."

"You've got that right," said the soldier Kap had pelted with the glass. He sat on the floor holding his broken nose, blood dripping between his fingers. "Should have just let us take the girl."

"Read the sign, jackass," Fussell said, hooking a thumb toward the bar. "Kap's is a neutral zone."

"The Imperium doesn't have neutral zones. You're all dead."

Fussell crossed his arms. "Big words from the guy sitting on the floor bleeding."

The soldier laughed. "We were supposed to do it quietly. Keep it simple. That won't be the case now. Look out a window."

Fussell glanced back at Kap. "I'll check, but we should probably secure him. And the others." He glanced around at the limp bodies on the floor. "If any of them are still alive." His gaze moved back to the two waitresses, and then back to Kap. "Pretty impressive help... You know, for just a bartender."

"And you don't seem as nervous now, smuggler."

Fussell grinned. "Once you're in the mess there's nothing to be scared of anymore."

"Right. Go ahead and check the window, Fussell. The girls will secure him and check to see if any of the others still live."

"You don't want to see?"

"I already know what's out there."

Fussell headed toward one of the exterior walls. Vera and Venias moved to secure the hostage.

Fussell passed Vaden on his way toward the wall and said, "How'd you like the show, bounty hunter?"

Vaden Mandordor nodded but didn't reply.

Kap watched as Fussell approached the window. The smuggler cursed and then ran back across the room to another window and cursed again. "There's an entire Imperium fleet out there! With enough ships to blow this whole station to bits. Or to drop a thousand ground troops." He laughed and pointed at the prisoner. "He's right. We're screwed."

"I was a fool," Indra said, burying her hands in her face. "I should've never come here."

"They've probably been tracking your movements for a while," Kap said, not sure if what he was about to say was going to be a lie. "If you'd been anywhere else, they'd have gotten you. You were lucky to end up here."

Still standing by the window, Fussell cursed again and took a step back. Kap looked up and realized a spy bot drone was looking at the bar from the window. In a matter of moments, every exterior window was surrounded with bots.

A number of soldiers appeared on the other side of the laser barricade at the door and took up positions. The front row, six men wide, dropped to their knees, and another six lined up behind them. These weren't plain-clothed guys with concealable blaster pistols but fully armored Imperium troopers with laser rifles. If the barrier dropped, they could shred everyone in seconds.

"This is Commander Varanis of the Imperium Fleet," a voice sounded through the bar. "You are all under arrest for assaulting Imperium officers. Stand down. There is no need for further violence."

Everyone in the bar stared at one another, unsure what to do.

"Be aware," Varanis's voice continued. "I am not a patient man. Now, everyone get on the floor. You're all going to be detained."

"We weren't all involved," a man near the door said, pointing toward Kap and the others. "It was them."

Varanis chuckled. "Perhaps, but there are enough of you in the bar who could have helped the officers. You chose not to. Therefore, every one of you is a party to treason. And for treason, there is only one penalty."

Surprised mumbles went up around the room.

"That's right," the soldier on the floor said, his hands now tied behind his back. "You're all traitors."

"As are you," Commander Varanis said. "You are being charged with treason and insubordination, soldier."

"What?" the man asked, his eyes widening. "We did exactly as you ordered!"

"No. You were ordered to subdue the girl. You did not, and therefore, you are guilty of insubordination as well as treason."

A stunned silence fell across the room as people realized the weight of the situation. If this Commander Varanis was going to have his own Imperium soldier executed, what of them? Most were just in the wrong place at the wrong time. It didn't matter. That was something Kap understood, but the others didn't, and the weight of it fell on him. He'd chosen this course. He could have given up the girl and saved them all. Instead, he'd sentenced them all to death.

Vaden Mandordor stood up from his seat and casually walked toward the bar. "Commander Varanis, this is Vaden Mandordor. I believe we've met."

"Yes," Varanis said, "I'm aware of who you are."

"I'm here to retrieve the outlaw smuggler, Fussell Halloran on behalf of the Imperium. Permission to detain and escort him out?"

There was a moment of silence before Varanis finally said, "Denied."

Silence hung on the air as the bounty hunter's dark visor turned toward one of the spy bots. He walked toward the window. The rest of the room was silent. Everyone knew who Vaden Mandordor was. He'd collected on hundreds of targets for the Imperium. Kap shook his head. This Varanis was an arrogant cuss. People feared Vaden nearly as much as they feared the Imperium.

Vaden stopped in front of the window, his dark visor staring into the camera. "Tell me, Varanis. Do you intend to arrest me for treason as well?"

Again there was a moment of silence as the Commander presumably thought if over. "You are a party to it as well. You of all people could have lent aid to the soldiers, yet you chose not to. That makes you the biggest traitor in the room, bounty hunter."

"This is a neutral zone," Vaden said, no emotion in his voice. "That is something which should be respected."

"The Imperium doesn't recognize such nonsense." Varanis laughed. "I never liked bounty hunters. Putting you to death will serve as a good warning to the rest of your kind."

"Woah," Fussell whispered, glancing over at Kap. "This Commander means business."

"What are we going to do?" Indra asked, quietly.

Kap shook his head. He didn't know.

Vaden Mandordor turned from the window and walked back toward the bar, his dark visor falling on Kap. Before he spoke, he pulled a device from his belt and pressed a button. "That should block them from hearing us."

"Woah," Fussell said. "Where'd you come up with something like that?"

"What's he saying?" Varanis demanded through the speakers. "Vaden, what have you done? Why can't we hear you?"

Vaden pressed the button again and said, "Shut up, Varanis. We're trying to talk."

"How dare you speak me to that way! I'm an Imperium—"

"You're a fool," Vaden said. "And I'm the last person you should have made an enemy of."

"You will pay for your insolence."

"We'll see," the bounty hunter replied, and pressed the button again, and then another. A static sound filled the speakers. "There. That will shut him up as well."

"What do we do?" Indra repeated.

"You're the rebel," Fussell said. "You tell us."

Indra paled. "I don't know."

"What about you?" Vaden asked, his visor aimed at Kap. "You have any ideas?"

"What would make you think I have any ideas? I'm just a bartender."

"No," he said. "You're Ward Dicero. Hero of the old rebellion."

"Fussell looked at Kap, then back to the bounty hunter. "Are you sure? He said he's not."

"He is," Vaden assured him.

"How do you know?" Indra asked.

"I knew it the moment I walked in," Vaden replied. "There's no point denying it. I hope you have a plan."

All eyes fell on Kap.

Even the other patrons, some of whom probably hadn't the faintest clue what was happening. Everyone looked at him. They were scared. Of course, they were scared, and rightly so. They were all about to be executed. And it was his fault.

But what could he do? Kap had left this life behind. It wasn't his fight anymore. Hell, there wasn't even a fight to be had. He just wanted to live out the rest of his years in peace and then die with the guilt he'd already stacked. He didn't want to add more to it.

He stared around the room. All of those faces, from different homeworlds, different species, different lives, all looking to him for answers.

And something snapped.

He turned to Fussell. "I'm assuming you've got a fast ship."

"Of course," Fussell said, grinning. "I've got the fastest ship in the galaxy, hidden away where no one can find it."

"And you?" Kap asked, turning to Vaden. "You have a ship?"

"Of course," Vaden replied. "Mine's even faster, and it's parked right beside his."

Fussell's grin faltered. "Really? How did you—"

"There's no time for that now," Kap said. "I'm assuming neither of your ships is on the station?"

They both shook their heads.

"Good," Kap said. "We're going to need them."

He turned to his waitresses. "Ladies?"

They both nodded, and Vera said, "Let's do it, boss."

"You're sure?"

"We're sure. We've always been sure," Venias said.

"We've just been waiting on you to come around," Vera added. "Why else would we work in this dingy bar?"

Kap couldn't help but grin. "Go get it ready."

Vera and Venias took off toward the back room.

He turned his attention to the whole bar. "Does everyone understand that the Imperium has signed our death warrants?"

Nods came from around the room.

"Does everyone understand that they've already scanned and logged us in their records as traitors? That no matter what we do, or where we go, that from this day forward, we are all sworn enemies of the Imperium?"

One person, a pink-skinned creature with tentacles, stepped forward. "But we didn't do anything!"

"Exactly," Kap said. "That's the problem with the Imperium and smug monsters like this Varanis. We all have but one choice left. Fight, or die. Does everyone understand that?"

It wasn't an epic speech, and it wasn't meant to inspire. It was meant to level set. To put it all on the table.

"So, is everyone in agreement that they'd rather fight than die?"

They all nodded.

Vera reappeared from the back room and said, "Ready."

"All right then," Kap said, turning to Vaden. "Un-mute the Commander and us."

Vaden complied, and Commander Varanis's voice said, "This is your final warning. Stand down, or all of you will be executed this instant!"

"Hello, Commander," Kap said. "I think it's time we had a chat."

"And just who are you?"

Kap chuckled. "Let's not play foolish games. You've already got a list of who everyone in the room is. But just in case, they call me Kap. I'm the bartender. This is my bar."

"Well, Kap, unless you want to watch everyone in your bar gunned down, you'd be wise to advise them to surrender."

"After you've told them they'll be sentenced to death? Not the best move on your part, Commander. You might have gotten a surrender out of us if you'd only lied about your intentions. The only reason you haven't shredded us yet is that you want poor Indra kept alive."

"Your point?"

"Are you broadcasting this communication back to the Imperium homeworld, Commander?"

"That is standard policy. Now, is there a point to all of this?"

"When Indra Hildebrand first walked into my bar she asked me a question. I want her to ask me again. And I want you to hear my answer. I want the whole Imperium to hear my answer."

Kap turned to Indra. "Go on, ask me again."

Indra met his gaze and rose to her full height. "What do you have for a rebellion?"

Kap smiled. "I have the daughter of the greatest rebel who ever lived. I have a smuggler the Imperium desperately wants to catch. I have the most feared bounty hunter in all the galaxy. I have the infamous assassins, the Vamillian sisters." Kap paused and looked down at the soldier. "I have an Imperium Special Forces soldier with no choice but to go rogue, and a room full of people with various skill sets and backgrounds. I have the makings of a rebellion."

Varanis snickered. "Well spoken, but what good is that going to do you when I take down the barrier and have you all gunned down? What then?"

"I wasn't done," Kap said. "Have you wondered why someone would open a bar on the exterior of a giant casino station? Or why someone would choose a bar as their choice of business to begin with?"

"I don't particularly care."

"Well, you should, Varanis."

"Why is that, Kap?"

"My name isn't Kap. My name is Ward Dicero. And I chose this location because it isn't just a bar. It's a ship. And I chose a bar because Imperium scanners will overlook large quantities of Flatarin fluid in a bar. The same fluid the Imperium uses to make missiles."

"What?" Varanis said an edge of panic in his voice. "You lie!"

Kap looked around the room. All eyes were still on him. He grinned. "Welcome to the new rebellion."

He reached under the bar and pressed a button. A door dropped in front of the laser barrier and was followed by a metal groan, and the whole bar shook as the ship disconnected from the station. The girls had already punched in hyperspace coordinates, and he'd had the missiles prepared for years. He always knew he might need to make a quick getaway.

There were several pressurized pops as the homemade missiles fired away from the ship and toward the Imperium vessels. The darkness of space became a blur of lights as the explosions started. He wasn't sure they'd be enough to take down most of the ships, but they were enough to cause a panic. At least a few of the Imperium ships would burn. Maybe all of them.

He pressed another button and the white stars of space stretched around them as they moved into lightspeed. Several people were flung from their feet, but after a few moments, the bar became incredibly silent. Everyone stared at each other for a few moments, then Indra started to cry, and Fussell began to laugh uncontrollably.

Vaden Mandordor pulled out his blaster and held it forward. "Ward Dicero, I pledge to you my weapon, for the purpose of ending the Imperium. For the rebellion."

Again, the bar fell into silence.

Fussell moved beside Vaden and raised his blaster. "Mine too. For the rebellion."

And around the room, they took up the cheer. "For the rebellion! For the rebellion!"

Ward Dicero nodded. There was no turning back now. It was going to be a fight for survival. But word would spread. People would know he'd returned. And they'd fight.

He smiled and joined the cheer. "For the rebellion!"

Sam 1701

Sam 1701 was dead tired. He stumbled toward the sleeping quarters, the door found while meandering through the stacks of files. As he reached the door, his shoulder bumped into a timeworn bookcase piled high with boxes. One crashed to the floor at his feet narrowly missing his left foot. He reached to push the box out of the way. The lid of the box fell off as he did so revealing the contents. Sam 1701 smiled in amazement there in the box were actual paper records written by someone using ink. He carefully picked the first folder up and leafed through the pages. "By all the known gods this could be old enough to have something to interest the Grand Master not to mention me." He thought. Clutching the prize documents he crossed the room behind the door to the bed and table on the other side.

Wearily he placed the folder on the table and dropped onto the bed. *"Could be something marvelous, but sleep must come and tomorrow is another day."* His eyes closed.

About The Authors

Aubrey Stephens is a retired teacher from Mississippi. He has Masters degrees in both theater and history, with certification in English, science, and special education. He is also a marine veteran and former military officer. The rumor that he has attempted to blow up the earth is just that, although he was on combat missile crew alert when the NORAD radar had a fail and reported that there were Soviet inbound missiles headed for the U.S. He is a trained martial artist with a second degree black belt in karate, brown belt in judo, and brown belt in Kendo, and taught European fencing for many years. His hobbies include recreating both the Middle Ages and the American Civil War. He is squired to one of the S.C.A.'s most well-known knights and at this time holds the rank of Captain in Co. A 24th Mississippi Cavalry. He has acted, written, directed, created set designs and construction for over 200 theatrical shows. Since his retirement, he has edited for Pro Se Press and been published as a writer. He enjoys swapping stories of the many sci-fi/fantasy conventions where he has worked, attended or been a guest, including one where he performed onstage with the late Grace Lee Whitney (Janice Rand of ST:TOS).

If you're looking for **Morgan McKay**, you'll usually find her sitting on top of a pile of books in a small little house out in the middle of nowhere, with two wolves and a knight in shining armor. Homegrown in the mud of the Mississippi River Bottom, Morgan enjoys both reading and writing fantastical stories of myths and legends, harrowing Sci Fi and occasionally the good'ol murder mystery. Working on her own collection of fictitious heroines, Morgan plans to have them published by the end of 2019, including characters such as Scheherazade, the Queen of Arabian Nights, and Marion Stone, the Knights' greatest Weapon.

Dale Kesterson was born in Manhattan, NY. She has lived in six widely diverse locations, from New Orleans to a town so small it doesn't have a red-yellow-green traffic light. She has been creating stories and putting them on paper since the age of seven, and she wrote, produced, and acted in her first play at age twelve. Life, however, kept her busy doing things such as majoring in science in college, teaching math and science, studying nursing, and managing a small home business with her husband. An avid Star Trek fan, she founded a Trek club and ended up running a convention – that's how she met her writing partner, Aubrey Stephens – one highlight of which was performing onstage with the late Grace Lee Whitney (Janice Rand, ST:TOS). A two-year stint with an opera company where she performed pantomime characters while singing with the chorus, and working in radio as an anchor and character voice artist are two of her accomplishments. In addition to writing (*Time Guards* series, *Tales of the Interstellar Bartenders Guild*), Dale is a seasoned traveler who is also a professional photographer; she lives in Kansas with her husband and their four hairless cats.

Kimberly B. Richardson is the author of *Tales From a Goth Librarian, The Decembrists, Tales From a Goth Librarian II, Mabon/Pomegranate, Open A,* and *The Path of a Tea Traveler.* She is the creator of the Agnes Viridian series, the Maven Chronicles, the Tea Traveler Chronicles, and the Order of the Black Silk trilogy. She is also the editor of *Realms of Imagination: An Urban Fantasy Anthology* and the Steampunk anthology series *Dreams of Steam,* and has stories in multiple anthologies. Ms. Richardson was the 2015 David McCrosky Volunteer Photographer in Residence for Elmwood Cemetery in Memphis, Tennessee. She is also the founder and Editor in Chief of the literary journal violet windows. Ms. Richardson is the founder and owner of Viridian Tea Company and a certified thanatologist.

Robert J. Krog is a native of Memphis, TN, where he still resides with his family. He has been a climber for his father's professional arborist company, a grocery store clerk, a waiter, an order out delivery guy, a legal runner, a substitute teacher, and a high school History teacher. He has a master's degree in Ancient History. He currently works for a chemical lawn care and organic services company in Memphis, TN. He is a devout Catholic, and this influences all of his writing. His published works include the collection, The Stone Maiden and Other Tales, the novella, A Bag Full of Eyes, and numerous short stories in anthologies from various publishers. He edited the anthology A Tall Ship, a Star, and Plunder for Dark Oak Press, and Potter's Field Five for Alban Lake Publishing. He is currently working as a freelance editor on Potter's Field Six for Alban Lake Press. A Bag Full of Eyes won the Darrell Award for Best Midsouth Novella in 2013. His short story, "The One's Who Remember," won the Darrell Award for Best Midsouth Short Story in 2016.

Mr. Krog continues to write and has numerous, previously-unpublished works slated for publication in the next year. He is currently working on a pair of novellas, a screenplay, and a couple of novels. He is a regular author guest at science fiction and fantasy conventions in and around the Midsouth.

Phillip Drayer Duncan is the author of 4 published novels and 12 short stories. He has work published with Yard Dog Press, Pro Se Productions, and Seventh Star Press.

His earliest books were acted out with action figures and scribbled into notebooks. Today he uses a computer like a real grown up. He would probably still play with the action figures if people wouldn't think he was crazy. He may be the only author that's ever sponsored a race car. His greatest dream in life is to become a Jedi, but since that hasn't happened yet he focuses on writing.

For more information about Phillip Drayer Duncan...

PhillipDrayerDuncan.com

H. David Blalock has been writing speculative fiction for decades. His fiction has appeared in novels, novellas, short stories, anthologies, and websites. He was awarded the Memphis Science Fiction Association's 2000 Darrell Award for Best Electronic Fiction and was nominated for the 2012 PulpArk Award for Best Short Story. His "High Kings" was finalist for the 2012 Darrell Award for Best Novella, his short story "Eclipse Over Elmwood" a finalist in 2014 for the Darrell Award for Best Short Story, and his story "Stolen Thunder" first runner-up in 2015. He was editor for "parABnormal Digest" from 2010 to 2012 and currently serves as an editor for Alban Lake Publishing.

Find out more about David and his work at his website (http://www.thrankeep.com) and his blog http://hdavidblalock.blogspot.com).

Herika R. Raymer began her writing career with a short story in Dragons Composed in March of 2009. In the following years, numerous short stories have appeared in several anthologies. Her first collection was published in November of 2016. She currently lives and dreams near Memphis, TN.

J.H. Fleming started her first novel in the 9th grade. That novel will never see the light of day, but it sparked something that has resulted in numerous short stories and 9 novels so far. She received a Bachelor's Degree in Creative Writing from the University of Central Arkansas, and it's very possible she'll try for a Master's at some point. She owns roughly 1,200 books and spends her free time befriending dragons, fighting goblins, and learning the craft of the bards. J.H. lives in Northwest Arkansas with three companions: a giant teddy bear, a miniature Cerberus, and a water dragon.

Terry Alexander and his wife Phyllis live on a small farm near Porum, Oklahoma. They have three children and nine grandchildren. Terry is a member of the Oklahoma Writers Federation, Ozark Writers League, Arkansas Ridge Writers and the Fictioneers. He has been published in various anthologies from Pro Se Productions, Meta Human Press, Airship 27, May December Publications, Hazardous Press, Rainstorm Press, Moonstone Books, and other publishers.

An award-winning author, **Bobby Nash** writes novels, comic books, short stories, novellas, graphic novels, and the occasional screenplay for a variety of publishers. He is a member of the International Association of Media Tie-in Writers and International Thriller Writers. On occasion, Bobby appears in movies and TV shows.
He was named Best Author in the 2013 Pulp Ark Awards. Rick Ruby, a character co-created by Bobby and author Sean Taylor also snagged a Pulp Ark Award for Best New Pulp Character of 2013. Bobby has also been nominated for the 2014 New Pulp Awards and Pulp Factory Awards for his work. Bobby's novel, Alexandra Holzer's Ghost Gal: The Wild Hunt won a Paranormal Literary Award in the 2015 Paranormal Awards. The Bobby Nash penned episode of Starship Farragut "Conspiracy of Innocence" won the Silver Award in the 2015 DC Film Festival. Bobby's story in The Ruby Files Vol. 2

"Takedown" was named Best Short Story in the 2018 Pulp Factory Awards, one of five nominations for The Ruby Files Vol. 2 (created by Bobby Nash & Sean Taylor). Bobby's digest novel, Snow Drive was nominated for Best Novel in the 2018 Pulp Factory Awards.

For more information on Bobby Nash please visit him at www.bobbynash.com and across social media.

Steeped in pulp magazines, old radio shows, and all things of that era's pop culture, **Tommy Hancock** lives in Arkansas with his wonderful wife and three children and obviously not enough to do. He is Partner in and Editor in Chief for Pro Se Productions, is an organizer of the New Pulp Movement, and has worked as an editor for various companies, including Moonstone and Dark Oak Press. He is also an award winning writer and has been published by various companies, including Airship 27, Mechanoid Press, Pulpwork Press, Dark Oak, Down and Out Books, and Moonstone. Tommy works as Project Coordinator for Moonstone.

R. L. Jones was born in Meridian MS. In the summer of 1951, but currently resided in the greater Northwest with various collections of friends, ancient and new, who all bow to the whims and needs of the local matriarch of the crowded house a Xoxoitzcuintle whom happens to have a full set of hair for a hairless breed of Mexican dogs. His adventures have seen all that military, university, and limited world travel through life has to offer and lived long enough to see most of his love of science fiction stories come to pass. Now it is time to have a drink at the farthest reaches of the universe and tell them anew.